Shifted By The Winds

August – December 1866

Book # 8 in The Bregdan Chronicles

Sequel to Glimmers of Change

Ginny Dye

D1608040

Shifted By The Winds

Copyright © 2015 by Ginny Dye
Published by
A Bregdan Publishing
Bellingham, WA 98229

www.BregdanChronicles.net

www.GinnyDye.com

www.BregdanPublishing.com

ISBN # 1544268505

Printed in the United States of America

For Jamie Whelan

She was a mother...
A daughter...
A granddaughter...
A niece...
A friend...
Most of all, she was
EXTRAORDINARY
to all she ever touched.

A Note from the Author

My great hope is that *Shifted By The Winds* will both entertain and challenge you. I hope you will learn as much as I did during the months of research it took to write this book. No one was more surprised than me when it ended up portraying just the last four months of 1866. As I move forward in the series, it seems there is so much going on in so many arenas, and I simply don't want to gloss over them.

When I ended the Civil War in *The Last, Long Night*, I knew virtually nothing about Reconstruction. I have been shocked and mesmerized by all I have learned. When I got to December of 1866, and I already had close to 600 pages, I knew I needed to close the door on 1866 and start fresh in 1867 with the next volume of *The Bregdan Chronicles*!

Though I now live in the Pacific Northwest, I grew up in the South and lived for eleven years in Richmond, VA. I spent countless hours exploring the plantations that still line the banks of the James River and became fascinated by the history.

But you know, it's not the events that fascinate me so much – it's the people. That's all history is, you know. History is the story of people's lives. History reflects the consequences of their choices and actions – both good and bad. History is what has given you the world you live in today – both good and bad.

This truth is why I named this series The Bregdan Chronicles. Bregdan is a Gaelic term for weaving: Braiding. Every life that has been lived until today is a part of the woven braid of life. It takes every person's story to create history. Your life will help determine the course of history. You may think you don't have much of an impact. You do. Every action you take will reflect in someone else's life. Someone else's decisions. Someone else's future. Both good and bad. That is the **Bregdan Principle**...

**Every life that has been lived until today is a
part of the woven braid of life.
It takes every person's story to
create history.
Your life will help determine the
course of history.
You may think you don't have
much of an impact.
You do.
Every action you take will reflect in
someone else's life.
Someone else's decisions.
Someone else's future.
Both good and bad.**

My great hope as you read this book, and all that will follow, is that you will acknowledge the power you have, every day, to change the world around you by your decisions and actions. Then I will know the research and writing were all worthwhile.

Oh, and I hope you enjoy every moment of it and learn to love the characters as much as I do!

I'm already being asked how many books will be in this series. I guess that depends on how long I live! My intention is to release two or three books a year – continuing to weave the lives of my characters into the times they lived. I hate to end a good book as much as anyone – always feeling so sad that I have to leave the characters. You shouldn't have to be sad for a long time!

You are now reading the 8th book - # 9 (*Always Forward*) will be released in the Winter of 2015. If you like what you read, you'll want to make sure you're on my mailing list at www.BregdanChronicles.net. I'll let you know each time a new one comes out so that you can take advantage of all my fun launch events, and you can enjoy my BLOG in between books!

Many more are coming!

Sincerely,
Ginny Dye

<u>Chapter One</u>
August 1866

Carrie Borden, her body tense with unnamed anticipation, took a reprieve from her back-breaking labor to look out the window of Moyamensing Hall, hoping for a breeze to cool the sweat running down her face and back. The air remained hot and stagnant, mocking her efforts to find relief. She took several slow breaths as she stared out at the never-ending view of three-story row houses and trash-filled streets. The putrid smell of outhouses made her nose crinkle. The clatter of horse hooves on the cobblestone streets mingled with yells and curses from men who looked as rough as they sounded. She inhaled deeply, trying to force her body to relax, but the odors invading her senses made her want to gag.

"Do you feel it?"

Carrie turned slowly and looked at Janie Saunders, trying to hide just how concerned she was.

Janie's soft blue eyes saw right through her. "Don't even bother attempting to come up with something encouraging to say," Janie scolded. "We've been friends for far too long. You can't fool me anymore."

Carrie managed a rueful smile, recognizing the beseeching look in her friend's eyes that begged her to say there was nothing to worry about. She regretted she couldn't do it. "Most of the time I'm glad you know me so well," she said lightly.

"So you feel it, too," Janie persisted, leaning forward to stare out the window as she wiped at the sweat dripping into her eyes.

"Trouble?" Carrie asked flatly, wishing she could deny it. "Yes," she admitted. "I feel it." She struggled to control the resentment flaring in her, but every particle of her being longed to be back on Cromwell Plantation. She *should* still have been home on the plantation for a holiday from medical school, but an emergency telegram delivered by special courier just two days before had changed everyone's plans. She, Janie, and their housemates,

Elizabeth, Alice, and Florence, had all been ripped from the fresh air of the plantation and forced to return to the cloying confines of Philadelphia.

"They're scared," Janie observed, as she gazed down at the angry faces scowling up at the building. She watched as the poorly dressed residents of Moyamensing talked among themselves, shaking their heads and pointing up at the windows.

"They have a right to be," Elizabeth Gilbert said as she came to stand next to them. Her blue dress, no longer crisp, was soiled and limp-looking. Tendrils of black hair escaped her bun, defying her efforts to shove them back into place. Her face, usually creamy white, was red from the suffocating heat in the building.

"I don't know how they expect cholera patients to survive in this heat," Carrie said grimly. Her heart ached at the thought of bringing sick people into this building. She knew it had served as a hospital for wounded soldiers during the war, but anyone who was forced to endure this building in August was going to be even more miserable than their illness already made them.

"They don't know where else to put them," Elizabeth replied, her tone both resigned and indignant. "It was just a matter of time before they had to make a hospital for patients. Since Moyamensing is in the poorest section of Philadelphia..."

"And since the first victim of cholera was found dead on the streets just a few blocks away..." Janie continued.

"And since sixteen more people have died in this area in the last few days," Carrie added, "I can understand why the city chose this location for the new cholera hospital."

"I ran into one of the city councilmen last night," Elizabeth revealed. "People are dying daily around the city, but Moyamensing is suffering a higher death toll. They wanted to put the hospital where it would be of the highest value."

"And also be as far away from *their* neighborhoods as possible," Carrie said wryly, her eyes narrowing as she saw something more lurking in Elizabeth's eyes. "What aren't you telling us?" she demanded.

Elizabeth averted her eyes for a long moment as she stared out the window at the growing throngs of people looking up at the hospital, and then swung back around to face them. "When the neighborhood found out the city's plans, the City Council was visited by James Campbell, a councilman from Moyamensing." She hesitated and looked away again.

"Tell us," Janie said. "Ignorance has never helped anyone. I want to know what we're up against."

Elizabeth nodded reluctantly. "Campbell told them that if they persist in their intention to turn Moyamensing Hall into a cholera hospital, the women and children of the neighborhood will burn it to the ground before a single patient is taken within its walls."

Carrie took a deep breath as she looked around the cluttered hall. Wagons of hospital bedding, furniture and provisions had arrived early that morning. She and her housemates, along with other students at the Women's Medical College of Philadelphia, had been hard at work all day, setting up beds, arranging provisions and doing whatever else was needed to prepare for what would certainly be a large number of cholera patients. "They burned the hospital on Staten Island eight years ago," she murmured, remembering what Dr. Benson from New York City's Metropolitan Board of Health had told her earlier that spring when cholera had come ashore in New York City.

Janie frowned. "There was a Yellow Fever outbreak in the neighborhoods surrounding the hospital on Staten Island. They believed it was caused by the hospital."

"Which it well could have been," Carrie replied. "Refuse from the hospital had to have ended up in surrounding water supplies. They didn't know then what we do now."

Elizabeth shuddered. "The men who burned the hospital on Staten Island had to have been so frightened for their families. It doesn't make what they did right," she hastened to add, "but I can understand their fear."

Carrie nodded, her thoughts racing. "Philadelphia's sanitation and water systems are so much better than New York's were," she murmured in weak protest. "We've learned so much about how the disease is spread, and even more about how to contain it."

"All of which these people don't have a clue about," Elizabeth said bluntly. "All they know is that a hospital full of people who are dying will soon be operating right next to their homes."

"So you agree with them?" Janie asked, her eyes wide with disbelief.

"Of course not," Elizabeth snapped. Her hand reached out to grip Janie's in apology as soon as the words flew from her mouth. "I'm sorry. I didn't mean to sound like that."

"We're all hot and tired," Carrie replied. "I believe you're saying that, while you don't agree with them, you understand their fear."

Elizabeth nodded. "I think it's very easy to pass judgment on people. I'm not at all sure I would feel any differently if I was the one watching this hospital be created." She gazed down at a tired-looking woman grasping two grubby, sweaty red-haired children by their hands. The mother's eyes were wide with fright as she spoke urgently with the equally frightened woman by her side. "Look at her. All she knows is that her children could be in terrible danger. She already lives in the poorest, most violent neighborhood in the city. She must worry about her children every day. And now this..."

Carrie laid her hand over Elizabeth's dirty fingers that were gripping the windowsill. "Something has to be done," she said steadily, her stomach clenching at the look of fear on the faces staring up at them. "No matter where the hospital is located, people will resist it and not understand it."

"I know," Elizabeth acknowledged. "But I can't help wondering if the City Council would have really even *considered* putting the hospital elsewhere." Her eyes flashed. "The elite in Philadelphia don't believe any resources should be used to help the people down here because they have already written them off as unsalvageable. I doubt they would feel any regret if most of this neighborhood died from cholera. They simply don't want it to spread."

Janie eyed her for a long moment. "You know a lot about Moyamensing," she observed. "I don't know that I was even aware this neighborhood existed until we were told to come equip the hospital."

Carrie realized Janie was right. "What's the connection, Elizabeth?" she asked quietly.

Elizabeth sighed, her eyes dark with worry. "My mother has a very good friend who lives down here. Mother has tried to talk her into leaving for years. She can well afford it, but she refuses to leave her people."

Carrie thought about what she had learned. "She's Irish," she guessed.

"Yes. She grew up in this area while it was still beautiful farmland. She refuses to leave. She says there is too much that needs to be done."

"Very admirable," Janie murmured.

"I agree," Elizabeth responded. "But evidently she is quite old."

Carrie thought about Old Sarah. She had refused to escape the plantation because she wanted to live out the rest of her days in the place she called home. Sam had felt the same way, choosing to stay until he died. "She's home," she said simply. "Moyamensing is her home."

"That's what I've told my mother," Elizabeth confirmed, "but she is still so very worried. I'm sure word of the cholera hospital has reached her. She is probably frantic."

"And her friend?" Janie questioned.

Elizabeth smiled for the first time. "From what my mother has told me, her friend would simply say she has lived a good life. If it's time for her to go, then she'll go in the place she calls home."

Carrie smiled. "She sounds like a wonderful woman. She also seems like she is making the best decision for herself, without worrying about what other people think."

"That would be Biddy," Elizabeth said, a fond smile on her face as she turned away. "We still have hours of work to do before we can leave. Patients start arriving tomorrow."

"If there is anything to bring them to," Janie said nervously as she looked out the window one more time. "The crowds are getting bigger."

A distant call across the room caused all of them to hurry over to help assemble the next set of beds. There was nothing they could do to stop what might be coming. They had work to do.

Robert felt a wave of contentment as he gazed out over the Cromwell pastures. All the spring foals had been weaned. The frantic neighs from the last three days had settled down into quiet as the colts and fillies learned life without their mothers wasn't nearly as bad as they had feared. They were all bunched together under the thick limbs of a spreading oak tree, resting in the shade after almost an hour of joyful play in the thick green grass. Most of them were lying down, their tails swishing rhythmically to keep the flies away.

Separated by a wide border of trees in another pasture, their mothers—once they had gotten over the separation anxiety—now seemed relieved to have a break.

"These babies sure seem a lot happier!"

Robert smiled at Amber as she clambered up on the fence attached to the barn, careful to stay in the shade. The mid-afternoon August sun was relentless as it beat down on the plantation. He eyed the horizon with a practiced eye. It was still two hours before the sun would dip below the line of trees in the distance. Anything with any sense would avoid its searing rays.

He felt a surge of pity as he thought of all the men, women and children toiling in the tobacco fields with no escape from the sun. Moses always started them early in the morning so they could take off a couple of hours in the hottest part of the day, but even the cooler parts of the day were still brutal during a Virginia summer. Huge barrels of water were placed in the fields every morning. For every cup that was poured down parched throats, even more was dumped onto sweaty heads.

"Do they still think about their mamas?" Amber asked, leaning forward to make sure she could see all the foals.

Robert thought about her question. "I imagine they do. It's only been a few days."

"Do they miss them as much as I would miss my mama if she were taken from me?"

"I think they did at first," Robert responded. "I think it's easier for them because it's the natural order of things, but I also decided a long time ago that just because people *think* they know what animals are feeling, that doesn't mean they really do."

"We just like to *think* we're smarter than they are," Amber said quickly, her ten-year-old eyes snapping with wisdom far beyond her years.

Robert gazed at her. "How do you figure?"

Amber met his eyes squarely. "We have to believe we're smarter than they are because it makes us feel better about taking control of their lives. If we knew what they were really thinking and feeling, we probably wouldn't do a lot of the things we do."

Robert blinked, disturbed by the feeling her words gave him. "Like what?" he managed.

"Like splitting up a mama from her baby. You said it's the natural order of things, but I don't see it that way. If they were out in the wild, there wouldn't be no way to separate them the way we do."

"But the mamas need a break from feeding them," Robert protested.

Amber looked at him with something like sympathy. "Don't you think they know that, Robert? I reckon they have a way of keeping that baby from continuing to suckle. Don't you think God would have taken care of something like that?"

Robert shifted uncomfortably under her piercing gaze. Amber had always been far wiser than her age. She had given him a reason to live—not just once, but twice. "What do you think we should do?" he finally asked.

"Oh, we can't do anything different than what we're doing," Amber said sadly. "This isn't the wild, and Clint and I got to start training these babies. I couldn't do that if they were still depending on their mamas." She patted Robert's hand. "I don't think you're a bad man, Robert. I just figure we'll treat our horses a whole lot better if we realize they are way smarter than we think they are." She paused, smiling as one of the colts kicked up his heels and skittered around under the tree. "We got to get these horses ready to sell. Isn't that the whole point of everything?"

Robert opened his mouth, but closed it, all the earlier contentment disappearing.

Amber frowned. "Did I say something wrong, Robert?" Her ebony face was wrinkled with concern as she leaned over to look at him more closely.

"Of course not," Robert said quickly. She was too young to be told what was worrying him. "I was thinking about how much we have to do before these babies will be ready to sell." He forced his voice to sound confident, but the considering look in Amber's eyes said she wasn't convinced.

Robert turned and waved his hand toward the group of foals. He knew he would have to distract her from asking more questions that he didn't want to answer. "Do you have a favorite yet?"

Amber gave him a knowing look but entered into the game, nodding her head quickly. Her eyes softened as they settled on a dark bay filly stretched out in the shade. "All My Heart."

"All my heart?" Robert asked quizzically. He had decided to wait until all the foals had been weaned before they were given their final names. "Are you talking about the filly with the perfect heart shape on her forehead?" Robert had known she was special the day she was born. Spirit blazed in her eyes, but she was gentle as a lamb.

"Yes," Amber said almost reverently. "From the day she came into this world, she done took all my heart."

Robert smiled. Amber was learning so much in school, but when she felt really strongly about something, she slipped back into the black dialect she had grown up with. "Then you'll be the one to train her," he announced, expecting a thrilled reaction. He was surprised when Amber shook her head slowly.

"I don't think that will be such a good idea, Robert," she said as her eyes strayed to the pasture.

Robert could feel the sadness flowing through her body as she looked back at him with wide eyes. "Why not? You obviously love her. I know she will respond easily to you," he said, confused by the look on his young friend's face.

"I reckon she would," Amber agreed, her eyes lighting with pride as they rested on the filly. "But it can't be me," she insisted. Her mouth tightened as the sadness returned to her eyes.

Robert laid a hand on her arm. "Tell me why, Amber," he said. He was certain he already knew, but he wanted her to say it.

Amber, after several minutes of silence, swung around to look at him. "I couldn't bear it, Robert," she said, desperation making her voice higher. "I couldn't stand to be the one to train her. She would learn to trust and love me, and then I would have to watch her leave with someone else." Her voice faltered as her dark eyes filled with tears. "I can stand it with the others, but not with her." She shook her head. "No, not with her." Her voice cracked with pain and certainty.

"She's already learned to trust and love you," Robert stated quietly.

Amber's eyes filled with alert confusion. "What do you mean?"

Robert smiled and squeezed her arm. "Do you think I don't know you're here early every morning talking to All My Heart, giving her extra grain, and grooming her until she shines?"

Amber gasped. "Did Clint tell you?"

Robert laughed. "Your brother would never have told your secret. He didn't have to. My bedroom window looks right out on the door of the barn, and I can see out over the whole pasture. I've watched you fall in love with that little filly for the last few months."

Amber stared at him, struggling to control the sadness twisting her face. She shook her head. "Then you know why I can't be the one to train her."

Robert felt a flash of joyful satisfaction. He had looked for a way to adequately thank the little girl who had saved his life and helped change his entire belief system. "What if she didn't leave?"

Amber blinked her eyes. "What do you mean?"

"What if All My Heart didn't leave?" Robert repeated, biting back his laugh.

Amber blinked again, a wild hope flaring in her eyes as she struggled to maintain her composure. "Maybe you should spell it out for me."

Robert made no attempt to hold back his laugh this time. Amber sounded exactly like her mama, Polly. He reached up, pulled Amber down from the fence, and held her close. He could not have loved this little girl more if she had been his own daughter. "I'm saying that All My Heart belongs to you, Amber."

"To me?" she whispered disbelievingly. "You're... giving me All My Heart?" she stammered.

"That's right," Robert confirmed, relishing the look of stunned, uncertain joy blooming on her face.

"She's worth an awful lot of money, Robert. Wouldn't it be best if you sold her?"

Robert smiled and knelt down to where he could gaze into her liquid eyes. "Yes, All My Heart is worth a lot of money, but she is worth far more to me if she makes the little girl I love best in the world happy."

Amber held her breath for a long moment. "You love me best in the world of any little girl?" she murmured. "*Me?*"

"You," Robert confirmed, squeezing both her hands tightly, his heart constricting with love. "And because I do, I want you to have All My Heart." He nodded toward the pasture. The filly had moved out from the shade and was trotting toward the fence. "She just figured out you're here. Don't you want to go see your horse?"

Amber stared at him for another moment and then tilted her head back as joyous laughter exploded from her mouth. She leapt forward to grab Robert in a hug and clung to his neck. "Thank you," she cried. "Thank you! Thank you!" She jumped back and did a wild little dance in the dusty dirt beneath the fence. "I ain't never been so happy in my whole life! I love you, Robert!"

Robert made no attempt to wipe away the tears stinging his eyes. He grinned and pushed her toward the gate. "I love you, too. Now go out there and spend some time with your horse, young lady."

Amber laughed even harder as she ran to the gate. Too excited to bother with the latch, she scaled it like a monkey, leapt down to the ground, and raced toward All My Heart. The perfectly formed bay filly waited as Amber flung her arms around her neck, and then she gave a glad little whinny.

Robert laughed as he watched them. They were the perfect pair. He couldn't help thinking about the bay colt he had fallen in love with when he was ten years old, almost exactly Amber's age. He had spent every spare moment with the colt, losing his heart a little more every day. At the end of the summer, his father, heedless of Robert's pleading, had sold the colt for a high price. Robert could still feel the agony that consumed him when the colt was hauled away in a wagon, his bewildered neighs ringing through the air as he watched the little boy he loved disappear from sight. One year later, his father died. Those years were still a blur of pain to him. Watching Amber's joy over All My Heart made the ache almost disappear.

"That was quite a gift," came a strong voice from the shadows.

Robert glanced over with a smile. "Hey, Moses. Don't they look great together?"

Moses came to stand by his side, his massive arms crossing as they rested on the top rung of the fence. "Like they belong together," he agreed. "I do believe Amber is the happiest little girl in Virginia today."

"She means the world to me," Robert murmured, joy radiating through his heart as he watched them together in the pasture. Now that the hugging had been taken care of, All My Heart was much more interested in playing. He watched as the filly pranced away, glancing backwards to see if Amber would follow. Amber, her laughter still ringing through the air, ran after her.

"Giving her that horse right now also provided the perfect distraction," Moses observed.

Robert glanced at him. "What are you talking about?"

Moses gave him a knowing look. "I've been in the barn a little while," he revealed. "I was coming to see you. When I heard you and Amber talking, I decided not to interrupt."

Robert frowned, the earlier worry flooding back into him. "I see..." he murmured. He continued to watch Amber and All My Heart cavorting in the field, trying to regain the contentment he had felt just moments earlier.

"What is it you didn't want to tell her?" Moses asked bluntly.

Robert sighed and looked at Moses. Even after a year, he was still astonished at the close friendship he had developed with the son of the slave who had killed his father when Robert was eleven years old. He seldom thought about it anymore, but the fact that he was about to reveal something that no one else knew caused him to reflect on how much he had changed. "No one will buy Cromwell horses," he responded with equal bluntness. He saw no reason to dance around the issue.

Moses' eyes narrowed, but he didn't look surprised. "Because of us."

Robert shrugged. "Because I no longer fit the parameters that other whites in the area believe I should fit. I no longer hate blacks. I no longer believe they are inferior. I choose to treat them fairly as equals." His voice faltered as he saw his dreams evaporating before his eyes.

"Do you regret it?"

Robert shook his head immediately. "Not a bit. I was miserable with hate and prejudice before Amber and her family helped me see the truth. I wouldn't change anything about who I have become, but it's impossible to make the stables profitable if no one will buy the horses." Worry flooded back into him. He had invested everything from the sale of Oak Meadows into his new breeding program. Abby had invested quite a bit as well. He hated the idea of her losing her investment even more than he hated the idea of losing his own. He had believed he was being given a chance to rebuild everything he lost during the war. Now he was watching that belief evaporate like early morning mist on the James River.

"Someone will buy these horses," Moses said, his deep voice communicating the conviction in his eyes.

Robert knew it was ridiculous, but he wanted to hold on to his friend's conviction. "Do you know something I don't?"

"I know God didn't open all these doors for you just to have some bigoted white people slam them all in your face."

"And you know this how?" Robert had changed a lot, but he still didn't truly comprehend Moses' belief in God. He was also thankful that it didn't seem to matter. The two men had grown to love and respect each other for who they were.

Moses grinned. "Sarah told me that. I haven't seen a reason to believe it's not true."

Robert laughed and shook his head. He had never met Rose's mama, but stories about her were legendary. "Sarah again..." He wished he had even a smidgen of the faith he heard about in the stories, but he just didn't understand it.

"Nobody thought I had a chance of being the first black spy for the Union Army," Moses reminded him. "I decided to believe what Sarah told me before I escaped." He shrugged, a smile twitching his lips. "You know how that turned out."

Robert grinned again, amazed they could joke about the war that had ended so recently and almost killed them both. He sobered as the memories swept through him.

Moses grew more serious. "I meant what I said, Robert. Someone is going to buy these horses. You just do your job. When the time is right, someone is going to purchase them. A door is going to swing open that you can't even envision."

"That last part is right," Robert muttered, turning to stare at the cluster of foals under the oak tree. His hope that his stud, Eclipse, would sire a sterling group of foals had been far surpassed by the reality. He had never seen such quality. In response, he had bought more mares in the last few months with the money from Oak Meadows. He knew the crop of foals they could look forward to in the spring would only enhance the reputation of Cromwell horses—assuming he could find someone to buy the ones he was looking at.

"Does Carrie know?"

Robert shook his head. "I was going to tell her, but they got called away. I didn't want to spring the news on her right before she left. She would just worry." He was glad not to have burdened her with the bad news, but he was also sad she missed the joy of giving All My Heart to Amber. They had planned on doing it together.

Moses nodded easily. "Looks like you're doing enough worrying for both of you."

Robert sighed. "I know worrying won't change anything."

"No, but you would be less than human if you didn't. The trick is to not let the worry paralyze you. You gots to feel it, let it go, and keep right on movin'."

Robert grinned as Moses slipped back into the black dialect. "Sarah?"

"Sarah." Moses slapped him on the back. "Let's go for a ride. There's something I want to talk to you about.

Carrie groaned as she and Janie finished putting the sheets on the last bed. "I don't think I've ever been so tired in my life. I have muscles hurting that I didn't even know existed."

"How easily we forget," Janie said, managing a weak smile as she pushed back limp strands of hair from her weary face.

"Forget?"

"There were times we worked twenty-four hours straight at Chimborazo," Janie reminded her. "We hardly knew our names when we walked out of there."

Carrie frowned. "You're right. I'm doing my best to forget those times." She knew she never would. It had gotten much better, but there were still times she had relentless nightmares of mangled bodies, rotting flesh, and glazed eyes burning with pain. She shuddered as she forced the images from her mind, and then turned to analyze the room. Her eyes narrowed. "Where is everyone else?" She'd been so absorbed in her work she hadn't been aware everyone else had disappeared.

Janie covered her mouth as she yawned. "They left a couple hours ago. Elizabeth, Alice, and Florence are finishing up on the first floor. The driver promised to come back for us. We told him we weren't willing to leave until the hospital was ready for all the patients tomorrow."

Carrie looked up as two men appeared in the doorway at the end of the long room. She recognized them as the watchmen she had seen earlier in the day.

"It's time for us to leave," one of the men called, "but we're not going to leave you women here by yourself. You're certainly not planning on staying all night, are you?"

Carrie shook her head. "Definitely not. Our driver should be here in a few minutes."

The watchman hesitated and looked at his companion. "We'll wait until he gets here," he said, only his eyes communicating how much he wanted to leave.

"You'll do nothing of the kind," Carrie responded. She was certain the men had family waiting at home for them. They must already be frantic with worry. She could feel Janie's alarm radiating from her eyes at the idea of being left alone, but it was not the watchmen's fault they had insisted on remaining. "You must go home. We will be fine."

The other watchman glanced out the window. "Things seem to have calmed down out there."

The first man still looked hesitant, his kind eyes dark with worry.

"Go home," Carrie insisted, although she wondered if she was making another unwise decision. The look of relief on the men's faces forced her to continue, however. "We will be fine. We'll wait right inside the building for our driver."

"And you'll make sure the doors are locked?"

"I promise," Carrie responded. "Go." She watched, struggling to push away a vague sense of panic when the two men disappeared, closing the door behind them as they left. Only then did she turn to look at Janie. "You think I made a mistake." She longed for Janie to disagree, but the knot forming in the pit of her stomach told her she had once again been too impulsive.

Janie tried to smile. "What I think doesn't really matter now. Let's finish putting out the water pitchers and glasses. Our driver should be here any minute."

Regret surged through Carrie. "Matthew will never forgive me if something happens to you." She grabbed Janie's hand. "I'm so sorry, Janie."

Janie's eyes softened at the mention of her fiancé's name, but she straightened her shoulders and glanced toward the window. "Matthew has told me far too many stories of what he has risked to tell the truth of what has happened in our country. He might be terrified, but he would also support us doing what we believe is the right thing."

"So you're not mad at me?"

Janie's smile was genuine this time. "If I got mad every time you did something impulsive, we would have ceased being friends a long time ago. Your impulsiveness is one of the things I love most about you. I've learned to deal with the fact that it sometimes gets us in trouble. Besides, it was your impulsivity that saved me the day we first met. Do you remember?"

"How could I forget you being attacked by a drunken idiot?" Carrie answered, forgetting their situation for a minute as her mind traveled backward. A loud noise outside jolted her out of her reverie. "What time is it?"

Alice Humphries, her blue eyes looking almost haggard beneath her blond curls, appeared in the door. "It's ten o'clock." She yawned as she looked at the watch she had pulled from her pocket.

Carrie's eyes widened. "Ten o'clock?" she echoed, amazed at how swiftly the day had flown by. "What time is our driver due to arrive?"

Florence Robinson, her other housemate, walked in and fell on one of the beds with a dramatic sigh. "He should have been here," she admitted. She stretched her long legs as she gazed up at her friends, her usually vivacious blue eyes glazed with fatigue. She pushed back stray strands of red waves. "Perhaps we should just stay here tonight. I'm so tired I could sleep anywhere."

Carrie pushed aside the appealing image of falling into one of the beds. "How late is the driver?" She was acutely aware she was responsible for sending the watchmen home. She was also quite certain it wasn't a good idea for five women to be alone in the hospital all night. She cast Janie an apologetic look.

"He should have been here thirty minutes ago," Elizabeth said as she walked in. "I decided to come wait up here on the second floor with the rest of you."

Carrie's heart sank. "Because you don't feel safe down there?"

"I like being further away from the street," Elizabeth replied, trying to hide her worry with a tired smile.

Carrie frowned and moved over to look out one of the windows. Once the sun had gone down, she had stopped keeping track of what was happening in the neighborhood. She and the rest had simply worked to get everything done. Her heart sank even further when she poked her head out. Every muscle tensed with sudden fright as she tried to interpret what she was seeing.

"What is it?" Janie murmured as she came to stand beside her.

Carrie stared at the clusters of people congregated on the hill beside the hospital. She could see blankets and buckets of food. Small children huddled sleepily against their mothers, while the older ones played in dim lantern light. "They seem to be preparing for a show of some kind," she muttered as she peered down at the crowd.

A sudden movement to the right caught her eye. It took her several moments to sort out the moving shadows from the darkness of the night. "Oh dear God..."

"Carrie?" Alice asked sharply. "You're scaring me."

Carrie took a deep breath and turned back to her housemates. "There are men carrying buckets of water to the rooftops of the surrounding homes."

Alice looked confused. "Why would they—?"

Florence leapt up from the bed. "Because they will use the water to extinguish any sparks from the flames," she snapped as all signs of fatigue swept from her face. "They're going to burn the hospital," she announced. "We have to get out of here."

"But our driver isn't here," Alice stammered. "Where will we go?"

Carrie berated herself for sending the watchmen home, though she was dimly aware she might have also saved their lives. Surely the men preparing to torch the building would have more compassion for five women. She also knew she had no time to regret her decision. They must act. "Florence is right," she said, looking out the window one final time before she headed to the stairs. "We must leave."

"Leave?" Alice echoed. "Surely our being here will keep them from setting fire to the building. Perhaps staying could save the hospital," she said bravely, even as her voice wavered with panic.

Carrie gazed at her with compassion, wishing she believed the same thing. The tension she had felt building through the day told her differently. "We must leave," she repeated."

"And go where?" Janie tried to control the fear on her face, but failed dismally.

Carrie said the first thing that popped in her mind. "Home."

Janie stared at her. "Home? How? We can't walk there. It's not safe."

"Safer than we are here," Florence said grimly. She fell in line with Carrie. "Let's go, my friends." She flashed them a confident smile. "It's time for an adventure."

Carrie ran down the stairs and unlocked the door. The night was still muggy and warm, but the searing heat had disappeared with the sun. She took a deep breath of dank air that somehow felt better than the cloying air that had embraced her all during the day. She pushed away the instant yearning for the plantation that swamped her as she waited for the other women to join her on the landing. They all looked hopefully down the road, but there was no evidence of a horse and carriage. The road, bustling all through the day, now seemed ominously empty. Something had happened to keep their driver from returning. She hoped he had not come to any harm, but she couldn't worry about that right now.

"Which way?" Alice asked, her eyes wide with fear, but her face set with determination.

Carrie was glad she had watched the sunset so she had a feel for the direction they must go. "We'll go right," she said. It was an unspoken agreement that kept everyone from mentioning they would have to walk over six miles on unknown roads through the dark night to get home. Linking arms with Janie and Florence, Carrie set off. She kept her head high and her step confident. Showing the fear she felt would only make them more vulnerable.

They were barely two blocks from the new hospital when they heard a triumphant yell and the sound of breaking glass.

Chapter Two

They whirled around just in time to see the first flames shoot from the windows.

Carrie ran straight back toward the hospital. People laughed and children danced with glee on the hill, their tiny shadows flickering in the light of the growing inferno. They reminded Carrie of little ghouls. "No!" she screamed. Her only thoughts were of the patients who so desperately needed a place to recover from cholera. It didn't matter that most of them would die—they needed a place to live out the remainder of their lives in dignity, and they needed a place where they might have a *chance* to survive.

A large group of men must have been hiding when Carrie and her friends left the building. As soon as the girls were out of range, the men had tossed in their homemade firebombs of rags, sticks, and kerosene. Carrie groaned as she envisioned all the new beds and supplies burning up in the blaze. She ran faster. There was no plan in her mind, but she knew she had to do something.

She gasped when a strong hand grabbed her arm and stopped her dead in her tracks. Frightened, she struggled to free herself. "Let me go!"

"I'm sorry, ma'am, but I can't do that."

In spite of her fear, Carrie was intrigued by the polite, firm voice. She turned her head to stare at her captor. The man gazing back was not much older than her. His face was tight with tension, but his eyes held nothing but concern. "I have to stop them," Carrie gasped, starting to struggle again. "You have to let me go."

"You can't stop it," the man said tersely.

Carrie felt a surge of hope when she saw a group of firemen rushing toward the blaze, their wagon clattering loudly as it swayed around the last corner. She sagged with relief. "The firemen will save the hospital!"

The man scowled but didn't refute her words. He held her firmly in place as her housemates ran up to join her.

"Carrie! What are you doing?" Janie scolded. "You can't possibly think you can put that fire out." She shot an anxious look at Carrie's captor, but seemed grateful someone had stopped her headlong dash.

Carrie watched as growing flames leapt from the windows and marveled at the heat she could feel reaching out to her from a block away. She hoped the hospital wasn't too far gone to save, but she had a growing awareness of the danger other homes were in. In spite of the buckets of water hauled to rooftops, it would be easy for other buildings to ignite.

She felt a spark of hope when the firemen hurried to attach hoses to the closest hydrants, but that hope died as she watched them. "What are they doing?" she asked. "That hose is far too short to reach the hospital."

"That it is," the man muttered. His face was set in angry lines, but his eyes were filled with a bitter futility, and his grasp didn't loosen.

Carrie stared at him for a moment and then swung back around to watch the fire just as a section of the roof exploded into flame. The roar of the inferno made it seem alive. Mixed in with the roar was the sound of cracking timbers and popping glass. "They're going to let it burn, aren't they?" she asked numbly.

"I'm afraid so," the man managed. He turned away and beckoned to the other women. "I have to get you out of here," he muttered. "You have to come with me."

"And why should we do that?" Florence asked in a crisp voice. Only her eyes showed the devastation she was feeling.

The man shrugged. "My granny told me to come get you. I never tell her no."

Carrie looked at him more closely. She liked the calm compassion she saw in his eyes, and she somewhat understood the urgency on his face, but she wasn't going to leave. She might not be able to stop the fire, but she was determined to see what happened. The fact that her obstinacy made no common sense was not registering in her mind. And, in spite of the fact that she liked what she saw in his eyes, it would be sheer lunacy to go into the darkness with a strange man. Perhaps it was no more ridiculous than thinking they could walk home alone through Philadelphia for six miles, but at least that was a choice they had made on their own. She was not going to allow herself and her friends to be hauled into a stranger's house in the middle of Moyamensing. She exchanged a long look with Janie.

"I suggest you go back and tell your granny that *we* said no," Janie said wryly.

"I'm not sure that's such a good idea," the man replied, pulling his hand through his hair as he eyed the angry expressions on the firemen's faces. "I'm afraid things are going to get ugly around here."

"They're *already* ugly," Carrie shot back as she twisted her arm free.

She felt another surge of hope when two more fire wagons rounded the corner and barreled down the street. "Here comes more help!" She held her breath and watched as the horses plunged to a stop. Men jumped from the wagons and deliberated briefly over the useless, short hoses.

"Get new hoses over here!" one of them yelled. Several of the firemen rushed forward with longer hoses that could reach the hospital from a block away.

Carrie knew it was too late for the entire building to be saved, but perhaps some of the supplies would be salvaged. Several of the firemen grabbed the long hose once it had been attached to the hydrant and began to run toward the burning building. Her alarm and anger exploded when several men from the first fire company emerged from the shadows with hatchets and immediately cut the hoses. Water gushed out onto the road, glowing from the light of the growing blaze.

"Stop!" Carrie shouted, rushing forward as fury propelled her into action. "You can't do that! You must stop the fire!"

Her indignation became fear when several of the men turned toward her with their hatchets raised and menacing looks on their faces. Carrie jolted to a stop, her mind racing as she realized she could be in grave danger.

"That's one of the women who was turning our hall into a hospital," a man called angrily.

"We let them leave before we torched the place, but if she wants to pick a fight, we'll show her what we think about women who want to bring cholera to our children," another man shouted through the noise and confusion, his voice harsh with fury.

"The rest of them women are right behind her," another called in a taunting voice. "Let's teach them *all* a lesson."

Carrie shuddered at the cold, deliberate rage in their voices and eyes. She tensed her body and prepared to run. She was relieved this time when she felt a firm hand grab her arm again. She knew without looking that it was the same man who had stopped her before. In just a few minutes, he had transformed from a stranger into their savior.

"I told you we had to get out of here," her rescuer growled.

"Lead the way," Carrie managed to say.

The man pulled hard on her arm and waved to her housemates to follow. They melted back into shadows that had lost their menacing look and instead become a sanctuary. They had only run a half-block when the man pulled her to the left, up some stairs, and through a door that was flung open from inside. She had no time to think before she and the rest were standing in a large parlor, breathing hard to regain some degree of composure as they stared around. Heavy furniture and rich, brocade fabrics barely registered in her mind.

"What took you so long, Arden?"

Carrie swung her head around and saw a tiny, wrinkled woman sitting in the corner. She was instantly mesmerized by the musical Irish brogue and compassionate blue eyes glittering up at them.

"They wouldn't come with me, Granny". Arden's face was set in a scowl, but his voice was respectful as he tilted his head toward Carrie. "I had to stop this one from running back to the hospital."

"Is that right?" The old lady studied Carrie for a long moment.

Carrie knew she was being examined and evaluated, and for some reason, it was important to her that this tiny woman approved of her. "Thank you for sending Arden out to rescue us," she murmured.

"Are you always so stubborn?"

"So I'm told," Carrie admitted, managing a smile. The woman had nothing but kindness in her eyes. In spite of her silvery hair, blue eyes, and creamy white skin, she reminded Carrie of Sarah.

"Who are you, girl?"

"My name is Carrie Borden."

"You're from the South."

Carrie nodded. "Virginia. My friends and I are students at the Female College of Medicine."

The woman's eyes sharpened as her gaze swept over all of them. "You're all going to be doctors?"

"That's the plan," Carrie replied as fatigue pressed down on her. Now that the danger seemed to be over, the weariness from a long day gripped her. She tried unsuccessfully to stifle a yawn. "And who do we have to thank for saving us?"

"The name would be Biddy Flannagan," the woman replied with a soft smile. "Welcome to my home."

Elizabeth gasped. "You're Biddy Flannagan?"

"Ever since I woke up this morning," the old woman responded, latching her eyes onto Elizabeth. "Who is asking?"

Elizabeth grinned and stepped forward. "Elizabeth Gilbert. I'm—"

A broad smile broke out on Biddy's face. "You would be Matilda Gilbert's oldest girl," she finished, her voice ripe with disbelief. "Girl, what are you doing down here in this sorry excuse of a neighborhood?"

"Granny!" Arden protested.

Biddy raised her hand. "You know it's true, boy. It's me home, but there's no reason in making it seem better than it is." Her gaze swung back to Elizabeth. "You're every bit as lovely as your mother."

Elizabeth sank down on one knee in front of her and grasped her hands. "Thank you for saving us. I was frightened half to death out there."

"As well you should have been. Your mama would be beside herself with worry if she knew what you were doing," Biddy snapped. She softened her voice as she shook her head sadly. "They're not all bad lads, but life seems to have sucked the goodness out of too many of them." She latched her eyes on Arden. "Who did this?"

"I'm figuring Boss McMullin's men set the fire. They were the first on the scene. They set up short hoses so the water couldn't reach the fire, and then his men cut the hoses when the other fire companies arrived."

"We'll talk about all that later," Biddy replied, still grasping Elizabeth's hands. She managed to sound calm in spite of the anger flashing in her eyes. "Right now we have some guests to take care of." She fastened her eyes on Elizabeth. "I bet we have about the same amount of questions for each other, but there is nothing that can't wait until the morning. You girls all look done in. You need some rest." She glanced up the stairs. "I won't be having much to offer you, but three of you can sleep in a bed. The other two will have to sleep on the floor. I'm real sorry about that."

"I'll sleep on the floor," Carrie answered quickly. She realized they could he halfway home by now if she hadn't turned around to run back to the fire. As she followed Biddy up the stairs, her mind was racing with questions, but she knew they would have to wait until the morning. Her brain was too fogged with fatigue to think any further than the appeal of sleep.

Robert was up early the next morning, drawn downstairs by the smell of frying bacon and fluffy biscuits. His mouth was watering when he entered the kitchen.

Annie looked up at him and smiled. "I figured you would be the first down."

Robert smiled back at Moses' mama. "Aren't I always?"

"You got a real good appetite," Annie agreed as she handed him a steaming cup of coffee.

"I don't normally wake up to tantalizing odors in the summertime. They pulled me out of bed." Robert took the cup and settled down in a chair next to the cavernous fireplace that was mercifully empty. Annie usually prepared meals in the cookhouse during the hot summer months, but an unusually cool night, combined with a strong breeze blowing through all the windows and open doors, had convinced her to fire up the woodstove in the kitchen.

"Looks like a storm is on the way," Annie commented as she pulled the biscuits from the oven, their golden tops confirming they were perfectly done.

"I hope so," Robert replied, his eyes locked on the biscuits. "We need the rain, and it will cool things off even more."

Annie handed him a hot biscuit wrapped in a napkin and then fixed him with her gaze. "I heard what you did for Amber yesterday, Robert. That was a right wonderful thing to do."

Robert grinned. He had seen Amber slip into the barn just after the sun rose. Right before she had entered, she had turned and given him a big wave of happiness. "She's a wonderful little girl. It was the least I could do."

Annie just kept gazing at him.

Robert squirmed under her examination. "Is there something you want to say, Annie?"

Annie studied him a few moments longer and then started pulling bacon out of the pans on the stove. "You keep right on changin'."

Robert didn't pretend not to know what she was talking about. "I suppose I do." The lines between whites and blacks faded a little more every day.

"That be causin' you any problems?" Annie asked shrewdly.

Robert tightened. He had told Moses about the horses in confidence. "What did Moses tell you?" he asked, trying to temper the sharpness in his voice.

"Moses ain't been tellin' me nothing," Annie replied. "I don't need nobody tellin' me somethin' to know there be trouble brewin'." She held him with her eyes. "I also ain't seen nobody comin' down that drive to buy horses. I was owned by a horseman for a right long time. This be the time of year folks should be comin' around to look at them fine babies."

Robert sighed, relieved in spite of himself that Annie suspected his problem. "People aren't keen on buying Cromwell horses," he admitted.

"Because of how you handlin' all the black people on the plantation," Annie observed.

"Yes."

Annie thought that over for a few moments. "Somebody gonna buy them horses."

"That's what Moses said." Robert took another sip of coffee in between bites of his biscuit. His eyes roamed out to the field where the foals, enjoying the cool of the morning, were prancing and running, their tails held high. He smiled. He never tired of watching them at play.

"You figure he's right?" Annie pressed.

"I want to believe him," Robert answered carefully. He had thought of Moses' certainty last night while he had struggled to sleep, but he couldn't honestly say he shared it.

"You figure it's best to just worry about it," Annie said blandly, her eyes kind as she watched him.

Robert thought about the conclusion he came to before he had drifted off to sleep. "I figure it won't do any good to worry, but it would be dishonest to say I truly believe it will all work out. I'm going to make sure those foals are well trained. What happens after that is not something I can control. I'm only going to focus on what I can do and then see what happens."

Annie smiled. "You're a good man, Robert Borden. You just keep movin' forward. I predict you gonna be real surprised one of these days."

Clattering feet ended their conversation. Robert grinned as John and Felicia burst through the door, followed moments later by Moses and Rose. Evidently, eight-month-old Hope was still sleeping. He had heard her crying late into the night, but it was the fatigue on Rose's face that really tipped him off. Moses didn't look much better. Both of them reached eagerly for the coffee Annie held out to them.

"Hi, Mr. Robert!" John crowed as he leapt up into Robert's lap and wrapped his chubby arms around his neck.

Robert managed to set down his coffee cup just in time for the assault. "Good morning, John." He was constantly amazed that a three-year-old could be so huge. He was definitely his daddy's son.

"I'm going to work with Daddy today," John proclaimed importantly.

Robert smiled. There were not many mornings that John didn't ride through the fields tucked in front of Moses in his saddle. "You're going to be too big for that pretty soon."

John frowned and turned around to eye Moses. "Is he right, Daddy? I'm gonna be too big to go to work with you?" His ebony eyes seemed to darken even more with worry.

Moses took a drink of coffee, closing his eyes briefly as the first swallow slid down his throat. "You'll never be too old to work with me, son," he promised. "But," he continued, "Robert is right that soon you'll be too big to ride in the saddle with me." His face held a faint hint of amazement that it was true.

"What will we do?" John demanded. He turned around to stare at Rose. "Fix it, Mama." His little voice sounded almost imperial.

Rose smiled and knelt down in front of him. "When you want something, John, you have to ask for it. Not demand it."

John stared at her, but the worried look didn't disappear from his face. "Mama, can you please fix this?" he implored. "I have to work with Daddy every day!"

Rose glanced up at Moses. "Will you please put this little boy out of his misery?"

Moses grinned and exchanged a look with Robert. At just that moment, there was a knock on the front door. Robert lifted John and set him down on the floor.

"Is it here?" ten-year-old Felicia asked eagerly, her eyes flashing with excitement.

"Is what here, Fe-Fe?" John demanded, advancing on her. "You know something I don't?"

"I just might," Felicia teased, her eyes dancing. She looked over John's shoulders at Robert. "Is it time?"

"I believe it is," Robert agreed, not able to stop the smile that spread across his face. He held out his hand to John. "Would you like to come with me?"

John grabbed his hand, but looked back at his mama and daddy.

"We're coming, too," Moses assured him.

"Is it a surprise?" John asked solemnly.

"Not for much longer, son. The only way you're going to find out what it is, is to go with Robert."

John grinned and pulled Robert toward the door. "Let's go, Mr. Robert," he yelled, his eyes snapping with excitement. "I want my surprise!"

Robert followed willingly. He had learned that while neighboring plantation owners weren't interested in buying his horses, they were more than willing to take his money. It was actually Moses' money, but no one would have sold to him, so Robert had handled the transaction.

When John flung the door open, he stared up at Clint towering over him. "Are you my surprise?" There was no mistaking the disappointment in his voice.

Eighteen-year-old Clint, his handsome face wreathed in a big smile, reached down and pulled John up into his arms. "Aren't I a good enough surprise for you, little man?" He laughed, and then turned around before John had to come up with an answer. "*There* is your surprise!"

Robert and the rest watched as John froze, his mouth forming a big "O" as he gaped at the driveway. His eyes grew wide and his mouth opened and closed several times, but he didn't seem capable of speech.

Moses laughed and stepped forward to pull his son from Clint's arms. "John, I would like you to meet Patches."

John continued to stare at the black and white pony standing patiently in the drive. "Patches?" he whispered, his eyes devouring the pony. He turned back around to look at Rose, a huge question in his eyes.

Rose's eyes filled with tears as she smiled at him and nodded. "Patches is yours, John. Your daddy bought him for you."

Robert hid his smile. He knew Rose wasn't at all sure John was old enough to ride by himself, but he had convinced her that he was riding before he was five, so John could, too.

John turned back to stare at Patches for another moment, and then he gave a crow of delight and squirmed to be let down. When Moses released him, John took a tentative step and held out his hand. "Patches," he said softly, his voice quivering with delight.

Robert watched. He had already taught John to move slowly and carefully around all the horses, and Amber always watched him like a hawk to make sure he did.

John stepped forward slowly and lifted his hand to touch the pony's neck. "Hello, Patches," he said reverently.

Patches turned his head and nudged John gently. Robert knew it was the first time John had ever been around a horse that didn't tower above him. He recognized the instant look of love that suffused the little boy's face. Robert had never forgotten his first pony—it had been love at first sight.

Moses moved forward and knelt down on one knee. "Do you like him, John?"

"I *love* him," John breathed, turning away just long enough to look into Moses' eyes before he swung back to stare at Patches. "He's mine, Daddy?"

"Yes."

"I can ride him?" John demanded. "All by myself?"

"I'm going to start teaching you after work today. Pretty soon you'll be able to ride in the fields with me." Moses' face glowed with satisfaction and pride.

"On my very own pony," John said, his eyes devouring Patches as he reached up to touch his face. He turned to look at Moses. "Thank you, Daddy." His eyes swung to Rose. "Thank you, Mama."

Annie stepped out onto the porch. "That be a real nice pony, John, but y'all need to get back inside this here house if you want something other than cold biscuits and bacon!"

Clint grinned as he reached for the bundle Annie held out to him. "Mama fed me before I left this morning, but I reckon I can eat more."

"Ain't never seen a time you couldn't," Annie snorted.

"You're taking Patches?" John said, alarm filling his eyes as Clint took the lead line and turned away.

"Just over to the barn," Robert assured him. "We built a special little stall for him. He'll be waiting for you after you finish breakfast."

John's eyes never left his new pony as Clint led him away. "Bye, Patches!" he called. "Bye!"

John was the first to speak when they sat down. "Fe-Fe, what about you? Where is *your* pony?"

Silence fell around the table as Rose waited for her answer. She and Moses had talked about getting Felicia a pony as well, but they weren't sure she would want one. She hoped they hadn't made a mistake.

Felicia smiled. "I don't want a pony," she said.

"Why not?" John asked, his astonishment clearly showing on his face.

"Because I want to spend my time doing other things," Felicia answered promptly, a mysterious glint in her eyes.

Moses and Rose exchanged a look. Felicia had truly become their daughter since the day Moses brought her home after her parents were killed in the Memphis riots, but they were still discovering things about her.

"Like what?" John persisted.

Felicia merely smiled. "Other things."

Rose knew John wouldn't give up his questioning unless she took charge. She would discover what was truly important to Felicia when it was time. Until then, she simply wanted to create a safe haven where the little girl could heal from all she had been through. Most of the time you wouldn't guess the laughing child with twinkling eyes had seen both of her parents killed in cold blood, but Rose had learned to recognize the pained numbness that filled Felicia's eyes at times. She turned to Robert. "I understand Moses talked to you about his idea yesterday?"

"About duplicating the Tournament and Ball the Blackwells used to host every year on their plantation? He did. I think it's a wonderful idea." Saying the words brought back a flood of memories—meeting Carrie; winning the tournament on Granite; crowning Carrie as his Queen of Love and Light; falling completely in love with her. For a moment, the ache of missing her was a physical pain. He was so proud of her for being in medical school, but there was never a moment he didn't long for her. Watching her depart four days early to return to Philadelphia had been excruciating. The only thing that made it bearable was knowing she felt the same way.

Rose smiled. "It will be a harvest celebration for everyone. They are all working so hard. They need something to look forward to." She turned back to Moses. "And you're sure you'll be finished with the harvest by the third week in October?"

"We'd better be," Moses responded. "Everything is going smoothly," he assured her. "We have a lot of work to do, but it's getting done right on schedule."

Rose exchanged an excited look with Annie.

"I already done talked to Polly and June," Annie said, answering Rose's question before she could even ask it. "They be just as excited as you are."

Moses hesitated. "It will be an awful lot of work, Mama."

Annie sniffed. "Ain't nothin' I can't handle, son. When I get too old to do things, I reckon I be tellin' you about it. That time ain't come yet. You ain't got nothin' to worry about."

Moses grinned. "Yes, ma'am," he said.

Annie snorted. "There ain't no meek bone in your body, boy. Now eat that breakfast and get out to the fields. We's gonna do our part on this side. It be up to you to make sure the harvest be done when you say it will be done."

Moses laughed and reached for another biscuit. "You heard her, John. We have work to do. When we're done, you're going to get your first riding lesson on Patches."

John bounced up and down in his seat as he stuffed a big chunk of buttery biscuit in his mouth and chewed as fast as he could.

Laughter rang through the house as the sun rose over the treetops and filled the dining room with glittering light.

Chapter Three

Sunlight was already streaming in through the windows when Carrie opened her eyes. She was confused by the feeling of hard wood beneath her until memories of the night before came flooding back. For several minutes she lay quietly, inspecting the room she had been too tired to notice the night before. The room was obviously a study. The walls were lined with elegant built-in shelves that bulged with books. Two rose-colored wingback chairs flanked a fireplace, and a massive desk was positioned so that whoever sat at it could look out the window onto the street. Remembering what Elizabeth had told her, she wondered if the desk used to look out over green pastures and trees. Surely it must be depressing to simply look out at trash and squalor now. Sounds from the street and aching muscles pulled her from her makeshift bed. In spite of what she knew she would see, she stood quietly and moved toward the window.

"It's gone," Florence said sadly.

Carrie turned. Florence was still covered by her sheet. The two had shared floor space in the study, allowing their three friends to have a bed. "You've been up?"

"Yes." Fatigue made Florence's voice gruff, and her eyes revealed her grief. "There is nothing left."

Carrie pushed the curtains aside. There was a perfect view down the street toward Moyamensing Hall. The three-story building had been reduced to charred embers. She could tell other buildings had caught flame, but the fires had been put out before they could destroy anything else. Only the hoped-for cholera hospital had not survived. She wondered how many people had no haven to come to today. She knew it was at least fifty, but she suspected it was far more. Beds had been assembled for three times that number. Carrie grappled with the mixture of rage and grief that consumed her. "What a waste," she snapped. "What a total waste."

"Not to them," came a quiet voice from the hallway.

Carrie spun around to see Biddy Flannagan framed in the doorway, her tiny, erect frame almost glowing in the morning sunlight.

Biddy stepped into the room. "I heard you moving around, so I decided to come up."

Carrie was once again mesmerized by the soft glow of compassion and life in the old woman's eyes. "I know they were scared," she admitted. "I suppose I would have been, too."

"Yes, they were scared," Biddy agreed, coming to stand beside her and look out at the blackened remains. "It was more than that, though. It's the residue of centuries of abuse for the Irish here in America," she murmured. "There is nothing right about what they did, but sometimes you can't stop the anger from spewing out."

Carrie stared at her. "Centuries of abuse?" She searched her brain for what she knew about the Irish. It took her only moments to realize it was next to nothing, other than what Matthew had told her about their part in the riots in Memphis and New Orleans. "I don't understand."

"No," Biddy said easily. "I don't suspect you would be knowing the truth about my people. It's been well hidden, it has." She looked directly into Carrie's eyes. "It's not been an easy life for the Irish here."

"You said centuries." Florence rose from her bed and came to stand beside them. "I thought Irish immigrants started coming over in the early part of *this* century."

Biddy laughed, but there was no amusement in her voice. "Oh, they were coming for a right long time before then, lass, but no one wants to talk much about the Irish slaves."

Carrie gasped. "Slaves? The *Irish*?" Her brow crinkled. "I'm afraid I have no idea what you are talking about." Her confusion made her totally forget about the fire.

Biddy nodded. "Come on downstairs. Elizabeth, Janie, and Alice are already up. Faith is making them porridge." She held up her hand when she saw the questions in Carrie's eyes. "I'll answer your questions downstairs. You need to eat something."

Carrie's stomach rumbled loudly in response. Biddy and Florence laughed as they linked arms and walked down the stairs. Carrie tried to guess her host's age, but the lively spirit and nimble body conflicted with the wrinkled face.

Carrie managed to hold her questions in while she ate two steaming bowls of porridge and two thick slices of hearty Irish brown bread slathered with butter. She hadn't realized how hungry she was until she started eating. Only when her stomach was full did she reach for the pot of steaming tea sending out its heady aroma.

"Elizabeth told me you girls have had nothing to eat since lunch yesterday," Biddy said.

Carrie thought back to the day before and realized she was right. "I guess that's why I was so hungry."

Janie chuckled. "I'm glad I ate before you came downstairs. The rest of us might not have gotten anything."

Carrie laughed and turned eagerly to Biddy. "Please explain what you were talking about upstairs."

Biddy eyed her for a long moment. "I'm thinking there must be a right good reason you girls got dumped into my house last night." She beckoned to Faith. "This story cannot be told without you, my friend. Come join us."

Faith, a slender black woman who seemed to be a few decades younger than Biddy, slipped into the remaining chair at the table.

Carrie studied her. She had assumed Faith was Biddy's housekeeper, but now she realized the two women were friends. She looked up to see Biddy watching her with knowing eyes.

"Faith Jacobs has been my housemate for over thirty years," Biddy said. "My housemate and my best friend."

Carrie smiled. "Rose Samuels is my best friend. She began life as a slave on my father's plantation."

"Until Carrie helped Rose and Moses escape," Janie added.

"Moses?" Biddy asked, her eyes wide with surprise.

"Rose's husband," Carrie answered. "They left the plantation on the Underground Railroad the year the war started. I didn't see her again until the war ended."

"Where is she now?" Biddy asked, keen interest shining in her eyes.

"They are living on our plantation with my husband, Robert. Rose is a schoolteacher. Moses has become the co-owner of the plantation with my father." Carrie decided not to go into the fact that Rose was actually her father's half-sister. She knew Biddy had more questions—they were burning in her eyes—but Carrie was too eager to learn more about Biddy's surprise statement. "Please, Biddy, help me understand what you were talking about earlier. What did you mean about the Irish being slaves?"

"Just what I said," Biddy answered, exchanging a long look with Faith. "Faith and I share that heritage in common."

Elizabeth gasped. "Slavery? My mother has always told me you had an extraordinary story, but she never told me any more than that."

Biddy nodded. "Most folks don't like to talk about it. It's as if they are thinking if they don't talk about it, it will mean it never happened. Pure poppycock it is!" She settled back in her chair and looked around at the women surrounding her. "I sent Arden to talk to the doctors who came down this morning to inspect what was to be the hospital. I didn't want anyone to worry about you women. They sent back word to rest here until you are recovered."

Carrie murmured her appreciation with the others but kept her eyes fastened on Biddy. The cholera hospital had faded away into almost insignificance in her mind. She didn't really understand her burning compulsion to know Biddy's story, but she somehow knew it was vitally important.

Biddy met Carrie's eyes squarely as she began to speak. "People like to think blacks were the first slaves in America, but that isn't true. Long before the first blacks were brought here, England was sending over white people to create the labor force this country needed."

"*White* people?" Alice gasped, her blue eyes growing wide. "From where?"

"It began in England," Biddy answered. "Things weren't going so well in the mother country. Famine and war had filled the streets with beggars, vagabonds, and criminals.

They decided that transportation was the way to handle it."

"Transportation?" Carrie echoed, wanting desperately to understand.

"That was their word for banishing the undesirable people from England," Biddy said bluntly. "Of course, that wasn't until they had sent the children over."

"Children?" Florence was the one to echo her this time.

"Children," Biddy confirmed. "It seems adults were having a very difficult time adjusting to southern heat. Too many of the first colonists were dying from heat, disease and starvation in the tobacco fields. They decided children would be more likely to survive the demands of the labor, so they began shipping them over, starting with a group of one hundred."

"But where did they get them?" Carrie demanded. "How old were they?"

"They ranged in age from eight to sixteen," Biddy answered. Her face tightened. "They took them from the streets of London."

"They kidnapped them?" Florence asked, the horror evident in her voice.

"That they did," Biddy answered grimly. "But that was just the beginning."

Carrie struggled to make sense of what she was hearing. "Don't you mean they were brought over as indentured servants?"

"That's what you were taught?" Biddy asked.

Carrie struggled to remember where she had heard about indentured servants. "I can't honestly say I was taught anything." She thought back to when she had first heard that term. "I remember my father talking about indentured servants helping to build our plantation. He never spoke much about it."

Biddy's face tightened with a quick anger but relaxed just as quickly, compassion returning to her eyes, along with a mixture of pity and sympathy. "How long has your family been here, Carrie?"

Carrie was silent for a long moment as she thought back. "My great-great-grandfather came over in the 1700s."

Biddy nodded. "Then they probably owned some of my people."

Carrie shook her head. "My family never owned white people."

"Just black folks?" Faith asked gently.

"Yes," Carrie acknowledged, unsure why her insides were churning so much. She also felt very much on display. Janie had grown up in the South, but her family never owned slaves. The rest of her housemates came from families who had heartily endorsed abolition for the slaves. Even though all her father's slaves had been set free before the war, she knew her family had stolen the lives of so many before that.

Biddy read the expression on her face. "Your family may have the most recent history of owning slaves, Carrie, but I can guarantee you that any of your families that have been here since the 1600s or 1700s have owned slaves." Her eyes touched all of their faces.

"That's not true!" Elizabeth cried. "My family has been here since the mid-1600s. We have never owned a slave."

Biddy smiled, but her voice was firm when she replied. "Did your mama ever tell you about the indentured servants your relatives used to build their life?"

Elizabeth frowned. "Mother has never said anything. It was my grandmother who told me about the people who came over from Europe looking for a new life. They didn't have money to come, so they agreed to work for a certain number of years to pay their transportation fare, and then they were given land or money to start over here in America. She told me they were very grateful."

"I suppose that's how it happened for a few," Biddy answered as she reached out to grasp Elizabeth's hand. "Your mama won't talk about it because she knows the truth."

"The *truth*?" Elizabeth had an almost frantic look on her face.

Carrie felt a surge of sympathy for her friend. "Please explain, Biddy."

Biddy took a deep breath. "I could give you quite a history lesson, but I would prefer to tell you my own story." She locked eyes with Faith.

"That's the best way," Faith agreed. "History is nothing more than a collection of people's stories. It's best told that way."

Biddy nodded and then got a faraway look on her face. "My family started here when my great-great-great-grandmother, Aileen, was kidnapped off the streets of Dublin in 1653. She was twelve years old."

Carrie gasped and covered her mouth. "Twelve? Where were her parents?"

Biddy smiled sadly. "They were taken as well. They weren't sent to America, however. They were sent to the sugar plantations in Barbados."

"The West Indies?" Janie asked.

"Yes. Sugar was quite a commodity, and the plantations required a lot of labor. Many of the Irish were sent to the West Indies, but the American colony was growing. Most came to America to work on the tobacco plantations, though up north they were mostly used for industrial labor." Biddy shook her head. "My great-great-great-great-grandparents were never heard from again. Aileen was put to work in the tobacco fields. Somehow she managed to survive."

"Meaning most of them didn't?" Alice asked.

Biddy nodded sadly. "Eight out of ten children never made it to adulthood. The work was too hard." She gazed at Carrie. "Does your family own a tobacco plantation?"

"Yes," Carrie whispered. She wanted to close her ears and not learn more, but something was demanding she know. "Please, continue."

Biddy eyed her with concern, but kept talking. "Aileen had four children. All four of them were sold to other planters in the area."

"Sold?" Janie gasped. "*Sold?*"

"They were *slaves*," Biddy reminded her. "People might want to clean up history by calling them indentured servants, but they were slaves just like the blacks who so recently won their freedom. They were bought and sold. They were beaten if they disobeyed. They were hunted down if they tried to run away. And most of them, in spite of the promises made to them, never received land. *If*— and it was a very big if—*if* they completed their servant contract, most of them were never given the land they were promised. They had to start over with almost nothing."

"But I know stories of indentured servants who went on to become very successful," Elizabeth argued. "My grandmother told me about them."

"Yes," Biddy agreed. "That is definitely true. A very small percentage ended up with good, kind, and fair people. They served their years, got their land or jobs, and started a new life here." She frowned. "The problem is that a good ending only happened to a very small percentage. Of course, those few were what they talked about in Europe. So many people were lured over by the chance to create a new life. The reality was usually something very different. It didn't take them long to understand they had been lied to, but it was too late to do anything about it. They had crossed the ocean and had no way to return. They simply struggled to survive."

Carrie tried to absorb what she was hearing, not certain why it was impacting her so deeply. Her housemates' faces showed their horror, but what she was hearing seemed to be connecting with her in a deeper place that she didn't understand. "Please continue with your story, Biddy," she urged.

"Aileen's oldest daughter, Bridget, was my great-great-grandmother. She grew up as a house servant on the plantation because she was such a great cook. Her life wasn't as hard as the field hands."

Carrie thought about her father's promise to make Rose a house servant so that her life would be easier.

"Bridget evidently had quite the favor with the plantation owner because he allowed her to marry another of his servants. Of course the marriage wasn't legal because indentured servants couldn't marry..."

"Just like the slaves," Carrie murmured.

"*Just* like them," Biddy confirmed. "My great-great-grandfather, Michael, was a Scottish survivor from the *Crown of London* disaster in 1679."

Carrie shook her head, more confused than ever. "Scottish? I thought the indentured servants were English or Irish."

Biddy sighed. "England was determined to colonize America. They weren't very particular about where the free labor came from. By the time it was all over, they had also enslaved many Scots, Germans and Dutch."

Carrie had a question still in mind. "You said Michael was a survivor of the *Crown of London*?"

"Yes. It was a ship," Biddy told her. "My great-great-grandfather was one of the rebels who tried to run the English out of Scotland. He had seen what happened in Ireland, and Michael was determined it wouldn't happen in his beloved Scotland." Her voice hardened. "He had seen hundreds of thousands of Irish men, women, and children stolen from their country and sent to America. He had watched the land ravaged by famine and disease. Many of the ones who somehow escaped transportation to America died from sickness and starvation. By the time it was all done, almost one-third of Ireland's population had been wiped out."

"But why?" Carrie asked between clenched teeth.

Biddy regarded her for a long moment. "Because the English were getting crowded in their own country. They decided their lords and earls and barons should be given Irish land for their grand estates. The only way for that to happen was for the Irish to be run out of their own country."

Biddy used the stunned silence to continue. "Grandfather Michael was captured during one of the battles. Many of the more than two thousand captured rebels died on the long march to prison. Most of the rest died from starvation or disease while they were incarcerated. The remaining prisoners, about two hundred and fifty of them, were loaded onto the *Crown of London*. The ship should have been headed south, but people suspect the captain had decided to sell the prisoners in England instead of incurring the expense of going to the West Indies. No one will ever really know why he was there on the northern coast of Scotland. What they do know is that a storm drove the ship onto the rocks right off the coast. The crew made it to shore safely by cutting a mast and using it as a bridge to land."

"And the prisoners?" Florence asked with wide eyes.

"They were going to leave them all to die," Biddy answered, "but one of the crew had enough heart to take an axe to the deck and cut an exit for them." Her eyes filled with sorrow. "Only about forty to fifty of them made it to land. The rest perished in the boat when it went down."

Carrie shuddered as she envisioned the terror of being trapped in the hold of the vessel while it was battered by waves. She wondered if their screams were heard above the wind. What a terrible way to die after all they had been through, simply for trying to save their country from destruction. Disgust boiled inside her, but she forced her thoughts back to Biddy's story. "And your great-great-grandfather Michael was one of the survivors?"

"Yes. But his troubles were hardly over. He was weakened by his months in prison, so he was easy to capture again. After that, he was banished from Scotland and put on a boat to America." Biddy shuddered. "It's a miracle he survived."

"Which is how he met Bridget," Alice said, leaping forward in the story. "Did they ever become free?"

Biddy shrugged. "I don't know. I've never been able to find out. I can only hope after all they went through that they experienced freedom for some part of their lives. What I do know is that Bridget had four children. Her owner liked her, but he couldn't resist the profit from the sale of her youngest daughter. Evidently, Darcy, who was my great-grandmother, was very beautiful. Even though she was only twelve years old, she would have brought a very high price."

Carrie remembered the slave auction she had attended years ago. The most attractive men and women had brought the highest prices. Bile filled her throat as she listened.

Biddy's voice became flat with a resigned anger. "Darcy had a terrible life. The man who bought her was a very angry drunk. He abused her horribly for almost thirty years." She cleared her throat and blinked her eyes. "She had four children from him, but all were sold away when they were very young. She had a brief time of happiness when she fell in love with one of the other servants, but he was murdered when he tried to protect her from being beaten by her master." Biddy's voice wavered.

"That's enough," Faith said firmly. "You can finish this story another time."

Carrie knew, as much as she wanted Biddy to continue, that Faith was right. Fatigue was written all over the old woman's face, and her eyes were numb with pain.

Biddy nodded slowly. "It all happened so long ago, but telling it makes it seem like I'm right there with them," she murmured.

So many questions were churning in Carrie's mind. She felt desperate for answers. "Can I ask you something, Faith?"

"Go right ahead. I reckon I've heard this story enough times to tell it myself."

"Biddy said Ireland was almost destroyed. If the English were trying to turn it into grand plantations of their own, why would they try to destroy it? It doesn't make sense."

Faith scowled. "That man hated everything Irish," she said. "Especially because they were Catholic. You see, Reformation had swept through Europe before then. England decided that Protestants were far superior to Catholics. They renounced Catholicism as their official religion and embraced the Protestant religion. He was a very devout Protestant, and very determined that Ireland would be swept clean of all Catholics. He did his best to make sure it happened. He almost destroyed the entire country."

"Who was he?" Florence asked.

It was the very question burning in Carrie's mind, but something had kept her from asking it. She didn't understand why everything inside her was tightening with dread as she leaned forward to hear the answer.

"I hate to give the man a name," she said scornfully. "Lord Cromwell hardly deserves to be remembered."

Carrie froze, her heart beating wildly as the words floated in the still air. She registered Janie's gasp, but her mind had gone completely numb.

Biddy was the first to reach out. "Carrie? What is it, girl? You look like you've seen a ghost."

Carrie's eyes moved to meet Biddy's, but she still couldn't form words. Long moments of silence passed before she could find her voice. "Lord Cromwell?" she whispered. "Lord Oliver Cromwell?"

Biddy eyed her sharply. "Yes. How would you know that?"

Carrie took a deep breath, forcing air into her lungs. "He was my sixth great-grandfather," she said faintly.

A shocked silence fell over the room. The only sounds were the clattering of wagon wheels, the shouts of men, and the laughter of playing children drifting in through the open windows.

Carrie stared at the swaying curtains, trying to make sense of what she had heard. Lord Oliver Cromwell had been an almost mythical person in her household. She had grown up hearing his name—Lord Cromwell, the Lord Protector of England who became the effective leader of England from 1653 to 1658. Her thoughts froze once more when she realized there were actually no stories. She knew nothing about him except that he was extremely influential in England for many years. She had heard over and over that she had a heritage she should be proud of.

"Carrie?" Janie moved her chair closer and put an arm around her shoulder.

Carrie leaned into her for a long moment, closing her eyes to savor the closeness. Why did she suddenly feel the whole world had been ripped out from beneath her feet? Why was she consumed with a sick shame? Why did she wish she was anything but a Cromwell?

"Oliver Cromwell lived two hundred years ago," Florence said, confusion evident in her voice. "His life had nothing to do with you now."

Carrie desperately wanted to believe that, but somehow, she knew it wasn't true. She stared straight into Biddy's penetrating blue eyes. The truth was staring back at her. Two hundred years may have passed, but the legacy bequeathed to her by Oliver Cromwell was still alive. She struggled to make sense of the feelings rampaging through her. "How do you know so much about my ancestor?" she asked.

Biddy smiled. "Those books in the study aren't just for looks, my girl. Most of them are history books. I've been collecting and reading them for a very long time."

"Why?" Elizabeth asked. "My grandmother told me it was best to let history be history. She told me there was no reason to drag the past into the present."

"And you think she's right?" Her earlier fatigue seemed to have melted away.

Elizabeth hesitated, and then her eyes dropped. "I did," she confessed. "Until right now."

"Why?" Biddy pressed.

Elizabeth shrugged. "I'm afraid I can't answer that," she responded honestly. "There is a very uncomfortable feeling I have that things in the past aren't really *just* in the past."

Biddy nodded with satisfaction. "I call it the Bregdan Principle."

Carrie was intrigued. "The Bregdan Principle?" Biddy settled back in her chair, but still held Carrie's hand. Carrie appreciated the strength she felt flowing from the old woman. "How old are you?" she asked suddenly. She wasn't sure why it mattered, but she wanted to know.

Biddy's eyes glinted with humor. "I turned ninety-seven last month."

Carrie gaped with disbelief.

Janie was the first to find her voice. "Ninety-seven? I don't believe it! You can't possibly be."

"Mother told me you were quite old, but I had no idea..." Elizabeth sputtered.

Biddy laughed loudly. "People have been waiting for years for me to crawl into a grave, but I reckon they will be waiting a while longer. I'm fit as a fiddle!"

Carrie smiled as she squeezed Biddy's hand. "I hope I'm like you when I'm your age," she said fervently.

Biddy turned to her, gazing deeply into her eyes. "I have a feeling you will be, my girl. Yes, indeed... I have a feeling you will be."

"Tell us about the Bregdan Principle," Carrie urged, sensing it held the key to her turmoil.

"It's simple, really," Biddy replied. "Bregdan is the Gaelic and Old English term for weaving and braiding. I realized long ago that every life that has been lived until today is a part of the woven braid of life."

Faith smiled as she broke in. "It takes every person's story to create history." She caught each eye around the table. "*Your* life will help determine the course of history."

Biddy picked it up again. "You may think you don't have much of an impact. You do," she said, pausing while she let her words sink in. "Every action you take will reflect in someone else's life. Someone else's decisions."

"Someone else's future," Faith said solemnly. "Both good and bad."

Silence fell over the table again while the words hung in the air.

"That's beautiful," Alice breathed. "The Bregdan Principle... It should be hanging on your wall somewhere."

Faith chuckled and stood up to pull down a framed scroll from the wall. "It just so happens that it is."

The Bregdan Principle

Every life that has been lived
until today is a part of the
woven braid of life.
It takes every person's
story to create history.
Your life will help determine the
course of history.
You may think you don't have much
of an impact.
You do.
Every action you take will reflect
in someone else's life.
Someone else's decisions.
Someone else's future.
Both good and bad.

Carrie reached for the frame and read the words again slowly. "Everything we do matters," she murmured, looking up to see Biddy watching her closely. "Oliver Cromwell's decisions are part of my history. *They are part...of what makes me...who I am.*" The halting words seemed to be pulled from her heart and filled her with an illuminating certainty.

Biddy nodded. "Just as his decisions are a part of what makes me who *I* am."

Carrie sensed a great truth rising inside her. Right on its heels was a sense of shame. Biddy's probing eyes demanded she reveal what she was thinking. She suddenly felt as if only the two of them were in the room together. Everyone else, including all the noises from the outside world, seemed to melt away. "I can't believe this is my heritage," she murmured. The last six years seemed to roll before her eyes, scene after scene flashing in front of her. "I've tried so hard to fight prejudice. I thought I was doing good things..." Her voice faltered. "To discover the truth about Oliver Cromwell mocks everything I have done." Her voice cracked as she acknowledged what was really bothering her. "I feel so responsible..."

Biddy nodded. "I felt the same way for a long time. I felt I was responsible for making right all the things that happened in my family."

"But everything was done *to* your family," Carrie objected, "not *by* your family." Her head reeled with images of the devastation Biddy had described.

Biddy chuckled. "I'm quite sure there were ancestors who weren't victims," she said. "But that's not the point."

"Then what *is* the point?" Carrie asked desperately.

Biddy's eyes softened. "While it's true that we carry some part of every generation inside us, it does not have to become a burdensome responsibility. I see it more as a privilege."

Carrie listened, but she couldn't stop the reel of horrible images in her mind. "A privilege? I don't understand."

"Of course you don't," Biddy responded. "You're still trying to deal with what you have learned."

Carrie nodded. She no longer tried to understand how Biddy knew what she was thinking—she just did.

"You can either consider this information a burdensome responsibility, or you can see it as a unique privilege to right some of the wrongs of what your—" Biddy hesitated, and then continued with a smile "—your ancestor did. I'm sorry, but I can't remember how many greats were in there."

Carrie managed to smile in return, but her insides were still clenched. Biddy reached forward to pat her cheek but remained silent, giving Carrie time to process what she was hearing. Carrie was amazed at how soft the woman's hands were.

After a long silence, Biddy continued. "Didn't you tell me you helped Rose and Moses escape?"

"Yes," Carrie whispered.

"What about the other slaves?"

"I gave them all their freedom," she admitted.

"Your father agreed with that?"

Carrie smiled at the memory. "No. Definitely not. He changed with time," she said fondly.

"No," Biddy said. "He changed because of you. Do you think he would have set all his slaves free before the defeat of the South made all of them automatically free?"

"No," Carrie said slowly. She was able to acknowledge it was her forcing the issue that had made her father change his beliefs and actions. "I don't think he would have."

"So you had the *privilege* of redeeming the past," Biddy said. "Are you fighting for equal rights for blacks and women now?" She waited for Carrie's nod. "You are having the *privilege* to redeem what happened in the past."

"But why me?" Carrie asked. That, perhaps, was the greatest mystery of all. There had been seven generations of Cromwells who had seemed very comfortable with slavery in all its forms. Why was she so different?

Biddy shrugged. "That I can't know any more than I know why I am the one who seems to have been chosen to redeem some of what has happened in my past. People think I'm crazy to still live here in Moyamensing." She glanced over at Elizabeth. "Including your mama," she said. "I know how much pain is trapped in the people around me. There are days I'm able to help people release that pain so they can move forward in their lives." A deeply sad expression filled her eyes. "And then there are times like last night when there is nothing I can do. All the pain explodes out."

"You saved us," Florence reminded her. "You sent Arden out for us. There's no telling what would have happened if you hadn't."

Biddy rewarded her with a bright smile. "That is the truth," she said with satisfaction. She turned back to

Carrie. "Have you always felt different from everyone else in your family?"

Carrie thought back to her conclusion long ago that she was simply a square peg trying to fit into a round hole. "Always," she agreed.

"I did, too," Biddy said. "Have you quit fighting it?" she pressed.

Carrie smiled. "I rather like being a square peg. Round pegs seem boring."

Biddy threw back her head and laughed. "Exactly." She reached forward and took Carrie's face in her hands. "We are very much alike, Carrie Borden. We carry a lot of dark things in our past. We have been chosen, through no effort of our own, to make some of them right." She cocked her head but didn't let go of Carrie's face. "Is your daddy a different man now?"

Carrie smiled when she thought of how much her father had changed. Images of black and white workers in the factory flashed through her mind. She thought of Moses running the plantation as co-owner. "Completely."

"That change will reverberate through all of history," Biddy replied. "Whole generations will be changed because you were willing to step out of the normal behavior for Southern women."

Carrie stared at her as images of Rose teaching a room full of eager children swarmed through her mind. She thought of Matthew writing articles that were changing the course of history. Would he have survived to write them if she hadn't intervened and helped him escape prison? How many black families would be forever changed because they were now being treated with equality on Cromwell Plantation? How many generations would be impacted because little Amber had given Robert the will to live? Understanding flooded into her. "We can change the course of history with every action we take," she said, the truth expanding inside her as she spoke.

"Yes!" Biddy said excitedly. Only then did she let go of Carrie's face and stare around the table. "Carrie may have the most famous person in her heritage, but every single one of us has people who have helped create who we are. Some of them contributed bad things, some contributed good things. We can't change the past. What we can do is acknowledge it, and then decide to make sure the heritage *we* pass down to generations to come is one we will feel good about."

"But it's even more than that," Faith added. "It's not only about the heritage of our families. Every single life you touch is important. A smile, a kind word can change someone's life, altering history at the same time. Likewise, a harsh word or an unkind deed can set something in motion that will cause horrible consequences." She let her words hang in the air turned to look at Carrie. "You said a minute ago that we *can* change the course of history with every action we take."

Carrie gazed at her, knowing that whatever she was going to say next was very important. "Yes," she acknowledged.

"Take out the word *can*," Faith said. "The truth is...*we change the course of history with every action we take.*"

Carrie laughed. The burden lifted from her and flew away like a monarch butterfly taking wing on a summer day. "I'm glad I know," she said. "I have been passionate for many years about equality for all people, but now that I know the truth of my past, I am going to be more passionate than ever." She jumped up and walked over to Faith, taking the scroll from her again. "The Bregdan Principle," she murmured. "What an incredible privilege I have to redeem what has been done in the past."

"I know just how you feel, Carrie," Faith said, a broad smile making her face radiant.

"And what are you redeeming?" Carrie was as eager to know Faith's story as she was to know the rest of Biddy's.

Faith smiled. "My fifth great-grandfather came to America as an indentured servant in 1619." She took a deep breath. "He was also one of the first men to own a black slave."

Carrie gasped. "But..."

Faith smiled. "Yes, he was black."

Carrie stared at her, once again at a complete loss for words. Everyone except Biddy was staring at Faith with wide, shocked eyes.

Chapter Four

A firm knock broke the spell in the dining room.

"Evidently the next story will have to wait," Faith said as she walked to the front door. In moments she was back, flanked by two stocky gentlemen dressed in rough workmen's clothing. Their faces were flushed with heat.

Biddy waved them into the room. "Hello, Seamus. Top of the morning to you, Connor. What are you doing here this fine day?"

Carrie took note of their presence, but her mind was still whirling with Faith's revelation.

"We came to take your guests back to their home in the city. We understand they had a bit of trouble last night. We're real sorry about that."

Biddy stared at the dark haired man who was speaking. "You know who set that fire, Seamus?"

Seamus shuffled his feet but met her gaze. "I'd rather not be saying, Mrs. Flannagan."

Biddy sniffed. "What? You think I wouldn't be already knowing it was McMullin?"

Seamus looked away. "He was thinking he was doing the right thing," he muttered. "You know he always looks after the neighborhood."

Biddy snorted openly, her blue eyes piercing his. "You tell McMullin he doesn't own Moyamensing. I was playing in these streets when they were still open pastures on my mama and daddy's farm. He could have burnt down the whole place, including the people he is *supposedly* taking care of."

"He was real careful, Mrs. Flannagan," Connor protested.

"And which of the lads threatened to harm these young women?" Biddy demanded.

Both men looked away now. "We made sure they escaped," Connor said weakly, obviously cowed by the old woman.

"That's pure nonsense," Biddy shot back. "Arden saved these two. And when they walked through the doors of my house, all you louts knew better than to trifle with them."

"That would be right, for sure," Seamus said, a smile touching his lips. "We're not fools."

Carrie was no longer thinking about Faith's ancestors. She was fascinated by the power Biddy seemed to have over these two intimidating men. She tried to remember if she had seen either of them the night before, but the darkness and chaos had made everything a blurry mystery.

Biddy eyed them sternly but her lips twitched. She glanced around the table. "I've been knowing both of these boys since they were in knickers playing in the streets with marbles. Marbles that I gave you," she reminded them sternly. "You still have those jobs I helped you get?" she asked. "You haven't messed it up, have you?"

Connor and Seamus both shook their heads, obviously relieved to be on a different topic. "We haven't messed it up," Connor said quickly. "We both got work down at the docks." His look of pride morphed into a scowl. "They still treat us like we're vermin, but they seem glad enough for our strong backs."

"You keep working hard," Biddy said, her eyes soft with understanding. "It won't always be like this. The Irish are going to prove themselves in this country. The day will come when the Irish will be seen as equals," she said. "It begins with each of us doing the right thing."

Carrie smiled. "The Bregdan Principle," she murmured.

Biddy heard her softly spoken words. "I teach it to everyone who walks through my doors," she confirmed. "If every single person in the world embraced it and lived by it, we would live in a world we could all be proud of."

Connor and Seamus nodded but were clearly impatient to be on their way.

"The doctors who came down to inspect the hospital this morning asked us to take the women back to their home. We have a wagon out front," Seamus said.

Carrie bit back her protest when she saw relief fill her friends' faces. She knew they'd probably had visions of walking back home in the searing heat. Whatever relief the evening had brought had long since disappeared, and heat shimmered in the air. Biddy's thick walls offered some relief, but she knew the other flimsy buildings must be like ovens by ten o'clock in the morning.

Biddy nodded. "Then you must take them home."

Carrie thought about the study lined with history books. "Could I stay one more day?"

Biddy studied her for a moment. "You still have questions."

"More than you can imagine," Carrie agreed.

"You might be surprised," Biddy responded. "Questions have driven me all my life." She looked at the two men with raised brows.

Connor shook his head. "We only got the wagon for today. The doctors gave us the money."

"I'll be happy to pay for another day," Carrie said quickly.

Seamus shook his head regretfully, his eyes saying he wished he could agree. "I'm sorry, ma'am, but we have to work tomorrow. If we're going to take you, we need to take you today."

Carrie realized she was doing nothing more than creating a new problem. Hadn't she already done enough of that? And she didn't really have any idea how Biddy and Faith felt about her staying longer. She smiled graciously and nodded her head. "Then we must go," she said as she pushed back from the table.

Biddy took her arm as everyone was walking outside. "You're welcome back anytime, Carrie. You can sit in my library for as long as you want."

"And hear the rest of your story?"

"Every bit of it," Biddy agreed.

Carrie smiled gratefully and caught Faith's eyes. "And I can hear *your* story?"

"Certainly," Faith assured her. She reached out and grasped Carrie's hands. "The blood of your ancestors runs in you, but you are proof that new actions and beliefs can completely change people's lives. They can completely change how our world operates. One day *you* will be the person that people look back on as their ancestor. It's a legacy you can be proud of."

"You know so little about me," Carrie said faintly.

"Not true," Faith said. "When you've lived as long as I have, you learn to tell who a person is by what is in their eyes. You learn to read their hearts. I've learned what I need to know to be sure you are determined to leave a legacy your ancestors can be proud of."

Carrie impulsively leaned forward and kissed Faith warmly on her cheek, and then did the same to Biddy. "Thank you. I will return as soon as I can." She saw the caution flare in Biddy's eyes. "And don't worry, I will have a driver bring me. I'm trying to learn not to let my impulses get me into danger."

Biddy laughed. "I suspect your impulses will get you into plenty more trouble, Carrie, but I'm glad you're going to use a driver. Most of the folks in Moyamensing are fine people who are struggling to survive in a system that barely considers them human, but there are some that have let their anger and resentment steal the goodness from their hearts. It's best to be wise."

Carrie opened her mouth to ask more questions, but a quick glance told her the other women had already seated themselves in the carriage. She knew the sun beating down on them must be brutal. "I must go," she murmured. "I'll be back as soon as I can."

"We'll be here waiting," Biddy said.

Moses rounded the curve on his gelding, Champ, his eyes glued to the front door of the plantation house. His smile erupted into a laugh when the door swung open less than a second later.

"Daddy!"

Moses urged Champ into a canter as John leapt off the porch and raced toward him. Rose emerged from the house behind him, an indulgent smile on her face as she shaded her eyes to watch her son.

"Daddy! Daddy!"

John flew into Moses' arms the instant he pulled his horse to a stop and vaulted from the saddle. Moses took a deep breath of happiness as his son's arms encircled his neck in a tight squeeze. Nothing could be more satisfying than this. He caught Rose's eyes over the top of John's head and knew she was feeling the same thing.

John squirmed to be let down. "I'm ready, Daddy! I'm ready! And so is Patches!"

Moses chuckled. John lived for his afternoon riding lessons on his beloved pony. He was improving so quickly. It had been almost impossible to put him to sleep the night before. All he could talk about was *working* with his daddy.

Amber appeared and reached for Champ's reins. "I'll take him, Mr. Moses."

Moses relinquished the reins willingly. "Thank you, Amber. Is—?

Amber didn't let him get the question out. "Patches is ready for you and John," she assured him.

"Now, Daddy, now!" John yelled, dancing around in the dusty dirt road.

Moses laughed and swung him back into his arms. "First, I go see your mother and sisters, young man." He saw Annie move out onto the porch with a platter of glasses. "And have some of that lemonade your granny fixed." He treasured the lemons Abby sent from Richmond on a regular basis.

"I helped squeeze the lemons," John said proudly. He cast a yearning look at the barn but seemed content to be carried.

"Then, I especially need to have some," Moses said, winking at Amber before he turned toward the house. His fatigue from a long day under the searing sun in the tobacco fields melted away as he strode up the steps. The fact that he was co-owner of Cromwell Plantation was still something that seemed utterly surreal. He took a moment to gaze at the elegant, white, three-story house graced with a tall columned porch. He was grateful for the towering oak trees that flanked both sides of the house, casting shade that protected it from the worst part of the heat. He was especially grateful his son would never know the unrelenting labor of slavery, nor bear the scars from whippings like his father.

Rose gave him a warm kiss and motioned him to his chair. "Your son has been watching for you almost since you left after lunch."

Moses smiled. He let John ride with him in the mornings but always brought him home before it got too hot. "Did you take your nap, son?"

"Yes, Daddy. I wanted to make sure I be ready for Patches."

"I wanted to make sure I *would* be ready for Patches," Rose corrected.

John sighed dramatically. "I'm only three, Mama."

Moses could see Rose bite back her laugh. Both of them knew his beloved Fe-Fe had taught him that.

"Just because you're only three doesn't mean you don't have to learn to speak correctly," Rose replied, reaching down to rub the top of his curly, black hair. The softness of his hair was the only testimony to the fact that Rose was half white, making her son one quarter white.

"Yes, Mama," John said meekly, his eyes dancing with fun as he squirmed in Moses' lap.

"Is Hope napping?"

"Yes," Rose said, relief evident in her voice. "I'm not sure if the crawling or the teething is going to do me in first. If it weren't for your mama, I don't think I could handle it." She wiped at the sweat on her forehead.

"And Felicia?"

"She disappeared right after lunch. I haven't seen her since."

Moses wasn't concerned, though Felicia was still somewhat of a mystery to him and Rose. He hoped the day would come when she would reveal what she secretly did, but they were content to leave the timing up to her. She was healthy, and she obviously loved them. That was enough for now.

He closed his eyes with relief as the lemonade soothed his parched throat. He drank water constantly when he was in the fields, but his mama's sweet lemonade was the only thing that could make him feel satisfied.

"The crops are good?" Rose asked.

"The best I've ever seen," Moses said with satisfaction. She asked him every single day. He knew it was more because she enjoyed his excitement than because she cared about tobacco, but he appreciated the opportunity to talk about it. "The flower heads have begun to form. Right now the men are still pulling the heads and the suckers off the plants, but we'll begin the actual harvest next week." He grinned at her. "Thomas is going to be pleased, and we're going to have a large amount of money for school next year."

Rose gazed at him. His dancing eyes said it would be more money than she could possibly imagine. Of course, that would not take much. The idea of both of them going to college was more than she could comprehend. She had been dreaming of going to college to truly become an educator for years. Moses' dream of becoming a lawyer so he could help their people was much newer, but the strength of his passion made up for the newness. "It doesn't seem real," she murmured.

Moses considered her words as John gazed longingly at the barn. John knew better than to interrupt when they were talking, but the tension in his little body said he was ready to leap into action at any moment. "No, I suppose it doesn't." He laughed. "Of course, *most* of our life seems like a fantasy right now, so it's just one more thing."

"I think about it all the time," Rose admitted. "I love my school, but I've dreamed of going to college for so long." Her eyes glittered. "It's such an amazing time to be alive, Moses."

Moses nodded, but he looked away, hoping she wouldn't see what was in his eyes.

"There's trouble?"

Moses looked back at her. He had promised to always be nothing but honest. "It's just something I feel," he protested. "Nothing has happened."

"But it's coming."

"It could be something else," Moses insisted. He wished he was better at hiding his feelings, but he'd never been able to hide anything from Rose. "I have no reason to believe trouble is on the way."

John frowned and patted his face. "Trouble, Daddy?" He turned to peer down the road. "Trouble's coming?"

"Absolutely not, son," he said confidently. He longed for his son to never know the trouble he had known growing up. He knew America was much too volatile for his wish to come true, but he would protect John as long as he could. He put down his glass, shifted John off his lap, and stood. "I say it's time for a riding lesson."

Just as Moses knew he would, John forgot all about the possibility of trouble. His face split with a wide grin before he turned and ran down the stairs. "Patches!" he yelled. "Patches!"

Rose laughed, forcing her heavy thoughts away. She lifted her face for Moses' kiss and smiled. "It doesn't matter what might be coming. We'll deal with whatever it is." Her eyes focused on John dancing at the base of the stairs. "Right now you have a son eager to go riding."

Rose listened carefully as she entered the house, relieved when only silence echoed around her. Hope was still sleeping. She lifted her head to sniff the aromas in the house. The rich smells told her Annie already had dinner well on its way to being prepared. She gave a tired sigh of relief and turned toward the library. It seemed like it had been months since she'd had time to spend in her haven. She frowned when she realized it actually *had* been months.

Her frown morphed into a smile as she remembered all the times Sam had protected her presence in the library when she was a little girl. He had shown her how to scoot under the table he had covered with a long tablecloth, and he had taught her how to listen with what he called "*both ears.*" She was always careful not to be caught in the library, believing Sam's warning that her status as Carrie's slave would not protect her from punishment, but there had been a few times when she had not had time to escape out the side door before Carrie's mother had come in. Each time, she had managed to slip under the table before she was discovered. One time she had to sit there quiet as a mouse for two hours while she heard Carrie calling for her. When she had finally been able to escape the library, she had been sent to bed with no supper as punishment, but she knew it would have been far more serious if they had actually caught her. Only Carrie knew that she had learned to read. Because it was forbidden for slaves to learn how to read, they had both been forced to keep it a secret.

Rose was humming quietly when she walked into the library. She stopped to take a deep breath. She never tired of the rich fragrance of books. She knew she was smelling the leather bindings, but she had always imagined it was the fragrance of knowledge filling the air.

She wasn't sure what alerted her to the fact that she wasn't alone. There wasn't a noise—it was more a feeling that made her walk over to the tall wingback chair that had been pulled close to the window. "Hello, Felicia," she said, smiling when she heard a sigh of resignation.

Felicia peered around the edge of the chair, her face puckered with worry. "Am I in trouble, Miss Rose?"

Rose had encouraged Felicia to call her "mama" whenever she was ready, but she wasn't sure the little girl with eyes much too old for her young face would ever do that. Moses had explained the horror she had experienced when she watched as her parents were murdered during the riots in Memphis. Felicia never talked about it, but the things she cried out in her sleep revealed her parents had been her whole world. She missed them dreadfully, and she carried vivid memories of their murder.

Rose sat down in the other chair. "Of course not, Felicia. Why would you think you would get in trouble for being in the library?" She knew Felicia had grown up in slavery, but she didn't know anything about the plantation she had come from.

Felicia frowned. "Everybody knows slaves aren't allowed in the library."

"You're not a slave," Rose said. "You are a free little girl."

Felicia frowned again. "That be an easy thing to say, but it's not a real easy thing to live."

Rose didn't bother to correct her language. The fact that Felicia was talking to her was far more important than her grammar. "That's true," she agreed. "I remember when I first escaped from the plantation, I didn't know how to live like a free person. It was hard to stop thinking and acting like a slave."

Felicia stared at her. "Really?"

"Really," Rose assured her. "It got easier every day, but it took me a long time to truly feel free."

"How long?" Felicia demanded.

Rose thought back. "I suppose it wasn't until I left Philadelphia and started teaching at the contraband camp. I guess it was about eight months." She closed her eyes and remembered. "The first day I stood in front of my own class as a teacher was the day I started to feel free. It kept growing from there."

Felicia considered her words. "How did you learn how to read, Miss Rose?"

"Right here in this library," Rose answered, not surprised when Felicia gazed at her with disbelief. "It's true. I was Carrie's slave. When she came to be tutored, I came with her. They certainly weren't teaching *me*, but I listened hard. Then I went back to my room and practiced what I heard. Pretty soon I was reading."

Felicia still looked like she didn't believe her. "What did you use to practice?"

"Books from this library," Rose revealed.

"How?" Felicia gasped.

Rose understood Felicia's shocked amazement, but what surprised her was the feeling of guilt that seeped into her own thoughts. Even after all these years, the shame and fear she had suffered as a child could rise up to taunt her. She lifted her chin. "I learned how to sneak in and borrow books from the library."

"You took them? From right here in the library?"

Rose nodded. "I was desperate to learn how to read. Once I did, I was desperate to learn everything I could."

The amazement faded from Felicia's eyes, only to be replaced by a burning scrutiny. "Did you ever get caught?"

Rose shook her head. "Sam made sure I never did," she said. Her mind was full of the man who had been like a father to her all her life.

"Sam?"

"He was the butler here on the plantation," Rose explained. "Sam died on Christmas Eve this past year."

Felicia looked at her sharply. "I thought Hope was born on Christmas Eve."

"She was," Rose confirmed. "It was a night of tremendous loss, and also unbelievable joy. Sam always took good care of me." She pushed aside the swell of sadness and told Felicia about how she had to hide under the table a few times to escape capture. She delighted in the little girl's laugh. When Felicia first arrived, she laughed more freely in spite of all she had been through. As time passed, however, she seemed to have become more withdrawn.

"How did you read at night? Slaves didn't have lights in their rooms."

Rose smiled. She understood Felicia's suspicion. "That's true. Sam used to take the remnants of candles and hide them under my mattress, along with some matches. I would sit in the corner so no one would see the light." Memories swamped her. "Sometimes I would read all night. I would be exhausted the next day, but it was worth it."

"Because you had to learn," Felicia said solemnly.

Rose gazed at the little girl, caught by the intensity of her expression. "Yes," she agreed. "I had to learn. It was like a hunger that ate inside of me all the time." The quick light in Felicia's eyes urged her to continue. "Just like I had been desperate to learn to read, I was desperate to study everything I could get my hands on. Sometimes I only had seconds to grab a book and hide it under my apron. I had no idea what I was taking, but it didn't matter. Whatever was in that book was something I wanted to know, because..." She paused to take a breath.

"Because you wanted to know *everything*," Felicia said passionately.

"Yes. I wanted to know everything." Rose waited patiently for Felicia to say something else.

The little girl stared out the window for a long time, her black eyes accentuated by the long braids surrounding her face. "I don't care about the horses," Felicia said suddenly.

"All right."

"And I don't care about tobacco," she said.

"Neither do I," Rose confessed. Felicia stared at her but didn't seem to have trouble believing her. Rose was thankful Moses was happy working in the tobacco fields, but if she never saw another stalk of tobacco, she would be perfectly happy. To her, it was just a way to help them achieve their dreams.

When the silence stretched out, Rose reached forward to take Felicia's hand. "What *do* you care about?" she asked tenderly.

Felicia kept staring out the window for several moments, but finally shifted around so she could meet Rose's eyes. "I care about knowledge," she said.

Rose knew the girl wasn't done, so she remained quiet.

"My mama used to tell me I was going to be so different because I was free. She wanted that for me more than anything. When we got to Memphis, she made sure I got to go to school. Even though she couldn't read a word, she stayed up with me until late at night while I learned. She made me read out loud to her every night." Felicia's eyes filled with tears. "My mama told me I could be anything I wanted to be."

Rose watched the little girl's face crumple under the weight of her memories.

Felicia took a deep breath as she fought for control. "I have to know what is happening in the world," she said. A strong light came into her eyes. "I read all those articles Mr. Matthew wrote about the riot in Memphis that killed my mama and daddy."

"You did?" Rose was astonished.

Felicia nodded. "All the newspapers are kept in that cabinet against the wall." She hesitated. "I've read them all."

It was Rose's turn to gape. "All of them?"

"All of them," Felicia confirmed. "Are you mad at me?"

"Of course not," Rose said faintly. Suddenly she understood. "This is where you come every time you disappear."

Felicia smiled and ducked her head. "I just want to learn, Miss Rose. I want to know everything. I've read books in here about astronomy and math. I've read about history and geology. I want to know all those things, but the way I figure it, I have to know what is going on in my country right *now*."

Rose was mesmerized by the light in Felicia's eyes. It was easy to forget she was only ten years old. She had lived far more life than any ten-year-old should live. "Why, Felicia?"

"Because I can't change things I don't know about," she stated matter-of-factly. "There is a lot going on in our country right now. It's not going to be easy for you and me to live as free people. There are a lot of people who want to make sure that never happens." Anger flashed in her eyes. "My mama and daddy were murdered just because they was black. I've got to help change the way things are in this country."

Rose felt a flash of alarm. "Honey," she said, "you're still a little girl. You can't carry that weight."

"I know I'm just a little girl," Felicia said somewhat impatiently, "but I won't always be. I'm going to grow up. I don't want to be ignorant until then. I want to learn everything I can so that when I'm grown up, I'll be ready to do something." She paused, her eyes imploring Rose to understand. "I owe that to my mama and daddy, Miss Rose."

Rose held back the tears that wanted to well in her eyes. She would not cry in the face of such courage. "How old are the papers you're reading?" she asked.

Felicia blinked. "I guess the last ones are a few months old."

Rose nodded, sure of her course of action. "I'll make sure you have all the current papers. I know Thomas orders many publications with news and current events. I'll have him send them out, as well."

Felicia stared at her. "Really?" She opened her mouth again, but no words came out.

Rose laughed. "Really." She leaned forward and tipped Felicia's face up so she could gaze into her eyes. "I am so very proud of you, Felicia. I will do everything I can to help you," she promised, her voice catching at the wild emotion she saw storming in the little girl's eyes.

Felicia launched herself out of the chair and flung her arms around Rose's neck. "Thank you!" she cried, joy replacing the earlier determination. "I was so afraid you would be angry that I didn't want to run around the plantation with the horses. It was fun learning how to ride with Amber, and I want to do it sometimes, but I would rather be right here."

"Let's make a deal," Rose said, realizing part of her job was to help Felicia live a balanced life. She was a little girl far wiser than her years, but she was still a little girl. She would grow up far too fast and carry the burdensome responsibilities of a black woman in the United States much too quickly. "I want you to play outside for at least an hour every single day." She understood the flare of resistance in Felicia's eyes. "Felicia, do you really think your mama and daddy would want you to never have fun again? Do you think they would want you to forget how to be a little girl because of what happened to them?" She watched the flickers of uncertainty penetrate the stubborn determination in the little girl's eyes.

Felicia grappled with the question and slowly shook her head. "I reckon not." A smile flitted across her lips. "My daddy used to play with me every night," she revealed. "He would put me on his back and run around the house. Sometimes we even ran out in the streets." The smile deepened and then seemed to be swallowed with sorrow. "I sure do miss my mama and daddy." She peered into Rose's face. "Will I always miss them this much?" she whispered.

Rose stroked her hair and pulled her close into an embrace. "You will always miss them," she said quietly, her heart swelling with love. "You loved them far too much for the ache to ever completely go away." Visions of her own mama swam through her mind. "The good thing, Felicia, is that they will always be with you. Sometimes you will hear things in your head that they said to you. You will remember what they looked like when they laughed or tucked you into bed. You will keep learning because you know how much it meant to your mama. But," she added soothingly, "the pain will be a little less every day. The moment will come when the memories don't hurt so much. And then the time will come when you can smile when you think about them."

Felicia leaned into her for a long moment. "You lost your mama, too, didn't you?"

"Yes," Rose answered. "I loved my mama very, very much. I think about her every single day. I will always wish she was with me, but now I can feel grateful that I had her for as long as I did."

Felicia considered that. "You had her for a lot longer than I had my mama," she said sadly.

"That's right," Rose agreed. She peered into Felicia's eyes. "You had her long enough, though."

Felicia looked doubtful. "I did?"

"You are a wonderful little girl. You have a heart that knows how to love, and you have a mind that is determined to gain knowledge. Your mama gave you that. I know you wish you had been with her longer. I wish you were still with her, too, but I have to believe God gave you everything you needed before she was taken from you."

Felicia still looked doubtful, sadness filling her eyes. "You think God took my mama and daddy from me?"

"No," Rose responded fervently. "I believe very bad men took your mama and daddy from you. But that doesn't mean God didn't know what was going on. I believe God cried when your parents died."

"You do?" Felicia whispered, a single tear rolling down her cheek.

"I do." Rose wiped away the tear. "And now God has brought you to us. I'm so very glad about that."

"You are?" Felicia asked, her voice still a whisper.

Rose pulled her back into a close embrace. "You are such a gift to us, Felicia. You always will be. Please know that." She was relieved when the tension released within the little girl's body. She was even more relieved when Felicia's arms stole around her neck again as sobs consumed her slender frame.

Rose held her tightly, rocking her gently, letting her cry out more of the pain she carried inside. It might take years for it to all be gone, but she would be right here to help. She had already known Felicia was a gift. Now she knew it with more certainty than ever. "I love you, Felicia," she said.

"I love you, too," Felicia whispered back.

Chapter Five

Abby walked out onto the porch, hoping for any movement of air to give her some relief. Philadelphia was brutal in the summer, but she had decided Richmond was even worse. The heat wrapped around her like a blanket and threatened to suffocate her. She stroked the velvety leaves of the magnolia tree shading the porch, trying to take her mind off how hot she was. She searched the horizon for any sign of storm clouds hovering above the surrounding houses, but the brilliant sky and blazing sun taunted her. The streets were empty. It was even too hot for the children to play. She knew they would return with the sunset, but for now it was almost deathly quiet. It seemed even the birds were hiding from the heat.

May stepped out onto the porch with a platter. "I figured you be needing this about now, Miss Abby."

Abby reached gratefully for the lemonade. It was too hot for food, but she knew their housekeeper would scold her if she didn't eat the scone she had brought. Abby picked it up and stared at it. She didn't have enough energy to actually bring it to her mouth. She had left the factory early that day, well aware Thomas realized how miserable she was. He had encouraged her to cut the day short. She needed no persuading. The calendar would soon declare it was September. She could only hope the new month would bring a respite.

"Hot as blazes, ain't it?" May said cheerfully.

Abby looked at her with a raised brow.

May chuckled but then sobered. "It's hot, sho 'nuff, but that ain't what's really bothering you." She plucked the scone out of Abby's hand, put it back on the platter, and set everything down on the table beside the porch swing. "You reckon talkin' about it would do any good?" Her kind black face framed piercing eyes.

Abby sighed. "Do you feel it all the time?"

May crinkled her brow. "Feel it?"

Abby nodded. "The danger," she said dully, unable to stop staring at the shimmering horizon. "I had my share of challenges in Philadelphia, but it's like Richmond has a black cloud hanging over it. I seem to be constantly waiting for the next horrible thing to happen." She hated the plaintive tone in her voice, but the combination of her feelings and the oppressive heat were weighing on her. She allowed herself a moment of longing for her Philadelphia home but knew she would never leave the husband she adored. That didn't mean she didn't hate the feeling of always seeming to dangle on a precipice.

"It can be tiresome," May said quietly. The pain in her eyes said far more.

Abby managed a tight smile. "I'm sorry, May. I feel like a whiny baby." She sat down on the porch swing and pulled her housekeeper down beside her.

May glanced up and down the street to see if anyone was watching, but she didn't jump back up. After a tense moment, she settled back against the swing. "I don't know how's I'll ever get used to not being treated less than," she admitted.

"Surely you've been with us long enough since the war ended," Abby objected.

"Eighteen months of freedom don't hardly make up for fifty-four years of slavery," May observed.

"No," Abby agreed heavily. "I don't imagine it does." She watched as an ornate carriage rolled down the street pulled by a beautiful horse drenched with sweat. She fought to free herself from the burden threatening to choke her. This wasn't like her.

"You want to tell me what's really going on?" May pressed. "Are things bad at the factory?"

"No," Abby said quickly. "The factory is doing well. We've hired more people to handle all the clothing orders coming in, and the tension between the workers seems to be lessening every day." She felt a surge of satisfaction as she thought about their black and white employees managing to work together. There would always be issues, but the lure of a well-paying job was forcing both races to work through them.

"That's good," May said simply.

Abby knew May was waiting for her answer. The two women had become friends in the year since Abby had married Thomas Cromwell. "I knew things would be difficult," she said, "but I was naïve enough to think they would get better more quickly once the war ended." She sighed. "In some ways they seem to have gotten worse."

"And you didn't have to see the trouble or hear about it every single day when you were living in Philadelphia," May observed astutely.

"That's true," Abby admitted. "I guess I lived more of a sheltered life in Philadelphia than I knew. I was committed to making a difference, but my home seemed far away from all the trouble." Her words came slowly as she faced what she was feeling. "I guess I always felt like I had a safe haven."

"And you don't feel that here?" May asked. "Somebody here been botherin' you, Miss Abby?"

"No, nothing like that." Abby tried to put her feelings into words. She realized as soon as she spoke, however, that she didn't truly feel safe. She suspected trouble could find her and Thomas at any moment, no matter where they were. Memories of Jeremy's beating still haunted her. She tried to bring sense to her rampaging feelings. "Philadelphia was more of a melting pot, I suppose."

"I feel like I be meltin' right now," May replied, her eyes dancing with fun in spite of the heat.

Abby chuckled but was pulled back into her thoughts quickly. "How do your people stand it?" she demanded. "Things have gotten worse since they burned the church in April. I know houses have burned down in the black quarters. People have been beaten." Restless, she stood up and gazed out over the streets. "I don't see it getting any better," she said helplessly, not sure if she was feeling more anger or sadness.

May patted the seat next to her. "Gettin' all hot and bothered ain't what you need on a day like this," she said matter-of-factly.

Abby whirled around and stared at her, too upset to sit back down. "How can you be so calm?"

"You think this trouble be comin' after you," May observed quietly.

Abby wished she could deny it. "I'm scared every day," she admitted, "but I'm *just* as scared for you and Micah. For Thomas and Jeremy. For Spencer and Marcus." Her heart beat wildly as she clutched at the porch column. "For Opal and Eddie. For all the kids..." Her voice slowed as she struggled to breathe. Her eyes widened as the humid heat threatened to drown her.

Alarmed, May stood up and reached for her arm. "This isn't like you, Miss Abby. Where does all this be comin' from?" She reached down and picked up a magazine from the table and began to fan her rapidly. "Now you just stop this nonsense and breathe easy." Her voice was sharp with worry.

Abby fought to slow her breathing. She knew she was letting fear consume her. Life had been so peaceful when they had been on the plantation a month earlier. She hadn't been ready to leave when they had to bring Carrie and the rest back to the city to catch the train to Philadelphia. Thomas had offered for them to return to the country, but she had insisted they stay because she knew he believed their absence affected the factory. She should have gone back.

Abby spun around to look into May's eyes. "It's going to get worse, isn't it?" she demanded. She wanted to hear the truth that her heart already knew. Perhaps if her mind and heart were on the same page, she would find a way to deal with it. She hated feeling weak and ineffective.

May regarded her steadily. "I reckon it will," she admitted, sadness cloaking her eyes. "But it ain't nothin' new, Miss Abby," she added. "We are used to it."

"*Used to it?*" Abby scoffed as frustration boiled in her. "How can you be used to being badly treated? How can you be used to knowing you could be beaten at any minute?" She knew she was asking not only for May, but also for herself and her family. Unable to control her explosive emotions, she slammed her hand against the porch column, biting back a cry when a splinter penetrated her hand.

"Well, for Pete's sake," May muttered. She grabbed Abby's hand and stared at the long splinter glaring out at her from Abby's soft white palm. "That will be enough of that, Miss Abby," she said. Turning, she pulled open the screen door and led Abby inside. "I gots to take care of that hand."

Abby was still scared and angry, but the burning pain in her hand was overshadowing some of it. "How foolish of me," she cried.

"Hush now," May said soothingly as she led Abby into the kitchen and settled her in one of the chairs. She brought out the medicine kit Carrie had put together, and pulled up a chair opposite from Abby. "This gonna hurt some, but it will feel better when I done got it out."

Abby bit her lip as May probed her delicate skin with the tweezers. She almost welcomed the pain that made her forget some of her earlier feelings. It also gave her a chance to get her emotions under control.

May spoke as she worked. "There is enough of the splinter sticking out that I should be able to pull it right out. It's gonna hurt like the dickens, but at least I don't have to dig around with a needle."

Abby shuddered but felt ashamed when she thought about how many people in the country were truly hurting. "It's nothing but a splinter," she said, filled with self-disgust.

May held her hand still, grabbed the end of the splinter, and gave a smooth, firm pull. She held up the splinter with a smile and then doused Abby's hand under water. "Now that that's done, I got some things to say to you, Miss Abby. You're being plum ridiculous," she scolded, her eyes flashing fire.

Abby blinked at her.

"You be one of the bravest women I know, but you be wallowing around in fear like you sit in it every day. I know for a fact you don't, so I be tryin' to figure out why you be sitting in it today."

Abby hoped May could tell her, because she was clueless. She just knew she couldn't break free from the emotions threatening to swallow her.

May cocked her head as the fire faded from her eyes. "I reckon you're trying to figure out a way to go right around all the fear and anger boiling up in you. The last years done been some real hard ones. You was needing a real break out there on that plantation, but you didn't get it. Now that you're back, everythin' be buildin' up inside you like that boiler that blew up on the steamship that almost killed Mr. Matthew. You ain't gonna be able to go around all you's feelin', Miss Abby." May took hold of her hand. "You gots to go right *through* it. You got to figure out what you really be afraid of and then you got to push right through it. Tryin' to go around it ain't gonna do nothing but make that steam build up inside you, because you ain't gonna be able to do it. Your heart knows that be true, but your mind tryin' to convince it of something else. Your heart ain't believin' it for even a second."

Abby considered her words. She recognized the truth, but still resisted it.

May wasn't done. "Fear is the brain's way of saying there is something important for you to overcome."

"It is?" Abby asked faintly. For most of the last several years, she had been the one helping others overcome *their* fears. The helpless feeling she now felt was as humiliating as it was terrifying. Yet she also felt an overwhelming gratitude that she wasn't alone with it, and she was also aware there was no judgement in May's eyes.

"You and Carrie taught me that, Miss Abby."

"We did?" Abby whispered, gazing into May's wise ebony eyes.

May nodded. "Before you got here, Carrie wanted me to learn to read. I was too scared because I knew I weren't gonna be able to do it. She sat me down in my kitchen one day and told me that courage didn't mean I wasn't plenty scared. It meant that I felt all that fear, and then I just did it anyway."

Abby smiled. She remembered the day she had told Carrie that very same thing. "So you did it," she said.

May nodded. "Now I read all the time, but I still had lots of things I was scared of. Right after you and Mr. Cromwell gots married, and you moved into the house, I was fretting over something that I can't even remember right now."

Abby nodded. Her memory of that day was very clear. The remembering, and the realization that May couldn't even recall what had her so frightened, began to shine a light onto her own fear.

"You told me that fear ain't nothing more than an obstacle that stands in the way of getting where I want to get. You told me that every time I feel the fear and keep moving forward, that I would get stronger and wiser."

Abby's smile was genuine this time. "That part was definitely true," she said warmly. "You have become so strong and wise."

May lowered her eyes for a minute. "It's going to get worse before it gets better, Miss Abby," she said bluntly.

Abby sighed. She recognized the truth, but she wished it weren't so.

"Just like it took a whole war to make all the slaves free, it's going to take a right long time for people to *treat* us like we're free. There be too many people—especially down here in the South—who don't think we ought to be free. They certainly don't think we ought to be treated equal. They's gonna fight it hard."

"And that doesn't scare you?" Abby probed.

"Well, of course it does," May said. "But my being afraid ain't gonna change it or help make it better. I can't stop no one from hurtin' me, and I reckon I can't stop somebody who decides to kill me..." Her voice wavered, but her chin lifted. "There gonna be plenty of people who's gonna die because them vigilantes don't think we got a right to be free. If I happen to be one of them, so be it," she said bravely. "I ain't got no death wish, Miss Abby, but I ain't gonna hide away from the world because I be afraid. Me and my people are just goin' to keep movin' forward. We have to believe that sometime it will get better. It might take a right long time, but at some point, it will get better." Her voice took on a slight edge of desperation. "It has to, Miss Abby. It just has to. Things be shifting in the world right now. It's just gonna take some time to shift all the way."

Abby listened with her whole heart, somehow knowing May was giving her the gift of courage that would carry her forward.

"You in as much danger as me, though," May added.

Abby didn't question her statement. She knew it was true. Southerners angry about the freed slaves were equally angry at the whites who chose to support and help them. In some cases the violence and hatred seemed to be even more extreme because they saw it as betrayal. Jeremy's beating had proven that. Abby had already been threatened, and she knew Thomas was at risk every day. The earlier fear that had almost rendered her paralyzed had disappeared into the background like a shadow disappearing from the rising sun. She didn't question what made it run for cover. She would analyze it later. Right now she was simply grateful it was no longer gripping her throat like a vise threatening to choke the life from her.

Abby gripped May's hand tightly. "Thank you, May," she said. "I know you are speaking the truth. Everyone who chooses to stand up for what is right in our country is in danger. You're right that many people are going to pay a high price." She smiled as she borrowed her friend's words. "So be it. I'm not going to hide away from the world.

I'm going to believe with you that someday it will get better."

May stared into her eyes for a long moment. Finally she sat back, a look of satisfaction on her face. "That's the Miss Abby I know."

"I'm so glad you were here today, May," Abby said, her breathing once more steady. "I haven't felt that kind of fear for a very long time."

May nodded. "We gots to stick together, Miss Abby. That's what you tell everyone. Women, especially, got to stick together."

Abby smiled. "Women have to stand up for themselves. We have to stand up for each other, and we have to stand up for justice for everyone. That's the only way things will truly change." She felt a surge of power as she spoke the words. Taking a deep breath, she rolled them over in her mind. "Yes, that is the answer." A sound in the distance pulled her thoughts away. She cocked her head and listened, a smile erupting on her face. "Was that...?"

"Yes, ma'am," May said, jumping up and moving toward the porch. "That be thunder rumblin'. I think we finally gonna get some rain to wash away some of this blisterin' heat."

Abby and May were standing on the porch luxuriating in the stiff wind blowing from the east in advance of the storm when Thomas and Jeremy pulled up in the carriage.

"Take the carriage around back, Spencer," she called. "The horse can stay dry in the stable." All her earlier fear had evaporated, disappearing like a vapor into the dark skies. She smiled broadly as Thomas and Jeremy jumped from the carriage and dashed up the stairs, barely making the porch before thick raindrops started to fall.

Abby hugged both of them and then leaned forward to watch the heavy drops generate spurts of dust as they hit the ground. She sighed happily as the drops came harder and faster. The sound of rain pounding on the roof and dancing on the magnolia leaves told her a cool breeze would assure sleep tonight for the first time in days.

May reappeared moments later with a tray loaded with lemonade, scones, and ham biscuits. "I don't see no reason for y'all to have to come inside," she said happily.

"Please join us," Thomas invited, reaching forward to take a biscuit, his handsome face lit with a smile of appreciation. He shrugged out of his jacket and draped it over the swing. The wind ruffled his collar and blew his graying hair.

"No thank you, sir," May said. "I's gonna cook some more biscuits while it be rainin'. The breeze blowing through the house will make it right nice in my kitchen for a change. Spencer already be eatin' a pile of biscuits I put out for him."

Jeremy grinned. "I'm not surprised he didn't get past the kitchen," he said with a smirk.

May eyed him. "You got something you want to say, Mr. Jeremy?"

Jeremy shrugged, an innocent look on his face. "Just making an observation, May. We've invited Spencer to join us for a meal many times. He never gets any further than your kitchen. I believe that means he really likes what is *in* the kitchen."

"He likes my cookin' just fine," May said, but the flustered look on her face didn't hide the glimmer in her eyes.

"He could get your cooking in the dining room," Thomas replied mildly, a smile dancing on his lips. "Spencer hasn't come any further than the kitchen ever since you treated him after the attack this spring."

"Yes," Jeremy agreed. "I do believe Spencer is sweet on you."

May opened her mouth to protest and then closed it, a satisfied look on her face. "That Spencer be a good man," she murmured. The screen door slammed behind her.

Abby turned to Thomas as soon as May entered the house. "Who are you waiting for?"

Thomas looked innocent. "What are you talking about?"

Abby looked at him expectantly. She had seen him glancing down the road several times.

"Oh, why even bother?" Jeremy asked with a laugh that was slightly muffled by a huge bite of a ham biscuit. His blue eyes danced with fun while the breeze ruffled his blond hair. "You know she always sees right through both of us."

Abby relaxed. They wouldn't be laughing and teasing if it was anything to worry about.

Thomas sighed. "Sometimes I wish I wasn't so transparent."

Abby tapped her foot, knowing her stern look was tempered by the smile twitching her lips.

"Fine," Thomas muttered. He turned away when the sound of carriage wheels rose above the rain. "Saved!" he cried triumphantly. "I told him I would keep it a secret!"

Abby moved to stand beside him, peering through the sheets of rain until the carriage drew close enough for her to identify the occupant. "Matthew!"

No one made an attempt to hide their laughter when Matthew ran up onto the porch, water streaming down his face. His clothes were soaked through, and his red hair was plastered to his head. The driver, eager to get home, had urged the carriage forward as soon as Matthew stepped out. It had already been swallowed by the storm.

Matthew looked down at himself ruefully before he joined in their laughter. "At least I'm not hot anymore," he said cheerfully. "The driver offered me an umbrella, but I turned it down. It felt wonderful!"

Jeremy clapped him on the shoulder. "I tried to persuade you to come with us, but no..."

Matthew shrugged. "I wanted to buy a train ticket before there were none available. It was worth getting wet." He grinned as he pulled a waterproof leather packet from his coat.

"Going to Philadelphia?" Abby guessed, thrilled by the excitement she saw in his eyes. He had pined for Carrie for such a long time.

"Yes," Matthew responded. "I can't stand being away from Janie any longer."

"Did you get the news about the cholera hospital being burned?"

"Yes. I stopped by the paper's office before I went to the train station to get the latest news. They found a building in another Philadelphia neighborhood. No one is happy to have it, but so far, it has been left alone. There are now over one hundred patients there. They are expecting many more."

"So it's spreading," Thomas said grimly.

Abby gripped her napkin tightly. It had been ten years since her first husband Charles died of cholera. She would never forget his agony, or how swiftly he had died.

Matthew frowned. "I'm afraid so. The railroad has made it spread even faster than the last epidemic. Cases have been reported in many cities. It's already made its way to Chicago, but it's also in New Orleans, and for the first time, it's in Texas."

"In just three months?" Abby protested. "It has never moved so quickly."

"It's never had the means to move so quickly."

"And Richmond?" Jeremy pressed.

Matthew nodded reluctantly. "The first case was reported on August twelfth."

"More than two weeks ago. Where?" Abby asked, certain she already knew.

Matthew met her eyes. "The black quarter. They are going to be hardest hit because of the lack of sanitation in that part of town."

Abby bit back a groan. Was there to be no end to the misery blacks would have to suffer? She knew the cholera would die out when cold temperatures returned, but tens of thousands could die before the first hard frosts came. The black quarters were bulging with refugees from the country who were convinced they would find a better life in the city. Her next thought was of Marietta. Her eyes flew to Jeremy's.

"We both know she won't quit going down there to teach," he said steadily.

Abby eyed him. "You knew about the cholera already."

"Marietta told me this morning when I walked her to school before I headed to the factory. I haven't had time to tell you. I tried to persuade her to take some time off, but of course she wouldn't hear of it. She insists she has learned enough from Carrie to both stay safe *and* help the people down there. She met with some people today about converting their school back to a hospital."

Abby nodded again. The paralyzing fear was gone, but the feeling of sorrow for all the suffering people was as strong as ever. "Your father would like knowing his church was being used as a hospital again."

Jeremy smiled. "Yes, I believe he would. He would hate the reason, but he would be very glad it was continuing to be useful. At least they won't be treated on dirt floors. Carrie and Janie will be glad to know some of the men put in wood floors this summer. They are busy building beds now."

"What about the students?" Matthew asked.

"They have freed up some of the classrooms in another church. I believe everyone realizes cholera is going to hit hard," he said. "The black population has grown so quickly. There is so much poverty and so little sanitation. Combine that with the heat and..."

Abby controlled her shudder as Jeremy's voice trailed off. She knew too much about cholera epidemics to not expect the worst. She wished she could pack up everyone she cared about and retreat to the plantation, but she knew that wasn't possible. The only way to handle this newest situation was to go *through it.* She squared her shoulders and turned to Thomas. "Please call a meeting of all the employees tomorrow. They must be taught how to protect themselves and their families." Then she looked at Jeremy. "Have Marcus set up meetings at the churches. Education is the best way to help people."

Jeremy nodded. "Marcus will be here shortly," he revealed. "He is walking Marietta home from school."

Abby took a deep breath. Spencer was in the kitchen, and Marcus would soon arrive. That could only mean more trouble was happening, or was on the way. "We're having a meeting tonight?" She hated the faint tremor in her voice but already knew she would choose to simply go through whatever the night revealed.

Jeremy met her eyes with a look of apology. "I'm sorry."

"Nonsense," Abby replied. "We must do whatever we can to help the freed slaves." She did not have to reveal that she was terrified by the price that might have to be paid. She had wallowed in her fear long enough. Now it was time to move forward in spite of her fear.

Thomas wrapped an arm around her shoulders and pulled her close. "Jeremy, why not give Matthew some dry clothes? His luggage is in the carriage in the barn, but there is no reason to get any wetter. Our red-headed friend looks quite drowned enough as it is," he said playfully.

Abby knew what he was doing. She turned to him as soon as the two men entered the house.

"You've had a difficult day," Thomas said tenderly, pulling her down on the porch swing with him.

Abby leaned into him, letting the moist, cool air envelop her. "It's become a much better day," she murmured.

Thomas pulled back to gaze at her, his eyes dark with concern. "I could tell you were tense all day. What's wrong?"

"Nothing that a little May therapy didn't take care of," she said. Thomas listened as she explained more fully.

He gripped her hand when she talked about her fears and smiled when she revealed what May had said. "So your words came back to you."

"They did," Abby agreed. "I had no idea how wise they were at the time."

Thomas chuckled. "It's good to be surrounded by people who love us enough to tell us the truth."

"You've changed so much," Abby said quietly as she snuggled closer, grateful for his solid warmth as the cool breeze washed over them.

Thomas considered her words. "You're surprised I would say that about someone who used to be my slave."

"Yes. I know how different you are, but sometimes, I'm so proud of you I feel I could burst."

Thomas smiled. "Sometimes I can hardly remember the person I used to be. I never want to forget how far I've come, though. It's going to take so many people changing, just as I have, to make things better." He pulled Abby close as a loud rumble of thunder rose above the pounding on the roof.

Abby sighed with contentment. She knew nothing would stop the storms, but she also knew she wasn't alone.

Dinner was a cold meal of vegetables straight from the garden. Thick slices of plump tomatoes joined a large platter of cucumbers soaked in vinegar brine. Carrots and radishes stored in the root cellar filled another platter. Thick slices of bread and ham completed the feast.

Silence fell as everyone devoured the food. Marietta and Marcus had joined them just before May placed the food on the table. A cool breeze still swirled the curtains, but the storm had passed. Sunlight had broken through the clouds perched on the horizon, turning them a glorious dark purple, but darkness was falling swiftly. It promised to be a refreshing evening—the first Richmond had known in many weeks.

As the last morsels of food vanished from the platters, the kitchen door swung open again. May, a broad smile on her face, carried another platter to the table. "Since that rain cooled things off, I decided to give all of you a special treat."

"Strawberry shortcake!" Matthew exclaimed, licking his lips with anticipation.

"You spoil us," Thomas said, grinning as he reached for his plate.

A fluffy biscuit had been cut in half, slathered with butter, and topped with a thick strawberry sauce. The melting butter streamed down into a yellow pool already being soaked up by the hot biscuit. The strawberries were sliding down to join it, mingling the rich flavors. The aroma filled the room.

"Micah picked these strawberries earlier today," May said with satisfaction. "I was going to give them to you cold, but I decided to make a sauce."

Jeremy took a big bite and rolled his eyes. "It's like a gift from heaven."

"Great!" Marietta said with a mock scowl. "How do you expect me to keep him happy after we're married, May? I am a great teacher, but I'm a lousy cook!"

"I'll suffer through it," Jeremy teased, his eyes bright with love. "It also helps that my father made me learn how to cook when I was growing up. It was either that or starve. He was a terrible cook. I celebrated on the nights his parishioners brought over food, but the rest of the time I was the source of our meals.   If your cooking is too terrible, I'll be able to step in."

Laughter rolled as the dessert quickly disappeared.

"I have news," Matthew announced. Silence fell on the table as everyone turned to him. He paused, enjoying the moment of anticipation. He could hardly wait to get here and tell everyone. "I heard from a publisher in New York City today. They want to publish *Glimmers of Change* when I have it written."

"That's wonderful!" Abby cried.

Everyone else quickly added their congratulations.

"What did you send to convince them?" Marietta asked.

Matthew smiled. "I told the story of a little girl who watched as both of her parents were murdered and is now being raised by a black couple who loves her like their own."

"Felicia," Abby murmured.

"Yes. It is a compelling story of how disaster can be turned around by people who care and who choose to do the right thing." Matthew paused. "I evidently convinced them I could fill a book with many more stories. They agree with me that all the negative things happening in our country need to be balanced with some of the good things." He grinned. "It will be a joy to write."

"And to read," Marietta said warmly. "It will be a gift to so many people."

"I'm also going to continue working for the *Philadelphia Inquirer*," Matthew revealed. He understood the silence that fell. Everyone present had seen his struggle when he returned from the riot in Louisiana. "New Orleans was terrible," he said, "but being on the plantation for the last three weeks has been so good for me."

"Not to mention Janie agreeing to be your wife," Jeremy said slyly.

"That, too," Matthew agreed. He was counting the minutes until he was with her again. He looked around the table, so thankful for the people who surrounded him. "The riot in New Orleans is something I will never forget, but hiding from what is going on in our country is not the answer. I am going to put most of my focus on telling the good things, but I have to balance it with the bad if I truly want to make a difference. I have to stay in the thick of things." He glanced at Abby apologetically. He knew how much she worried about him.

Abby reached out and covered his hand with hers. "Of course you do," she said. "You have reached your limit before, Matthew, but your determination to tell the truth has always pulled you back. I didn't expect it would be any different this time."

"Sometimes I forget how well you know me, or how *long* you have known me."

Abby squeezed his hand tightly. "I wish to God none of us would ever have to experience things like what you went through in New Orleans, but I'm afraid this is just the beginning."

Matthew gazed at her, trying to read her expression. Thomas had told him he was concerned about the growing tension in his wife. He didn't see any of that now.

Abby smiled, seeming to read his thoughts. "It would be so nice if we could all hide away from the hatred and bigotry, but I know that's not possible." She took a deep breath. "I'm done being afraid." She locked eyes with May, who had come in to clear the table. "May reminded me that I can't walk around what is happening in our country. I can only walk *through* it. We all have to shift with the winds." Her gaze swept the table. "That's all any of us can do."

A somber silence fell on the table.

Marcus cleared his throat. "I guess this is a good time to talk about the Black Militia we're forming."

"Things are getting worse?" Thomas asked.

Micah, who had been gone for most of the day, walked into the dining room in time to hear Marcus' announcement. "I'm sorry to be getting back so late, Mr. Cromwell," he said.

Thomas nodded. "Tell us what you found out."

Abby looked at her husband sharply. She had known Micah was gone all day. She didn't realize until now that Thomas had sent him on a mission.

Micah exchanged a long look with Marcus and then settled in at the table. He accepted the cup of coffee May handed him with a grateful smile, but waved off the food. "I'll eat later," he said. "I been through most of the black quarter today," he announced. "In the last month, fifty-two homes have been burned. At least one hundred men have been beaten, and at least forty women have been raped."

Abby gasped and covered her mouth.

Micah glanced at her. "I'm real sorry, Miss Abby..."

Abby shook her head. "We have to know the truth," she managed.

He nodded gravely. "It's gonna get worse," he said. "The vigilante groups are growing. Not only here in Richmond, but everywhere. They's determined to stop black folks from having the rights President Lincoln gave us."

"That's why we're forming the militia groups," Marcus growled. "We're not going to sit back and let it happen anymore. There are a lot of black men here who fought for the Union. We have weapons." His eyes narrowed. "We know how to use them. We're going to make folks think twice before they come down to hurt us."

Abby bit back a protest. She hated the thought of more violence, but she also knew things would only get worse for the blacks if they did nothing. The Richmond government was either powerless to stop what was happening, or they simply didn't care. It made her sick to realize it was probably the latter of the two.

Chapter Six

Abby gazed at Matthew. "Please tell me something is going to happen in Congress to change the situation in the South."

Matthew nodded. "I can do that," he said. "President Johnson has virtually lost all power with Congress."

"What about the National Union Convention that met earlier this month?" Thomas asked. "I was hoping you would be able to give us news of that."

"I can." It gave Matthew a deep sense of satisfaction to know that his series of articles after the riots in Memphis and New Orleans had played a part in changing the mood of the country. "The convention was called with the hope that President Johnson's friends who are fond of his pro-South Reconstruction policies could rally support for him."

"Please tell me it failed," Jeremy pleaded.

"It failed," Matthew assured him. "About seven thousand prominent politicians and activists attended the convention." He glanced at Marcus, aware he wouldn't have been privy to much national news before the end of the war. "The National Union Party was the name used by the Republican Party during the war. They wanted to stress the national character of the war and make it more than just a North-South thing. Unfortunately, it was also this thinking that resulted in President Johnson being our vice presidential nominee. Since he was from Tennessee, the hope was that more people would rally behind the ticket during the elections."

"It worked," Marcus commented.

"Yes," Matthew agreed with a scowl, "but it also backfired when Johnson became president." He took a deep breath as he pulled his thoughts together. "This latest convention was an attempt to maintain a coalition of Johnson supporters. They tried to bring together moderate and conservative Republicans, as well as defecting Democrats."

"So they could push through Johnson's Reconstruction policies," Thomas observed.

"Yes." Matthew gave a slight smile. "It was a dismal failure. Too much of the country has seen the results of President Johnson's policies."

"Because of your articles," Marietta pointed out proudly.

"My voice was just one of many."

"But none as powerful as yours," Abby insisted. "You were one of the few journalists in the thick of things who had the courage to tell the truth. Which is, of course, why you must continue doing so."

Matthew squeezed her hand with gratitude.

"What happens now?" Marcus asked. "Is there any hope things will change for black folks down here?"

Matthew grimaced. "I believe so, but I don't believe the answer will come as quickly as we all want it, or need it to. I am confident President Johnson is going to lose all power, but it won't be until after the November election. And then it is going to take time for the Congress to enact change."

A solemn silence fell on the table.

Marcus was the first to break it. "So we'll have to take care of things ourselves," he said grimly.

Matthew met his eyes. "I'm afraid you're right."

Jeremy's gut was churning as he walked Marietta home through the dark neighborhoods. He was grateful for the glimmering light of the street lanterns. It wasn't safe to travel in total darkness in Richmond anymore. He missed the easy days of his youth when he would spend hours roaming the streets of the city, never once feeling any danger. He bit back a sigh as he realized anew that those days were long gone. That realization only made his gut churn harder.

The rain had moved on to the mountains, but a refreshing breeze made the limbs of the oak and maple trees create a dance of shadows on the road. He wasn't ready for fall yet, but he was grateful for a break in the heat. It would probably return tomorrow with worse humidity than before, but he was going to enjoy the respite. He tucked Marietta's arm more securely through his and smiled down at her.

"You're just going to smile at me?" Marietta asked.

Jeremy gazed down into her vibrant blue eyes, admiring the sheen of her red hair in the glow from the street lanterns. "You'd rather I not smile?" he teased.

Marietta didn't return his smile. "I'd *rather* you tell me what is really going on inside of you."

Jeremy frowned as he searched for words. He was certain he had hidden the true state of his emotions. Evidently, he had not succeeded.

Marietta stopped and pulled him to face her. "I know you constantly want to protect me. I realize it may take some time for you to understand I am not a fragile Southern belle who longs for a man to take care of her, but I thought we had come further than this, Jeremy." Her expression was one of frustrated exasperation.

Jeremy felt a surge of remorse, as well as regret that she had sensed his turmoil, but he still didn't know what to say. He glanced away as a carriage rattled down the street. He watched it until it was out of sight before turning back to her.

Marietta stamped her foot as her eyes flashed. "Out with it, Jeremy! We are getting married in four months. I will not have a husband who treats me like a delicate doll."

Jeremy sucked in his breath, wishing she wasn't so adorable when she was angry. He knew what he needed to do, but she wasn't making it any easier. "Perhaps you should reconsider your decision," he said, every part of him aching as he forced out the words.

Marietta stared at him. "What?"

"Are you sure you want to be my wife, Marietta?" What he really meant to say was that they were making a mistake getting married, but he couldn't bring himself to utter the words. Feeling a surge of self-contempt for his cowardice, he continued. "You heard Micah and Marcus. Things are getting worse. We both know my being mulatto—especially being one who looks completely white—makes me even more of a target. The vigilantes see me as a bigger threat." His eyes darkened with memories of the beating he had suffered that spring. The scars had faded, but the images had not left his mind. "Women are being attacked, too," he continued, as he tried unsuccessfully to control the desperation he felt. "Your being with me, combined with the fact that you're a Northern teacher, is only going to make you more of a target."

"We're still talking about this?"

Jeremy took a breath, trying to read her expression. He could see danger flashing behind the calm demeanor, but he had to make her understand. "It's getting worse," he repeated. "I have let my love for you become more important than your safety…"

"And my love for you?" Marietta broke in. "Is that not to be considered?" She didn't give him time to answer. "Do you love me so little that you would simply cast me aside when it's not convenient?"

Jeremy flushed and opened his mouth to answer, but she cut him off.

"Clearly you have decided that you no longer see me as your equal," she said angrily.

"That's not true!" Jeremy exclaimed. "You are definitely my equal, but…"

"But nothing," Marietta said. "I either am, or I am not. There is no middle ground. Have you been lying to me all this time?" she pressed.

Jeremy thought his insides would split open when the anger in her beautiful eyes was replaced by pain. "I've never lied to you," he said.

Just as quickly as the pain had flashed in Marietta's eyes, it disappeared and was replaced by triumph. "Exactly."

Jeremy was lost. "Excuse me?"

Marietta stepped forward. Heedless of whoever might be peering from the windows of the surrounding homes, she planted a warm kiss on his lips. "You're being ridiculous, Jeremy. I knew the risks when I fell in love with you. I knew the risks when I agreed to marry you. I have certainly not forgotten the risks now that things are becoming more dangerous." She paused. "I think of them every day," she admitted.

"Then you know..."

Marietta put a hand on his lips to stop him from talking. "What I *know* is that I love you more today than when I fell in love with you. I know that I love you more today than I did when I agreed to marry you." She stepped back and straightened her shoulders. "I also know that one or more of us may be injured or killed in the battle that is raging through America," she said, her eyes gazing into his.

Jeremy's gut clenched with pain.

"Not loving each other will *not* change that," Marietta continued. "Refusing to get married will not change that. The choices we have made will have us both on the front lines for as long as there is a battle to be fought." She took a deep breath. "The only way we will both get through the time ahead is to rely on each other. We must trust the love we share. Don't you see?" she pleaded. "You can't protect me, Jeremy, any more than I can protect you. Our only choice is to love each other with every fiber of our being. It is too late to turn back the clock."

Jeremy stared into her eyes. He wanted to deny his inability to protect her, but he also knew she was speaking the truth.

Marietta's voice grew gentler. "I love you, Jeremy Anthony. You have made a choice to live as a mulatto because you have also made a choice to fight for what is right. You are fighting for Rose and Moses. You are fighting for your nieces and nephew. You are fighting for Marcus and Micah and Spencer." She gripped his hand tightly. "I have made the same choice. I could run away to the North and teach school where I would be safe. I *choose* not to. I might be able to convince you to come north with me to escape the danger. I *choose* not to try. This is my battle, too." She took another fortifying breath. "Our only protection is our love."

Jeremy gazed at the courageous light burning in her eyes for a long moment and then crushed her to his chest. As he held her tight, he could feel their hearts beating against each other. He could no more imagine life without Marietta than he could imagine breathing under water. They had both made their choices—now they would both have to live with them.

Marietta pressed herself against him for a long moment. When she pushed back, the street lamp played across her face. "Can we officially be done with this conversation? Forever?"

Jeremy smiled and pulled her back to him. "We are getting married in four months," he said. "Until then, we are going to love each other, worry about each other, and support each other in every way we can." He paused. "I'm also going to hire someone to take you home when you're done at the school. Spencer will be there every chance he can, but he has already recommended someone else that he trusts completely. I will continue to drive you to school each morning." He held his breath, not at all sure of her reaction, but knowing this was not something he was willing to compromise on.

Marietta laughed, her eyes glowing with love. "And I'm smart enough not to argue with you about that. Just because I'm determined to stay and make a difference does not mean I will also choose to be foolish. Having someone to accompany me will be most welcome, sir."

Jeremy sighed with relief. He had expected her to fight him on his plan. Once again he recognized that Marietta was as smart as she was beautiful. "Thank you," he murmured. His heart swelled with love as he caressed her cheek. "I never want to lose you."

Marietta sighed with contentment, snuggling closer. "And I never want to lose you, my darling." She tilted her face up. "Should we scandalize the neighbors a little more?"

Jeremy lowered his head and claimed her lips in a passionate kiss. He didn't care who was watching or what they would think. He was going to make the most of every moment because he never knew when the joy he felt might be snatched away.

A sudden movement down a side street made him jerk to attention. Holding a finger to his lips in warning, he pulled Marietta back into the shadow of a large tree. She remained silent, peering in the direction he pointed. They stood motionless as a group of ten white men emerged from the darkness. Rifles and pistols reflected the street lanterns. The expressions on the men's faces as they turned and moved in the direction of the black quarter were all Jeremy and Marietta needed to see.

"Quickly," Marietta whispered. "We can take this side alley to my boarding house."

Jeremy nodded, breaking into a run as they moved further into the darkness. Neither said another word until they were standing in front of Marietta's residence, their sides heaving from their dash through the night.

Marietta placed a finger to his lips. "Go!" she said urgently. "Warn who you can. You'll beat them there because you know the area better." Her voice tightened with love. "Be safe..."

Jeremy turned and ran.

Marietta watched until he disappeared around a corner, her heart pounding with fear. She had meant every word she had uttered earlier. Both of them had made choices that put them in grave danger. She had no regrets, but that certainly didn't mean she wouldn't feel fear. She waited a long moment and then reluctantly entered her building, praying Jeremy would find one of the patrol members quickly. It was going to be a long night.

Marietta climbed the stairs to her second-floor room. She smiled at her boarding house keeper when the old lady cracked open her door and peered out at her. In spite of Marietta's admonitions not to do it, the woman never went to bed until she was safely at home. Marietta hated the worry she caused, but she also relished the knowledge someone was looking out for her.

She entered her room but didn't bother to turn on the light. Neither did she undress to get ready for bed. Thankful her room was not sweltering with heat, she quietly pulled a chair over to the window and settled down to wait.

Jeremy knew her well enough to know she would be sitting beside her window until he returned. When he walked home and waved at her, she would allow herself to go to bed. Until then, she would watch and pray.

Eddie sucked in his breath as a light tap sounded at the door. The warning system in the black quarter was simple but effective. He strode across the room and quickly extinguished the candle on the table. Amber Lou and Carl, both hunched over their homework on the floor, blew out the candle in front of them and stood to move into the back room to warn Cindy and George. Eddie was sure his two children were frightened, but the four cousins knew what to do. If things got bad, they would all slip out the ground floor window and run for help and protection.

Opal appeared at his side, taking his hand in a firm grip. "Does the door have the latch on?" she whispered.

"Yes," Eddie replied, though he knew the door could easily be bashed in.

Jewel materialized from the darkness. She had been upstairs sewing. "All the candles are out," she reported, her voice trembling with fear.

Eddie clenched his teeth when he heard the terror in his sister-in-law's voice. He was sick of the pervasive fear in the quarter, but grateful for the system in place. He wondered who had warned him this time.

"Where is Clark?" Jewel whispered. "He be at a meetin'?"

Eddie reached for her hand. "He is on patrol." He understood when Jewel sucked in her breath. Being on patrol meant her husband was in more danger because whatever was coming was more likely to find him. "My brother is gonna be fine," he said reassuringly. "He knows this area better than anyone." Jewel clutched his hand but remained silent.

Eddie moved closer to the window. If trouble was coming, he wanted to see it before it reached them. Experience had taught the quarter residents that dark homes were less likely to be attacked. All the men out on patrol, as soon as they suspected trouble, raced from one house to the next, tapping lightly to sound the alarm. He looked up and down the street, relieved when he didn't see the flicker of even one candle or oil lamp. Opal and Jewel pressed in even closer to him. They all waited quietly.

Eddie felt the trouble coming minutes before he saw it. The dark forms of the vigilante group emerged from the black night. There were no streetlights in the quarters. Usually that worked against the residents, but tonight it made it almost impossible for the vigilantes to see more than a few feet in front of them. There was no moon, and every shanty and building on the road was shrouded in darkness.

"What happened to all the niggers?" he heard one man growl.

"They must have been warned," he heard another one mutter, his voice tight with nervousness.

Eddie smiled grimly. These men had no idea how nervous they should be. He knew there were men on patrol watching from the cracks between the houses. Right now they were powerless, but that would change soon. He had been at the earlier meeting that finalized the creation of the Black Militia. He wouldn't be part of it because he had not served in the Union Army, but he was going to handle the administration. His years in prison had toughened him, but they hadn't given him firearm skills. He knew, though, that the part he would play in it was equally important.

"Do you suppose they're watching us?" the man with the nervous voice asked.

"Hush!" another man whispered. "We don't want to give away our position."

Eddie bit back a laugh. There were hundreds of eyes trained on the men right at that moment. The residents had been warned to stay inside no matter what, but they needed no urging. Every black person in the city was aware of the beatings that were happening on an almost daily basis.

Eddie relaxed a little as the men walked slowly up the street. They seemed completely confused by the total darkness. Opal leaned into him, but he squeezed her hand to remind her to stay silent. He was taking no chances. He could imagine the children huddled in the corner of their room, trembling with fear. His anger flared as he once again questioned his and Opal's decision to leave Philadelphia to return to Richmond. They had both wanted to get away from the crowded, lonely city after their restaurant had burned—taking Susie, Zeke, and the two Sadies with it—but the constant fear pervading the air in the old capital of the Confederacy was wearing on all of them.

Time ticked away as the three of them remained at their window post. They knew the men could turn around and retrace their steps at any moment. Now was not the time to let their guard down, though Eddie knew there was little they would be able to do against ten men with whips and guns. His teeth clenched as the night crept forward.

It seemed like an eternity before Eddie saw another dark form slip through the night, stopping at every dwelling. He breathed a sigh of relief when a light tap told him the vigilante group had left their area. He silently prayed no one else would be harmed, but for the moment, he was simply grateful no one in his family had been threatened, injured, or killed. He was quite sure he and Opal couldn't take any more death.

By unspoken agreement, no one lit a candle. There was no reason to take the risk. The patrol thought the vigilantes were gone, but it was also possible one or two of the men would double back to try to catch anyone foolish enough to let their guard down.

Opal and Jewel slipped into the bedroom to tell the children the danger had passed, and to tuck them into their beds. Eddie heard the soft murmur of Opal's voice. A short time later he felt her soft body press against his.

"See anything?" she whispered.

"No," Eddie whispered back hesitantly.

"Eddie?"

"Did we make a mistake?" Eddie asked. "Should we have stayed in Pennsylvania?"

"No," Opal said quietly but firmly. "We might be in danger down here, but we're with family. One thing I found out, Eddie, is that trouble can find you wherever you are. These are our people, and this is our city. We're not gonna let hatred and fear run us out."

Eddie marveled that this was the same woman who had arrived in Richmond from Cromwell Plantation the year the war started. She was still plump, but that was the only resemblance. Her timidity had been forged into bold courage by all she had gone through.

"What are you thinking, Eddie?" Opal asked after a long silence.

"How proud Fannie would be of you," he replied tenderly. He would never forget his first wife who had been killed in an armory explosion, but he knew that wherever she was, she was smiling down on them. He liked the idea of her, Susie, and Sadie Lou all together. He knew it wasn't possible to truly know what happened when you died, but he liked his version just fine.

"And of you," Opal said, squeezing his hand. "It's gonna be a fine day when we're all together again. I still miss her, you know. I didn't have my cousin for long enough."

Eddie remained silent, knowing words wouldn't change anything.

Carrie pushed away from her books and rubbed the back of her neck. A quick glance at the clock told her it was almost one in the morning. She smiled as she listened to the patter of rain on the roof, then extinguished her oil lamp and walked to the window. A cool breeze blew in as she stretched her arms and back. She swung around when she heard her door crack open, not surprised when Janie stuck her head in.

"I thought I heard you moving around."

Carrie sat down on the window seat and patted the cushion next to her.

Janie settled down with a sigh. "I'm so glad for the rain."

Carrie nodded but kept staring out the window.

"A penny for your thoughts," Janie prompted.

"I'm wondering if it rained on the plantation," Carrie admitted. "Remember the storm we had when we were last home? Robert and I went out very late that night and walked in the rain. We were soaked, but we didn't care. The rain felt so wonderful." She smiled as she remembered. "When we passed the horse pasture, Granite was racing around." Her smile turned into laughter. "He ran up to us, snorted, and then took off again. I know the rain felt so good to him, too."

Janie chuckled. "Matthew and I were out in it, too. He took me down by the river. I thought it was crazy to be on the water in case there was lightning, but there was something magical about watching the storm swirl across the water. When it finally stopped, the tree we were sitting under lit up with the light of what seemed to be thousands of fireflies. I've never seen anything more beautiful in my life."

"Are you sure it wasn't just beautiful because you're in love?" Carrie teased.

"It *is* wonderful, isn't it?" Janie breathed. "I never dreamed of feeling this way." Her voice trailed off before she continued. "I thought I loved Clifford, but I never felt for him the way I feel about Matthew."

Carrie grinned. "Matthew is coming tomorrow, isn't he?"

"Yes!" Janie said excitedly. "His letter said he thought he would be in Philadelphia through all of September. Though he'll be traveling for the newspaper and for his book, this will be his home base again."

"That's wonderful," Carrie said, pushing down an uncomfortable feeling of envy.

"You miss Robert," Janie stated after a lingering silence.

"More than I thought possible," Carrie admitted as a wave of longing swept over her.

"Being here isn't enough?"

Carrie sighed. Sometimes Janie knew her too well. "It's harder than I thought it would be. I miss Robert terribly, but I also miss the plantation. I miss Rose and Moses. I miss Granite."

"You miss home."

"I miss home so much," Carrie said passionately. "I thought being in school would consume me but..." Her homesick feelings swirled with confusion.

"But...?" Janie pressed. "This is me, Carrie. I know you're feeling something more than homesickness. Out with it."

Carrie pushed black curls away from her face. She had been struggling with her feelings almost since the day she had arrived at school, but she had been able to push them aside. It was becoming more difficult. Still, she couldn't find a way to put them into words—at least not words she was willing to say.

"Carrie?" Janie's voice was warm and concerned.

"I don't know..." Carrie started helplessly, pushing back the curtains to stare up at the dark sky. Streetlights glimmered on the puddles the rain was making, but the murky blackness more accurately portrayed her feelings. The golden pools collecting on the road seemed nothing more than a mockery.

"You're not happy at school," Janie said quietly.

Carrie gasped and spun around. "How did you know?" She managed a chuckle when Janie remained silent. "Okay, I know that was a silly question. You know me almost as well as I know myself. Sometimes I'm sure you know me *better* than I know myself." She frowned in the darkness, still not ready to communicate what she was feeling. Why was it so difficult to understand her own mind sometimes?

"Tell me what it is," Janie invited after another silence.

"I believe so differently than the doctors at the school do," Carrie said, almost cringing when she heard the words. How could she so disagree with the very women she had come to learn from? When Janie remained silent, Carrie knew she was being given time to express her feelings. She relaxed and searched for the right words.

"I've been feeling this way almost from the beginning, but I tried to tell myself I was being arrogant because things are so different."

"What exactly is so different?" Janie asked.

Carrie listened closely, but she heard no judgement. "Don't you know?"

Janie took a deep breath. "You're upset because they turn their nose up at herbal remedies and anything homeopathic."

"Yes," Carrie cried. Hearing Janie say the words unleashed a torrent of emotion inside her. "I realize medicine has made many advances, and"—her mind flashed to all she had learned from Dr. Wild—"surgery changed so much during the war." Other memories filled her mind as her thoughts congealed. "But if not for the herbs the doctors here turn their noses up at, many of the patients at Chimborazo would have died. All of the patients down at the black hospital would have died." Everything she had been pushing down rose to the surface. "So many of the things they call remedies now are pure nonsense."

"Like?"

Carrie spun around and stared at Janie. "Don't you know?" she asked again, wishing the darkness was not shrouding her friend's face. "You were there with me all through the war, Janie. You know what we did!"

Janie sighed. "Yes, I know."

Carrie peered at her, trying to analyze what she was hearing. "It doesn't bother you?"

"And if it does?" Janie asked, a helpless note in her voice. "What difference will it make? This is the only medical school for women in Philadelphia. What good will it do to disagree? I want to become a doctor," she said. "When I get my degree, I can run my practice the way I want to, but until then I need to learn what they are teaching. I guess it really doesn't matter to me if I agree or not."

Carrie knew there was truth in what Janie was saying, but she chafed at what she was being asked to do.

Janie felt her angst. "First do no harm," she murmured in understanding.

Carrie shook her head. "Actually, that is not part of the Hippocratic Oath. At least not the original one." She could feel Janie's stare. "It's true. I found a book in the library a few days ago. The phrase, 'First, do no harm,' came from an English physician named Thomas Inman."

Janie cocked her head. "The English physician who is still alive?"

"Yes. I agree with what he said, but it was not part of the original oath."

"I didn't know that," Janie murmured.

Carrie warmed to her subject, eager to get away from her earlier thoughts. "Hippocrates has often been called the father of medicine. It is believed that either he or one of his students wrote the oath in the fifth century BC." She stood and walked to her desk and pulled down a book from the shelf next to it. She turned on her light and flipped the pages. "I won't read all of it, but this is the part I find most important:

> "*With regard to healing the sick, I will devise and order for them the best diet, according to my judgment and means; and I will take care that they suffer no hurt or damage.*
>
> *Nor shall any man's entreaty prevail upon me to administer poison to anyone; neither will I counsel any man to do so. Moreover, I will give no sort of medicine to any pregnant woman, with a view to destroy the child.*
>
> *Further, I will comport myself and use my knowledge in a godly manner.*
>
> *Whatsoever house I may enter, my visit shall be for the convenience and advantage of the patient; and I will willingly refrain from doing any injury or wrong from falsehood, and (in an especial manner) from acts of an amorous nature, whatever may be the rank of those who it may be my duty to cure, whether mistress or servant, bond or free.*

Whatever, in the course of my practice, I may see or hear (even when not invited), whatever I may happen to obtain knowledge of, if it be not proper to repeat it, I will keep sacred and secret within my own breast.

If I faithfully observe this oath, may I thrive and prosper in my fortune and profession, and live in the estimation of posterity; or on breach thereof, may the reverse be my fate!"

Carrie put the book back on her desk. *"And I will take care that they suffer no hurt or damage,"* she repeated quietly. She knew by the look on Janie's face that she was remembering what they had talked about in class today. "Can you honestly say that bloodletting does not inflict hurt or damage?" she asked angrily. "Withdrawing large quantities of blood from a patient to cure or prevent illness and disease is ridiculous."

"Doctor Jamison said it was being questioned and not used so much anymore," Janie protested as she looked away uncomfortably.

"Yes," Carrie agreed, "but she didn't make clear how much damage has been done by the practice, and she didn't tell us it has no place in modern medicine!" Her heart pounded as she reached for another book and opened it to the marker she had placed in it. "'Bloodletting has been used to treat almost every disease. It's been used to treat acne, asthma, coma, convulsions, epilepsy, gangrene, gout, herpes, indigestion, insanity...'" Her voice rose with disgust. *"Insanity!"* she snorted. "I've never heard such nonsense." She looked back at her book and continued to read. "'Jaundice, leprosy, plague, pneumonia, scurvy, smallpox...'" She snapped the book closed. "And that is only part of it. It goes on to list about one hundred more."

"Are you certain it has no value?" Janie asked quietly.

"What I'm certain of," Carrie snapped, "is that doctors that had no idea how to cure patients decided *any* treatment was better than nothing at all. Even draining large amounts of their blood!" She stared at Janie, vaguely aware her friend wasn't sharing her outrage, but now that she had started to talk, she couldn't stop. "Do you know George Washington died after he was bled heavily?"

Janie shook her head, her eyes curious. "No."

"Our first president asked to be bled heavily after he developed a throat infection from weather exposure. Within a ten-hour period, they took close to a gallon of his blood." Carrie's voice was tight with fury. "A *gallon* of his blood. How did they expect the man to live?" she demanded. She answered the question in Janie's eyes. "He died. They blamed it on the throat infection, but the truth is he had nothing to fight it off because of all the blood they had taken. I believe bloodletting weakens patients and facilitates infection."

"He asked them to do it," Janie said weakly.

Carrie looked at Janie, unable to believe what she was hearing.

"How can you be sure you're right? Why do you think you know more than the doctors who are teaching us?"

Carrie knew it was a fair question. "Because I've seen it," she said promptly. "The surgeons at Chimborazo did it to most of the patients. Sarah taught me that blood is life, so I convinced Dr. Wild not to perform bloodletting on his patients."

"And how did Sarah *know* that?"

"I don't know," Carrie confessed. "But neither do I know how she knew yarrow relieves fever and helps with digestion. All I know is that she was right. When Dr. Wild stopped draining our patients of their blood, many more of them lived." She stood and paced the room. "You know that is true, Janie! Our ward had the highest survival rate at the hospital."

Janie didn't refute Carrie's challenge, but she seemed to draw within herself on the window seat. "I'm not like you," she said, her voice tight and anxious.

"What does that mean?" Carrie fought to remain patient. How could she see it so clearly, and Janie not see it at all? She grabbed up the book again. "Do you know that in medieval Europe doctors believed surgery was beneath them? Physicians tended to be academics. They worked in universities, and most dealt with patients as an observer or consultant. They didn't want to get their hands dirty," she scoffed. "They used *barber* surgeons."

Janie blinked. "Barber surgeons?"

"Yes," Carrie said. "Barber surgeons were the most common medical practitioners back then. Their job was to look after soldiers during or after a battle. They, of course, all had sharp-bladed razors. They were expected to do everything from cutting hair to amputating limbs. The death rate was already staggering due to loss of blood and infection. They increased it by taking even more of their patients' blood."

"I'm sure they thought they were helping, Carrie," Janie protested, her face white with horror.

Carrie nodded. "I'm sure you're right," she said, "but doctors have been telling people since the 1600s that it is harmful. Instead of listening, doctors who have no real clue how to make people well keep cutting them and sucking the very life from them!"

A long silence filled the room.

"I envy you," Janie murmured. "I'm also scared for you."

Carrie shook her head. "Scared for me?"

"Yes. It's already so difficult for a woman to become a doctor. We are ridiculed and looked down upon. We have to fight for any kind of respect. Now you want to challenge everything we are being taught by both male and female doctors."

"Not all of it," Carrie shot back. "Just the part that is wrong."

"That's why I'm scared for you," Janie said insistently. "The medical establishment here in Philadelphia is already trying to prove women have no place in medicine. They are fighting us at every turn. Now you are going to tell them they are wrong about one of their most established practices?" She paused. "What do you think is going to happen?"

Carrie sighed heavily. "I don't know." Anger surged through her in a renewed wave. "All I know is that I have to do what I believe is right." She frowned and studied Janie's face. "Do you know that bloodletting is a prescribed remedy for cholera patients?"

Janie stiffened. "No."

"They are doing it to the cholera patients at the new hospital," Carrie said bluntly.

Janie shook her head. "But they're already so dehydrated. How can the doctors—"

"Take more fluid? Drain the blood that might give patients the ability to fight off the disease?" Carrie clenched her fists. She stood and paced the room for a minute before she spun around to look at Janie again. "It's not like I enjoy creating problems. I don't enjoy being a square peg in a round hole," she said helplessly.

"It's who you are," Janie said. "You can't help it."

"I suppose I can't," Carrie agreed, a deep fatigue settling over her.

Suddenly, she knew what she needed to do.

Marietta had not moved away from her position at the window for several hours. She tried to breathe steadily as she prayed, but her fear was growing. In spite of her best efforts, her breath was starting to come in uneven gasps as exhaustion tightened its grip. She had seen no telltale flicker of flames on the horizon, but that didn't mean the situation was good in the black quarter. Her mind filled with vivid images. Jeremy figured in every one of them.

She stiffened and leaned forward when a man materialized from the darkness and moved toward her. She forgot to breathe as he came closer. The curtain swirled around her head and shoulders as she pressed forward. When the man drew next to the streetlamp closest to her boarding house, he looked up. "Jeremy!" she gasped, a laugh breaking through the sob caught in her throat. "Jeremy..." Her voice was a whisper as her heart filled with joy and relief.

Jeremy stopped under the streetlight and raised his hand, his eyes trained on her window. He waited until she drew the curtains back and stuck her hand out the window to wave. Then he smiled broadly and continued walking until he was once more swallowed by the night.

Marietta had so many questions, but she knew they would have to wait until the morning. Her heart full of gratitude, she crept to her bed, pulled back the covers, and climbed in. Within moments, she was asleep.

Chapter Seven

Carrie hoped her assumption that ninety-seven-year-old women didn't go out much was accurate. She peered at the windows as her carriage pulled up in front of the home where Biddy lived. She didn't see any movement, but there was no reason to expect any. The street, even so early in the day, was already full of carriages and wagons. Laughter and calls filled the air as hordes of dirty, raggedly dressed children played with careless abandon on the side streets. Women hung laundry while they chatted with neighbors, and Carrie could smell the fragrant aroma of bread swirling around her. Her mouth watered as she suddenly remembered she hadn't taken time to eat before she left.

Carrie leaned forward to speak to her driver. "Will you please wait here until I discover if anyone is home?" The look Chester gave her made it clear he thought she was crazy for coming all this way without already being sure of a reception. She quite agreed with him, but there hadn't been time to send a telegram and wait for a reply. As soon as the sun was up, she had walked down to the livery station to hire her transportation. If she was going to take advantage of no classes on a Saturday, she simply had to take the chance.

"Yes, ma'am," Chester said, his tone respectful even though his eyes communicated something else.

Carrie hid her smile as she climbed out of the carriage. She knew that all her driver really cared about was being paid. Her trip might be fruitless, but Chester would still put money in his pocket. It was actually to his benefit for Biddy to be home because Carrie was paying him to wait until she was ready to leave. She hurried up the steps, rapped on the door, and held her breath. A broad smile spread across her face when she heard footsteps inside.

"Why, land sakes!" Faith cried as she opened the door. She called over her shoulder. "Biddy, Carrie Borden is here!"

Carrie hesitated, surprised at how nervous she felt. "I know you weren't expecting me..."

Faith snorted. "Girl, you get yourself in this house. We've been looking for you to come back every day since you left. You certainly took your sweet time about it. It's been almost a month!"

"Get that girl back here!" Biddy called from the parlor.

Carrie grinned with relief and turned back toward the carriage. "I will be staying," she called loudly.

Chester waved his hand and moved forward.

Carrie interpreted the look on Faith's face. "I already made arrangements for the driver to wait in that tavern a few buildings down if y'all were home," she assured. "He will take me back when I'm ready."

"Good," Faith said, the relief evident in her voice. "We'll send one of the children in the neighborhood to fetch him when we're willing to let you go." She beckoned for Carrie to come inside and then enveloped her in a warm hug. "It could be a while before we're willing," she warned.

Carrie sighed, more sure than ever that she had made the right decision. "It's so good to see you," she murmured as Faith kept hold of her arm to lead her into the parlor.

"Why has it taken you so long to come see us?" Faith asked in a scolding tone.

Biddy was sitting in her same chair when Carrie and Faith entered. "Leave that girl alone," she admonished in her musical brogue. "She is right here now, isn't she?"

Carrie hurried forward and planted a kiss on the soft, wrinkled face that framed the blazing blue eyes she remembered so well. They drew her as much now as they had when she'd first met this remarkable woman. "Hello, Biddy. It's so good to see you again."

Biddy smiled and waved her into the chair next to the window. "Have a seat, Carrie. Faith will bring some tea and cookies."

Faith happily bustled from the room.

Biddy eyed her for a moment. "We were afraid we had scared you off with all our stories."

"Absolutely not," Carrie replied. "Classes and study have kept me busy every single minute. I wanted to get away so many times, but something always happened."

"So what pushed you over the edge today?" Biddy asked, watching her with wise eyes.

Carrie flushed, not ready to talk it. She shook her head instead. "I came to hear more of your story." She looked up as Faith entered the room carrying a tray. "And to hear Faith's story," she added, glad for the distraction. The look in Biddy's eyes said the old woman would press her on that question again, but she was going to hold it off as long as she could. Carrie was looking for a way to navigate her latest struggle. She could only hope she would recognize it when it came her way. Whether she would find it here in Moyamensing, she had no idea, but she had learned not to ignore the impulse that had directed her here.

Biddy eyed her for a moment longer and then reached for the cup of tea Faith held out to her. "This is the first break in the weather for months," she said casually.

Carrie relaxed. "I feel like I can breathe again," she agreed, accepting the plate Faith held out to her. "These cookies look wonderful," she murmured, her stomach growling in anticipation.

"You're about to sink your teeth into some Irish oatmeal cookies," Biddy explained. "This recipe has been passed down through the generations."

Carrie took a bite and closed her eyes with a moan of delight as her teeth sank into the moist, chewy sweetness. "Oh..." she breathed. "They are wonderful."

Biddy grinned, her eyes dancing with satisfaction. "The secret is plumping up those raisins with some strong Irish whiskey," she whispered dramatically. "It takes an Irish cook to know how to make oatmeal cookies!"

"Or a black cook who knows the secret," Faith said wryly.

"That, too," Biddy agreed.

Carrie took another bite. "I can't wait to tell the rest of my housemates about these cookies."

"You'll take some home to them," Faith said.

"I was so hoping you would insist," Carrie said demurely.

Biddy and Faith laughed, their eyes sparkling with approval.

Faith settled down into the other chair in the room. "I told Biddy you weren't a figment of our imagination," she said.

Carrie smiled, so glad she had come. She had simply told her housemates she was going out for the day. She didn't feel like explaining her reasons, and she didn't want anyone else to join her. Janie, excited about Matthew's arrival, had looked at her closely but said nothing.

Biddy nodded at Faith. "Carrie wants to hear your story."

Faith smiled. "I'll be happy to tell my story, but first you need to finish yours. We don't want everything to get all jumbled up in her mind."

"Which wouldn't take much at this point," Carrie said.

Biddy closed her eyes for a moment. "My ninety-seven-year-old mind doesn't remember where I left off when you were here before," she confessed when she opened them again.

"You stopped at the point where Darcy's lover was murdered when he tried to save her from more abuse by her owner," Carrie replied promptly.

"That's right," Biddy said. She closed her eyes for another moment, obviously pulling memories forward. "Even though the courts mostly let owners do whatever they wanted—because they were themselves landowners who had their own contracted servants—the things Darcy's owner did to her were even more horrible than they could bear. After Great-Grandfather Ian was murdered, the courts set her free."

"That's wonderful!" Carrie cried, glad there was a happy ending. The realization of what the woman must have gone through had made her feel ill many times during the last month.

"Being set free was definitely an improvement," Biddy agreed, "but she had nothing and nowhere to go. A neighbor took pity on her and sent her up here to friends in Philadelphia so that her old owner couldn't find her. About the time she got here, she realized she was pregnant from her lover."

Carrie gasped. "Pregnant? She must have had so many mixed feelings."

"I imagine she did. She had lost the man she loved, but at least she was going to have his child."

"And she didn't have to worry about the child being sold away from her," Carrie said with relief.

Biddy frowned. "Not true. A family took Darcy in and cared for her during her pregnancy, but when my grandmother was born, she was taken as an indentured servant as payment."

"What?" Carrie grappled with what she was hearing. "After all Darcy had been through? How awful!"

Biddy nodded. "Darcy stayed with the family because she wouldn't leave her daughter, Fiona. She was, for all purposes, still a slave, but the difference was that they were kind to her."

"How long?"

"Until Fiona was eighteen. She was set free then, but Darcy was already dead. Too many years of abuse had finally taken their toll on her health. She died from pneumonia the winter when Fiona was fifteen."

Carrie squeezed her eyes closed for a moment, sorrow for the woman she never knew surging through her heart. "What happened to Fiona?"

"Fiona remained free," Biddy said proudly. "She became a seamstress to very wealthy Philadelphians. She married another man from Ireland who had served out his contract, and had eight children."

"Which one was your mother?" Carrie asked.

"Keela. She was the third child, and the oldest of the four girls." Biddy smiled fondly. "My mother was a very beautiful woman, and also very intelligent. She learned from all Grandma Fiona told her and inherited Grandma's dressmaking talents. Instead of making clothes, though, she opened a fashion consulting shop that outfitted the finest women in Philadelphia society. She was very much in demand."

"How wonderful!" Carrie said, vastly relieved to know the terrible cycle of slavery and abuse had been broken. She looked around the house. "Didn't you say you were born here?"

Biddy shook her head. "No, but I was only two years old when Mama and Father moved out here and bought the farm. Father was a very successful banker. He adored me and Mama and didn't want me growing up in the city. He wanted me to have room to run and play outside like he did as a boy on the farm he grew up on in upstate New York."

Carrie glanced out the window at the crowded, bustling street. "So Moyamensing really used to be a farm?" It was difficult to believe.

Biddy nodded, her eyes glowing with memories. "The prettiest farm you ever did see. There were more than a hundred acres of rolling pasture. We grew apple trees and raised dairy cows. Father hired men to take care of everything. This house was surrounded by large trees and the flower gardens that were my mother's pride and joy."

"What happened?" Carrie asked. She flushed when she realized how her question must sound.

Biddy smiled. "It's a fair question. I grew up on the farm while it was still considered an estate, but my father lost all his money in a bad business deal." She frowned briefly. "He would never tell me what happened. I just knew that one day we had a glorious life, and the next day he was selling our life out from under us. A little bit at a time, he sold off our land. I watched as the farm filled with buildings and houses. By the time he was so desperate he had to sell all the land right around the house, the only thing being built was tenement houses for the poor Irish population." Biddy closed her eyes. "It broke my father's heart, but he didn't know what else to do. My mother wanted to go back to the city and build up her fashion business again, but he wouldn't hear of it. He died when I was twenty-four."

"What did your mother do?" Carrie asked, fascinated by the story she was hearing.

"Her spirit was broken by then. There wasn't enough left in her to build up her business again. We didn't have much, but we had enough. She used what little money was left to make sure I continued my education."

Carrie gazed at her. "I didn't know women could go to college then."

"They couldn't," Biddy replied. "The first women weren't allowed into colleges until right after the war. You and your friends are helping pave the way. Not only by being in school, but especially by being in medical school. That's something I could only dream about when I was your age."

Carrie looked at her. "You wanted to be a doctor?"

"More than anything," Biddy answered, her voice tinged with regret. Then she waved her hand in the air. "It doesn't do any good to moan about the past. My mama knew how badly I wanted to learn, so she did the only thing she could do and brought in tutors of every kind to teach me. If any of the teachers—all of them men—treated me with any degree of condescension, they were gone the next day." She smiled. "I lost a lot of teachers, but I also had some very wonderful ones who understood women could do anything men could. They treated me like that, and I thrived."

Carrie thought about the stuffed bookshelves in the library above her head. "And your father? Did he support your desire to learn?"

Biddy smiled slightly. "I suspect Father thought it was a frivolous waste of time and money, but he adored my mother and would do anything for her. She wanted me to be educated, so he went along with it. He never discouraged me, but he certainly never encouraged me," she mused. She looked at Carrie. "And you? Women medical students are very rare in the North. I suspect they are even rarer in the South. How did you attain your education?"

Carrie smiled. "My mother was convinced I only needed training to become a typical plantation mistress. My father understood the very idea made me ill, so he championed me. He made sure I had tutors, and he gave me free run of the plantation on my horse, Granite."

Biddy pursed her lips in a soundless whistle. "He sounds like quite an extraordinary man."

"He most certainly is," Carrie said fervently. "It took him a little while to come around on the slavery issue, but he embraced women's equality long before anyone else in the South did."

"And your mother?" Faith asked.

Carrie met her eyes. "My mother died the year before the war started. I hated losing her, but I suspect our country at war would have been more than my mother could have handled." She smiled fondly. "She was rather fragile."

"The two of you made peace before she died," Biddy observed.

Carrie met her eyes, not surprised she would know that. "Yes. She didn't understand me any more than she had before, but she wanted me to be happy, and she encouraged my dreams of becoming a doctor. It was the last conversation we had," she murmured.

"I'm sure she is so proud of you," Faith said quietly.

Carrie nodded. "I believe she is."

"So your father is alone then?" Biddy asked.

Carrie smiled brightly. "No. He married a wonderful woman from right here in Philadelphia. I had met her before the war, and we became close friends. We corresponded until the war made it impossible, but we reconnected as soon as the war was over. I was thrilled when she and my father fell in love."

"Your family is here in Philadelphia?" Faith asked, a look of surprise on her face.

"No," Carrie answered. "My father and Abby live in Richmond now. They own a clothing factory that they started when the war ended."

Biddy looked at her sharply. "*Abby? A clothing factory?* What was Abby's last name before she married your father?"

Carrie felt a glimmer of anticipation as she answered. "Her name was Abigail Livingston." She was somehow not surprised when a broad smile spread across Biddy's face. "You know Abby?"

"That we do," Faith answered. "We were all at the first Women's Rights Convention in 1848."

"At Seneca Falls, New York," Carrie said with a laugh. "I should be shocked, but I'm not."

Biddy grinned. "Powerful women tend to find each other, Carrie. You will understand that more and more as you get older. Abigail Livingston made life better for so many women in this city, and she was a leader in the abolition movement. Your stepmother is an extraordinary woman."

"Now *that* I already know," Carrie replied with a wide grin. "Abby was already one of my closest friends, and my mentor. To have her become my stepmother was simply icing on the cake."

"Did she sell her factories here in the city?" Faith asked.

"No, she has managers to handle them. She comes up periodically to check on them."

"And you and the rest are living in her house," Faith guessed.

Carrie nodded, her heart full with the knowledge that her life had been entwined with these two wonderful women. She could hardly wait to tell Abby the news. "She will be so excited to visit when she is here again."

"Will that be soon?" Faith asked.

Carrie frowned as she remembered the letter she had received two days earlier. "I don't know. Life is very difficult in Richmond right now." She'd had to read between the lines of Abby's letter, but she was certain she hadn't missed the unspoken message. "I believe Abby is rather afraid to leave my father right now. They are both in danger because of their stance on black people."

Carrie was happy to talk more at another time, but she still had questions of her own. "Why did you stay here, Biddy? Moyamensing has become such a dangerous place to live. Couldn't you have left?"

Biddy smiled. "I suppose I could have," she replied. "Especially once I was married. My husband tried to convince me many times, especially once it really started to grow as new immigrants poured in. Peter had a job in the city, and he hated the distance he had to drive to work, but he let me have my way."

"Your husband was Irish?"

"Oh yes, but he was born here in America. He started as an indentured servant, but his master thought of Peter as a son. He made sure Peter received education when he was growing up, and when he died, it turns out he left Peter everything he had. It wasn't a tremendous amount, but it allowed him to go to college. He was a businessman all during our marriage." Her eyes softened as she remembered. "Peter and I had four fine sons."

"Where are they now?" Carrie asked.

Biddy's eyes glimmered with painful memory. "They all died in the cholera epidemic of 1842."

Carrie gasped with horror. "*All* of them?"

Biddy nodded sadly. "It hit Moyamensing especially badly."

"That's the reason the hospital was burned," Carrie murmured. Understanding swept through her and wiped out the remnants of anger about the destruction of the hospital.

"They were afraid," Faith said simply.

"Of course they were," Carrie replied. She looked back at Biddy. "I'm so very sorry." She was almost afraid to ask her next question. "What about your grandchildren? Does Arden live nearby?"

Biddy smiled. "Arden is my great-grandchild. He is nothing but a gift to me." Her smile faded as she closed her eyes again. "I had seven grandchildren. All boys. God evidently didn't think any more females were needed in my family. I didn't care. I was happy with all my men around me." She paused. "They were all killed in the war. Arden is all I have left." Her voice caught as she looked out the window.

Carrie was at a complete loss for words as she stared at Biddy. "I don't know what to say." Her voice was faint as her eyes filled with tears.

Biddy reached forward to take her hand. "Life is a series of loss and grief, but it is also a source of unbelievable joy, Carrie. I wish with all my heart that I still had my family with me, but I am grateful for the love we shared and all the memories I carry in my heart."

Carrie still had no idea what to say. She simply couldn't comprehend that amount of loss. She knew Sarah had suffered so terribly, but what Biddy had been through was more than she could wrap her mind around.

Biddy squeezed her hand. "I hope you never have reason to understand what I've experienced," she said, "but I do hope you fill your life with as much love and laughter as you can, because you never know when it will be taken from you. I've learned not to take one single thing for granted."

Carrie couldn't control the tears that filled her eyes.

"I choose to be happy every single day," Biddy said. "Yes, I've suffered great losses, but I also have so many wonderful things in my life. I can focus on the losses, or I can focus on what is."

Faith reached over and put a hand on Biddy's shoulder. "I can assure you Biddy focuses on what is. She has also used her losses to make her more compassionate toward all people."

Carrie thought about the love the old lady had for her community. "You stayed in Moyamensing so you can make a difference."

Biddy nodded. "Yes. This country has taken so much from the Irish. It started out as an English wrongdoing, but it didn't end when America became an independent nation. Forcing the Irish to become indentured servants eventually faded away because it became more financially profitable to enslave the blacks, but it didn't change the attitudes toward the Irish. They have always been seen as inferior. That hasn't changed."

"How are you changing it?" Carrie asked.

Biddy waved her to the window. "Look outside," she invited.

Carrie looked, seeing only what she always saw— wagons, carriages, and hordes of children. She turned back to Biddy with a question in her eyes.

"All those children you see start school next week," she said proudly. "Every child in Moyamensing is in school...if we can get them to go, that is.

"How?" Carrie murmured. She knew Philadelphia's City Council was certainly not funding education in this area. "Public education is available to only a very small percentage of youth. Who teaches them?"

"There are schools in each of the churches, and many of the businesses have back rooms where classes are held. We have hired teachers who understand these children have as much potential to learn as any other children."

Carrie processed this information with astonishment. "Who pays for it?"

"Biddy does," Faith said proudly.

Carrie stared at Biddy with her mouth open. Finally she found her voice. "You pay for all these children to go to school? *All* the children in Moyamensing?"

It was Faith who answered when Biddy shrugged her shoulders modestly. "Biddy's husband became a very wealthy man," she said. "When he died, Biddy used her mama's business sense and invested most of that money."

Carrie stared at Biddy. "You're rich?"

Biddy chuckled. "I prefer to think I'm able to give away quite a bit to make things better for the people here."

Carrie stared out at the street again. Biddy could live anywhere. She could be in a grand neighborhood... She could live in a peaceful place... Carrie's thoughts were jumbled.

Biddy read her mind. "I'm where I want to be, Carrie. I could put all these children in school even if I wasn't living here, but then I wouldn't be with my people. A huge injustice has been done to the Irish for many centuries. I can turn my back on all that and live my life in comfort and solitude, or I can have the joy of being here with them."

Joy. Carrie mulled over the word Biddy chose to use. "This gives you joy?"

Biddy's smile was radiant. "More than you can imagine. I encourage the children every chance I get. I talk to them from the window, but they also come inside for Faith's cookies."

"I bake a lot of cookies," Faith admitted happily. "I can't think of a better way to spend my time because it ensures we always have young ones around."

"I also have the opportunity to find employment for many of the men down here through my business connections," Biddy added.

"She makes them believe things can be different," Faith said. "Burning the hospital wasn't the right thing to do maybe, but it shows that the folks in this neighborhood are beginning to believe they're better than the way others see them. They are beginning to understand that being Irish is something to be proud of."

Suddenly it all clicked together in Carrie's mind. "You're fulfilling the destiny your heritage left for you."

Biddy's eyes met hers. "What makes you say that?" she asked keenly.

Carrie knew the old lady was inviting her to go deeper. "A part of every one of your ancestors lives in you," she said. "Everything that ever happened to them lives on in you," she said more firmly as her understanding solidified.

"Is that your medical opinion?" Biddy probed.

"No." Carrie's mind was spinning, trying to fit the pieces together like she used to fit together wooden jigsaw puzzles when she was a child. "So many horrible things happened to your family, but they were survivors. Somehow they kept the lineage going, and they kept passing down the courage it took to make that happen." She stared at Biddy. "It would have been so easy to live your life in luxury once the horrible things stopped happening."

"Except that would have been the most horrible thing of all," Biddy responded. "Up to that point, most of the horrible things had been done *to* my family. What a waste if I had simply turned my back on all of that so I could live a life of ease."

"Yes," Carrie murmured. She turned back around to look at all the children, seeing them completely differently now. Each child was an opportunity for Biddy to redeem the pain of the past.

Biddy was watching her closely. "You got what you came for," she said quietly.

Carrie nodded. "Yes, I believe I did." It stunned her to realize it was true. It had taken no more than Biddy telling her the rest of her story for understanding to bloom in her confused mind.

Faith smiled when she turned to her. "You need to take what you've learned today and live it for a while before you put anything more in. My story should wait. Stories aren't meant to be told just for the telling."

Carrie understood. "They're meant to be told so the people hearing them can change the present and the future."

Biddy held up her hand. "I know you're thinking you need to explain what brought you here. You don't. Oh, I would love to know what has happened in you when the time is right, but it's all too new for you to try to express it. It needs to sit with you for a while. It needs to sink into your heart until it becomes part of you. Then you'll be ready to talk about it."

Carrie stared at her. Biddy was just like Old Sarah. Life could have destroyed her, but instead, she had chosen to let it refine her like a beautiful piece of glowing glass. The wisdom and love shining from her eyes was a testimony to her choice not to let life make her bitter. "Can I return soon?" she asked. Somehow she knew this house pressed into an impoverished neighborhood was a vital key to her life in Philadelphia.

"Any time you wish," Biddy replied. "Consider this another home."

It was late in the afternoon when Carrie finally left. The rest of her time there had been spent in easy conversation and laughter. There had been no more storytelling and no more questions. Carrie understood that deep transformation needed time to take root and grow. It couldn't be hurried.

Faith had fixed a delicious lunch, and at least a dozen children had appeared at the back door eager for her oatmeal cookies. She listened quietly as Biddy and Faith talked to *their* children, sending each of them away with a confident shine in their eyes.

When Chester pulled the carriage to a stop in front of the house, Carrie was reluctant to leave. For the first time ever, she felt uncomfortable about going home. The conversation with Janie had been playing in her mind all day. She was certain of what she needed to do, but she was dreading it.

Chapter Eight

Janie was waiting on the porch when Matthew's carriage arrived. Her heart almost exploded with joy when a wide grin split his face as soon as he saw her. There had been times when she was sure she had merely imagined the tender moments they'd had on the plantation before she had been called away. Perhaps she had only dreamed the proposal. The look in his eyes when he leapt from the carriage, however, said it was all real.

"Janie!" Matthew ran up the stairs and swept her into his arms.

Janie closed her eyes in sheer delight. She had never felt the joy of being treasured before, and had never expected to experience it during her lifetime. To find it after the traumatic marriage to Clifford made it even more precious to her. "You're here," she breathed. "I've missed you so much."

Matthew held her back just far enough to claim her lips in a warm kiss. "The good thing about being back in the North is that no one will be shocked to see me kiss my fiancée on the porch," he said when he finally pulled away and grinned down at her. "They may turn their noses up, but no one will pull out their smelling salts." His smile faded. "I missed you, too," he said quietly.

Janie understood the yearning look in his eyes. They would already be married if the decision was up to him. She knew she loved this man with all her heart, but she also knew she wasn't ready. Matthew was nothing like Clifford, but she was still jolted awake far too often from the nightmares her marriage had bequeathed her. She had fought so hard for her independence. It might be selfish not to be ready to give it up yet, but so be it. Matthew said he understood. She would have to trust he was telling the truth.

Matthew lifted his nose and sniffed. His eyes widened with delight. "Do I really smell an apple pie?"

Janie laughed and pushed at him. "I do believe you're part hound dog. Does it come from being born in West Virginia? I remember Hobbs had the same kind of nose."

Matthew looked smug, his blue eyes dancing with fun. "I prefer to consider it sensitivity to the finer things in life," he drawled.

"Right," Janie teased back, her joy almost pounding out of her chest. She nodded toward the carriage. "Are you going to make your driver wait all day, or are you going to let him go?"

"I totally forgot him," he admitted. "That's what you do to me, young lady."

It was Janie's turn to look smug. "I'm certainly not going to apologize," she shot back.

Matthew ran down the stairs to claim his two bags from the carriage and pay the driver. When he turned back around, Janie was looking at his bags with a raised brow. "No, I'm not moving in," he said, answering the question in her eyes. "But neither am I willing to be very far from you when I'm in town." He nodded his head toward the elegant yellow home two doors down. "Abby convinced a friend of hers to let a battered newspaper reporter board with her."

"You're living two doors down?" Janie gasped. "That's wonderful!" Again, she saw a look flash through Matthew's eyes. He wanted to marry her so they could be together, but he was giving her the time she needed. She knew she couldn't truly understand how difficult it must be for him, but it made her love him even more. "And I will not hear anything about you being a battered newspaper reporter. *You* are on your way to being a celebrated author."

Matthew grinned. "You got my letter. I wasn't sure it would get here before I did."

"It came a few hours ago," Janie said happily. "I'm so excited for you! *Glimmers of Change* is going to be an excellent book. More importantly, it is going to change how people see things in our country. Your stories are so needed, Matthew."

"And the part about me still doing newspaper work?" Matthew asked hesitantly. He watched her eyes closely.

"I knew you couldn't walk away," Janie replied easily. "To not have your finger on the pulse of this nation would have driven you crazy. You needed to heal from your experience in New Orleans, but I knew you would be right back in the fray."

"And you don't mind?"

Janie regarded him for a long moment, melting at the look of vulnerability on his strong face. "I won't pretend I won't worry, but I also won't ask you to be less than you are."

Matthew reached out and pulled her close. "I have fallen in love with an angel," he said thickly.

"And don't you forget it," Janie replied, her heart catching as she thought about the night before.

Matthew sensed the shift in her feelings. He held her away and gazed down into her face. "What is it?"

"I'm afraid I'm far from being an angel," Janie said quietly. "Carrie and I had a disagreement," she admitted. "We've never felt so differently about things before." She fell silent and looked down the street, wondering for what must be the hundredth time where Carrie had disappeared to this morning.

"You haven't talked about it?" Matthew asked after a long moment.

"We haven't had a chance," Janie replied. She explained how Carrie had left earlier with no explanation about where she was going.

"Are you worried about her?"

Janie shook her head slowly. "No. I suspect she has gone down to visit the two women who saved us when the cholera hospital was burned but..." Her voice trailed away. "I'm afraid she is very disappointed in me."

Matthew frowned, but he didn't refute her statement. "Do you want to tell me about it?"

Janie looked down the road again, but she didn't see Carrie coming. "It's getting late," she muttered. In spite of what she had said, worry was beginning to build.

"It will still be light for more than an hour," Matthew assured her. "Did Carrie go wherever she was going with a driver?"

"I believe so. She said something to Elizabeth about going to the livery this morning." Janie wished she could push the concern from her mind. "I shouldn't be so worried."

"Oh, I don't know," Matthew replied with a smile. "Our friend Carrie has quite a solid reputation for being both impulsive and rash."

The glint in his eyes made Janie laugh. "That is true. Still," she said, "I have no reason to believe anything is wrong. I think she just needed to get away so she could think."

"About what the two of you fought about last night?"

"I wouldn't call it a fight," Janie protested. "I would call it more of a philosophical disagreement." Matthew raised a brow and looked at her. "All right," she amended. "I guess it was more like a fight. All I've done all day is think about you coming, and all the things Carrie and I said last night. It was a total mix of joy and regret."

"And you made an apple pie," Matthew added, obviously trying to take her mind off the argument with her closest friend.

"I'm afraid I can't take credit for that. Alice saw how you fawned over Annie's pies on the plantation. She brought home some fresh apples that came into the city from the mountains, and she insisted on making two pies."

"I will try my best to do them justice."

Janie laughed again, so very glad he was there. "Would you like to go for a walk?" she asked suddenly. She needed to get away from the house and clear her head. Staring at the road was not going to make Carrie miraculously appear.

Matthew promptly deposited his bags in the foyer of Abby's house and joined her on the porch again. "Lead the way, my love."

Janie shivered. "I don't know that I'll ever get used to hearing you say that," she said. "I loved you for so long."

Matthew pulled her close again and claimed her lips in another kiss. "Then we've got a lot of time to make up for," he said tenderly. He ended the kiss and tucked her hand in the crook of his arm. "Tell me whatever you want me to know."

Janie discovered she wanted him to know everything. They had walked quite a long way before the entire story had spilled from her. Matthew merely nodded his head occasionally to indicate he was listening closely. She felt herself relaxing as she talked. She and Clifford had been able to talk like this once, but it had been for such a short time after their marriage. The Confederacy's defeat had made him bitter and angry—completely changing the man she had fallen in love with. Matthew had already been through the worst and come out each time a better man. Janie knew she could trust her future with him.

The cool front that had brought in the storm the night before had kept the temperatures mild. The searing humidity had escaped out to sea as if the tides had simply pulled it away. Laughter and conversation flowed from porches as they strolled beneath the overhanging trees.

Window boxes were still full of colorful flowers, and the smell of apples and cinnamon gave testimony to the recent influx of fruit from the Pocono Mountains.

Janie finished her story, edging right to miss a hoop rolling down the street. It was being madly pursued by a young girl with long braids, her face flushed with exertion.

"Sorry, ma'am!" she yelled, a grin revealing a gap in her teeth.

"I spent hours playing hoops when I was a young girl," Janie said with a chuckle as she watched the child dash off, expertly spinning the hoop.

"And I never saw one until I left the mountains of West Virginia," Matthew replied. "All my free time was spent in the woods with my dog."

Janie eyed him. "We *are* from different worlds," she murmured with an appraising glance. "I guess it was all that time in the woods that made you so strong and handsome, so I'm not going to complain. I will take on the responsibility of teaching our children how to roll hoops," she said playfully, before sobering as her mind was pulled back to their conversation. "So, what do you think?"

"Of our children playing hoops?" Matthew answered. "I'm all for it." He reached down and squeezed her hand. "Or about Carrie and what the two of you talked about?"

"The latter," Janie said. She squirmed under his sudden scrutiny but was so glad to have someone to talk it through with. She hadn't felt she could talk to any of her housemates because she didn't want them to feel they were in the middle of it, and she was also concerned with how they would react.

"What do *you* think?" Matthew pressed. "You've told me what was said, but you haven't really told me how you feel about it."

"I'm still trying to figure that out," Janie admitted. "I know I feel terrible about having such a strong disagreement with Carrie..." Her voice trailed away as she tried to face her feelings.

"Because you believe you were wrong, or because you hate to have conflict with her?"

Janie searched her heart. "I certainly hate having conflict." She paused for a long moment. "I haven't decided if I believe I was wrong." She stopped in front of a brick building and stared up at it, glad for a distraction. "Do you know what this is?"

"The Philadelphia School of Design for Women."

Janie stared with surprise at what must have once been someone's mansion. "For *women*?"

"Yes. It was established about twenty years ago by Sarah Peter. It is actually the first art school in the United States."

Janie stepped back and looked at the building with new eyes. "Are these women treated as badly as we are?"

"I don't believe so," Matthew replied. "They are taught to design articles for domestic use, like patterns for wallpaper, carpet, and woodwork moldings. Mrs. Peter realized the industrial revolution in the North could mean new opportunities for women. She has been a widow twice. Though she had financial means, she realized most single or widowed women have few resources. She wanted to change that."

"And there are so many more of them since the war," Janie murmured.

"Yes. Women have proven they can excel in these fields," Matthew continued. "Most of the women who graduate from here have no trouble finding jobs."

"Because they are doing something men believe is acceptable for women," Janie stated. She was aware of the bitterness in her voice, but she realized that she wasn't interested in trying to hide it. She had been forced to be someone she wasn't when she was married to Clifford. Those days were behind her. She would never be anyone but herself again.

"You knew becoming a doctor would be difficult," Matthew said.

"Did I?" Janie asked. "Or did I simply do it because Carrie was doing it, and because I didn't know what else to do?"

"You're the only one who can answer that question," Matthew said gently, "but I do know you are quite gifted in medicine."

Janie considered that for a moment, wondering if it was true. She sighed heavily and repeated what she had said to Carrie the night before. "The medical establishment here in Philadelphia is already trying to prove women have no place in medicine. They are fighting us at every turn. Now, Carrie is going to tell them they are wrong about one of their most established practices?" Her voice rose. "And that's just one of the things, Matthew. She disagrees with much more."

"And you think she is wrong?"

Janie was quiet for several moments, forcing herself to answer honestly. "I'm afraid to admit she is right," she finally confessed, her cheeks burning as she faced the truth.

"Why?"

Janie chuckled. "I should have known falling in love with a journalist would be dangerous. Do you always ask so many questions?"

Matthew smiled. "I've learned it's the only way to get information. I could tell you what I think, but it isn't important. The only thing that matters is what *you* think."

"I *do* want to know what you think," Janie protested.

"And I'll be happy to tell you, but not before you know what you think yourself."

Janie managed a small smile when she saw the twinkle in Matthew's eyes. "I think Carrie is absolutely correct," she said, finding relief in speaking her mind.

"And you're sad about that?"

Janie shrugged. "Left to my own devices, I don't believe I would choose to rock the boat. I don't necessarily believe that's a good thing, but it's the truth. Once it has been rocked, however, and the wrongs have been pointed out to me, it would be nothing but cowardice to look the other way. That doesn't mean I don't wish I could do just that, though." She stepped back and stared up at the School of Design. "They couldn't have had it easy," she murmured as Matthew turned and began to walk back in the direction of the house.

"No. They didn't fight the same deep prejudices you and Carrie are fighting, but they were taking jobs that had always been considered to be for men. Of course, it helped that so many of our men died fighting in the war. Industry was forced to consider a different option if they were to continue moving forward at the same pace as before."

"Do you think I'm an awful coward?"

"Never," Matthew said fervently. "You are a strong, beautiful, talented woman."

Janie heard the words, and she appreciated his support, but she didn't see herself that way. She let her thoughts take her where they wanted to as they walked through the deepening dusk. "Carrie is right," she said, growing more certain by the moment. "But I still don't know what that means. If we want to become doctors, we have to graduate from medical school. How can we do that if we don't believe what the doctors are teaching us?" She ground her teeth with frustration.

"There might be another way," Matthew informed her, "but I think we'll have to continue this conversation later."

"Why?" Janie looked at him with surprise.

"We're back at the house," Matthew replied, "and Carrie is sitting on the porch."

Janie gasped. She had been so lost in her thoughts, she'd had no idea they were so close to the house. A quick glance told her Matthew was right. Carrie was watching them from the porch, but Janie couldn't read her expression because dusk had cloaked her in shadows. It didn't matter. She knew what she had to do. "Carrie!" Janie dropped Matthew's arm and ran forward to envelop her friend in a warm hug. "I was an idiot last night. Will you please forgive me?"

"You were not an idiot, and there is nothing to forgive," Carrie replied. "We had a difference of opinion. Certainly our friendship is strong enough to handle that." She kissed Janie on the cheek, and then turned to Matthew. "Welcome home."

Matthew smiled. "Yes, it *is* home, isn't it?"

"Is it?" Carrie teased. "I saw your bags in the foyer. Northern society is more accepting, but they may frown upon a single man with five women."

"Wouldn't it be fun to give them something to talk about?" Matthew asked with a laugh, before explaining his boarding situation two doors down.

"Wonderful!" Carrie exclaimed. "And you're here for a month?"

"That's the plan, but we all know things could change. That's the reality of life for a newspaper reporter."

"But not for an author," Carrie protested.

"How did you—"

"Know about your book deal? You couldn't possibly think Janie didn't announce it to our housemates as soon as she got your letter. They spilled the beans when I got home."

"Home from...?" Janie asked tentatively.

"I'm sorry I worried you," Carrie said contritely. "I went to visit Biddy and Faith today. I needed some time to think, and I needed to hear the rest of their story."

"And did you?" Janie watched her closely.

"Have time to think? Yes. Hear the rest of their stories? I heard the rest of Biddy's. Faith wanted hers to wait for another time. I think she knew I had quite enough to process."

"And did you find what you were looking for?"

Carrie hesitated. "Let's say I know what I need to do, but I'm not at all sure how to go about doing it."

"Matthew has an idea," Janie said quickly, grasping Carrie's hand. "I'm so sorry about last night. I was feeling particularly scared," she admitted. "I knew what you were saying was right, but I didn't want to rock the boat. After everything that happened during the war, experiencing the difficulty of being a woman in medical school felt like quite enough. I had no desire to make life more difficult."

Carrie gazed at her with soft compassion. "That's completely understandable."

"Stop it!" Janie scolded, laughing when Carrie's eyes widened. "I was acting like a coward last night, but that is no reason to treat me like I might break. I'm not a natural-born rebel like you are, but that doesn't mean I can't see the light. You were absolutely right. I was absolutely wrong. Can we leave it at that and move on?"

"Certainly," Carrie said with a grin. "I love being right sometimes." Her smile faded. "But I still don't know what to do. You were right about the need to graduate from medical school if I want to be a doctor."

"What if you became a different kind of doctor?" Matthew asked.

Carrie cocked her head, a quick question lighting her eyes. "Go on," she invited.

"Have you heard of the Homeopathic Medical College of Philadelphia?"

Carrie frowned. "I barely even know the term. I certainly didn't know there was another medical school here in Philadelphia."

"I'm not surprised," Matthew said easily. "Homeopathy is becoming very popular in the United States, but the more popular it becomes, the more the traditional medical field fights it."

"Why?" Janie asked.

"I suspect it's because they don't want competition," Matthew replied. "The American Institute of Homeopathy was founded by homeopathic physicians from New York, Philadelphia, and Boston in 1844. It was actually the first medical organization in the United States."

"I had no idea," Carrie murmured.

"It was created to promote standardization of the practice and teaching of homeopathy. Anyway, the regular doctors were not thrilled with this development, so they founded the American Medical Association three years later. Their charter contains very specific language against homeopathy, and all its members are forbidden to consult with homeopathic physicians."

"Why?" Janie asked again. "I don't understand."

"Because homeopathy doesn't support their beliefs in drugs and practices like bloodletting," Carrie answered.

Matthew raised his eyebrows. "I thought you didn't know anything about homeopathy."

"I don't, but I am gaining a very clear understanding of how conventional medicine works," Carrie said flatly. "They're against anything that doesn't conform to their accepted standard of doing things."

"Which is your specialty," Matthew teased.

"Evidently," Carrie sighed. "I've decided being a square peg is a wonderful thing. I lost my vision for a while, but it has returned."

"Because of Biddy?" Janie guessed.

Florence stuck her head out the door. "Are the three of you going to talk in the dark all night, or are you going to come in and eat some dinner?"

Janie hesitated. She didn't want to interrupt their conversation, but Matthew's eager look toward the house told her he was hungry. "We're coming," she responded. She turned to Carrie when Florence's head popped back inside. "Can we finish talking later?"

Carrie looked puzzled. "You don't think this is dinner conversation? Surely our housemates will be interested in this."

"I don't know," Janie said slowly, trying to figure out what she was feeling. "Elizabeth and Alice both have a physician for a father. I imagine they have heard a lot of negative things about homeopathy."

Carrie thought for a long moment before she nodded. "You're right. I don't mind disagreeing with someone, but I prefer to have some idea of what I'm talking about before I do."

Janie nodded with relief. "I say we just enjoy a meal of baked chicken and apple pie."

Carrie's eyes widened. "Apple pie? That smell really is coming from our house? I thought surely it was from the house next door."

"Alice has two pies waiting inside for us," Matthew said wistfully, his eyes large and pleading.

Carrie and Janie looked at each other and burst into laughter. Linking their arms around each other's waists, they entered the house.

Carrie leaned her head against the windowsill, relishing the feel of the cool breeze on her body. She knew it wouldn't be long before the refreshing flow became a brutal blast of cold air against tightly closed windows, but she was enjoying the respite from the heat and very happy fall was on the way. The air drifting in carried the aroma of baking, flowers, and industrial smoke. While it wasn't necessarily distasteful, it made her long for the fresh air on the plantation. She fought against the wave of homesickness that tried to take her again. It was her decision to come to Philadelphia, and she didn't want to waste her time here wishing for what she had willingly left behind. Biddy's story had helped her to understand that.

She was not surprised when Janie opened the door and stuck her head in tentatively. "I'm awake," she said.

Janie joined her on the window seat. "I have a reason to be up late now that Matthew is in town. I thought you would be asleep."

"My body wants to sleep," Carrie said wearily, "but my mind doesn't seem willing to shut down."

"What are you thinking about?"

Carrie rolled her eyes. "A better question would be, what am I *not* thinking about? My mind seems to be swirling in circles. Just when I think I may come close to figuring everything out, it dances out of reach and swirls in another direction."

Janie nodded and took hold of her hand. "What is bothering you most?"

Carrie felt a surge of comfort. "This is just like our late night talks during the war. You were the only thing that kept me going most of the time."

"We did that for each other." Janie pushed back her hair and looked out the window unseeingly. "It seems like we have quite a dilemma," she said with a heavy sigh.

"Like what do we do about medical school?" Carrie asked. "Yes, I'd say that is a dilemma."

Janie stared at her. "Are you thinking about leaving?"

Carrie searched for words. "I don't know. I honestly can't decide what I'm thinking, but I did some reading when I came up from dinner."

"About homeopathy?" Janie guessed.

"It's in one of the books Aunt Abby gave me years ago," Carrie answered. "I didn't even realize I had it until I went searching for answers to my questions."

"What did you learn?"

"I learned a lot, but the crux of the matter is that homeopathy reflects my beliefs and experiences much more than conventional medicine."

Janie waited for a moment before she prompted her. "But...?"

"But I also know the need for surgery at times, and I've seen some aspects of conventional medicine work wonders," Carrie said. "That's my problem. There are many things I'm learning right now that I don't feel good about, but it seems silly to throw it all away because I don't agree with *all* of it."

"Tell me what you learned," Janie invited.

Carrie settled back against the cushions and organized her thoughts. "Most homeopaths were former conventional doctors, what they call allopaths, who abandoned conventional medicine because they found homeopathy to be more successful in battling cholera, typhus, yellow fever, diphtheria, and influenza—just for starters."

Janie whistled. "Then why is it so looked down upon?"

Carrie frowned. "Homeopathy was founded by Samuel Hahnemann, a German doctor who was also a respected chemist. Evidently, he was forced to move several times during his life because the local German apothecaries objected to the fact that he created his own medicines rather than use theirs."

Janie absorbed that for a moment. "It all came down to money," she said with disgust.

"From what I can tell," Carrie agreed. "Though I suppose it was a mix of money and male pride. The doctors of the day didn't take kindly to homeopaths saying they had found a better way of doing things. Doctors were rather revered figures."

"I'm still not sure I understand exactly what it is," Janie murmured.

"I'm just beginning to figure it out," Carrie replied. "It's not that easy to explain." She paused a moment. "I'll do my best. Homeopathy is based on a single law of therapeutics called the *Law of Similars*. Basically, this law says that a substance that can cause the symptoms of a disease can also cure it." She reached for the book she had been reading, turned up the oil on her lantern, and opened to a page she had marked. "'Homeo' means similar. 'Pathos' means disease, or suffering."

"Similar disease, or similar suffering," Janie said thoughtfully.

"Yes. From what I can tell, the reason homeopaths run into trouble with skeptics revolves around how the remedies are prepared. Obviously, many of the substances that can cause the symptoms of the disease are dangerous. Administering them becomes quite a challenge."

"I would imagine." Janie's eyes were bright with curiosity.

Carrie smiled. "Dr. Hahnemann tried different things until he learned how to dilute his medicines. First, he would take the substance of a plant or mineral and steep it in alcohol. He called it the mother tincture. He would take that and add a tiny amount to a mixture of distilled water and ethyl alcohol. Once he had it diluted, he shook it vigorously. He called the shaking process succussion. He discovered succussion enhanced the effects of the dilution," Carrie said, warming to her topic. "He would take that tincture, add it to another mixture of distilled water and alcohol, and then succuss it again. He learned that doing that would lessen any potential negative side effects."

Janie absorbed what she had said. "It doesn't sound that different from what Old Sarah taught you," she concluded.

"Exactly!"

"Does it work? I've seen Old Sarah's remedies work, but what about these?"

"I wondered the same thing," Carrie admitted. She and Janie might ultimately end up disagreeing, but at least they were able to talk about it. "The whole thing is so fascinating," she said as she flipped through pages to find what she was looking for. "Dr. Hahnemann was viewed as little more than a quack until 1812. He was living in Leipzig, Germany when Napoleon was driven from his country. The battles to reclaim their country resulted in eighty thousand dead, with another eighty thousand wounded, but it also created a typhus outbreak." She took a quick breath as her excitement grew. "Every physician in Germany was pressed into service. Dr. Hahnemann arrived with twenty-six different homeopathic medicines that he believed would work. He achieved remarkable results." Carrie's eyes flashed. "Of the one hundred eighty typhus patients he treated, only two died."

"Two?" Janie echoed. "That's astounding."

"I know!" Carrie flipped pages quickly. "Listen to this. Homeopathy has been used with a high degree of success in both the treatment and prevention of cholera." She smiled when Janie leaned closer. "We know cholera killed more than ten thousand people in London in 1854. What we've never been taught is that patients were much more likely to survive if they were treated by homeopathy rather than with conventional medicine."

"How much more likely?" Janie demanded.

Carrie grinned. "The death rate for those treated homeopathically was only nine percent, compared to..." She paused for dramatic effect. "Compared to over *fifty-nine percent* of those treated conventionally."

Janie stared at her. "That's a huge difference."

"I know!"

"Why aren't we taught this?" Janie asked angrily.

"I'm as disgusted as you are," Carrie replied. "The results were so embarrassing to the Medical Council of England that they tried to suppress the information by omitting it from their report to Parliament. Fortunately, one of the members of Parliament had been saved by homeopathic treatment during the epidemic so he demanded the full records be obtained. The Medical Council obliged, but they made sure the homeopathic figures were in a different report, and they also made sure that report was not easily obtainable."

"So it works," Janie said.

"All my research says it does."

"And your experience says it does."

Carrie nodded. "Yes. This is so very similar to the solutions Sarah taught me how to make. Why use drugs that can cause harm when you can use natural things that will cure?"

"Are drugs really harmful?"

"I believe most of them are, but I've got so much to learn. I'm going to keep reading, and I'm also going to make an appointment to meet with someone at the Homeopathic College. Do you want to come with me?"

"Yes," Janie said after a moment's hesitation.

Carrie understood. They were on the verge of turning their worlds completely upside down.

Chapter Nine

It was late in the afternoon before Moses finally headed back to the house. Work would continue until it was too dark to see, but he had promised he would bring John out into the fields with him for the last two hours. He smiled as he thought of his son's eagerness to be with him every moment. The feeling was definitely mutual.

John and Patches were as well known on the plantation as he was. Moses felt a flash of pride as he thought of his little boy's easy confidence, but gratitude was his primary emotion. It was too easy to dredge up the memories of his own childhood. He had already felt the lash before his fifth birthday. He couldn't remember what he had done wrong, but he still had vivid memories of the bite of the whip into his tender back. He had seen his father beaten many times, and he had toiled for hours under the brutal sun picking worms from the tobacco. He shuddered as visions exploded in his head of Sadie screaming during the beating that left her crippled.

Moses took a deep breath as he forced his thoughts back to the present. The past was over. Knowing his son would never have to repeat his experiences meant more than words could ever say. It made every hardship during the war worth it. The pain fled as pride in his contribution swelled his chest.

Amber appeared in the distance, walking down the road with All My Heart. The setting sun created a halo effect that glimmered around them like a curtain of gold. Just the sight of them made Moses smile. The bay filly had quickly accepted the halter and just as quickly learned how to lead, but there was hardly a need. The two adored each other. All My Heart would follow Amber anywhere. When the little girl left at night to go home, the filly would hang her head over the wooden railing and whinny pitifully for her to return. Amber usually walked backward, waving and calling to All My Heart until she disappeared around the bend.

"Hello, Moses!" Amber called, waving excitedly.

"Hello, Amber. Where are you and that filly headed off to?"

Amber's eyes danced with excitement. "Robert told me I could take her down to the river today. All My Heart has never seen it. I can hardly wait to show her!"

Moses laughed. "You be careful down there."

Amber nodded gravely, though her expression said she was not the least bit concerned. "I will, Moses." Her face broke into a wide grin. "See you later!"

Moses watched them for a moment and then continued on to the house. He wasn't going to eat dinner until his day was done, but he knew his mama would have cookies and lemonade waiting for him. Just the thought made his stomach growl with anticipation. He chuckled and nudged his horse into a canter, suddenly eager to be home.

Rose was waiting on the porch for Moses when he rode up. When he raised a brow, she nodded toward the barn. "You have a very impatient son. He already has Patches bridled and saddled."

"By himself?" Moses asked with surprise. John was big for his age, but that would be a tough challenge for him.

Rose shook her head. "Amber helped him, but only with the bridle. He stood on a box and put the saddle on all by himself."

Moses grinned with unconcealed pride. "That's my boy!"

Rose waited until Moses tied his horse and settled into a chair on the porch before she turned to him. "I have an idea."

Moses took a long drink of lemonade and stuffed a large oatmeal cookie in his mouth before he looked at her. "What?" he mumbled around his cookie.

Annie appeared behind him, shaking her head. "I know I taught you better than to be talkin' when your mouth be full. You spit crumbs on this clean porch, and you'll be the one cleaning it up."

"Yes, Mama," Moses said meekly, winking at Rose as he tried to swallow the rest of his mouthful.

Annie glared at him, a smile lurking on her lips, before she turned to Rose. "So you be wantin' that picnic or not?"

Rose hid her frown. She had wanted to surprise Moses with her idea. Pushing down her disappointment, she turned to him. "That will be up to Moses." His look invited her to continue. "School starts tomorrow..."

"Yes."

"And there is almost a full moon tonight..."

Annie shook her head again and made a clucking noise before she opened the screen door. "Once you get around to tellin' him what you want to do, you let me know. I ain't got enough time to listen while you creep your way toward it like a scared fish roaming around a baited hook." The screen door slammed behind her.

Rose grinned as Annie's footsteps faded into the distance. Her strategy had worked. Patience was not one of her mother-in-law's strong points. She turned to Moses eagerly now that she no longer had an audience. "I would like to take you for a moonlight ride tonight," she said. "Annie is going to watch the kids, and she is fixing a picnic for us to take." She hesitated, hating the fact that she felt the need to, but she knew the demands of harvest time. "I know you're probably tired after a long day..."

"I'm never too tired for an invitation like that," Moses said, his dark eyes boring into hers. "Is there going to be a blanket with that picnic?"

Rose met his eyes squarely, a smile of delight dancing across her lips. "Why, Mr. Samuels, I do believe there will be."

Moses stuffed two more cookies into his pockets, drained his glass, and stood. "John and I will be back as soon as we can." He leaned down to give her a warm kiss and then moved swiftly toward the barn. "Make sure Mama puts more cookies in that picnic," he called over his shoulder.

Amber walked along easily, contentment flooding her body as All My Heart's head bobbed against her shoulder. She could still hardly believe this beautiful filly belonged to her. She was at the barn every morning as soon as it was light, her pockets stuffed with fresh carrots and ham biscuits her mama left out for her every night. She would settle down with All My Heart under a tree, and they would each savor their treats. Most times, her filly would curl up right next to her on the ground while she talked to her. Clint said she was spoiling her, but All My Heart would do anything Amber wanted, so she suspected he was just jealous. Robert was overjoyed with the filly's progress.

She took a deep breath as the breeze cooled her body. Late September had brought an end to the unbearable humidity, but it was still plenty warm. She smelled the rich, freshly cut tobacco mixed with the pungent aroma of curing tobacco and wood smoke. The furnace blazed in the drying barn all the time now. She had thought the mountains of firewood cut that summer would surely go to waste, or be used in the big house over the winter, but they were dwindling before her eyes every single day. She had even heard Moses asking some of the men to cut more.

Amber had finished her work for the day, but an uneasy, guilty feeling swept through her as she gazed at all the men working in the fields. She stopped for a moment and watched as several of them used a machete to split the tobacco stalks three-quarters of the way down, and then cut the plants off above the ground.

Other men were standing by, holding a big stick they had cut from five-foot-long pine logs. Once five or six of the plants had been placed on the sticks, they would carry them on their shoulders to the drying barn where they would hang them to dry. Other men would quickly take their place. There seemed to be a constant stream of workers heading toward the barn. Moses had said it was a good crop this year. It must be, because all the men looked tired, but they also looked happy.

Robert and her daddy had warned her to stay away from the drying barn. She was only too happy to comply. Her life was in the stables. She didn't want anyone getting the idea that she should also help with the tobacco. Just the thought was enough to make her keep walking. This was her last night of freedom before school started, and she knew her mama would make her come home early to study every night. She would still help in the stables after school, but she wouldn't have nearly as much time with All My Heart.

"Come on, girl," she murmured, her heart leaping forward to the river. Tomorrow would come, but she still had today. Her mama was always telling her not to waste today by pining away over what might happen tomorrow. "I have a surprise for you, little one." All My Heart nickered and nudged her shoulder as if to hurry her. Amber walked faster, her feet kicking up little spurts of dust.

She could feel the river before she could actually see it. The air cooled just a little, but it was the smell that told her they were close. Amber didn't know how to explain the smell of the river, but it had a special rich and earthy smell all its own. To her, it carried the aroma of life itself. It didn't matter if she could explain it. As she took a deep breath, the unspoiled, pristine, pure aroma gave her a heady feeling.

All My Heart snorted and pranced a little, her delicate head lifted high and her ears pricked forward as she gazed down the trail. "You can smell it, too, can't you girl?" Amber asked. She broke into a run, All My Heart floating along beside her. Moments later, they were standing on the bank of the river.

All My Heart stared, her ears twitching back and forth as she swung her head to take it all in.

"This is the James River," Amber told her. "It starts way up in the mountains and goes all the way down to the ocean. I don't know if you'll ever see the ocean because I haven't even seen it, but I've read about it in books. It sounds wonderful. I will see it one day," she vowed. Stroking the filly's neck, she watched the shimmer of the setting sun on the calm, smooth waters. She wasn't eager for the sun to go down, but she drew a sharp breath of appreciation when the glowing orb transformed the clouds, turning them gold and purple, shafts of sunlight bursting through like a halo.

"Ain't it beautiful, All My Heart?" she murmured. The scene unfolding before her made her heart catch. "I reckon we be in the best place in the whole world right now." Amber was glad no one was around to correct her English. She wanted to learn how to speak correctly, but sometimes she wanted to open her mouth and have words come out without having to think about them. When she was alone with her filly, she felt like she was in her own little world where no one else could touch her.

All My Heart snorted and bobbed her head, pulling against the lead line to get closer to the water.

Amber walked forward. "I brought you to a smooth bank so you can go in."

The filly moved forward slowly, staring wide-eyed at the vast expanse of water that reached as far as the eye could see. A distant line of trees could be seen on the far bank, but glistening water was the only thing visible to the left and right. All My Heart edged closer, stretching her neck out until her velvety muzzle touched the water that reflected back at her like a mirror. She jerked and stared when a fish jumped in the distance, but nickered again and moved closer until she was actually standing in the river. Snorting loudly, she lifted her right front leg and began pawing at the water.

Amber laughed with delight as droplets of water exploded, catching the sun like tiny, dancing diamonds. She laughed even harder when All My Heart started bobbing her head as she pawed the water. Soon the filly was standing chest deep in the water, her head swinging as she gazed in each direction. The look on her face was easy to read—she loved the river.

Amber hitched up her skirts and walked out to join her, sighing in ecstasy as the warm water wrapped around her legs. She went still at the same moment All My Heart did, both of them alerted by a sound in the distance. Side by side, their eyes to the sky, they watched as a large flock of geese flew overhead in a perfect V, their loud honking signaling the imminent arrival of fall. "Other than the day Robert gave you to me, I think this be the best day of my life," Amber whispered as she stared up at the sky. All My Heart lowered her head to rest it on Amber's shoulder.

Amber stroked her muzzle, her heart almost bursting with joy and love.

The two stood quietly until the sun dipped far enough below the horizon to signal they had to return home if they didn't want to incur someone's wrath. "We'll be back, girl," Amber promised. "We'll be back many, many times." Her heart pulsed with anticipation as they navigated the shadowed trail back to the road. "And one day I will be riding you!"

Rose cuddled Hope close as she watched Moses and John walk from the barn toward the house. She was sure she would never grow tired of watching her husband and son together. John ran in circles around his father, waving his arms excitedly as he talked about something Rose couldn't decipher. Moses' booming laugh lifted toward her through the still evening air, telling her all was well.

Annie appeared on the porch beside her. "Give me that little girl."

Rose kissed Hope's warm, pudgy cheek before she handed her over. "She just had dinner. She will be fine until I return. I think she'll go right to sleep." She prayed she was right. John had been such an easy baby. Hope was much fussier and demanding, but her smile when it burst forth filled Rose's heart every time.

Annie smiled down at Hope's toothless grin. "My grandbaby will be just fine. If she gets hungry, I have some fine porridge I can give her. I can't believe this baby girl already be eatin'. It seems like yesterday that she was born."

Rose smiled. "Almost nine months old. Can you believe it?" She smiled but felt a flicker of sadness. "I so wish Sam could have seen her."

"Sam be up there lookin' down on our little girl," Annie said. "You can count on that. He probably went home that same night so he could look down on this baby and take care of her the same way he took care of you all those years. He knew he was too old to chase after her down here on earth."

Rose smiled, the image creating warm comfort. "I think you might be right," she murmured.

Moses had drawn close enough to hear. "Don't you know my mama is *always* right?" he teased. "At least that's what she has been telling me all my life."

"You learned things the right way," Annie said. She reached for John's hand. "I got dinner waiting for you, little man."

John gazed up at his father. "Are you coming, Daddy?"

Moses knelt down to look into his eyes. "Not tonight, John. Remember that I told you I was going on a picnic with your mama?"

John's eyes flooded with disappointment before they took on a hopeful glint. "Can I come, too?"

"Not tonight," Moses said with a chuckle. "I told you this is a special time for just me and Mama."

John's face crumpled. Annie swooped him up before he could begin to cry. "Come on now, John. You can't be eatin' none of my fine blackberry cobbler if you be cryin'."

John's tears vanished before they had even begun to fall. "Blackberry cobbler? For dinner?"

"For *after* dinner," Annie said. She winked at Moses and Rose. "At least that's what I got to tell you while your folks be listening. Once they leave..." She let her voice trail off.

John's eyes widened with quick understanding. "Maybe you and Mama should go ahead now, Daddy."

Rose mouthed "thank you" to Annie as Moses picked up the picnic basket and hoisted it easily.

Annie grinned, took the hand John offered her, and disappeared into the house with Hope snuggled in the crook of her other arm.

"She's an angel."

Moses nodded. "We spent too many years apart," he said gruffly. "We're all making up for lost time."

Rose took her husband's hand and smiled into his eyes. "That's what I'm doing, too," she said. She knew she couldn't expect much until the end of harvest, but she was determined to claim this one night before the classroom swallowed all her time again. Moses was gone from sunup to sundown nearly every single day. She was thrilled with how well the crop was doing, and she was grateful to be able to snuggle up beside her husband every night, but she missed him. She was already longing for the barren, cold winter that would give her more time with him.

"I've missed you, too," Moses answered, reading her thoughts perfectly. "One more question, and then tonight will only be about us."

"Felicia is in the library," Rose said, anticipating his question. "The courier from town arrived today with all of Thomas' magazines and newspapers. She is like a kid in a Philadelphia candy store. I'm sure I'll have to drag her out of the library when we get home."

"Did she get a letter?" Moses asked.

Rose stared at him. "How would you know anything about a letter?"

"Does that mean it came?"

"Yes, but Felicia wouldn't tell me a thing. She just got a smile on her face and ran upstairs with it." Rose stopped walking. "Do you know what was in that letter?"

Moses shrugged innocently. "I might, but I'm not really sure."

Rose stamped her foot. "Moses Samuels!" She had been dying of curiosity ever since it had arrived.

Moses laughed loudly. "I'm sworn to secrecy."

Rose hated the little twinge of jealousy and hurt.

Moses read her look instantly. "She wants to be the one to tell you, Rose, but she doesn't want to talk about it until she knows for sure."

Rose stuffed aside her hurt feelings. She knew she was being small and petty, and she also recognized Felicia and Moses shared a special bond because he had been the one to save her in Memphis. She and Felicia had become closer since their time talking in the library, but the little girl still kept her at arm's length. "I'll look forward to her news," she said, "but that is enough about our children. As much as I love them, I love their father just as much. Tonight is ours."

Moses lifted her chin and kissed her lips. "Where to?" He looked around. "Are we walking or riding?"

"Walking," Rose answered as she headed toward a trail down to the river.

Moses looked suspiciously at the basket. "This isn't big enough to have a blanket in it."

Rose blinked. "We need a blanket?"

Moses opened his mouth to protest, but quickly read the look in her eyes. "Lead the way."

Rose walked briskly, glad for the last remaining vestiges of light that made the path barely visible, although she knew the woods on the plantation as well as she knew the back of her hand. She'd had to.

"Remember the night I met you?" Moses asked. "You led me through the woods to your secret school. I thought I was certainly going to die that night. I didn't believe you could get away with teaching. I was terrified."

"I remember," Rose answered. "What *I* remember the most, though, was being scared to death I was going to fall in love with you."

"It hasn't been so terrible, has it?"

"It's been the best thing in my life," Rose said as they broke out onto a secluded beach along the river.

"You've been busy," Moses murmured, his eyes bright with appreciation.

Rose moved forward to light the fire she had built earlier. The blanket was already laid out. She shooed a frog off the edge of it, reached for the picnic basket, and motioned for Moses to sit down.

Moses stared hopefully at the basket as he lowered himself to the blanket. "Is some of my mama's fried chicken in that basket?"

Rose chuckled. "Along with potato salad and deviled eggs."

"And some of her cookies?"

"Cookies and warm bread with butter," Rose confirmed. "Along with a jug of cold tea. I knew you would be starving."

"It's good to have a wife who knows her man," Moses said happily, patting his stomach as he reached out for the plate she handed to him.

Rose ate, but mostly she watched Moses devour enough food for three men. It never ceased to amaze her how much he could eat, but she also realized it must take a lot to fill up someone so tall and strong.

"What are you thinking about?" Moses asked as he reached for another cookie.

"That I hope we'll be able to feed both you and John one day. If he eats like his father, we could be in trouble."

"Guess his mama better make good money as a schoolteacher," Moses replied.

"And his daddy better make good money as a lawyer," Rose shot back playfully. "But that's not all I was thinking about..."

"No?" Moses gazed at her, pushing aside the picnic remnants from the blanket.

When he reached for her, Rose jumped up. "Wait!" She lit the fire, knowing it would keep the mosquitoes away. She waited a moment to make sure it was going to burn easily, and then turned back to Moses. The look in his eyes made her catch her breath. All her efforts and planning had been worth it.

"Come here," Moses commanded, his eyes never leaving her.

Rose went willingly, her heart melting as he pulled her close and claimed her lips. She reached up and cradled his face. "I love you so much," she whispered.

"Just how much?"

Rose smiled. "I'll be happy to show you."

The fire had died down to glowing embers before Moses stood and added wood. Crackling flames soon illuminated the night and shot sparks high into the air. The breeze caught them and carried them over the black water that reflected back their glimmering dance before they floated into a watery grave.

Rose lay where she was, afraid movement would break the magic. She gazed at his broad shoulders outlined against the night sky, and then gasped with delight. Moses swung around to look at her, but she merely held out her hand to him. When he was settled down beside her again, she pointed east. The moon was now perched on top of the tree line, its silvery glow bringing the woods to life.

Moses, sensing her desire for closeness, pulled her tightly to his side. They watched as the moon slowly slid up in the sky, wispy clouds scuttling across its face as the wind picked up. Soon it was high enough to illuminate the ripples on the James River. Bullfrogs and crickets sang a welcome while fireflies darted through the grasses and the trees surrounding them.

Rose smiled, her heart full. "This has been a perfect night," she whispered.

Moses pressed his cheek against her head. "Thank you for making it happen. The only thing more beautiful than this night is my wife."

Rose sighed with contentment as she stared up at the silvery orb. "The moon is such a mystery."

"It looks like it's sitting right in the Big Dipper."

Rose pulled back to stare at him. "The Big Dipper?"

"It's a constellation," Moses explained. He pointed toward the sky. "See, it looks like a big ladle. That's why they call it the Big Dipper. During the spring and summer, it is much higher in the sky. Now that it's almost fall, it's lower on the horizon."

"And you know this how?" Rose asked, completely surprised by his knowledge.

"Felicia told me."

Rose chuckled. "Of course she did. Let me guess. She found it in some of Thomas' books."

Moses nodded, pointing again. "That's the Little Dipper. The brightest star is the North Star. Sailors have used that to navigate ever since they started using boats."

Rose stared at the sky with fascination, eager to know more about the mysteries it held. "When did Felicia teach you all this?"

"When she told me about the letter that might be coming," he confessed. "Don't ask me any more questions. She wants to tell you herself."

Rose was content with his answer. She was happy to stare at the sky and see millions of stars twinkling at her. She was too relaxed and peaceful to make an attempt to see more than that. She pushed aside the thought of how much she could teach her students if she learned more. Tonight she wasn't a schoolteacher. Tonight she was a woman in love with her husband.

When Moses tried to stifle a yawn, Rose knew it was time to go. She knew it was late because the moon was high in the sky, lighting up the night and dancing over the water and rocks. Part of her wanted to stay right there and never move. Another part of her was eager to get back to her babies. She was sure they were sleeping peacefully, but she wanted to see it for herself. "It's time to go home," she whispered, not willing to break the quiet of their sanctuary.

Moses pulled her close, kissed her one more time, and then lifted her to her feet. He repacked the picnic basket while she shook out the blanket and folded it. When he reached for the blanket, she handed it over willingly, and then led them toward the path.

Within moments, the thick woods had swallowed the moonlight. Rose moved forward confidently, not at all alarmed by the total blackness and the sound of scurrying feet. The woods had become her friend years ago. The fact that Moses was with her only made her more confident. It took but a few minutes for them to walk the trail and draw near to the road that led back to the house, and also down to the old quarters where the temporary workers were now living.

She stiffened and stopped.

"Rose?"

Rose held up her hand and listened intently. "There is someone on the road," she whispered. She could feel Moses frown even though she could see nothing but a large shape that stepped up to stand beside her.

"Are you sure?"

Rose nodded her head, annoyed with how hard her heart was beating. This was the plantation. Surely the vigilantes wouldn't come right onto the plantation with so many men around. But as soon as she had the thought, she knew they might well do that. She fought to swallow her fear.

Moses took her hand and continued to move forward.

"Moses!" she hissed, hating her terror, but unable to stop it. She had heard too many stories. "Don't go out there!"

"There is only one way to find out what's on the road. I refuse to be afraid."

Rose bit back her protest and gripped his hand as they moved toward the glow of the moonlight. Whether she agreed with him or not, she would not allow her husband to walk into trouble alone.

Chapter Ten

Moses stopped before they broke out of the woods, watching the group of men carefully. He couldn't identify faces, but their bodies were outlined in stark contrast by the light of the moon. He was certain they were not any of his workers, but neither were there any alarm bells going off in his mind. He was content to watch the ten men clustered in the middle of the road. They were talking quietly but urgently, their arms waving as different ones made their point. "They don't seem to be trying to hide," Moses whispered. "If they were planning on trouble, I'd think they would be less conspicuous. They're probably just men looking for work."

"In the middle of the night?" Rose was still suspicious, but she felt her heart beat slowing as she acknowledged Moses was probably right. She was curious to find out who the men were, but something still held her in place. She felt protected by the dark embrace of the woods. Once they stepped out into the bright moonlight, it would be too late to try to hide.

One of the men's voices carried to them on the breeze. "I told you it be too late to come here. We can't find Moses at night."

"They know you!" Rose whispered. "Is that a good thing?"

"It is tonight," Moses said with a chuckle as he stepped out of the woods. "Is that you, Jeb?" he called.

The man who had been speaking whirled around. "Moses?"

"Depends on who is asking," Moses responded as a grin broke out on his face.

The man, who stood almost as tall as Moses but not as broad, stepped forward. "It's Jeb! From your old unit."

"Then I reckon I'm Moses," he said with a laugh. He pulled Rose forward. "And this is..."

"Rose!" another man yelled, breaking loose from the group. "I remember you from Fort Monroe. I was with the unit when Moses surprised you for Christmas!"

They were suddenly surrounded by men, all eager to explain why they were on Cromwell Plantation so late at night. Moses laughed as he realized every one of the group had served with him in his army unit. He called out greetings as they strode forward to shake his hand or slap his back.

Rose watched with a smile on her face, but she was still curious why they had arrived in the middle of the night.

Moses finally held up his hand to stop the talk because none of it was making any sense. "One at a time!" he called.

Rose smiled at the authoritative tone of his voice and realized how effective he must have been as a leader, because every one of the men stopped talking and stood tall.

Moses fixed his eyes on Jeb. "You do realize it's past midnight, don't you, Jeb?"

"We do," Jeb said apologetically. His voice grew tight and nervous. "We've learned it's best not to travel during the day. Groups of black men tend to make white people nervous."

"They can certainly do that," Moses replied.

"We were going to bed down outside the entrance to Cromwell tonight," Jeb continued, "but four white men on horseback rode by. They didn't see us, but we got the feeling they were up to no good."

Rose stiffened, her eyes searching the horizon. She was relieved when there was no orange glow to indicate a fire at the schoolhouse. "Could you hear what they were saying?" she asked. She was sure the four horsemen knew school was scheduled to start again tomorrow. They had all night to cause trouble.

"No, ma'am," Jeb responded. He offered her a gentle smile. "I've heard a lot of good things about you, Mrs. Samuels. It's real nice to meet you."

Rose smiled warmly. "It's nice to meet you, too, Jeb. Welcome to Cromwell Plantation." Her mind shot back to the horsemen. "So, you couldn't hear what they were saying? Not any of it?" She hoped that someday the image of her school in flames would fade from her memory, but it wasn't going to be tonight.

"No, ma'am, but they didn't sound happy. We decided it would probably be a good idea if we just came on in to the plantation. We were planning on sleeping in the woods until morning. We didn't expect the two of you to be out roaming around in the middle of the night."

Rose chuckled, glad she didn't have to explain what they had been doing, but she was startled when she heard angry muttering from someone in the group.

Moses stepped forward. "Is there a problem?" he asked evenly.

Rose could feel Moses stiffen when a small, wiry man separated himself from the group.

"Hello, Trevor."

Rose, only because she knew her husband so well, could hear the strained tone in his voice. She waited quietly, knowing time would reveal the cause of his tension. Since her husband was more than twice Trevor's size, and because he didn't appear to be armed, she felt no alarm. Moses could take care of himself.

"Long time, Moses," Trevor drawled.

Rose held back a shiver at the barely concealed anger in the little man's voice. Was he angry with Moses, or just life in general?

"Yes, it has been. Is there a problem?" Moses repeated.

"This country is full of nothin' *but* problems," Trevor said bitterly, his shoulders slumped with fatigue. "We's hopin' you can help us. We've come a mighty long way."

Rose felt Moses relax marginally.

"What do you hope I can do?"

Jeb stepped forward again. Evidently he had been designated the spokesperson for the group. Trevor shot a sour look at him but stepped back.

Rose realized Moses gave his attention to Jeb but was still carefully watching Trevor. What was going on? She couldn't help seeing the hopeful look on the other men's faces, but she could tell Moses was wary of Trevor.

"Trevor is right that the country is full of problems," Jeb said, only his eyes showing his anxiety. "We got mustered out of the army about two months ago down in Texas. We were all real careful to save the money we made, figurin' we could buy some land when the fightin' was all done and they let us out. It ain't worked out that way."

Moses nodded. "You can't find anyone who will sell you land."

"You know how it is?" Jeb asked.

"Unfortunately, yes. You're not the first I've heard this from." He turned and looked at the group. "All of you have money?"

"Just barely," Jeb said, not trying to conceal his anger this time. "We got ambushed one night about a month ago. Thankfully we had been warned, so all our money was hid up in the trees above where we were sleepin'. The men threatened to rough us up some if we didn't give them everything we had, but they figured out real quick we were ready to fight back. Those cowards hiding under them white hoods rode off pretty quick when they realized we had guns. We learned to keep hidin' our money after that. That's why we try to mostly travel at night. We figure we won't draw as much attention."

"White hoods?" Moses asked. "Where were you?"

Rose held her breath, remembering what Matthew had told them.

"Coming through Tennessee," Jeb answered. "You ever heard of a thing called the Ku Klux Klan?"

Moses frowned deeply. "I have. A friend told me a group had formed that could mean trouble for our people."

"Oh, they mean trouble all right," Trevor snarled. "But theys ain't the only ones. We ran into vigilante groups all through the South. They ain't happy about black folks being treated like people."

Jeb shot Trevor a warning look but nodded. "Trevor is right. These groups are killing black people everywhere. I figure thousands of us have been killed in Texas since the war. Louisiana and Mississippi seem to be as bad. We headed north, hoping Tennessee would be better since it was a border state, but that's where they almost got us. We hide out during the day now."

"That's terrible!" Rose cried.

"Yes, ma'am," Jeb agreed, "but it's the way things be. We all be stickin' together, hoping we can find a way to make our lives better. We heard through some folks how things are here on Cromwell Plantation." He looked closely at Moses. "It be true that you own half this plantation now, and that the men who first started with you after the war all have their own places now?" His voice made it clear he didn't think the rumors could possibly be true.

"It's true," Moses answered, giving no more information than that.

Rose understood when excited muttering broke out from the group. They had come a long way to find out if their information was correct.

Jeb straightened even more. "Moses, we was hopin' you had room for some more of your old unit. If we can't find nothing to buy, we's at least hoping we can work where we can get treated fairly." He paused. "We heard about them riots in Memphis and New Orleans. We also heard they might just cook President Johnson's goose. We's hoping things will get better if he ain't got no real power."

"I believe things are going to get better, but it's not going to be right away," Moses said carefully.

"So you got a place for us here?" Trevor broke in to ask.

Moses shook his head. "I'm sorry to say the answer is no. I have all the full-time hands I can afford right now. Our harvest workers will only be here a few more weeks and then they will have to move on."

Rose's heart swelled with sympathy at the despairing look that filled the men's eyes. They had traveled so far, hoping they would find a place to settle. "One of the houses is empty down in the old quarters," she said quickly. "You will stay there for the next few days while we see if we can figure out a way to help."

Jeb stared at her. "I appreciate that ma'am, but if you ain't got work, you ain't got work. There doesn't seem to be any sense in hanging around," he said wearily. "We should be moving on."

"My wife is right," Moses said. "We'll take you down to the quarters and get you settled. You'll be a little cramped, but it will be better than what you had in the old days. And you'll have plenty of food." Jeb still hesitated. Moses stared at the group, imagining what they had experienced as they crossed the country in the dead of night. "We fought more battles together than we care to remember. Just because I don't have enough jobs for all of you doesn't mean I can't help. We can try to figure something out."

Rose watched hope ignite in the men's eyes again.

Jeb saw it, too. "I appreciate that, Moses."

It took them almost an hour to get all the men settled into the cabin. Rose wasn't surprised when women had appeared from the other dwellings with food and water for the travelers. They had all walked the same road. It didn't matter that it was the middle of the night. Their people had learned to stick together to survive.

"I'm glad we could help them," Rose said as she and Moses walked back toward the house. Her husband nodded but remained silent. "What's bothering you?"

"Trevor could be trouble," Moses said reluctantly.

"You've had trouble with him before?"

"Let's just say there is potential," he answered carefully. "He never disobeyed any orders during the war, but I've always felt he was like a keg of dynamite on the edge of exploding. I don't think it would take much to set him off."

"Do you know why?" Rose had been watching Trevor carefully when they were in the quarters. The oil lanterns that had been carried out with the food allowed her to examine his eyes. She had seen what seemed to be equal amounts of anger and pain etched into his very soul. Just looking at him had made her heart ache.

Moses shrugged. "He's not much for talking, but he revealed some things during the Siege of Petersburg the last year of the war. His years as a slave were bad ones."

Rose frowned. More than anything he could have said, the flat tone in Moses' voice told her how bad those years must have been. "He ran away?"

"Yes. They caught him and brought him back twice."

Rose shuddered as she imagined what his punishment must have been like.

"The second time he ran away, his master killed his youngest child and sold off his wife and other children. He had run away so he could start a better life for them, but they were all gone when he was brought back. Evidently he hasn't been able to find them."

"No!" Rose whispered with horror.

"When he ran away the third time, I think they gave up on sending the slave hunters after him. They knew he would run again. I don't think he's a bad man," Moses continued, "but when you have that much hate and anger in you, it can make you do bad things."

Rose wished there were more light so she could see the expression in his eyes. "What are you afraid he will do?"

Moses shrugged. "That's the thing. I don't have a basis for being afraid at all. It's just something I feel..."

"And we've both learned to trust our feelings and intuition," Rose answered quietly. "What are you going to do?" The final decision should be up to him. He knew the men in his old unit.

"I'm going to let it play out and see what happens," Moses replied after a long silence. "All of those men have been through terrible times. They fought for their freedom, and now they're forced to fight to have any kind of life at all. Any one of them could end up being trouble, but that's no different from the other harvest workers I hired. The only men I completely trust are the first ones who came with me." He stared up at the moon falling lower on the horizon. "I'm going to do what I can to help them. That may end up being nothing, but at least they have a safe haven for a while."

Rose nodded. "They're all horribly skinny. At least we can feed them."

Robert took a deep breath of the cool morning air. Summer seemed to have left for good. They may have a bout of Indian summer, but the ushering in of October seemed to have eliminated the searing heat. He smiled as he watched the colts and fillies cavorting around the pasture.

The only thing to mar his joy was the constant ache of missing Carrie. He knew how happy she would be on a morning like this. She would already be on Granite, riding off to take advantage of a beautiful day. He could envision her black hair flowing down her slim back, a brilliant smile on her face as she waved to him. They would have spent the night snuggling together under covers that were needed for the first time in months. He shook his head to clear it of his lonely thoughts. She had promised to be there for the Harvest Festival. At least he had something to look forward to.

"Sure is a fine morning," Clint said cheerfully as he led two of the colts from the barn.

"That it is," Robert agreed, pushing aside his feelings as he turned to face his assistant. "And you're doing a fine job with those two."

Clint nodded, a bright smile lighting his face. "They make me look good," he said easily. "All of these babies have the temperament of their sire. Eclipse is a fine stud."

"That he is. I thank God every day that you had Abby buy him." Robert walked around the two colts. "They are both going to be natural athletes," he murmured, running his hand gently down their shoulders and legs, satisfied with their early training when he noted they watched him with no trace of fear.

He jerked his head up when a sharp whinny broke the still air. "Has All My Heart been hanging over that fence since Amber left?" he asked with a laugh.

Clint nodded. "She came by the stables this morning as soon as it was light, just like she always does. When she left to go to school, that filly watched her until she disappeared into the woods. She hasn't quit watching that spot since then."

"That filly is more like a dog than a horse," Robert muttered.

"I keep telling Amber she's spoiling her," Clint proclaimed.

"Not a bit," Robert said. "They adore each other, and All My Heart does whatever Amber asks. She is already leading and walking perfectly. Winning an animal's trust is the best way to train them—especially with horses. Far too many of today's trainers think they have to discipline them into obedience. Amber naturally knows that love is the best way. Just like you do." Robert's belief that Clint was a natural horseman had been confirmed many times over since he had arrived on the plantation with his family. Robert had worked closely to ingrain his own training methods into the boy, but he also knew how easily a man's pride could get in the way of gentle training.

Clint nodded, seeming relieved that Robert agreed with Amber's methods. He grinned suddenly. "I have something to show you."

"What is it?"

Instead of answering, Clint tied one of the colts to a hitching post and moved forward with the other one, a colt named Pegasus who promised to be the biggest of the crop of babies. Clint stroked the colt's neck for a moment, whispering in his ear before moving in front of him. He waited a moment and then held out his right hand. Pegasus promptly lifted his right leg and placed his hoof in Clint's hand. "Good boy!" Clint murmured.

He stepped back a little further. "How old are you, Pegasus?" The willing colt flicked his ears forward, lifted his right leg and pawed the ground once. "Good boy!" Clint repeated, pulling a piece of carrot out of his pocket for Pegasus to devour.

Robert laughed. "How long did it take for you to teach him that?"

Clint shrugged. "Only a few days. He's a smart one," he said proudly.

Robert could see the truth in Clint's eyes. He had been waiting for a good time to talk to his assistant. Now that Amber was in school, that time had finally come. "I've been wanting to talk to you about All My Heart and Amber," he began.

"No need," Clint replied.

"But..."

"I know the bond you and Amber have," Clint said quickly. "And I know the time will probably come when you decide to give me a horse, too. I don't want you to," he said, planting his feet and squaring his shoulders as he met Robert's eyes.

Robert blinked and waited for him to continue.

"I want to buy Pegasus from you," Clint continued. "I know you'll get a good price for him, but I've been saving every penny since I started working for you. I knew the day would come when I found the horse I wanted to train to be mine." He stroked Pegasus' neck as he talked. "Pegasus is the one, but I don't want to buy him yet. I have to know what a fair price is."

Robert was speechless, remembering the bitter young man who had hated him on sight. "I'm listening," he finally managed to say.

Clint continued to meet his eyes. "You still don't have any buyers for the horses do you?"

Robert didn't look away, but he also didn't know how to answer the question. How did Clint know?

Clint offered a small smile. "No one told me, but I read horse publications all the time, and I know buyers usually line up for the year's crop of foals sometime in the summer. No one has shown up, so I figure you're being shunned because of what you're doing with all the freed slaves."

Robert stared at him for a long moment. "When did you get to be so smart?" he muttered.

"Someone is going to be smart enough to understand these are the finest fillies and colts in Virginia."

Robert decided to be honest. "I wish I shared your confidence," he confessed. Sleep had come slowly the night before. Between missing Carrie and wondering what he was going to do if no one bought any of his stock, he had tossed and turned until late in the night.

"Mama told me not to worry about it," Clint replied. "Mama always knows what is going to happen." He saw the look in Robert's eyes. "She saved your life, didn't she? She told me and Daddy you could be trusted, didn't she? She said you would walk again, didn't she?"

Robert couldn't refute the truth of what he was saying.

"So, Mama says somebody is going to come and buy all these horses," Clint said. "I believe her."

Robert felt a surge of comfort, but he couldn't say he had any confidence in Polly's prediction. Regardless, all he could do was make sure his stock was ready if a buyer did appear. "Back to Pegasus..."

"When the buyer comes, I'm going to know what a fair price for Pegasus is. Then I'll make you an offer and buy him."

Robert calculated in his head the amount of money Clint could have accumulated since he had arrived, and then he thought about the amount Eclipse's progeny should bring. He was willing to let Pegasus go for far below his value, but he knew Clint's pride wouldn't allow that. He had to respect the boy who had grown into a young man he was proud of, but he also wanted to figure out a way to make it possible for Clint to own the colt he so obviously loved. There would be plenty more horses in the years ahead that he could sell for top dollar. He searched his mind for how to respond.

Clint read his thoughts. "If I don't have enough, I'll only ask you to give me some time to pay what he is worth."

Robert stepped forward to shake his hand. "Done." He knew he could stretch the payments out for a very long time.

Clint looked dazed. "Really? I can buy him from you?"

"Absolutely. He's going to be a fine horse." Robert walked around him slowly. "If I don't miss my guess, he's going to be as big as Eclipse."

"I think so, too," Clint said. "And he's already faster than any of the rest of them." His eyes sparkled as he laid a hand on Pegasus' neck. "I'll take real good care of him."

"That I'm sure of," Robert said. "The two of you deserve each other."

A sudden noise caught Robert's attention. He turned to stare down the drive, certain he heard a carriage approaching. He knew they weren't expecting company that day. "Keep working," he said quickly. "I'll go see who is coming."

Clint started to turn away but hesitated. "You want me to come with you?"

Robert was the one to hesitate now. Moses had told him early that morning about the unexpected arrival of his men. Could there be vigilantes who were after them? He shook off that thought as soon as it popped in his mind. Vigilantes intent on secrecy were hardly going to drive up in a carriage in the middle of the day. He bit back a sigh, wondering if life would ever return to the way it had been before the war split his country in half and left too many people afraid and paranoid. He shrugged off that thought as well. Given the choice, he wouldn't go back to a country built on slavery, and he wouldn't go back to the blind hatred that had ruled him. Everyone would simply have to navigate through the country they had now.

Clint made the decision for him. "I'm coming," he said, tying Pegasus to a post and stepping up beside Robert.

Robert felt better with Clint by his side as they strode toward the house to meet whomever was coming. The reality was that they all lived in a country full of hatred and turmoil. At the very least, they had to choose to be wise.

Annie joined them on the porch as they waited for the carriage. "You know who it be?"

Robert shook his head. "Where are the children?"

"John went down to play with the other children in the quarters. Hope is just stirrin'. Rose fed her before she left for school, and then that sweet little girl went right back to sleep."

Robert's eyes were trained on the curve of the driveway. "Go on inside with her," he suggested. "Clint and I can handle whatever this is."

"The rifles are just inside the door," Annie murmured as she turned and disappeared.

Robert stepped up to the edge of the porch.

"Want the guns out here?" Clint asked.

"Won't do us much good if they're sitting inside," Robert replied, hoping with all his heart they wouldn't be needed.

Chapter Eleven

Robert was relieved by the sound of the guns being deposited on the table beside him. He was also grateful he had taken the time to teach Clint and his father, Gabe, how to handle a rifle. His pulse quickened as he waited for the carriage to round the curve.

When it did, it was still too far away to identify the occupants, but he was relieved to see there were only two people. There were no additional horsemen to indicate an increased threat. Still, he waited patiently, every muscle tensed for action. When the carriage drew closer, the first thing he felt was confusion. "Is that...?"

"Who is it?" Clint asked. "Looks like one of them is a woman."

"That it is," Robert agreed, stepping off the porch to wait for the carriage to pull up to the house. "We're not in any danger."

The carriage rolled up before he could explain further.

"Hello, Louisa," he called courteously. "And I'm assuming the man with you is your husband, Perry Appleton?" He laughed when a third head popped up, blond hair glistening in the sun. The boy was the spitting image of his father. "And this must be your son."

Louisa smiled brightly. "Robert Borden! I'm so glad to know you survived the war."

"As am I," Robert said mildly. Louisa was as beautiful as ever, though fine lines around her eyes at twenty-four said the years had been full of stress and hardships. "To what do we owe the pleasure of this visit?" His brain whirled with questions, but he needed to let them tell their own story. The last he knew, Louisa and Perry were in Georgia. The Blackwell Plantation had sat empty for the entirety of the war. As far as he knew, it was still unoccupied. It had not been destroyed, but he was sure everything worth taking had been raided by Union troops when Richmond was under siege.

Clint stepped forward. "I'll be happy to take your carriage to the barn and give your horse some water."

"I would appreciate that," Perry said, his voice and manner dismissive.

Robert narrowed his eyes. "This is Clint. He is my stable manager and right-hand man. Your horse will be in good hands."

Perry shot him a look Robert couldn't interpret as he stepped from the carriage. Carrie had told him Louisa's husband had lost his leg during the war, but still he winced.

Perry caught his expression. "It doesn't bother me anymore," he said. "I've learned there is very little I can't do on a wooden stump. Sometimes it takes me a little longer, but it still gets done."

"My husband is amazing," Louisa said proudly as she walked to the base of the porch and gazed up. "Cromwell Plantation is still so beautiful," she said. "It's almost as if the war never happened. Nothing has changed."

Robert understood the envy in her voice. He was also grateful there was none of the angry vindictiveness he had grown to associate with her. "We've been very fortunate," he agreed.

"Mama! Can I get out?"

Louisa smiled and reached out her arms to swing her son to the ground. "This is Nathan."

"Two years old?" Robert guessed.

"He'll be three this winter," Louisa answered, her eyes soft with love and pride as she watched Nathan dash up the stairs. "He was born in the middle of a terrible snowstorm in Georgia. He and Perry are the greatest joys of my life."

Robert smiled. Carrie had been right. The self-centered plantation daughter had changed.

Louisa looked at the house eagerly. "Is Carrie here?"

"She's in medical school in Philadelphia."

Louisa's eyes widened, and she smiled. "I suspected she would make her dream come true."

"And you're all right with your wife being away?" Perry asked.

Robert met his eyes evenly, not sure yet what he thought of Louisa's husband, but suspecting they believed differently about many things. "I miss her every day, but I knew from the first week I met her that she wanted to be a doctor. I would never stand in the way of what she wants to do. I'm very proud of her."

"Of course," Perry said hastily, looking away to scan the pasture. "Those are some beautiful horses."

Robert nodded. Now that the babies were weaned and their mother's milk was dried up, he had allowed the mares to rejoin them in the fields. He knew what a beautiful sight they were because he stood right where Perry was and admired them every morning. "Thank you. Cromwell operates now as a horse breeding facility, as well as a tobacco plantation."

"Congratulations," Louisa said warmly. "Robert, the last time I saw you I was totally horrid. In fact, *all* the times I saw you I was horrid. I'm so very sorry for how I treated you. I'm hoping you can forgive me and start fresh."

Robert didn't bother to refute her statements, but he was more than willing to accept her apology. "The war changed us all," he said graciously. "I'm not proud of who I was before the war, either."

Louisa nodded, her eyes radiating her gratitude.

Robert was still puzzled, however. "I thought y'all were living in Georgia now. What are you doing up in Virginia? Have you returned to check on your family's plantation?"

"There's not much in Georgia for us now," Perry said bitterly.

Robert looked at him sympathetically. "Your farm was in the way of Sherman's Army?" he guessed.

"They destroyed almost everything. Louisa's quick thinking saved some of it." Perry's expression was a mixture of shame and pride. "I was hiding back in the woods with our livestock and as much food as we could load up. Louisa stayed behind, believing they would not burn our home if there was a lone pregnant woman in it."

Robert's heart caught at the look in his eyes. "I can't imagine..." He knew how hard it would have been for him if he had been the one hiding while Carrie stayed behind.

"It worked," Louisa said. "Our home and most of our food were saved."

"But they still destroyed our barns and the cotton gin I was counting on to rebuild after the war. Perry's voice was thick with anger. "Sherman's plan was to bring Georgia to its knees. He succeeded."

Annie opened the door and walked out on the porch with a tray of tea and cookies. "I hear there be a little boy out here who might want a cookie," she called.

Nathan grinned and scampered across the porch on his chubby legs. "Me!" he yelled. "I love cookies!"

Louisa smiled, but also looked confused as she gazed at Annie.

Robert interpreted her look. "Annie, this is Perry and Louisa Appleton. Perry and Louisa, I'm pleased to introduce Moses' mother, Annie."

"I'm so pleased to meet you," Louisa said, but her face was still perplexed.

Again, Robert understood. He didn't know what the rumor mill had already told them, so he would have to try to clarify things. "Rose and Moses used to be slaves here on the plantation."

Louisa nodded slowly. "Rose was Carrie's slave. I remember now."

"Yes. Now Moses and Rose are co-owners of Cromwell Plantation." He stifled a laugh as both Perry and Louisa stared at him, their mouths gaping open with shock. "Moses' mother, Annie, lives here with us and takes care of the kitchen and children."

Annie grinned, obviously enjoying the look on their guests' faces. "I do believe I hear a little girl hollering," she said. "Y'all sit down and enjoy this tea and cookies."

Robert continued to hide his smile. "Moses and Rose have a three-year-old son and a ten-month-old baby girl. As well as a ten-year-old they adopted after the race riots in Memphis back in May."

Perry was the first to find words. "I see."

Robert made no attempt to hide his laughter now. "Surely you had heard things were rather unconventional on Cromwell Plantation."

Louisa nodded. "We had," she said faintly. "We just hadn't heard the whole story."

Carrie could smell death before they entered the cholera hospital. Classes and clinic work had kept her going nonstop in the last several weeks. She was still struggling with what to do, but she'd had no time to explore further or make any decisions. Or maybe she was using the activity as an excuse to avoid the issue.

The death rate from cholera was rising. In spite of her misgivings, she had volunteered to use her one free afternoon to visit the hospital. The city had provided nurses and doctors. Carrie knew she wouldn't be welcome if it was discovered she was from the Female Medical School, but she couldn't stay away.

She smiled warmly when a harried, weary-looking nurse met her at the door. "Hello."

The nurse had a kind face, but it was evident she was completely overwhelmed. "What can I do for you, ma'am? You do realize this is the cholera hospital, don't you?"

"I do," Carrie assured her. She had decided to do whatever it took to get inside. She had to see what was happening for herself. Up to this point, she'd only heard stories. "I served as a nurse during the war." At least that much was true. She didn't feel the need to say it was a Confederate hospital, or that she had actually worked as a doctor. "I'd like to help."

"The city has sent nurses," the woman replied.

"Yes, but do you have enough?" Carrie knew by the look on the woman's face that they were woefully understaffed. "I have experience with cholera patients." She didn't feel the need to explain that her experience was only from the books she had been devouring in the last weeks. She hid her smile when the woman's eyes lit with quick interest.

"Experience?"

Carrie nodded. "I work in one of the other hospitals, so I don't have a lot of time to give, but I'd like to help if I can."

The nurse, evidently accepting her explanation, led her back toward one of the rooms. "There's not much we can do but try to make them comfortable," she said sadly.

"How many are dying?" Carrie asked, trying to keep the concern from making her voice sharp.

"All of them."

Carrie jolted to a stop. "*All* of them?" Her heart pounded wildly. "*Every* patient is dying?"

The nurse shrugged her shoulders helplessly. "There is nothing to do for them. When they get here, the disease has already claimed them. We keep them warm and try to give them some fluid, but that doesn't stop their death." Her eyes filled with tears. "At least they aren't alone," she murmured, turning toward the room again.

Carrie followed her numbly, her brain spinning. Modern medicine had offered many remedies in previous epidemics that had proven completely useless. She had the thought that perhaps she should at least be grateful they were not bleeding the patients here, but the stench of death filling her nostrils as soon as she entered the room wiped away any feelings of gratitude. Her eyes fell on the long rows of beds, where most of the patients seemed to indeed be on the very verge of death. Their eyes, if they were open, were blurred and numb. Pale faces with blue-tinged lips hovered above bodies racked with spasms. Hoarse voices called weakly for help as hands fluttered feebly.

Nurses moved from bed to bed with pitchers of water— and nothing else—their set faces pinched with worry and pain.

"My God," Carrie whispered.

The nurse nodded. "I know. These poor people don't have a chance."

"Where are they from?" Carrie asked.

"Where are they *from*?" the nurse echoed. "Here in the city, of course."

"What parts of Philadelphia?" It was critically important that Carrie know.

"A large number of them came from Moyamensing." The nurse gazed out over what looked to be hundreds of beds. "Other neighborhoods have been hit, but none this hard. The city is hoping to keep it from spreading anymore."

Carrie felt sick as she absorbed the news. She was looking at a room full of mostly Irish people in the last moments of their lives. Thoughts of Oliver Cromwell filled her mind. Her own ancestor had been vastly responsible for destroying the Irish way of life when they landed on the shores of America to live mostly in poverty. Now an epidemic running rampant in England had breached the shores of America and reached out to destroy more Irish lives. She bit back a desire to scream with frustration, but the heavy weight of responsibility settled in her gut. Surely she had discovered the truth about her ancestor for a reason. There must be something she could do to make a difference.

"Are you all right?" The nurse in charge took hold of her arm. "Ma'am? You look ill."

Carrie stared at her, barely registering the words. "How long do they have?" She ground her teeth when the nurse stared back without comprehension. "How long do they have to live?"

"By the time we get them here, they don't have very long. Usually a day or two at the most. Cholera takes people quickly."

Carrie swallowed, the taste of bile in her throat, and forced herself to focus. "How many have died?"

"I don't see how that matters," the nurse said. "Didn't you say you were here to help?" Her dark eyes narrowed with suspicion. "Or are you just some newspaper reporter looking for a story?"

Carrie shook her head quickly. "I promise I am not with a newspaper. And I am here to help. Please, tell me what I can do."

The nurse shrugged. "Patients aren't allowed visitors. You can hand out water and talk to the people who are still aware so they don't feel so alone. That's all anyone can do."

"I don't believe that." Carrie fought the rage boiling inside her. This nurse was doing the best she could, and her face said she cared. "I don't believe that," she repeated, her certainty growing.

"I'm sorry?" the nurse asked in an astonished voice. "What are you talking about?"

Carrie shook her head and stepped back. "I'm sorry, but I can't stay. I have to go somewhere." She regretted the astonished look on the nurse's face as she spun and walked away, but she refused to sit beside a patient's bed and watch them die. She must, at least, make an attempt to help.

She knew of only one way to do that.

Carrie left the stench of death and headed for 1105 Filbert Street. She was resigned to the fact that she might not help the hundreds filling the hospital in that moment, but she was determined to return with information that would help them recover from cholera—not just hold their hands and watch them die.

She walked briskly through the streets of Philadelphia, her mind working too fast to notice the changing leaves as summer bowed in submission to fall. Her schedule had kept her too busy to make an appointment to talk to anyone. And yet, there was suddenly nothing more important than finding an answer to the disease that was killing thousands of Philadelphians, seemingly most of them Irish.

Her thoughts whirled as she envisioned the repercussions of her actions, but the more she pondered it, the more she realized she simply didn't care. The not caring, however, did not protect her from the pounding headache that assaulted her as she thought of the hordes of playing children surrounding Biddy and Faith's home. The pounding intensified as she envisioned either of her dear friends struck down with cholera.

"Watch out, lady!"

Carrie jolted back into awareness as she felt someone shove her from the path of a carriage. She muttered a thank you, but didn't slow her pace. Nothing was more important than getting to the Homeopathic Medical College. She pushed her way past vendors, ignoring the smell of bread and cookies wafting out from the bakeries she passed, and completely dismissing the people who stared at her as she rushed down the street in a very unladylike manner. The images of burning eyes on the verge of death pushed her forward.

She stopped just long enough to get her breath when she arrived at her destination. While she fought to control her breathing, she gazed up at the elegant four-story building towering above her. She knew the Homeopathic College had started out in the same location where she now went to school. Matthew told her they had moved to these larger quarters in 1850. As her breathing and pulse slowed, she had a brief thought as to whether she was on a fool's mission. What if no one would see her? As soon as she had the thought, she pushed it aside and strode up the stairs. She would quite simply *make* someone see her.

That determination carried her up the stairs, but when she entered the cavernous, echoing foyer, she ground to a halt again, doubts assailing her. Several people walked past, but she was hesitant to stop one of them. Carrie scolded her timidity, knowing her mission was vitally important. She also realized the possible consequences of her actions were the true root of her fear. "Oh, for pity's sake," she muttered.

"Excuse me?"

Carrie spun around, unaware a woman had been standing right behind her. "Oh..." she breathed, frantically trying to force intelligent words from her mouth. As she stood there opening and closing her mouth, she realized it wasn't just the fear of possible consequences but the sudden acceptance that she was somehow staring at her future, and she didn't want to mess it up.

"My name is Carolyn Blakely," the woman said.

At least Carrie could respond to that. "My name is Carrie Borden," she replied, glad her voice didn't carry the trembling vibrating through her body. Something about the woman with salt-and-pepper gray hair and light blue eyes soothed her. "I need to speak with someone," she said boldly.

"About what?" Carolyn probed.

Carrie felt herself relaxing more as Carolyn's eyes communicated calm compassion. She managed a low laugh. "I really am capable of speech. I'm just a little overwhelmed right now. It is very important I speak with someone about homeopathic treatment for cholera."

Carolyn's eyes softened with sympathy. "Is someone in your family ill?"

"No. I have volunteered to help at the city's cholera hospital," Carrie explained. "The conditions there are deplorable. They are simply letting people die. I must help them."

Carolyn's eyes widened. "I see."

Carrie laughed. Now that she had communicated her goal, she simply had to press through until she got what she came for. "I realize this may be a little unorthodox."

Carolyn continued to gaze at her for another moment. "You are a nurse?"

"I'm a student at the Female Medical College."

Carolyn's eyes narrowed. "Yes, this is rather unorthodox." There was no judgment in her voice, only a slight bewilderment.

Carrie laughed again. "I would love to explain. Can you tell me who I need to talk with? I'm afraid I don't have much time. There are too many people who need help."

Carolyn's face indicated she had many questions, but she nodded quickly. "I believe Dr. Strikener is in his office."

"Dr. Lucas Strikener?"

"You know him?"

"Is he the same doctor who inspected the hospitals in Richmond after the war to make sure they met Union standards?" Carrie's thoughts were whirling again. She'd had no indication Dr. Strikener was anything but a regular doctor. Surely...

"He's the same man," Carolyn responded. "Though he has changed quite a bit."

Carrie opened her mouth to ask her own questions, but a voice ringing across the foyer stopped her.

"Carrie Borden?"

Carrie spun around, a smile spreading across her face. "Dr. Strikener!"

Dr. Lucas Strikener crossed to her with a welcoming smile on his face. "I thought that was you. What are you doing here?"

"I could ask the same thing," Carrie responded, "but the short answer is that, evidently, I am here to speak to you."

"She wants to talk about homeopathic cures for cholera," Carolyn inserted. "She is a student at the Female Medical College."

Dr. Strikener raised his eyebrows. "Are you now?" He waved his hand toward a closed door on the other side of the foyer. "I was just on the way to my office. Please join me. We'll answer each other's questions."

Carolyn stepped forward. "May I join you, as well?" she asked hesitantly.

Dr. Strikener laughed. "I'm sure you recognize a good story when you see one," he said easily. He glanced at Carrie.

"I'd love for you to join us, Carolyn," Carrie said quickly. She already sensed this woman would become an ally and friend, and she'd rather not explain her story twice.

As they crossed the lobby, she tingled with both excitement and nervousness. Without words to explain, she was quite sure she was casting herself out into a turbulent ocean. Once again, the winds of change were about to shift everything in her world.

Chapter Twelve

Dr. Strikener pulled off his suit jacket and hung it from a hook before he settled down in the leather chair behind his ornate desk.

Carrie gazed around his office, glad it communicated the same warmth she saw radiating from the doctor's light brown eyes. He was every bit as handsome as she remembered, but his hair was much grayer than when she had known him right after the war. Only a year and a half had passed. She wondered what had happened to age him so quickly. She had watched her father go gray far earlier than he should have because of wartime stresses and tragedy.

Dr. Strikener smiled as she inspected him. "You're wondering why I have aged so much."

Carrie flushed, embarrassed he had read her thoughts, and wishing anew her face didn't reveal everything going on in her mind. She searched for a response. "I..."

The doctor's smile widened into a cheerful grin. "Without knowing what you are here to talk about, I am going to hazard a guess it is the same reason I have gone gray so quickly."

Carrie stared at him, completely at a loss for words. She opened her mouth, but nothing came out.

Dr. Strikener threw back his head in a loud laugh, and then waved both her and Carolyn into the comfortable chairs across from his desk. "Carolyn, Carrie Borden is a very unique young woman. She is the daughter of a wealthy plantation owner from the Richmond area. Her father served in the Confederate government, while Carrie served as a doctor for the Confederate Army at Chimborazo Hospital. She kept the hospital supplied with herbal medicines when the blockade kept anything else from coming through, and she also began, and ran, the only hospital for black patients."

Carolyn's mouth was the one to hang open then. "I see..." She turned to Carrie with wide eyes. "And now you're a medical student?"

"I am," Carrie said. She could fill in all the gaps for Carolyn at a later time. "An unhappy one, I'm afraid."

"Because you don't agree with the methods being taught and used by the regular medical profession?" Dr. Strikener asked shrewdly.

Carrie swung back around to gaze at him. "Yes. Am I safe in assuming you are here because you found yourself in the same predicament?"

"You are. It had bothered me before the war started, but then every moment was consumed with taking care of our men wounded in battle. I treated them somewhat differently from my colleagues, but I was still feeling my way forward. All I knew was that I could no longer, in good conscience, treat my patients the way I had before. I was quite sure that in many instances I was doing more harm than good."

Carrie remained quiet, hungry to hear every word he had to say.

"Shortly after I saw you in Richmond," he continued, "one of my daughters was taken gravely ill. I was sure I would lose her the same way I lost my wife. I did everything I knew to do, but she didn't get better."

"And that's when your hair went gray," Carrie murmured.

"Yes," Dr. Strikener confirmed. "Another of my daughters, influenced by Elizabeth Stanton, convinced me to consult with a homeopathic physician. My daughter recovered completely and is now a student here."

Carrie's eyes widened at the mention of the leader of the women's rights movement, whom she had met in New York, but she didn't interrupt.

"Mrs. Stanton has been a leading force in the homeopathic movement. Women in general have had a huge influence because they have been given a way to keep their families healthy, and they want to share their knowledge. As the women's movement has grown, their voices have grown louder in their demands for more effective medicine."

Carrie leaned forward eagerly. "And is it? More effective, I mean? Homeopathy?"

Dr. Strikener glanced at Carolyn.

"You've come to the right place, Carrie," Carolyn assured her. "I was a nurse all during the war. The rates of death and suffering caused by our medical methods sickened me." She paused. "Do you know Louisa May Alcott?"

Carrie nodded, wondering what this had to do with her question but willing to see where the conversation went. "I don't know her personally, but I have heard much about her. My stepmother has talked about her being a leader in both the abolitionist and women's rights movements. If I'm correct, I also believe I have read some of her writing— a collection of her letters home from when she served as a nurse for a short time during the war." She crinkled her brow as she remembered. "I believe she wrote about the mismanagement of hospitals and the indifference and callousness of some of the surgeons she encountered. I recall them being a combination of astute observation and humor," she added with a smile. "I also completely agreed with her."

Carolyn nodded, a smile lighting her eyes. "That would be my friend, Louisa. What you may not know is that Louisa became very ill with typhoid when she was serving in the hospital during the war."

"I do remember hearing that," Carrie answered. "I also heard she recovered."

Carolyn's smile morphed into a scowl. "No thanks to her doctors," she said grimly. "They almost killed her. Doctors are quite impressed with their use of mercury to treat diseases like typhoid fever and syphilis." Disgust dripped from Carolyn's voice. "They refuse to acknowledge they are doing little but poisoning their patients. When the poisoning symptoms appear, they blame it on the worsening of the disease they are treating."

Carrie listened closely. "I've read some things that question the use of mercury."

"Not books you have gotten from your professors."

"No," Carrie agreed. "I do quite a bit of reading outside the curriculum. Please finish with your story about Louisa May Alcott."

"Her doctors treated her with mercury. A homeopathic doctor stepped in, saved her life, and is still treating her for the long-term consequences of mercury poisoning. I suspect she will always have health issues, but she is well enough to do the thing she loves best—write."

"How did the homeopathic doctor save her?" Carrie pressed. She desperately wanted to believe the things she was hearing, but they had to give her enough reasons.

Dr. Strikener stepped in. "Homeopathy is a very complete way of treating a patient, Carrie. We could talk for hours, but I know you came here for a specific reason. Let me just say that homeopathy is an intelligent form of medicine that treats each patient as an individual. It focuses not only on the physical aspects of a disease but also the mental and emotional. We believe each illness identifies itself through the symptoms it causes. Modern medicine tries to erase the symptoms, but we believe we can use them to determine which homeopathic remedy best suits the patient."

"I've done enough reading to understand that," Carrie responded, "but what remedy was used for Louisa May Alcott?" She thought she had an adequate understanding of principles. It was time for specifics.

"Natrum muriaticum," Dr. Strikener answered.

Carrie blinked. She had no clue what he was talking about, but she wasn't here to understand mercury poisoning. "And what about a cholera remedy?"

"Cholera?" Dr. Strikener asked with a raised brow.

"Carrie is here because she has volunteered to help at the cholera hospital established by the city," Carolyn told him.

"The Cholera Death Trap?!"

"It's terrible," Carrie cried. "They are simply bringing people in to die!" Unable to control the flood of emotions, she stood and walked to the window, taking several deep breaths before she spun back around. "Is there a way to help them? Please, tell me there is."

Dr. Strikener stared at her. "In the hospital? I'm quite certain they won't let you try anything I might tell you."

"But..."

Dr. Strikener held up his hand. "There is a wide rift between allopaths and homeopaths," he said bluntly. "The regular medical profession is determined to make us be seen as little more than quacks. When my daughter was completely healed, and when I had to face the truth that my wife would have probably lived if she had been treated correctly, I dug deeply into homeopathy. I couldn't deny the results I had seen, and what I learned told me I would continue to do great harm if I didn't change my methods. That is when I made the shift. My practice is now one hundred percent homeopathic, and I have just recently been asked to serve on the faculty of the hospital."

Carrie felt surer than ever that she was in the right place, but she had more questions before she returned to the cholera situation. "Are homeopathy and herbal medicine basically the same thing? Is that what Sarah taught me?"

"No," Dr. Strikener answered. "You'd learn the difference on a much deeper level if you went to school here, but the simple answer is that herbs nourish a certain part of the body. Homeopathy works by stimulating your immune system."

Carrie considered his response, as well as all she had learned from her reading. "A plant like milk thistle is used to treat the liver. Homeopathy is more like a vaccine for the entire body that treats a particular illness," she finally said.

"Yes," Carolyn agreed. "The basic principle is that 'like supports like.' Our remedies are like a weakened or killed disease similar to what the patient already has. The remedy primes the person's immune response so the body is prepared to deal with the real thing."

Carrie listened closely to learn all she could, but the vision of hundreds of dying faces from the hospital crowded into her thoughts. She knew Dr. Strikener might be correct that she couldn't help the ones dying in the rows of beds, but another thought had come to her. "And cholera? Is there a remedy? I read that homeopathy had a tremendous result in Europe during the last epidemic. Surely—"

"Stop, Carrie," Dr. Strikener said abruptly. He stood and walked around his desk to where she was standing. His voice was firm, but his eyes were soft with compassion. "Are you aware you may lose your place at the Female Medical College if you pursue this?"

Carrie had faced that reality when she had walked to the Homeopathic College. She met his eyes squarely. "Yes," she replied. "I have learned a lot, and I will always be grateful for the surgical experience I received during the war, but I didn't decide to become a doctor because I wanted to be a surgeon. I chose to be a doctor so I can make people well. I've seen herbal medicine do that, but I realize homeopathic medicine has gone even further in understanding the true nature of illness and how to treat it. I want to be a part of it." She paused but didn't look away. "I'm prepared to leave the Female Medical College and apply here. But first I want to help the people of Moyamensing."

Dr. Strikener nodded slowly. "I understand cholera has hit them especially hard."

"Most of the people dying in the hospital are from Moyamensing," Carrie said. "I have good friends down there. Is there a way for me to help them?"

Dr. Strikener held her gaze. His eyes revealed his awareness that there was more to the story than she was telling, but he didn't press further. He turned toward the bulging bookcases lining three sides of his office and reached for a very thin leather-bound volume. He handed it to her without a word.

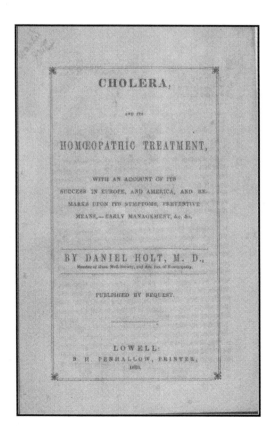

Carrie's eyes widened when she saw the title: *Cholera, Homeopathic Treatment.* She took a slow breath, feasting her eyes on the rich leather. "And it works?" she breathed.

"It works," Dr. Strikener confirmed.

Carrie stared at the book and went rigid with anger. "Then why is it not being used?" Her head pounded as she thought of the hopeless stares of the hundreds dying in the hospital. "Because of pride? Because of money? This is criminal!"

"I would agree," Dr. Strikener said, "but I suspect you don't have time to hear my feelings on that very issue. We'll have plenty of time to talk in the future."

Carrie held the book closely. "Where do I get the remedy?"

"There is a dispensary just down the street," Carolyn answered. She hesitated. "May I help you? I have some experience with this."

Carrie turned to her eagerly. "Of course! I have no problem admitting when I don't have a clue what I'm doing." She managed a small smile before she glanced out the window and realized the afternoon light was ebbing away. "I'm afraid it's too late to go down today. I will hire a carriage and pick you up early tomorrow morning. Say eight o'clock?"

"I'll be ready," Carolyn promised. "The dispensaries open then as well. Spend the evening reading the book..."

"And these, too." Dr. Strikener handed her several more books and pamphlets. "The more you know, the better you will be able to help, though you will probably be appalled when you realize how very simple it is." He put his hand on her shoulder. "I know you have to figure out your course of action, Carrie. Come back when you are ready to make a change. I can assure you you'll be accepted. The Homeopathic College will be lucky to have you as a student."

Carrie's heart surged with gratitude. She smiled brightly as she gave him a hug. "You are an angel, Dr. Strikener. My focus right now is on helping the Irish in Moyamensing, but I'm also well aware my entire life path has been changed by this visit. I can't thank you enough for everything."

Dr. Strikener nodded, hesitating before he asked, "How is Mrs. Livingston?"

Carrie smiled. "Mrs. Cromwell now. Abby married my father last summer." She remembered suddenly that there had been an attraction between Dr. Strikener and her beautiful stepmother, but his response, when it came, was genuine.

"That's wonderful! She is a very special woman, and if your father raised you, he must be a very special man."

"He is," Carrie agreed. "We have so much to talk about."

"But it will wait until after you have crammed your head with as much knowledge about cholera as you possibly can, and after you have seen what wonders homeopathy can work for Moyamensing," he finished. He moved toward the door. "My driver is waiting outside. I have plenty of work to keep me busy for another hour or so. I'm going to have him drive you home and then return for me."

"Thank you," Carrie replied gratefully. She had not looked forward to navigating the streets in the dark.

Dr. Strikener started to walk away, but turned back. "You have set a difficult course for yourself."

Carrie laughed easily. "When have I ever *not* set a difficult course for myself? It seems to be the only way I know how to live." She was absolutely certain she was making the right decision, but that didn't keep images of her housemates from floating through her thoughts. She was confident Janie would support her actions, but she wasn't sure about the rest of them. Regardless, she would do what was right for her and then deal with the consequences.

Dr. Strikener walked her outside to where his carriage was waiting. "The doctors at the Female Medical College are in a very difficult position, Carrie. Many of them have great respect for homeopathic medicine, but they are under constant scrutiny by the American Medical Association. If they go against protocol in any way, they will lose any chance of equality with the male doctors in their profession."

Carrie raised a brow. "Even if it means letting patients die needlessly?"

"Perhaps there is a place for both," he said. "It is very easy to judge someone when we are not walking in their shoes. Perhaps it is necessary for women doctors to make these concessions now in order to impact medicine for centuries to come. We've certainly learned how necessary women are in homeopathic medicine, but it's only been recently." He paused, laying a hand on her shoulder lightly. "You have to do what is right for you, Carrie. If you're like me, you wish others would simply respect your position and decision."

"Yes," Carrie replied immediately. She opened her mouth to say how much she doubted it would happen, but Dr. Strikener wasn't done.

"Then isn't it reasonable for them to want and expect the same from you? It's not about all the other women being wrong, Carrie. It's about you simply doing what is right for you, without bitterness and anger."

Carrie closed her mouth quickly. She looked toward the horizon where the sun was slowly sinking below a dark bank of clouds, forcing herself to take a slow breath of the cool evening air. "Do you talk sense into all your daughters, as well?"

Dr. Strikener laughed. "I try. I also acknowledge that sometimes they talk sense into me. They are quite extraordinary women. As are you, Carrie Borden," he added quietly. "All of us are navigating very difficult times, but as long as we choose to respond to the people around us with as much compassion and understanding as we can, I believe we will make it through to a better place in our country. I've seen what anger and refusal to communicate did to America. I never want something like that again."

Carrie shuddered. "I completely agree with you." She clutched the stack of books closer to her chest and stepped into the carriage. "One thing I am certain of is that I will be back here as a student. If for no other reason than to work with you, Doctor. Thank you for everything."

Robert settled back into the rocking chair, relishing the cool air that flowed over him. He watched as the foals frolicked in the field, their mamas contentedly eating grass as the last rays of light seemed to be absorbed into the dark trees surrounding the pasture. He watched until it was impossible to pick out the horse shapes in the gloom. There was nothing that gave him more joy than his horses. As soon as the thought entered his mind, he knew it wasn't true. Carrie gave him far more joy, but she was also far away from his world. He had hoped for a letter, but nothing had arrived with all the journals and publications sent out for Felicia. He tried to swallow the deep feeling of loneliness that welled up in him.

The snap of the screen door closing made him glance up. "Hello, Perry."

"It's a beautiful night," Perry responded as he sank down into one of the other rocking chairs.

"I see Annie provided you with fresh cookies. Care to share?"

Perry glanced down at his handkerchief full of warm oatmeal cookies.

Robert grinned. "Giving up one won't kill you."

Perry looked doubtful. "Don't tell Louisa, but I think these may be the best cookies I have ever had."

"Irish whiskey," Robert replied, smiling at the look of confusion in Perry's eyes. "I received a letter from Carrie a short while ago telling us she had learned a new recipe from some Irish friends. Evidently, the secret to the best oatmeal cookies in the world is to plump the raisins with Irish whiskey before you mix them in. Annie has decided she has Irish blood mixed in with the black."

Perry held up a cookie in the dim light of the porch lantern. "All I know is that I have never felt like paying homage to a cookie before," he answered. "I guess telling me the secret has earned you *one*."

Robert laughed as he reached for one, but at the last moment he paused, indicating the full plate of cookies beside him. His body had hidden them until he shifted. "I just wondered if I could get one out of you."

Perry laughed and stuffed another cookie in his mouth. When he finished, his eyes were serious. "Can I ask you a question?"

"Ask away," Robert responded, wondering if he was about to discover the real reason Perry and Louisa were in Virginia.

"Is the plantation profitable?"

"More than ever."

Perry stared at him. "More than *ever*?" he echoed. "More profitable than before the war?" The disbelief in his voice made his words almost harsh. "That isn't possible."

"It's possible." Moses, just in from a long day in the fields, stepped up onto the porch and grabbed the plate of cookies off the table.

"Hey!" Robert protested.

"My mama made them," Moses responded, shoving one into his mouth. "And I'm starving."

"But..."

Annie pushed through the door. "I should have known I couldn't be puttin' three men onto a porch with my cookies without you fightin' over them. Pitiful," she said with a sniff. "Good thing I have sympathy for pitiful men." She pulled her arm from behind her back and placed another plate of cookies on the table.

"Yes!" Moses crowed as he reached for another, yelping when Annie slapped his hand away.

"I gots dinner for you comin' right out. I ain't gonna have you spoiling it with cookies."

Moses opened his mouth to protest, but Annie glared at him. He settled back in his chair with a sigh, waited several moments until his mama retreated into the house, and then reached for another cookie. "Women don't understand starving men," he growled as he bit in, a smile spreading across his face as he chewed. "This is more like it." He turned to Perry. "It's true by the way. The plantation is more profitable than ever."

Perry peered at him. "How?"

Moses shrugged, chewing rapidly before he drank a swig of Robert's water. "It's simple. People respond well when you treat them well. The workers here are free to come and go, all their children are in school, and no one is beaten," he said. "But it's much more than that. No one is just a worker. Everyone receives a share of the profits when the harvest is done. My year-round workers receive a higher percentage, but even the seasonal workers receive something, as long as the harvest profits create more income than the wages I pay them now. They work hard because they know they will be rewarded."

Perry gaped at him. "You share the profits?"

Robert looked at him with sympathy. He didn't think Perry was a cold, mean man, but it was quite clear he couldn't begin to comprehend such a system. "Did you own slaves before the war, Perry?"

"Only a few," Perry responded. "Nothing like Louisa's family, but I couldn't have made a go of my cotton business if I hadn't," he insisted.

"I know it's hard to change that way of thinking," Robert replied, "but it really is true the plantation is more profitable than ever. That means the plantation is making more money than all the years when Thomas owned slaves." He let Perry mull his words over for a few moments. "Plantation owners, if they still have their land, are struggling, because they want things to be the same as before the war. They expect to have complete control of the blacks even though they are free. They want to treat them the same as they did before the war, but now the freed slaves have a choice."

"They are refusing to work," Perry said angrily.

"Which is their choice," Moses said.

Robert could tell anger was simmering in Moses' eyes, but his deep voice was level.

"But how is the South supposed to rebuild?" Perry demanded.

"The freed slaves will work if they are treated fairly," Moses replied. "They want fair wages, and they want to be treated as equals."

"That's preposterous!" Perry snapped. "No black will ever be equal to a white man."

As soon as the words came out of his mouth, his expression was apologetic, but Robert knew he had meant it.

The heavy silence was interrupted by Annie stepping back out onto the porch with a dinner tray for Moses. She could tell something was awry, but all she said before she left was, "Rose be upstairs puttin' the little ones down. Felicia be in the library."

"Thanks, Mama," Moses answered.

Perry cleared his throat. "I'm sorry I said that," he mumbled.

"There's nothing wrong with saying what you believe," Moses replied. "The problem comes with the fact you believe it."

Perry's eyes narrowed, but he remained silent.

"The South is going to struggle for a long time," Moses continued. "Whether you believe a black man will ever be equal to you doesn't change the fact that we are all free now. You have the right to keep on believing the way you do, but that will only make it harder for you to accomplish what you want to accomplish."

"What do you know about what I want to accomplish?"

Robert watched the exchange between the two men quietly. His own understanding had only come through great hardship and suffering, and he knew true change in the South could only be accomplished in the same way. He could also tell by the bewildered anger in Perry's eyes that he had never had this kind of discussion with a black man before.

Moses shrugged again. "You wouldn't be up here if things were going well in Georgia. You would still be busy with harvesting and ginning cotton. I imagine you and Louisa are up here to decide if Blackwell Plantation can be made profitable again."

A long silence filled the porch before Perry responded. "And if we are?"

"Then you're going to have a real hard time accomplishing it with your attitude."

Robert bit back a smile as fury flared in Perry's eyes. He wasn't concerned about violence, so he was content to watch things play out. If he was asked his opinion, he would give one, but it was more interesting to watch the sparring between Moses and Perry. He didn't know Perry well enough to know if he would move beyond his prejudices, or stay mired in the beliefs of a life that was gone forever.

Another long hush filled the porch. Bullfrogs sang their night song, accompanied by an occasional hoot owl. Horses whinnying and snuffling added to the chorus. They heard Hope's sharp cry for several moments, but it died away quickly, followed by John's easy laughter floating through the open window of the children's bedroom.

In spite of the intense conversation, Robert felt an easy peace fill his soul. He thought of Carrie trapped within the noisy confines of bustling Philadelphia. He missed her, but there was not one iota of him that wanted to be anywhere else. After the terrible years of the war, he wanted nothing more than to live in peace. He had a sudden image of how quickly it could all disappear if he didn't sell the horses, but he pushed it aside immediately.

He was learning not to worry about things he couldn't change. Every youngster on the farm was coming along quickly in their training, and they were exhibiting the excellence of their sire and dams. That was all he could expect for now.

Perry's voice broke the quiet. "We're here to decide whether we want to sell Blackwell Plantation, or come back here." He turned to Robert. "What do you think?"

Robert shrugged. "I'm a horseman," he responded. "You should be asking Moses. He's the farmer. He runs every single part of the operations on the plantation."

Perry stared at him with hard eyes for a long moment before he reluctantly turned toward Moses. "What do you think, Moses?" The words, delivered with bitterness, seemed to have been wrung from him.

Robert continued to watch quietly. He could tell by the angry set of Moses' shoulders that he wanted nothing more than to stand up and walk into his home, but he continued to rock as he stared out into the darkness. Robert had no real clue of how difficult this conversation must be for his friend, but it was one that was going to have to take place many, many times if the South was ever going to change.

Moses finally finished chewing his ham biscuit, wiped his mouth, and turned to Perry. "You could probably sell it, but you won't get much for it. The prices are severely depressed. There are Northerners who will buy plantations, but you won't get a fair price. They figure they have you over a barrel."

Perry's face tightened. "They do," he spat.

Moses met his eyes. "Not as much as you think. Oh, it would be difficult to bring Blackwell Plantation back, but it could be done."

"How?" Perry shot back. "I have nothing to work with."

Moses nodded. "Not many Southerners do. How much land is there?"

"Almost three thousand acres," Perry responded.

Moses sat silently for a moment as he mulled it over. "You don't need all that to make the plantation profitable if you handle it correctly."

Perry's eyes narrowed with anger once more. In a different situation, Moses would not have gotten away with suggesting a white man might not handle something correctly, but there was nothing Perry could do when he was a guest sitting on the porch of Cromwell Plantation. "Which would be how?" Perry snapped.

Moses pretended not to notice the mounting anger. "You could sell off five hundred acres of your land and still have plenty to work. Selling the land would give you working capital to rebuild the plantation."

Perry blinked. "You said no one would give me a fair price."

"I said no *Northerner* would give you a fair price. I happen to know some men who would."

Robert smiled, glad Perry was not looking his way. He had talked through all of this with Moses that morning. He had grave doubts it could work, but it would be interesting to see what happened.

"Who?" It was obvious Perry's desperation was forcing him to push beyond his resistance to ask advice from a black man.

"I happen to know a group of men with money enough to buy fifty acres each at a fair price. I also happen to know they would be willing to work on your plantation in return for wages and a share of the profits."

Perry seemed to freeze. "Black men?" he finally ground from between his clenched teeth.

"Yes. Ten men from my old unit."

Perry slammed his fist down on the table beside him and bolted to his feet. "You are suggesting I sell parts of Blackwell Plantation to niggers who fought against the South? And then hire them to work in the same ridiculous way you are running Cromwell Plantation? Are you insane? I would rather die first."

"Well, I hardly think you'll die, but I'm pretty sure the plantation will." Moses rose to his feet. Perry was not a small man, but Moses towered over him, his massive size diminishing the furious cotton ginner. He turned to Robert. "I told you it wouldn't work."

Robert shrugged. "It was worth a try," he said blandly. "It sure will be a shame to see Blackwell Plantation snapped up by some carpetbaggers, but it might be the best solution. They'll probably be easier to get along with as neighbors."

Perry gaped at him, his eyes almost wild with fury. "You agree with this insane plan?"

"I agree that nothing will ever be the same in the South," Robert responded, forcing his voice to remain calm even though he was every bit as disgusted as Moses. "Except the sanctity of Southern hospitality." Robert watched as the meaning of his words sunk home.

Perry took a slow, deep breath. "I'm sorry," he said tightly. "I realize I am a guest in your home."

"Yes, you are," Robert answered. "But you are also a guest in Moses' home."

Perry's eyes bored into his before he turned to Moses and bowed stiffly. "My apologies. I'm afraid I was out of line."

Moses nodded, his black eyes still snapping with anger. "Apology accepted."

Perry stepped to the edge of the porch and stared out into the darkness. A half-moon was beginning its dance along the treetops on the horizon. Its glimmering light outlined the horses, bringing them to life in the darkened pasture as they grazed or slept.

Robert welcomed the silence, hoping the peace of the night would work its way into Perry's heart. He knew the man was desperate. He also knew Moses' solution was the only thing that would save Blackwell Plantation.

Perry finally turned back to look at them. "Will the men work for me?"

"Not now," Moses answered.

"Why not?" Perry demanded.

"Because I'll tell them not to. These are good men who have been treated badly all their lives. They don't need more of it." He drained his glass and placed it on the table. "Good night."

The only sound for a very long time was the slap of the screen door when Moses disappeared into the house.

Robert was the first to speak. "You and Louisa are welcome to stay for a while, Perry." He interpreted the look on Perry's face. "Moses agrees."

"I don't know that we can do that," Perry snapped.

Robert shrugged. "It's up to you, but Blackwell isn't exactly livable for Louisa and your son." Perry opened his mouth to refuse, but the truth of Robert's statement hit home.

"I understand your feelings far better than you realize, Perry."

As the moon slowly rose above the trees, Robert told his guest about the long journey that had completely changed his feelings about blacks and slavery. Perry listened, but his face revealed nothing of his feelings.

When Robert finished with his story, Perry settled back in his chair. "That's quite a tale," he murmured. "I'll admit I have absolutely no ability to understand it, and I can't imagine that I would ever come to the same place." The anger was gone from his face, replaced with an almost sad resignation. "Everything I've ever known is gone."

Robert had been disgusted with Perry's earlier reaction, but his sympathy for him now was just as strong. "Give it some time, Perry. You might be right. You also might be wrong. You can't take Louisa and Nathan to Blackwell Plantation right now. They will be safe and cared for here. Consider yourselves guests for as long as you need."

"Why?" Perry asked. "Why would you do this? And why would Moses be okay with it?"

Robert thought back to the months he had lain paralyzed in Gabe and Polly's bed. "Because someone once did it for me. There has been enough hatred, Perry. I know it's going to take a long time for things to change, and I don't think the change will come easily. I also know the only thing I have any control over is my own actions. I can't control what happens outside the gates of this plantation, but I can definitely make sure I don't respond to things with the same hatred and bitterness boiling in our country right now." He paused to let his words sink in before he stood. "You and your family are welcome to stay. Think about it." He was almost at the door when Perry spoke.

"Thank you, Robert. We will stay until I can figure things out."

Chapter Thirteen

Carolyn was waiting outside the Homeopathic College when Carrie pulled up in the carriage the next morning. The sun was up but tucked behind a thick blanket of gray clouds. A brisk breeze carried the briny smell of the ocean through the city streets, but the smells of bread and pastries from surrounding bakeries were doing their best to cover it. The streets teemed with delivery wagons moving at a slower pace than they would be by mid-afternoon. The sidewalks were full of women carrying baskets full of produce and bread and men carrying satchels as they hurried toward their jobs. Summer's release on the city seemed to have brought everything back to life. Even the colorful blooms in the city's flowerboxes seemed to be glowing with a greater joy as their heads tossed in the wind. Carrie was grateful for the light jacket she had grabbed on her way out.

"You look exhausted," Carolyn said cheerfully after she had settled into the seat.

Carrie grinned. "My body is exhausted, but my mind is more exhilarated than it has been in a very long time." A glance in the mirror before she left had revealed tired, blood-shot eyes—the legacy of a night spent reading and studying. She had not gone to sleep until almost four o'clock that morning, and was grateful she had asked Janie to wake her.

Carolyn hesitated. "I thought you might have someone else with you."

Carrie shook her head. "Janie supports what I'm doing, but she had a major exam today. Even if she leaves, she wants to walk away with integrity. She'll be waiting for me tonight to get every bit of information she can."

"And Janie is?"

"We worked together at Chimborazo Hospital during the war. Janie is one of my closest friends. I am quite sure that one day we will open a homeopathic practice together."

"And the others?" Carolyn pressed. "Didn't you mention having more housemates who are all medical students?"

Before Carrie could answer, her new friend leaned forward and gave directions to the driver. She frowned, thinking about her reply. "In truth, I don't know what to expect from them. Any woman willing to go to medical school has more than a touch of rebel in her, but two of the three also have fathers who are physicians. I've chosen not to say anything at this point, but I know that will have to change soon when I take action. All I cared about last night was learning as much about how to treat cholera as possible. I'm missing classes today, but I simply don't care." She knew Carolyn would understand her passion to help dying people.

"And did you learn what you needed to know?"

Carrie grinned happily. "I did!" She glanced toward the road. "Are we headed toward the dispensary to pick up veratrum and camphor?"

Carolyn eyed her with approval. "We are if you can tell me what they do and how you are going to use them."

"Veratrum is created from the hellebore plant," Carrie responded. "Sarah called it Indian poke or itch-weed. It grows in swamps, low grounds and moist meadows. There wasn't a lot of it on the plantation, but we were able to collect enough to make powder we used in an ointment for itches when people came down with bad cases of poison ivy." She paused, collecting her thoughts. "Indian poke is extremely poisonous, but the symptoms it evokes if ingested are very similar to the cholera symptoms of nausea and diarrhea. Veratrum is a diluted form of the plant that almost immediately stops the symptoms."

"Why?" Carolyn asked.

"Because like impacts like," Carrie answered. "You told me yesterday that homeopathic remedies are like a weakened or killed disease similar to what the patient already has. In this case, cholera. The remedy primes the person's immune response so the body is prepared to deal with the real thing."

Carolyn nodded her approval. "Good. If veratrum will deal with the cholera symptoms, why do you want to also buy camphor?"

"Veratrum is the right remedy for every person in the cholera hospital because the disease is so advanced, but for people who have not yet started exhibiting symptoms, veratrum would do nothing but make them gravely ill. If a person is starting to exhibit illness but is not yet vomiting or having diarrhea, then camphor is the correct remedy. It is also very effective in making sure people who are around the illness will not get it. It can be used safely in either case."

"And how is it given?" Carolyn pressed.

Carrie felt a flash of satisfaction that she had learned the answers to all Carolyn's questions. She might be exhausted, but her almost-sleepless night had been worth it. "The patient should be put to bed immediately and kept warm with hot bricks to the feet if necessary. Two or three drops of the camphor should be given in tepid water every five to ten minutes until they improve."

"And if they can't swallow the water?"

"Then you can wet a cloth with camphor and apply it to their nose," Carrie replied.

"How do you know if it's working?"

"If the patient starts to perspire and become warm, that's good. They should start feeling better pretty quickly. If they don't respond or if they start vomiting, have diarrhea, or have spasms, then veratrum is called for. The results of veratrum treatment, when used correctly, are very quick." She had a vision of the nearly comatose patients in the cholera hospital but pushed it aside. She knew what she needed to do for now.

Carolyn grinned. "Excellent. Did you get *any* sleep last night, Carrie?"

The warm light of approval in Carolyn's eyes meant even more to Carrie than Dr. Wild's approval had during the war, because she was now certain homeopathy was the best way to treat most illnesses. If a man lost a leg, surgery was called for, but other illnesses would be best treated in a natural, homeopathic way. Her deepening understanding during the long night of study had confirmed she was finally on the right path. "I'm fine," Carrie assured her.

After a stop at the dispensary, the carriage rolled into Moyamensing. Carrie could feel sorrow and grief permeating the air. Gray faces and shuttered eyes spoke of fear and loss. The streets were still busy, but people were almost silent. No children seemed to be in sight. She didn't know if it was because the children were in school, or because they were ill in bed. Her lips tightened as she thought of all these people had suffered. She wanted to lean forward and urge the driver to go faster, but she knew he was navigating the clogged streets as best he could. And really, she didn't know what she expected to do. She simply had hope she could make a difference.

"There is the house," Carrie said when they rounded the corner onto Biddy's street. She had told Carolyn the story of Biddy's life, including the loss of her husband and sons to cholera in the last epidemic, but had not included the revelation about Oliver Cromwell. She was determined to do all she could to right the wrongs of her ancestor, but the shame continued to keep her quiet. Telling herself she need not carry the burden of actions taken hundreds of years earlier seemed to have no impact on her feelings now that cholera was decimating the people Lord Cromwell had forced to America. There were moments when the knowledge was a privilege. There were others when she wanted nothing more than to forget she had ever learned it.

Carolyn eyed the ornate home that stood out starkly from the squalor surrounding it. "Biddy must be a remarkable woman."

"That she is," Carrie agreed fervently, wondering why her gut was tightening the closer they got to the house. She searched the windows for some explanation, but the blank panes revealed nothing. "Something is wrong."

"Sickness is in the air," Carolyn agreed sadly.

Carrie knew it was more than that. She controlled her impulse to jump from the carriage and run to the house when they less than a block away. She squirmed impatiently as the driver waited for a knot of wagons to clear the road. It would do no good to arrive without the box of remedies nestled at her feet.

As soon as the carriage rolled to a stop, Carrie sprang out and reached for the box Carolyn held out to her. "You'll wait?" she asked the driver. She had specifically requested a driver who was not afraid to take her into Moyamensing, and had then explained their mission on the way over.

"I'll be here, ma'am," he promised. "Don't forget I have a sister and nephew a couple streets over."

"I won't. I'll do my best to find them," Carrie assured him. She turned toward the house, disturbed that Faith hadn't already swung the door open in welcome. Her gut clenched even tighter as she walked briskly up the steps with Carolyn at her side. She rapped sharply.

Her concern grew when no sound came from inside the house. She had just reached forward to turn the knob when she heard someone slowly moving toward the door. Carrie exchanged a long look with Carolyn, certain both of them were feeling the same thing. Something was dreadfully wrong.

It was Biddy who slowly swung the door open. Her soft, wrinkled face was tightened into a mask of fear, her bright blue eyes shrouded with dread. "Carrie!" she gasped, reaching out a shaky hand. "What are you doing here?"

"I'm here to take care of whatever is wrong," Carrie replied, grabbing both of Biddy's hands, shocked by how cold they were. "What is going on?"

Biddy stared into her eyes wildly. "It's Faith. She's sick."

"Cholera?" Carrie asked.

Biddy nodded, seeming to shrink into herself even more once the word was out and floating through her house. "I'm afraid so." Her voice trembled. "We never should have stayed when the cholera struck. It's my fault."

"How long has she been sick?" Carolyn asked.

"We're here to help, Biddy. I have medicine that will help Faith." She knew they needed to move quickly.

Biddy gazed at her, a tiny spark of hope breaking through the fear. "I thought there was nothing…"

"I'll explain later," Carrie answered. "Take us to Faith."

Biddy turned and began to walk. "She started feeling poorly yesterday afternoon. She insisted she was just coming down with a cold, but she got sicker last night."

"Is she vomiting?" Carolyn asked, tightening her lips when Biddy nodded. "Diarrhea?"

"It started about an hour ago," Biddy whispered.

Carrie's heart swelled with sympathy, but she felt a powerful gratitude that what she carried could save Faith. "We can help her, Biddy," she said confidently. She knew from reading the material from Dr. Strikener that Faith had moved beyond the first stage into the second stage, but they were still catching it early.

"Will she have to go to the hospital?" Biddy asked, her blue eyes deepening with even more pain as she imagined it.

"No," Carrie replied, knowing the stories coming back from the hospital must be horrifying. She stopped at the parlor and led Biddy to her chair. "We will take care of Faith. She is going to get well." Carrie prayed she was right and that homeopathy did what the literature said it would do. "You wait here. I'll come down with an update soon."

Biddy looked as if she wanted to protest but sank down in the chair gratefully, her eyes fixed on Carrie.

Carrie took only long enough to remove the pitcher of water on the side table, thinking of Faith placing it there before she started to feel badly. "This isn't safe to drink," she announced. "I'll bring you more soon." Then she kissed the old woman on the cheek and led Carolyn upstairs to Faith's room.

Her heart sank when she walked in and saw Faith hovered over a bucket, vomiting clear fluid, her dark skin almost gray. She rushed to her side and held her head, taking the wet cloth Carolyn handed her. She wiped Faith's face and bit back a cry of dismay when she saw how full the bucket was.

"Carrie..." Faith whispered. "You...shouldn't...be here..." she said weakly.

Carrie helped her back to the bed and laid her down gently. "I'm here to help, Faith."

"Sick... Cholera..." Faith mumbled, her lips ashy with fever. "Go..."

"I'm going nowhere," Carrie answered. "You're very sick, but you're going to get better."

Faith shuddered. "No...Can't..."

"No more talking," Carrie commanded, reaching for another pillow to put under Faith's head. She was determined not to show how horrified she was at the severity of Faith's illness. She could hear Carolyn unpacking the bottles of remedy as she got her friend settled. When Carolyn left the room, Carrie knew she had gone back for the box of water jugs the driver had promised to deposit on the porch. It was simply not safe to use any of the water in Moyamensing. Cholera was passed through unclean water, and it would do no good to put the veratrum into tainted, diseased fluid.

Carrie stroked Faith's head, covering her with another blanket to make sure she was warm. She was glad when the older woman closed her desperate, fevered eyes and sank back against the pillows, nearly disappearing into their silky, gray softness. Everything she had read said the vomiting and diarrhea would return quickly, unless...

Carolyn strode into the room, carrying a large pitcher of water. She pushed aside the one on the table and handed Carrie a small bottle. "How much do you put in?"

"Two or three drops," Carrie replied, realizing her voice was a little shaky.

Carolyn took hold of her hand. "We got here in time, Carrie. Faith is very sick, but she's going to be fine."

Carrie gazed into Carolyn's eyes. She saw nothing but a compassionate confidence that relaxed her immediately. "Thank you," she said as she reached for the bottle of remedy. "I believe I should start with three drops."

"Why?"

Carrie was glad she was being forced to concentrate on something other than Faith's pallor. "Because she is already vomiting and having diarrhea, but mostly because the vomit has become a clear liquid. She is on the verge of dehydration, which could cause her organs to shut down. We need to stop it quickly."

"Good," Carolyn replied, handing her a glass of water. "Put the remedy in. I will hold her shoulders up so she can drink."

Faith opened her eyes slightly, but gave no other sign that indicated she was being propped up. One hand fluttered like a wounded sparrow and then went still.

Carrie added three drops of the remedy and stirred it quickly. "Drink as much of this as you can, Faith," Carrie said. She tipped the glass, and Faith swallowed weakly. It took more than a minute for her to drink the liquid, but she got it all down and then closed her eyes again. Carrie continued to hold her hand, sinking gratefully into a chair Carolyn pulled next to the bed. The remedy should stop the vomiting almost immediately.

"Breathe, Carrie," Carolyn said as she came to stand beside her. "It will work."

Carrie was indeed holding her breath. She released it in a quick gasp, wishing she had thought to bring a watch with her. Every second that passed seemed like hours. Unwilling to look away even for a moment, she fastened her eyes on Faith's face. If the remedy was going to work, she wanted to see the change. As she watched, she thought of all the people dying all over the city. Hope and anger warred in her heart. Hope that she could save many of the sick people in Moyamensing. Anger that so many were dying senselessly if it were true that the veratrum worked.

She lost track of time, but she was immediately aware when Faith's breathing eased. She stared in astonishment as the gray pallor began to disappear and the warmth returned to Faith's hand. "It's working," she whispered. "It's really working!"

"It will take her some time to get her strength back," Carolyn said, "but she will be fine."

Carrie gazed at Faith, almost unable to believe it when her even breathing said she was sleeping. "Will she need more veratrum?" she whispered. She held up the small bottle, amazed just three drops of the liquid had worked what she considered a miracle.

"No," Carolyn responded. "It has done its job. Now we have to get water back in her to fight the dehydration. And get good food into her when she is able to eat." She stood and turned toward the door. "We need to check on Biddy now. Faith will sleep."

Carrie hurried to the parlor.

Biddy was sitting motionless, her eyes fixed on the door. "Faith?" Her voice quavered.

"She's going to be fine," Carrie assured her. "She is sleeping now."

Biddy blinked, her face a mixture of confusion and disbelief. "Fine...? How...?" She reached out and clutched Carrie's hand as she shook her head. "It's not possible. You must tell me the truth, Carrie." Her voice was firm now.

Carrie smiled and covered Biddy's hand with both of her own. She understood Biddy's reaction. The old lady was watching many people die on a daily basis. "I'm telling you the truth, Biddy. Faith is going to be fine. The vomiting and diarrhea have stopped."

"But how?" Biddy pressed, her hands still trembling. "So many are getting sick and dying. Just like it was in 1842."

Carrie's gut tightened with anger again. "I know. That's why I'm here. I will explain it all to you soon, but for right now, know there is a homeopathic remedy that will keep people from becoming sick, and it can also help most of the ones who are already ill." Her voice sharpened with urgency as Carolyn pressed her shoulder. "But only if we can help them quickly," she added. "There is no time for long explanations."

"The hospital?" Biddy said hopefully. "Can you help those people, too?"

Carrie shook her head with regret. "I'm afraid they won't let me try to help," she replied. She wasn't going to describe the horrific specter of death that hung over the hospital, but she suspected Biddy knew it all too well. "But we can save so many before they end up there, Biddy. Starting with you."

"Me?" Biddy shook her head. "I'm not sick."

"And you're not going to get that way, either," Carrie said. "When did you last eat?" She knew Faith did all the cooking.

Biddy shrugged. "Yesterday sometime," she said. "I haven't been hungry."

Carolyn appeared beside Carrie with a pitcher of water and a bottle of camphor. "Give her this."

Carrie poured a glass of water and added five drops of camphor. "Drink this, Biddy".

Biddy reached for the glass and drank it down quickly. "Can I see Faith?"

"In a little while," Carrie promised. "She needs to sleep, and you have to eat something. In ten minutes I'm going to give you another glass of water."

"What are the drops you put in it?"

Carrie remembered Biddy's old dream of being a doctor. "Are you familiar with homeopathic medicine?"

"I've heard something of it, but I can't really say I know what it is."

Carrie nodded. "I would have said the same thing not too long ago. There is a lot I want to tell you, but first we want to help as many people as we can."

Biddy's eyes lifted over Carrie's shoulder as she nodded. "Who are you?"

Carrie pulled Carolyn forward. "This is Carolyn Blakely. She is a student at the Homeopathic College here in Philadelphia."

"A different school than yours?" Biddy looked confused.

"I'll explain it all later." Carrie needed to heed the urgency she felt. "I'll be back with some food in a minute. And then I want you to take a nap."

Biddy stared at her. "Are you always so bossy?" she demanded, a smile flitting across her lips.

Carrie smiled back. "Only with the people I love best."

She was cutting up some tomatoes for Biddy when she heard a soft rap at the back door. A young boy's head appeared around the corner. He frowned when he saw her standing in the kitchen.

"Who are you?" he demanded suspiciously as his eyes darted around the kitchen.

"My name is Carrie Borden."

"Where is Faith?" he asked brusquely.

Carrie felt a rush of warmth when she recognized his protective stance. "She's been sick."

The boy's eyes darkened. "She got the cholera? She gonna die?"

"No. She is not going to die. She'll be making cookies for you again soon."

"How come she ain't dying?" the boy said. "Lots of people are dying." His frown melted into quivering lips. "My daddy already died, and my brother has been throwing up all day. Mama made me leave the house." His blue eyes were too old for the freckled face topped by rusty red hair. "Faith gonna die, too," he said, suddenly looking exactly like the seven-year-old she guessed him to be.

Carrie moved forward and squatted down. "She is not going to die," she repeated as she smoothed the hair away from his sorrowful, knowledgeable eyes. "And neither is your brother. I want you to take me to your home in a few minutes." She pulled him forward. "But first I need you to do something for me while I fix Miss Biddy some food."

She could tell the little boy didn't believe her, but he was listening. "What do you need me to do?"

"What's your name?"

"Paddy."

"It's nice to meet you, Paddy. Do you know where Miss Biddy's grandson, Arden, lives?"

"Yep."

"Will you go to his house and tell him he needs to come help take care of Biddy?"

"Yep."

Carrie bit back a smile when he didn't budge. "Could you do it now?"

Paddy cocked his head, considering. "You be here when I get back? And then you'll come make my brother better?"

"Yes," Carrie promised, breathing a sigh of relief when Paddy turned and vanished out the door. She heard pounding feet for a second, and then all was silent in the kitchen again. She finished fixing Biddy a meal of fresh tomatoes and cucumbers from the garden that Faith had carved out of the little postage stamp yard—all that was left of what had once been a magnificent farm. Then she quickly cut up potatoes and onions to join the rest of the vegetables she had prepared. The sound of Carolyn's feet on the floor above accompanied her while she concocted a large pot of soup with some of the bottled water. Faith would need some nourishing food when she woke.

Twenty minutes passed before she heard the sound of running feet again and Arden and Paddy burst through the door. Arden ground to a halt when he saw Carrie. "What is going on? Is Granny sick?"

"No," Carrie said, knowing that whatever Paddy told Arden had probably scared him to death. "And she's not going to be." She waited for the fear in Arden's eyes to die away. "Faith has been extremely ill. She is going to be fine, but she won't be able to take care of Biddy for a while, and your great-granny is too tired and distraught to take care of herself. I've made her some food, and I have a pot of soup that will be ready in an hour or so. Can you stay here and take care of her?"

Arden nodded. "Of course I will." He paused. "Paddy said Faith had the cholera, but you said she is going to be fine..." His voice trailed away as he stared at her. "Why isn't she dying like the rest?"

"I'll explain later," Carrie said. She stepped to the table, poured two glasses of water, and added the drops of camphor to both of them. "Drink this."

Arden blinked, but did as he was told. Paddy stared at the water suspiciously.

"It won't hurt you, Paddy. It will keep you from getting sick." Carrie waited until he drank it, pinching his nose closed first. She almost laughed as he screwed his face with distaste. The liquid was tasteless. She turned to Arden. "I want both of you to drink three more glasses in the next hour—one every twenty minutes. Add five drops of camphor to each glass."

"I wish you had been as easy to get along with the night of the fire as I am right now."

Carrie chuckled, glad to have the humor to lighten the atmosphere. "Me, too," she agreed. "I'm going to have Paddy show me where he lives and then he will come right back here."

"Why do I have to come back?" Paddy demanded. "My little brother needs me," he said, his eyes firing with protest.

"He'll need you tomorrow after he gets some rest," Carrie said. "And so will your mama. Right now they're going to need the house real quiet, and they need you to not get sick."

Paddy eyed the table. "And that stuff will keep me from getting sick?"

"Yes."

"Promise?"

Carrie remembered Faith's almost instantaneous response to the veratrum. "I promise."

Paddy held her gaze for a long moment. "I'll be back, Arden." He headed for the door. "I'll take you to my brother now."

Janie was waiting on the front porch when Carrie finally arrived home long after dark had fallen. An almost sleepless night, followed by a very intense day, had her stumbling when she stepped down from the carriage.

Janie ran down the stairs and steadied her just as the driver leapt off his seat to take her arm. "Carrie, are you okay?"

"It's been a long day." Carrie squeezed Janie's hand and turned to the lanky, dark-haired man. "Thank you."

"I'm the one to be thanking you, Mrs. Borden. If not for you, my sister and nephew would probably be dying in that hospital right now." He tipped his hat. "You ever need anything at all, you let me know," he said.

"I'm just glad they're going to be okay," Carrie murmured.

"You sure you want me to pick you up tomorrow morning? You look like you need some rest."

Carrie nodded. "Absolutely. There is still so much to be done." She pushed away the images filling her mind, knowing there was nothing else she could do until she had some rest and food.

"I have dinner waiting for you," Janie said as they walked slowly up the stairs.

Matthew appeared at the door, his eyes darkening with concern when he saw Carrie, but he said nothing as he stepped back to let them enter. "I guess I really do have to share my soup with her, don't I?"

Carrie managed a smile, so very glad to be home. She wouldn't have traded the day she'd had for anything, but she had nothing left to give. The sight of Matthew and Janie's faces filled her with warm gratitude.

Thirty minutes later, she could feel life ebbing back in. She pushed away the remnants of her third bowl of thick soup but continued to nibble on bread slathered with the apple butter Alice had made a few days earlier. She grasped the hot cup of tea Janie shoved toward her and finally leaned back in her chair.

"Long day?" Janie asked.

Carrie nodded. They had let her eat in silence. Now she felt ready to form words. "Yes," she agreed, "but it was also one of the best days of my entire life."

Janie's eyes widened. "Do you have enough energy to tell us about it?"

"No," Carrie admitted, "but I will tell you nothing is more satisfying than knowing I have the power to heal people of a disease that is killing thousands all over the city, and even more across the country."

"The cholera?" Janie breathed. "The remedy worked?"

Carrie closed her eyes for a moment. "Like a miracle," she replied. "So many were sick." She told Janie and Matthew about Faith. "She is still weak, but she was eating soup when I left, and she looks almost back to normal." She shook her head. "I was sure she was going to die when I saw her vomiting into a bucket." Shuddering, she pushed the thought from her mind. "A few drops of veratrum gave her back her life."

"We saw Sarah's herbal medicines bring people back, too," Janie said. "What makes this so different?"

"I don't know that I can explain it yet," Carrie confessed, realizing she was too exhausted to make the effort. She just wanted to enjoy the company of her friends. She and Carolyn had administered camphor to hundreds who were just beginning to feel ill, leaving bottles of remedy with each family. Biddy had insisted on paying for every drop of it, placing an order for as much as the dispensary could create. They were formulating remedy as fast as they could.

Carrie and Carolyn had treated at least thirty patients who were as gravely ill as Faith had been. Each of them had responded to the veratrum. Carrie had enlisted the help of neighborhood women to cook up huge vats of soup that would be delivered to everyone that was ill. Men had been sent to bring back jugs and bottles of water from areas of Philadelphia protected by the sanitation system. There was still a lot of work to be done, but she knew she had made a difference.

She smiled at Janie and Matthew. "I'll tell you all about it later. Right now I want to be distracted by something else. I have been so immersed in study that I realized at some point on the way home that I know absolutely nothing about what is going on in the world." She fixed her gaze on Matthew. "I'm betting you can fix that for me."

Matthew watched her for a long moment. He must have been satisfied with what he saw, because he gave her an easy grin. "You've come to the right place," he assured her.

Janie stood and moved toward the icebox. "Do you have room for some more food?"

"Only if it is some of Alice's apple pie," Carrie answered. "How does that woman find time to bake apple pies and make apple butter?" she asked with a frown.

"Not everyone spends fourteen hours a day in class or with their nose in a book," Janie retorted as she placed an apple pie on the table.

Carrie stared at it, suddenly hungry again as Janie cut through the flaky crust, releasing the aroma of apples and cinnamon into the kitchen.

"Can *you* make pie like this, Janie?" Matthew asked as he stared at the piece she cut and laid on his plate.

Janie laughed. "Will *you* be able to afford a cook for us when you're a wealthy writer?"

"Does that mean the answer is no?"

Carrie laughed at the morose sound in his voice. "Men are pathetic. Why should Janie be the one to make the pie?"

Matthew cocked his head and eyed her thoughtfully. "You have a point. My mama always made the pies in our house, but the world is changing so fast I suppose this is another thing that could change." He glanced toward the ceiling. "Do you think Alice will teach me?"

"Oh, fine," Janie said, only her twitching lips giving her away. "I tell you what. We'll have Alice teach both of us. Between the two of us, we should be able to make sure there is some kind of pie around for what will be our otherwise neglected children."

"Children? I simply want pie around for the aspiring author. I'm quite sure I will write better if I have constant access to delicious pie. I understand it stimulates the brain cells."

"Or you'll become so huge you won't be able to move from behind your desk."

"At least that means I will get a lot of writing done."

Carrie laughed, more of the fatigue melting away as the warmth of the kitchen and the easy banter of her friends restored her. "Enough! Are you going to tell me what is going on or not?"

Matthew nodded, his smile tightening. "It's not all good," he warned.

"I quit hoping for *all good* years ago," Carrie responded. "I'll settle for the truth."

Chapter Fourteen

"The good news is that President Johnson's tenure is as good as dead," Matthew began.

Carrie pushed her thoughts past her fatigue. "His 'Swing Around the Circle' campaign did not go well?"

"That would be putting it mildly," Matthew said. "A more appropriate word would be disastrous. It's been about two weeks since it concluded. The repercussions have grown stronger as the news has reported over and over again how damaging it was. Our president believed he could regain the trust of moderate Republicans by exploiting tensions between them and their radical counterparts on the tour."

"He only alienated them more?" Carrie guessed. She had long ago lost any respect for the man who had taken Lincoln's place.

"I doubt the end result would have been any different, but it would have been far better for Johnson if the tour had never been made. Having said that, I am thrilled for the country that he decided to do it. He doesn't have a chance of maintaining control of Congress next month." Matthew looked thoughtful. "It's sad, actually. I believe when Johnson first began his reconstruction approach, he meant to fulfill Lincoln's promise to benevolently bind up the nation's wounds after the war."

"That all changed when Congress began enacting legislation to guarantee the rights of the freed slaves," Janie observed.

"Yes," Matthew agreed. "Johnson was happy to be forgiving with the whites, but when it came right down to it, our president was not able to move beyond his own prejudice and bigotry to do what was right for the country."

"His power corrupted him?" Carrie asked

Matthew considered her question. "I believe he gradually realized he had the power to push forward the agenda he had never stopped believing in. I think he tried to push it aside for a brief time, but the reality of black equality—once it was staring him in the face—was more than he could handle."

"So he did everything he could to stop it." Carrie said.

"Yes, but it backfired on him. There are many in the North who don't believe blacks are equal, but they do believe they should be treated fairly. They are also aware they lost hundreds of thousands of their sons and husbands in a war ignited by the South. If for no other reason than their belief the South should be punished and held accountable for its actions, they have grown sick and tired of their commander-in-chief."

"Was *every* stop on the tour harmful to him?" Janie asked.

"No," Matthew admitted. "It actually started rather well for him. He was well received in Baltimore, New York and right here in Philadelphia."

"Here? In Philadelphia?" Carrie was surprised. "Did you go to the speech?" She watched as Matthew's eyes narrowed with disgust. "I take it you did, and that you weren't impressed?"

"His speech was fairly benign until he compared himself to Jesus Christ."

Carrie and Janie gaped at him.

"What?" Carrie managed to ask, hoping she was not hearing Matthew correctly.

"He recounted his rise from the tailor's bench to the presidency," Matthew said. "Then he compared himself to Jesus Christ and explained that, like the Savior, he too liked to pardon repentant sinners. The problem, he revealed, was that Congress and radicals still wanted to break up the Union. An effort he was trying to prevent."

A long silence fell on the kitchen when he finished speaking.

"I see," Carrie said, trying to absorb what he was saying, but hardly able to wrap her brain around something so ludicrous. "And the people of Philadelphia supported him? I find that difficult to believe."

"Well, *some* of them," Matthew reminded her. "I think our city has far more people that know how destructive this man is to our country. The tide turned against him in the Midwest. The crowds were much more hostile. Johnson lost his temper several times and said things his advisors cringed at." His voice grew tight with anger. "When he was in St. Louis, he accused the Radical Republicans of inciting the New Orleans riot. He compared himself to Jesus again, saying the Republicans were betraying him like Judas had Christ."

Carrie wasn't sure whether to laugh or be angry. "You're serious?" she breathed. Her mind filled with images of the stories Matthew had told of the New Orleans riot. She was sure he had protected them from the most heinous acts, but the ones he had shared had made her blood boil.

"When he got to Indianapolis the next day, the crowd was so loud and hostile he couldn't speak. When he left, violence broke out between his supporters and opponents. One man was shot and killed." Matthew took another bite of pie, chewing it thoughtfully before he continued. "The press has crucified him." Satisfaction filled his voice.

"Fitting, since he compares himself to Jesus Christ," Janie muttered.

"What is going to happen?" Carrie asked. "You say there is bad news, but I have to admit, Johnson's failure is nothing but good news to me."

"And to me," Matthew said, "but nothing is going to be resolved easily or quickly. I believe the Republicans will take Congress in a landslide victory in November, but Johnson will still be president. It is going to be a long series of battles."

"But the Republicans will have control," Carrie argued. "They can block Johnson's bills and override vetoes."

"They can, and I believe they will," Matthew agreed.

Carrie stared at him, fatigue pressing down on her again. "Then what are you not telling me?"

Matthew sighed and glanced at Janie.

"Did you really think she wouldn't demand to know everything?"

Carrie took a deep breath and waited for the rest of what Matthew had to say.

Matthew rocked back in his chair and leaned against the wall for a minute, his red hair contrasting badly with the purple flowers on the wallpaper. "It's going to get much worse before it gets better," he said. "The Republicans are not the only ones who know they are going to be victorious. Southerners know they are about to lose their ally in the White House. They know they are going to have many of their newly re-established powers taken back from them as the new reconstruction policies take shape early next year. They realize they are going to be forced to treat the black man as an equal." He paused. "They are terrified, and they are determined to fight back. If President Johnson can no longer help them, they are going to take action on their own."

"How?" Carrie demanded, her throat tightening around the word with dread.

"Vigilante groups are gaining power in the South," Matthew said. "Reports have been coming in from journalists. Southerners believe Radical Reconstruction is little more than the social and political emasculation of whites and the exaltation of blacks. They say the Ku Klux Klan and the other groups have been created as a necessary self-defense movement. They proclaim they have to take action to protect themselves, their families, and what is left of the South."

Carrie was reminded of just how protected she was here in Philadelphia. "How?" she repeated, knowing her voice sounded harsh in the quiet kitchen. She remembered hearing about the Ku Klux Klan before. Matthew and Peter indicated they feared it could become something more, but she had been too buried in school to keep up with it. Matthew's expression told her it had indeed become something more.

"Some of it is a play for control. The Klan has become more active since the riots in New Orleans and Memphis. What started as a social club that played pranks has transformed into a true vigilante movement. The whites are afraid of losing total control of the South. And, like with Johnson, the power the KKK members feel when they dress up in their costumes has made them aspire to more vicious activities. But they are not the only ones," he added. "There are many other groups made up of what seems to be mostly Confederate veterans eager to continue violence among the freed blacks."

"How?" Carrie repeated once more. "Quit trying to protect me," she demanded, pushing back her fatigue again, but realizing it was draining her ability to be patient. "I simply want to know the truth. The sooner you tell me, the quicker I can quit haranguing you."

Matthew met her eyes squarely. "They are going out to cabins at night and confiscating firearms. They are breaking up prayer meetings and social gatherings."

"That's annoying, but..."

"They are whipping people, raping women, and killing blacks around the country," Matthew finished, his voice pinched with anger and pain. "Over one thousand have been murdered in Texas already, but every state has a growing number of deaths. It's going to get worse."

Carrie closed her eyes in a futile attempt to block out the images, but forced them back open. She had demanded to know the truth. She was not going to hide from it. "What can be done?"

Shadows filled Matthew's eyes. "Until President Johnson loses the last of his control in November? Until the new Congress can pass new Reconstruction acts and step in to take control of things in the South?" His voice tightened. "Nothing. Every black person simply has to try to stay safe."

Carrie gasped. Her thoughts flew to the plantation. "Rose... Moses... The children..." Her voice cracked. "All of them are in danger?"

"As are your father, Abby, Jeremy, Marietta, and any white person who stands for equality for the blacks." Matthew's eyes sparked with anger. "And as soon as you step foot back on Southern soil, you will be, too."

Carrie sat back in her chair, her stunned mind absorbing the information. She had known it was bad, but her Philadelphia cocoon, and the focus on school and the cholera epidemic, had virtually closed her mind to other realities. "Abby sent me a letter recently," she murmured. "She tried to hide it, but I think she is scared."

"As she should be. I have warned them they must be extremely careful."

Carrie fought to comprehend what she was hearing. She was aware of Janie taking her hand, but she remained silent for a long time. The combination of fear and exhaustion was making it difficult to think. "It's not over," she whispered, understanding flooding in as all the pieces clicked together.

"It's not over?" Janie asked, confusion lacing her voice.

"The war. It's not over. The surrender at Appomattox supposedly ended things, but it didn't. The South may have surrendered its armies, but the soldiers and many of the citizens are determined to fight on. That means the government is going to have to continue to fight against a white insurgency that relies on murder and intimidation to undo what their defeat in the war created." Words tumbled out of her mouth. "The war is not over," she repeated, looking to Matthew for confirmation, though she had a wild hope he could prove her wrong.

"You're right," Matthew agreed heavily, dashing her flimsy hopes. "President Johnson tried to officially end the war this summer. Congress seized control of his war powers and denied him the right to do it. They know the war has done nothing but enter a new phase. And it's just beginning."

Eddie moved through the dark streets easily. He was alert, but the ever-present fear had disappeared with the emergence of the Black Militia units. He felt hope pouring into his soul as he thought about how things had improved. For the first time since moving to Richmond, he and his family were safe. No one had let down their guard, but neither were they hiding in their houses each night from fear of attack.

"Howdy, Eddie."

Eddie moved toward the four men from the Irrepressibles who were stationed on the corner across from the Second African Baptist Church, which had been burned that spring on the eve of the Emancipation Day Celebration. It had taken less than two months for the black community to lay the cornerstone for a new church building. Now it towered in defiance of those who would threaten to destroy it. "Seen anything tonight?"

"Nah. Them white boys know better than to come down here and bother us now."

Eddie nodded. It certainly seemed to be true. At least five black militia units had been formed, but the Irrepressibles, with more than two hundred members, was the most prominent. All of them had served in the Union Army. They loved nothing better than to march around the city and the black quarters in full military regalia, their rifles and cavalry sabers held defiantly. "Make anybody angry tonight?" he asked with a chuckle.

One of the men laughed. "I reckon we did. About a hundred of us were out on the edges of the quarter before it got dark. I don't reckon anybody be coming to bother us tonight. The fear on them white faces felt right nice." Satisfaction deepened his voice.

Eddie understood. The man's house had been broken into in early summer. His wife and children had been forced to watch while vigilantes beat him, threatening to come back for his family if he didn't leave the city. Not willing to sacrifice his family, he had been ready to follow their orders, until he'd heard news of the militia units. Since then, he'd been out on the streets every single night, proud of the fact he was protecting his family and many others.

Eddie had been reading almost daily reports in the *Richmond Dispatch* that complained about the militias, but he didn't care. Not one white gang attack on blacks had happened since the militia went into effect two months earlier. "Keep up the good work," he called cheerfully. He turned the corner and walked toward his house.

The smell of collard greens and cornbread assaulted him when he opened the door. He took a deep breath, smiling at the warm glow of oil lanterns illuminating his children.

Amber Lou looked up and smiled. "Hi, Daddy!" she called brightly.

Carl scrambled up and raced to give him a hug. "We had some chess pie tonight, Daddy."

Eddie returned the hug, relieved beyond words that his children's eyes were no longer shuttered with fear and grief. "Is that right? Did you save me some?"

"No, Daddy." Carl said, but his dancing eyes told a different story.

"You know that ain't true!" Amber Lou scolded.

"*Isn't* true," Opal corrected as she handed Eddie a plate of hot food.

"Well, it *isn't* true, either," Amber Lou answered, her eyes flashing with indignation. "Daddy, you know we wouldn't eat all the pie!" She glared at Carl.

Carl smirked at her, his face unrepentant. "Why do you have to be so serious all the time, Amber Lou?"

Carl's question made Eddie's heart catch. He remembered how cheerful and fun-loving Amber Lou had been as a little girl, back when she had been called just Amber. All the suffering seemed to have sucked it right out of her. She had started to come back to life after the war when they had the restaurant in Philadelphia. Losing the Sadies in the fire, along with Susie and Zeke, had ripped it right back out. Her sister Sadie had insisted on being called Sadie Lou to distinguish her from her best friend. Amber had added the Lou to her name in honor of her sister. She refused to let anyone call her by just Amber anymore. The fear seemed to be gone, but Eddie wasn't sure the dark heaviness that aged her eyes would ever disappear. "Leave your sister alone," he admonished, reaching down to pat Amber Lou's head. "Thanks for making sure I have pie, honey."

Amber Lou nodded with satisfaction and bent back to her book. She and her cousin Cindy talked all the time about being the first girls in their family to go to college. The two Sadies had made plans to attend, but the restaurant fire had snuffed them out. Amber Lou was determined to fulfill her sister's desire. Her commitment had ignited a passion for education that no amount of learning seemed to be able to quench. Marietta gave her extra tutoring every chance she had, but Amber Lou kept asking for more.

"How did it go at the factory today?" Opal asked.

"Same as usual," Eddie responded. "More and more orders are coming in. Thomas knows I want as much overtime as I can get."

"You getting too tired?" Opal pressed. "Fourteen hours in a day is an awful long time to work."

Eddie shrugged. "Nothing seems very hard after those years in prison. I'm glad to have the chance to work. Besides, I don't think I'll have to do this all my life." He took a bite of collards and reached for the cornbread slathered in butter, knowing his overtime made it possible for them to eat so well.

Opal and Jewel's garden had produced a bountiful harvest this year. What they hadn't eaten lined the walls of the pantry, filled the closets, and was stuffed under every low bed. All the signs said it was going to be another brutal winter, but they wouldn't go hungry.

Eddie swallowed his bite and asked, "Any luck finding a place for your new restaurant?" Until recently, Opal had worked at the factory, as well, but they had decided she would quit so they could pursue their dream.

Opal frowned and shook her head. "Not yet," she admitted. "I'd feel a lot safer if it was right here in the quarter, but Miss Abby is still telling me I should put it in the white part of the town because they can afford to eat my food, and also pay higher prices. She says my cooking will pull in a lot of customers. I don't know, though," she murmured. "Am I wrong to be afraid?"

"Nope," Eddie replied. "I think things are going to keep getting better here in the city, but any black person with sense would be afraid."

"So you think I should put it here in the black quarter?" Opal asked, her voice both hopeful and also faintly disappointed.

Eddie shook his head. "I didn't say that. Things are changing," he continued. "I wish sometimes we could hide away and never see a white face again, but that would mean things gonna be the same for our children." His gaze drifted toward Amber Lou and Carl hunched over their books. "We want our children to have a better life. That means things have to change."

"And it means we have to take risks," Opal agreed, courage blooming on her face again.

"Yep. I've been talking with Thomas and Jeremy some. They believe Congress is gonna make things better down here for us."

"*Going* to," Amber Lou called from across the room. "They're not gonna, Daddy. They are *going to.*"

Eddie swallowed a sigh. He was trying hard to undo years of bad habits, but it wasn't easy. There were times he got plain disgusted with the necessity to even make the attempt. If white folks looked at him as less than because he didn't talk as fancy as they did, he didn't know if he cared.

"It's not your place to correct your Daddy," Opal scolded mildly.

"Why not?" Amber Lou asked, her face genuinely puzzled. "You're correcting *me* all the time."

Eddie broke in. "I don't mind you correcting me, Amber Lou. Just know it's going to be harder for me because I've been speaking this way for a real long time."

"But you're older, Daddy. Doesn't that mean you're smarter?"

Eddie chuckled. "Sometimes it does. Sometimes it doesn't. Speaking right isn't only about being smart. For Opal and me, it means unlearning how we spoke all our lives." He tried to think of an example she would understand. "How do you get out of bed every morning, Amber Lou?"

Amber Lou stared at him. "I just get out of bed, Daddy."

"But *how* do you do it?" Eddie asked.

Amber Lou gave him an exasperated look, but she closed her eyes for a moment before they flew back open. "I throw back the covers, I swing my legs over the edge, and I stand up."

Eddie nodded. "What if the floor wasn't there one day?"

Amber Lou's look said she questioned his sanity. "The floor will *always* be there."

"But what if it wasn't?"

"Then I better get out of bed another way."

"And do you think it would be easy to change that habit of swinging your legs out of bed after doing it for so many years?"

"Of course!" Amber Lou said, but then her face clouded with doubt. "Maybe it would take a *little* while to change," she admitted.

Eddie waited, watching the thoughts flit across his daughter's face.

Finally Amber Lou met his eyes. "I see what you're saying, Daddy. I think it might be real hard to learn a different way to get up every morning. I don't think about it when I wake up. I just do it." She paused. "Having to think about what you say all the time must make you real tired."

"There are times it does," Eddie replied.

Amber Lou stared at him for a long moment, remorse flooding her eyes. She jumped up and ran to throw her arms around him. "I'm sorry, Daddy. I won't say anything else. I promise!'"

Eddie shook his head. "That's not why I said that to you. I want to learn how to speak right. I don't mind if you correct me, but it's important you do it with compassion and understanding." He tilted her chin up until their eyes met. "It's real easy to judge people, Amber Lou. The world don't need more of that, honey."

"*Doesn't* need," Amber Lou replied, her eyes twinkling. "And I promise I won't judge people."

Eddie laughed. "The world *doesn't* need any more judgment, Amber Lou." He would take every opportunity he could to drill that into her.

Abby snuggled into the blanket covering her and Thomas, savoring the feel of the cool breeze that rustled the leaves that were just beginning to take on the delightful colors of fall. They had come out to the porch swing to enjoy the beautiful night. She squeezed Thomas' hand and leaned into his shoulder, sighing with contentment when he kissed the top of her head.

The militias had brought peace to more than the black quarter. Because so many of the men in the quarter worked at Cromwell Factory, the militias always posted at least ten of their men around the building. The tight fear that had almost suffocated Abby all summer had released its hold—just as summer had bowed in submission to fall. She could still feel tension in the air, and she knew the South was moving into more troubled times after the Congressional elections, but she no longer felt the threat aimed directly at her or those she loved. She was sure there were people who still wished them harm, but she felt protected.

Thanks to her and Marietta's efforts, the cholera impact was not as terrible as feared. There were people who had died, but the number was much smaller than they had envisioned when it first struck. The first hard frosts would end it. Until then, they would keep educating people on how to keep from falling ill. The people in the black quarter had no idea how much they owed to Carrie for all the instructions she had sent from Philadelphia.

"I can hardly wait to go out to the plantation," Abby murmured. She had been anticipating the Harvest Celebration since the moment she had received notice.

"I hope Carrie and the girls will be able to join us," Thomas replied.

"I got a letter from Carrie today. She is certain they will be able to get away, since they had to return to Philadelphia so early this summer after the cholera outbreak." She spoke lightly, but she felt Thomas raise his head to look down on her.

"But...?"

Abby sighed. "Must you always know my every thought?"

"Evidently. Unless you decide to work a little harder to hide them," Thomas replied.

Abby shook her head. "That requires far too much energy, and besides, I rather like being known this well."

"So...?" Thomas prompted.

"It wasn't anything Carrie said in her letter," Abby said. "It was more of a feeling I got that something is going on up there."

"Some kind of trouble?" Thomas asked.

"No," Abby assured him. "I just got the feeling that things are changing for her. And really, Thomas, it's just a feeling. There was absolutely nothing in her letter that indicated that or gave me reason for alarm."

"More of that women's intuition," Thomas said dryly.

"It does seem to be rather effective."

"I can't argue with that. Besides, Carrie doesn't seem to be happy unless things are changing. She seems to thrive on it."

Abby wasn't sure if Thomas' voice indicated pleasure or displeasure at the thought. "Independent women prefer to call it 'remaining flexible to the seasons of life,' " she said coyly. "Remember what Janie's grandmother told her—that it's usually in the winds of change that we find our direction? I find I love the idea of shifting with the wind."

She felt Thomas' sudden tension release as he laughed. "Oh, do you? Isn't that just a way of justifying being a natural rebel and never doing the things people expect of you?"

"Well, certainly!" Abby said. "It's why you love your daughter, and it's why you fell in love with me. You can pretend you don't like it, but then you'll have to explain why you have surrounded yourself with women who do just that." She leaned back to glare at him.

"Other women are boring," Thomas chuckled, pulling her back close to his side. "Carrie will tell us what is going on when she gets here. Until then, we can wonder."

"I'm far too busy for that," Abby responded. "Rose sent me a letter asking me to design the awards for the tournament. She wants them to be quite elaborate. I'm having fun creating them."

Thomas nodded. "It will be interesting to see who wins the tournament this year. The last one I attended at Blackwell seems like another life."

Abby understood when a shadow crossed his face. "It *was* another life, Thomas. Do you miss it terribly?"

Thomas sat silently for several moments before he shook his head. "I thought I would," he murmured. "Before the war I couldn't imagine another life. When my first wife died, I couldn't escape the plantation fast enough. After the war, all I wanted was to go back to it. I enjoy our visits now, but the plantation is no longer my life. Even if things hadn't changed so drastically in the country, *I* have changed drastically. I did farming one way my entire life. I know I could have changed, but I no longer had the desire. I was ready to create a new life with you here in the city."

"I'm glad you don't have any regrets," Abby murmured.

"Not a single one," Thomas assured her. "Especially now that the tension has eased some. The one regret I struggled with for months was the knowledge that living in Richmond was putting you into extreme danger. I felt selfish for not having us move to Philadelphia."

Abby sniffed. "I believe it was my choice to be here as well," she reminded him. She was touched by his concern, but her need for independence was strong.

Thomas laughed. "That it was, but can't a man love his wife enough to not want her to be in danger?"

Abby relaxed. Both of them were learning how to love each other, while also respecting the other's needs. "You're right," she agreed. She returned to the earlier topic. "Didn't Robert win the tournament last time?"

"He did," Thomas answered. "And then he crowned Carrie as his Queen of Beauty and Love. It was quite a special night. My beautiful daughter was the belle of the ball."

Abby smiled as she remembered the story Carrie had told her.

"I predict the tournament will be a hard fought battle between the men this year," Thomas said with a laugh.

Abby leaned back and gazed up at him. "Only between the men?"

Thomas started to nod and then stopped himself. "Oops. I'm about to make another mistake, aren't I?"

"You could be," Abby agreed sweetly.

Thomas threw back his head with a hearty laugh. "You're absolutely right, my love. I'm sure Carrie has plans to win this year. It will be fun to see if any other women materialize to challenge her. She'll be at a disadvantage because there will be no opportunity to practice in the city, but it might not keep her from winning. She used to practice for hours when she was young, telling me that one day *she* would ride in a tournament. And now she can," he added. "Times are indeed changing." His voice deepened as he pulled Abby even closer. "I like it."

Abby opened her mouth to ask him if he was sure, but snuggled closer instead. She was a smart woman. She was simply going to be grateful.

Chapter Fifteen

Rose was glad for the fire crackling in the woodstove. She knew the afternoon would be warm and mild, but the morning air was chilly enough to make the flames welcome. She pulled her sweater close, relieved the long, humid summer was over. At least when the weather was cold, she could build a fire and stay warm. There was no escape from the brutal summer heat. She would probably be longing for the warmth in a few months, but right now she was simply glad not to be miserably hot.

"Hurry, Amber!"

Rose smiled as Felicia and Amber broke out of the woods behind the school. They always walked on the path from the plantation. Amber was moving slowly, her face indicating she wished she was still back at the stable with her beloved filly. Felicia ran ahead, her face showing even more eagerness than usual to get to school.

"Good morning, Miss Rose!" Felicia chirped as she ran in the door, skidding to a halt in front of her desk.

Rose grinned at her, knowing exactly why she was so excited. "Are you ready, Felicia?" It had been hard to get the little girl to eat that morning, but she had finally refused to let Felicia go to school with her until she ate some breakfast. Annie had stood over her with a stern look while she grumbled and shoved in spoonfuls of porridge.

Felicia nodded her head, her braids slapping against her back. "Yes, ma'am. I'm ready!"

"Are you nervous?"

Felicia shook her head just as hard. "No, ma'am. I'm just real excited to tell what I've been learning." She glanced out the window and saw that Amber was busy playing with some other children in the schoolyard.

Rose waited, sensing Felicia had something she wanted to say.

Felicia looked out the window again, evidently made up her mind, and then turned to Rose. "There's something I would like to tell you."

Rose nodded. "All right."

Felicia flashed a bright smile that turned her from a serious little girl into a beautiful young woman. Rose caught her breath, amazed a smile could work such a total transformation. Felicia had followed her directive that she play for an hour every day, but once she had fulfilled the requirement, she headed straight for the library. Rose knew that as Felicia got older it would be harder and harder to stay far enough ahead of her to teach her, but she welcomed the challenge.

Felicia took a step closer. "I've been selected to be a meteor observer," she said proudly.

Rose stared at her. "A meteor observer? I'm afraid I don't know anything about that."

Felicia nodded. "Most people don't," she replied. "My mama and I used to watch the stars every single night from our plantation. We would go out when it was good and dark and watch how the sky changed. Sometimes we saw white flashes of light across the sky. They scared us because we didn't know what they were, but we finally realized they weren't going to hurt us. It became a game to see how many would appear each night."

"Meteors," Rose murmured. Watching them streak across the sky was one of her favorite things, too.

"Yes!" Felicia said, her eyes snapping with excitement. "I never get tired of looking for them."

"Which is why you climb out the window at night sometimes to sit on the roof," Rose said as understanding dawned.

Felicia stared at her. "You know about that?" Her face puckered with a frown. "Am I in trouble?"

Rose smiled. "If you were in trouble for it, you would have known long before now. I figured you were doing something important. That part of the roof isn't very steep, so I decided not to say anything." Truth be told, she had imagined Felicia crawling out on the roof with the hopes of being closer to her dead parents. It was a relief to know she was stargazing.

"Mama and I used to watch the stars move around the sky in different places, but we didn't know anything about constellations and how the earth rotates around the sun.

That's what made us see different stars at different times of the year, you know."

Rose gazed at her. "I can learn a lot from you," she admitted. "I don't know very much about the stars."

Felicia's grin exploded again. "I'll be real happy to teach you. I go out almost every night now so that I can record meteor activity. Not many people get accepted as observers because you have to take very careful calculations. Once a month I mail in my observations. I'm sending the letters back to Richmond when the courier delivers Mr. Cromwell's journals and publications." Her smile disappeared into a frown. "I could do a better job with a telescope, but I do the best I can."

Rose tucked that piece of information away for later thought. "I would be honored to watch them with you some nights." She was thrilled she had found a way to connect with the little girl, but she also had to be a parent. "But you have to make sure you get enough sleep each night," she cautioned, hiding her smile when she saw the flare of resistance in Felicia's eyes.

"You told me you used to stay up almost all night reading sometimes," Felicia protested. "Sleep is really not that important."

Rose allowed her smile to emerge and decided not to point out that her status as a slave meant that was her *only* time to learn. "I know you believe that right now, but I happen to know that's not true."

"How?" Felicia demanded.

Rose didn't mind the questions. She wanted Felicia to learn how to think for herself. "I've been teaching for almost four years. I know how much better a student learns when they get enough rest. I don't believe your brain works as well if you are not getting enough sleep."

Felicia nodded thoughtfully. "I suppose that could be true," she murmured. "I'll make sure I get enough sleep," she promised. "At least most of the time," she added impishly.

Rose leaned forward and gave her a hug. "Congratulations on being selected as a meteor observer." A glance at her watch told her it was time to start school. "What are you going to talk about today?"

Felicia hesitated. "Can I keep it a surprise?"

Rose raised a brow but had no objection. "If you wish. I trust you to do an excellent job."

Felicia stared at her. "You do?" she breathed. "Really?"

"Really," Rose assured her, touched by the little girl's hunger for her approval. She knew Felicia still held back her wholehearted love because she was afraid of being disloyal to her dead mother, but the walls were breaking down a little more each day. Rose could see her own mama's gleaming eyes encouraging her to keep loving Felicia. "I am looking forward to what you have to share."

Reading and spelling had been completed when Rose raised her hand to get everyone's attention. "I have a surprise for all of you today," she said. She watched sixty-five students snap to attention. Abby had told her the Missionary Society was trying to find another teacher to help her, but their efforts so far had been unsuccessful. She would welcome the help, but her students were so well-behaved, the large class of many different ages wasn't a problem. Everyone helped each other, and all the children were eager to learn.

"This is story day," one of the children called. "Is that the surprise?"

"It is indeed story day," Rose responded, "but the surprise is that I'm not going to be the one telling the story. Felicia is." She motioned for Felicia to come forward, and then moved to sit at Felicia's tiny desk. She wanted to be able to watch her daughter's face.

Felicia grinned and walked forward to the front of the room. The quick flash of nervousness in her eyes was concealed by the bright smile. "I'm going to tell you today about Maria Mitchell. She was the first American woman to work as a professional astronomer."

"What's an astron...omer?" one little girl asked, stumbling over the long word.

"An astronomer is someone who studies things up in space," Felicia answered. "Things like the sun, the moon, and stars and *comets*," she finished.

"A black woman was an astronomer?" Clay, a thin twelve-year-old boy who liked to tease Felicia asked.

"No. Maria Mitchell was a white woman," Felicia announced matter-of-factly.

Rose was quiet as a silence fell on the room.

"Why are you going to tell us about a white woman?" Clay asked. "We be black."

"We *are* black," Rose corrected, waiting to see how Felicia would respond.

The little girl held her ground. "What's wrong with being white? Some white folks are very bad people, but there are others who aren't. If we want people to like us even though we're black, shouldn't we like folks even though they are white?"

Rose watched the faces of the other children, encouraged when many of them nodded. Felicia's simple statement had said it all. The fact that it had been said by someone their own age meant they were more likely to believe it. She nodded encouragement when Felicia looked her way.

"Like I said," Felicia continued, not missing a beat, "Maria Mitchell was the first American woman to work as an astronomer. She was born way back in 1818. She was actually very lucky because her parents believed she was equal to boys, so she got the same education they did."

"She was white," Clay snorted. "Of course she did."

Rose stood. "There is no interrupting when I teach, and there will be none while Felicia is teaching. If she decides to take questions after she is done, she will let you know. For now, you will give her the same respect you give me," she said. Felicia raised her head even higher, her eyes expressing her gratitude when they met Rose's.

"Women today, whether they are white or black, are fighting for equality," Felicia announced, obviously emboldened by Rose standing up for her. "You boys may think you're better than us, but you're not."

Rose heard the boys shifting in their seats, but no one else interrupted.

"Maria Mitchell went to school from the time she was very young. When she was eleven, her father built his own school. She was a student, but she was also a teaching assistant." Felicia's eyes glowed with excitement. "Her father taught her astronomy at home. When she was twelve years old, just two years older than me, she helped her father calculate the exact moment of an annular eclipse. An annular eclipse is when the sun and moon are exactly in line during the day. The moon slides over the sun, but it appears to be a little smaller, so the sun looks like a bright ring around the moon."

The class was silent now, mesmerized by one of their own teaching them something they had never heard about. Some of them glanced toward the sun shining brightly through the windows, but then turned back quickly so they wouldn't miss anything she was saying.

"Maria Mitchell became a teacher. She was actually one of the first teachers to let *black* children come to her school up in Massachusetts. That's a state way north of here. Lots of slaves ran away to there before the war started. There were lots of people who didn't like her teaching blacks, but that didn't stop her. She knew it was the right thing to do because black children are just as smart as white children," she added.

Rose was impressed by Felicia's knowledge, but she was equally impressed by her teaching style. Felicia knew she was speaking of things most of the other children knew nothing about. The little girl was eager to share what she had learned, but she wanted to make sure everyone could understand her.

"In 1847, almost twenty years ago, Maria Mitchell discovered a comet. She found it on October 1st, at ten thirty at night, with a telescope." Excitement made Felicia's voice higher.

Rose decided not to point out that no one in the room knew what a comet was. There would be plenty of time for Felicia to teach them.

"King Christian the Eighth of Denmark gave her a gold medal for discovering that comet and now she is famous all over the world. They named the comet after her. Mitchell's Comet!" She paused, evidently seeing the confused look on some faces. "Denmark is a country in Europe, all the way across the ocean." She looked at Rose. "Can I bring in a map of the world tomorrow so everyone can see where it is?"

"Certainly," Rose murmured, a sudden idea taking shape as she watched Felicia teach.

"Maria Mitchell became the first woman elected Fellow of the American Academy of Arts and Sciences. And last year she became a professor of astronomy at Vassar College." If possible, even more excitement snapped in Felicia's eyes. "Vassar College is the first real college just for women," she announced. A tiny frown crinkled her brows. "Right now they don't let black women enroll, but that will change in time," she said confidently. "Maybe I will go to school there one day, but there is something very exciting that is going to happen next month," she announced. "Right here on the plantation..."

Rose looked at her with surprise. She knew she was about to discover the most important part of what Felicia had wanted to wait to reveal.

"...Something very special happens every November. It's called the Leonid Meteor Shower. When I go out at night to watch meteors—" Felicia stopped, realizing she had lost everyone again. She bit her lip and thought for a moment. "How many of you have ever seen what looked to be a shooting star streaking across the sky?" She was relieved when most of the hands in the room went up. "It's not really a star," she proclaimed. "Those are *meteors*. They are very big chunks of rock that break off of a comet. When they get close to Earth, gravity makes them start moving really fast until they catch fire. The heat melts them away so they don't hit the Earth. That's what makes them *look* like a shooting star."

"How do you know all this?" Clay demanded, unable to remain silent. "I only seen a few of those in my entire life. I always thought they would come down and crash on me."

Other children nodded their heads in agreement, their eyes wide with wonder and curiosity.

"I only see a few of them on a good night of watching," Felicia agreed, "but on November thirteenth and fourteenth—just next month—the Leonid Meteor Shower happens." She paused and took a long breath, watching the other students carefully. Felicia knew she had everyone's full attention. She was making them hungry to hear what she had to say.

Rose smiled with amazement as the little girl drew out the suspense.

"Those two nights we'll be able to see hundreds, maybe even *thousands* of shooting stars in the sky," Felicia announced.

"Really?" Rose couldn't hold back the question. Her mind filled with the image Felicia was creating. She longed to see it for herself.

"Really," Felicia said happily. "I thought it would be a wonderful thing if all the students in the school met on the plantation to watch them together." She caught Rose's eyes, looking tentative for the first time.

"That's a wonderful idea," Rose responded. She had a clear vision of parents and children lined up on blankets, their faces lifted to the sky. She said a quick prayer it would be a clear night with no clouds. "We'll have a family picnic and then watch the meteor shower together," she announced. Her mind began to work through the details.

Felicia's face exploded with a grin. "And that's all I have to say about Maria Mitchell," she finished.

Rose stood as Felicia came to claim her seat. "That was wonderful, Felicia," she said, her heart melting at the pride and satisfaction shining in Felicia's eyes. Then she turned to the rest of the class. "I know I said all of you could ask Felicia questions, but I think it would be better if we just have Felicia teach us something new every day about astronomy. When the Leonid Meteor Shower happens, we'll all know what we are seeing. What do all of you think?"

A chorus of agreement rose from every child in the room. Felicia's face bloomed with a smile brighter than the sunshine streaming in through the windows.

Rose beckoned to Felicia to remain behind when she released the rest of the children at the end of the day. She waited until the schoolyard emptied, and then she turned to Felicia. "How would you like to be my teaching assistant?"

Felicia stared at her with disbelief. "Could you say that again?"

Rose smiled, completely understanding the stunned joy in the little girl's eyes. "I would like you to become my teaching assistant. You are a natural teacher, and you know so much about so many things. You can teach the students about astronomy, but you can also keep them up-to-date on things happening in the country. I don't have time to stay as current as you do. It would help me as much as everyone else," she admitted.

The idea that had hatched while she was listening to Felicia teach had blossomed into a complete plan by the end of the day. "You'll have to stay current with all your studies, and you still have to take time to play every day," she warned. "It may be too much for you, but I'd like to give it a try."

Felicia was nodding her head so hard her braids were slapping against her back. "Yes!" she cried. "It will be just like Maria Mitchell being a teaching assistant for her father. Only I'll be a teaching assistant for my mama!"

Rose caught her breath. This was the first time Felicia had ever referred to Rose as her mother.

Felicia realized it at the exact same moment. She caught her breath and stared deeply into Rose's eyes. "I've been real afraid to call you mama," she murmured. There was a look of pain and loss that shadowed her eyes for a brief moment as she remembered the mama and daddy she had lost, but it was quickly swallowed by a look of intense longing. "Will it be okay if I call you that, Miss Rose?" she asked.

Rose's answer was to hold out her arms and envelop the little girl in a close hug. "I can't think of anything I would like better," she whispered, tears burning her eyes as Felicia threw her arms around her waist and clung to her. "I love you, Felicia."

"I love you, too, Mama," Felicia whispered back.

Rose was exhausted when she finished class that night. The men were all busy finishing up the harvest, but the women had returned to school two weeks earlier. They worked in the fields during the day but left in time to come to school. Her insistence about the importance of education was paying off. Her school was full, not only of the women from the plantation, but also the surrounding area. She had gone home with Felicia after school but returned after eating dinner with her family, as she did almost every night, to teach the adults.

"We're done for the night," Rose announced. "I'm proud of all of you," she said. "Every single woman in this room is reading now. Congratulations!" She felt a surge of anxiety when the women remained seated, their bodies cramped into small desks built for children. She could tell by the looks on many of their faces that something was wrong. She had felt glimmers of it through the night, but she had pushed it aside to focus on teaching.

Now she perched on the edge of her desk as her eyes swept the room. There were thirty-five women looking back at her. They ranged in age from twenty-five to eighty years old. All of their eyes carried the weight of years of slavery, but they also carried the pride of education. "What is it?" she asked.

Morah, the youngest one in the group, stood. Her eyes were fearful but determined. She had obviously been selected to be the spokesperson. "We need your help, Rose. Our men ain't treating us right."

Rose decided now was not the time to correct her speaking. She was disturbed by the pain and anger radiating from the eyes of the woman almost her age. "What do you mean?" she asked, though she was certain she already knew.

"When me and Abraham were slaves together before the war and we was married, things felt pretty equal," Morah replied. "We were both slaves. We were both treated badly, but we made it through because we had each other.

I thought when slavery ended that it meant things would be better for me." She scowled. "Some things are worse."

Rose's gut tightened as most of the other women nodded their heads.

"Abraham came home a while back and told me he was now the *head of the house*," she said, disgust evident in her voice. "From that point forward he been treating me like he's better than me." Pain shadowed the anger in her eyes. "It used to be a lot of yelling, but now he's taken to hitting me and the children when he don't like something." She waved her hand across the room. "The same thing is happening with a bunch of us. We didn't leave the beatings we done had in slavery just to be treated bad by our men!"

Rose sighed. She had suspected something like this may happen ever since Moses brought word that a brochure from the Freedmen's Bureau designating males as the heads of their households had landed in his men's hands.

June opened the door and stepped inside. "I'm sorry I missed class," she said. "Little Simon is sick." She interpreted the look on Rose's face. "He's going to be fine," she assured her, "but I didn't want to leave him alone. Polly came by and offered to stay with him so I could come to the meeting."

The meeting? Rose realized things must be serious if all the women had *planned* a meeting. She waited for Morah to continue, praying she would know what to say.

Morah took a deep breath. "We need your help, Rose. Things can't keep going like they be going. You be Moses' wife, and you be the teacher. Can you do something?"

Rose swallowed hard. She had read the brochure that seemed to have sparked all the trouble.

"Change is hard," she began. "When all of us were slaves, the master was the one in charge, so most of us felt more equal. There was not one person earning money, because none of us did. We were all equally powerless."

"But..." Morah began to protest.

Rose raised her hand. "Let me finish, and then we'll talk about what we're going to do." Morah nodded and sat back. "Now that we're free, our men are starting to think more like white men," she admitted. "Many of them have decided men and women are different." She sighed heavily. "Actually, a lot of them have decided they are better than women."

"Nonsense," Morah snorted.

Some of the other women looked doubtful. Rose understood. A lifetime of slavery had already made them feel less than. Most of them were used to being abused and controlled by their masters and their overseers. It would be frightfully easy for them to concede control of their lives to abusive husbands. Anger flared in her as she stared into eyes that had seen so much suffering. They were working so hard to learn and to make their lives better. "Morah is right," she said. "It is pure nonsense." Her declaration made most of the women sit up straighter. It also loosened their tongues.

"My man told me he was going to run things now because he served as a soldier. He said that makes him better than me, and that I have to let him control things now." The statement was offered up by a mousy-looking woman who had lived as a slave for most of her fifty years.

"My husband told me about a brochure that says men are the only ones who can sign contracts for their whole family. It ain't happening here on Cromwell, but he said men were going to be paid more than women for the same work," another chimed in. "He said that makes him better than me, and the one who should be in charge. I figure if I'm out sweating in the tobacco fields the same as him, that I ought to get paid the same!"

A murmur of agreement rose from the rest of the room.

"Ain't gonna do nothing but get worse if black men get the vote like Congress is trying to make happen," Hettie added. "I be eighty years old. I lived long enough to know men like to think they are in charge. The black man always been pushed down, but if they get that right to vote, it's gonna make things even harder for us."

"You don't think they should vote?" Rose asked, wanting to keep the conversation going. She hoped it would give her time to think of an adequate response.

"Oh, I reckon they should vote, but they ain't got no more right to vote than I do," Hettie snapped. "It ain't right that white women can't vote, and it ain't right that black women can't vote. I figure men done quite enough to mess up things in this country. It's gonna take women to make things right again. I reckon I've lived long enough to figure that much out!"

Rose couldn't have agreed more, but she recognized the more immediate need of dealing with the abuse in the community.

"Does Moses treat you badly?" Morah asked, eyeing her sharply.

"Never," Rose said. She smiled. "He wouldn't dare." There was a ripple of laughter, but serious concern remained on every face as they stared back at her. "I know Moses is unique, but it's only because he learned another way of treating women."

"How?" Morah demanded.

It was a good question. Rose thought through her answer. "I think my mama probably put the fear of God in him before she died." Her tone was light, but she realized that her mama *had* probably made it very clear how she expected him to treat her daughter. "It was more than that, though. All of you have heard the story about how Carrie Borden helped us escape through the Underground Railroad. Watching how she struggled to do the right thing and make the right decisions about slavery made him think about his own beliefs." She paused. "Then we got to Philadelphia, and he met Abby Cromwell—only she was Abby Livingston then. He saw a woman who owned her own business, and who was succeeding in a man's world. He developed even more respect for women." Her gaze swept the room. "He grew up in slavery just like all your men did. But he turned into a different man."

"My Abraham told me I was supposed to *submit* to him," Morah said. "I ain't a slave anymore. I know how to read now, and I work every bit as hard as he does. There ain't gonna be no *submitting*." She fairly growled the words.

"Can you help us, Rose?" Hettie asked, her eyes resting on Morah. "I ain't got no man telling me what to do because my man died years ago, but the other women here need help."

Rose nodded. "You're right." She took a deep breath. "Women all over the country, both white and black, are fighting for their rights." She had gotten a letter from Carrie about that very thing last week. "It's going to be a tough battle, but we're not going to quit fighting until we have the right to vote."

Morah snorted. "You really think men gonna let that happen?"

Rose waited until every eye in the room was looking at her closely. "I think the day will come when they won't be able to stop it," she said. "Women will get the right to vote."

"Not in my lifetime," Hettie observed.

"Perhaps not," Rose replied. "And it may not even be in my lifetime. I sincerely hope that is not true, but the thing I do know to be true is that women simply won't quit fighting for equality and the right to vote."

A somber silence fell on the room as all the women contemplated her statement. Courage filled their faces, and their shoulders straightened, but Morah's next statement just as quickly deflated them.

"That's all fine and good, Rose, but how's that gonna stop our men from treating us badly right now? I'm tired of Abraham treating me bad. I thought I left all that behind me. I told my children they would never be treated wrong again. Now it's their daddy doing it." Anger dripped from her voice, but her eyes were cloaked with something verging on hopelessness.

Rose knew she was right. "I'll talk to Moses," she promised. The husband of almost every woman in the school worked for Moses. It wouldn't address all their problems, but it would be a place to begin. She pushed aside the thought that most of them would be moving on at the end of the harvest. It was imperative they do something *now*. "He will talk to the men and tell them things have to change."

"What about when we have to move on?" Morah demanded. "We gots to leave here when the harvest is done and look for different work."

Rose sighed. "I wish I could tell you Moses can make everything different, but I can't honestly promise you that," she admitted. "It will be a start, though," she said.

"Your men respect my husband, and they need the job he is giving them. That alone will insure they will at least listen. Some of them will change when they know Moses doesn't agree with them."

"And the rest of them?" Morah demanded, fear spiking her voice.

Rose suddenly understood things must be very bad for her. This kind of fear didn't come from being hit occasionally, though any kind of abuse was inexcusable. She stepped over and took Morah's hands. "You're being beaten." It was not a question.

Morah's face flamed with shame before she dropped her gaze to the floor. "Abraham ain't the same man he was before the war," she mumbled. "He came back hard and mean. He was the gentlest man I ever knew before he went off to fight for the North. That's gone," she said.

Rose knew men all over the country, both Union and Confederate, had returned home as changed men. Moses still had nightmares, and there were nights she heard Robert cry out in his sleep. June had told her Simon still wasn't the same, but she knew he wasn't abusive to her sister-in-law. "Everyone changed," she said, "but that doesn't give him an excuse to beat you."

Morah shrugged. "We'll see if Moses can change things." Her face tightened with fear again. "What if Abraham figures out I told about him?" She began to tremble. "It will only make things worse."

"We're *all* here telling," Hettie reminded her.

A chorus of agreement rose from the room.

"We've had enough."

"They's got to treat us better."

"We ain't putting up with no more of this!"

Rose gazed at the resolute faces that reflected both fear and determination. "I will talk to Moses tonight," she promised.

Moses listened quietly as Rose recounted what the women had told her after class.

"It's terrible for some of them," Rose cried. "They've already suffered so much. Will you talk to the men?" She took a deep breath. "I promised them you would."

Moses took a deep breath of his own. "I'll talk to them," he agreed.

Rose wished there was more light on the porch so she could see his face more clearly, but she knew him well enough now to hear every nuance in his voice. She had waited until everyone had gone to bed before she broached the subject. "What are you not saying?"

"Some of the men are very angry," Moses said. "Talking to them might make them angrier, because they are going to believe their wives said something."

Rose squirmed as she thought of Morah's fear.

"I can control what happens on the plantation," Moses said, "but when they leave, I can't do anything."

"I know," Rose admitted, "but we have to try. We can't just do nothing." The look on the women's faces as they implored her for help was engraved on her mind. "We have to do something, Moses."

Moses nodded. "I know." He stood and walked to the edge of the porch, staring out into the night for a long moment before he swung around. "I want you to be careful, though."

Rose stared at him. "What?"

Moses sat down next to her and took both her hands. "The men know the women respect you and come to you for advice. They know you are teaching them and giving them a self-confidence they never had before."

"Those are good things!" Rose cried.

"Yes, but certain men also see it as a threat to their manhood," he said. "They might decide to take it out on you."

"Let them try," Rose retorted, but she felt a flash of discomfort. Every man working for Moses had served in the Union Army. They had the potential to be dangerous. She gripped Moses' hands. "I'll be careful," she said, struck by the look of love on his face.

"You'll do more than that," Moses replied. "From now on, I would like you to carry a pistol with you at all times."

Rose gasped. He hadn't asked her to do that even with the threat of vigilantes. "You really think one of them would hurt me? I'm your wife!" Unbidden, an image of the anger and pain in Trevor's eyes floated into her mind.

"And that should be enough," Moses agreed, "but men who have been through battle are sometimes never the same. I'm giving all these men a chance, but that doesn't mean I trust all of them. I've taught you how to shoot. Will you carry the pistol?"

Rose nodded slowly. "Yes," she said. "And you will talk to the men?"

"I will talk to them," Moses promised.

Chapter 16

The sun was still tucked beneath the treetops when Moses rode Champ out of the stables. The cobalt blue sky was just beginning to take on the hue of dawn when he reached the tobacco fields. He had told Rose he needed to check on the final stages of harvest. The truth was that he needed time to think. He agreed with her that something needed to be done to help the women in the community, but he felt uncomfortable with the knowledge that the weight of the responsibility seemed to rest on his shoulders. He had come to grips with the idea of being a leader for his people, but the demands of the tobacco season had allowed him the luxury of pushing that reality far to the back of his mind. It was a future possibility, not a present thing. Rose's revelation had brought it roaring back with an intensity that threatened to overwhelm him. He knew that whatever he chose to say could make things better for these women. It could also make them worse.

A riotous chorus of birds broke through his thoughts. He managed to smile as cardinals flitted through the trees. It was easy to spot the bright red of the males, but he was just as adept at identifying the softer ocher color of the females. Their identical dark orange beaks made them stand out, but it was their calls that pulled his heart this morning. *Waaait... Waaait... Cheer...Cheer ...Cheer...Cheer.* He wished he could follow their heed and wait to talk to his men, and then he hoped someone would cheer him after he lowered the boom on them. Somehow he was certain neither thing was going to happen.

Moses sighed, shifting easily as Champ shied away from a wide-eyed deer that bounded out of the woods. Champ snorted but stood steady as the doe turned and raced back into the trees. Moses couldn't see it, but he was sure there was a fawn joining its mama in the race from danger. The fawn's spots would have all faded by now as its coat thickened in preparation for winter.

In spite of his anxiety, the peace of the plantation began to work its way into his soul. He turned his head and gazed out over the fields. Every field, once standing tall with fluttering tobacco plants, was bare. Just the tough green stalks, cut almost to the ground, remained behind as testimony to Cromwell Plantation's biggest ever tobacco harvest. All the tobacco was now either packed into barrels headed downriver to Norfolk for export, or to Richmond by wagon to be turned into chewing and pipe tobacco or cigarettes. Moses smiled with satisfaction as he thought of Thomas' stunned response to his final report on the harvest. He planned on waiting until the Harvest Celebration to let the workers know the final results of their hard labor, but he had shared it with Thomas as soon as he had calculated the final numbers.

A flurry of raucous calls from deep within the pine and cedar trees made him turn his head in time to see a flock of ten blue jays darting through the woods. He never tired of their bright azure blue color, though there were times he could do without their noisy, harsh calls. He remembered the day his father had told him these crafty birds could also imitate the call of a hawk. He had watched for years to find one doing it, but so far he had come up empty. He would keep looking, because he knew his father wouldn't have told him something that wasn't true.

Another burst of song made him smile. He had always loved the robin's trilling whistle heralding the arrival of spring. *Cheer-up, cheery me... Cheer-up, cheery me...* He knew most of the robins would soon be migrating further south to avoid the snow, but listening to them now made him feel better. Their constant cheer had helped him through many long days of toiling in the tobacco fields as a boy.

His father had taught him all the birds he knew, telling Moses their songs would help him get through the longest days. He had been right—until he had seen his father hanged from a tree. The birdsongs had ceased to comfort him after that. They were nothing but a stark reminder of what he had lost...until recently. The joy had returned, bringing with it the memories of a man who had given his all to try to offer freedom to his family.

Moses took a deep breath, feeling courage surge into his heart. He could almost feel Big Sam right there with him. He wished his father could have lived to experience freedom. Now he just hoped his father knew his wife and children were finally free. Big Sam would not have stood by if he knew a wrong was being done. He would have done the right thing, no matter the consequences. Now it was Moses' turn.

Moses was relaxed as he watched everyone arrive. The sun had begun its ascent above the treetops, casting a golden glow over the morning. Now that the heat of summer had abated and the harvest was almost done, it was not necessary for everyone to begin work at dawn. The fields were bare, but the final remnants of the tobacco were drying, and there was still a large amount waiting transport. The rest of the men were going to be busy repairing tools and equipment broken during the season. There was still a lot to be done before the Harvest Celebration, but everything was on schedule.

Some of the workers had ridden in from their homes. Others had walked in from the quarters where they were living. More had come in from the surrounding community. The men from his old unit who had appeared in the middle of the night, and who were now sequestered in the quarters, were also working. They had insisted they work for room and board. Every man arriving was grateful for a job, and every one of them worked hard. He watched them as they gathered, wondering which ones were abusing their wives and family. The very thought made his blood boil, but he knew he had to handle things carefully.

Shuffling feet and anxious looks revealed they wondered what was going on. Different groups were usually pulled together in the morning to be given their assignments, but not since the beginning of the season had he brought them together as one unit.

Simon walked over. "What's going on, Moses?"

"There's not time to explain. It will all be clear when I'm done." His brother-in-law eyed him closely, but nodded and stepped back. Moses was grateful for their effortless relationship, forged by their time together on the battlefield.

He stepped onto a box he had placed on the ground so he'd be able to see every man's face as he was speaking. "Good morning," he called. An instant hush fell over the group as every eye turned toward him. It was interesting to view who looked anxious and who looked merely curious. He would analyze that later.

"I'm not ready to give a final report yet, but I want everyone here to know that the Cromwell tobacco harvest has broken every record ever set here. Other plantations all over the South are struggling. You men have proven what can be done when everyone has a chance to work together...reaping the benefits *together*." He smiled as excited murmurs rose into the morning air. He let the comments continue for several moments, and then raised his hand for silence.

"Our time working together is almost over," he continued. "Some of you will be staying, but most of you will have to move on and look for other work. I wish I could keep all of you, but it's not possible." He wasn't telling the men anything they didn't already know, but he was trying to lay a foundation for what he was going to say next. "Freedom is not easy," he said, understanding the confused looks on the faces staring back at him. They thought they had been pulled together to talk about work.

"There was nothing about slavery that prepared you for freedom. You were beaten. You were told what to do every moment of your life. You were not allowed to make any choices of your own. You were held in ignorance, and you were punished if you tried to be something more than the animals most slave owners believed you to be."

Moses prayed he would find the right words as he continued. "When Rose and I ran away, I didn't know anything about being free. I knew I wanted it, and I knew I would do anything to have it, but I didn't really know what it meant. Freedom was just a shining light that had pulled me forward for a long time. When I got it, there were times when it was overwhelming, and there were times I hoped I didn't mess up my opportunity to live another kind of life." He paused, certain the men were listening closely.

"The whites are waiting for us to mess up," he said. "They believe we are animals. That means they believe we don't have the ability to live as free men. They believe we can't take care of ourselves. They believe we won't work to take care of our families. They believe we don't care enough to get educated." Moses' voice rose, carrying his words through the still, crisp air with a strength and clarity that held everyone spellbound. "They believe we will all simply die off because we don't have the ability to live life on our own, without them controlling us."

He waited for the angry murmurs to die down before he raised his voice again. "They are wrong, of course, but one of the things I decided when I became free was that I was going to do whatever it took to prove I was different from what they believed. People in the North don't look at us the same way as Southerners, but most of them still don't believe we are equal—they just don't believe we should be slaves." He let his words sink in, understanding the anger suffusing the faces staring back at him. He waited for a long minute, glad when he saw anger being morphed into determination on most faces. He paused long enough to identify the men who remained nothing but angry, rage shimmering in their eyes and on their faces.

His voice became stronger as he spoke, slightly awestruck at the words coming from him. He'd done nothing to prepare because he had no idea what he should say. He had simply prayed a desperate prayer and then stepped onto the box. The words were coming from a place he couldn't identify, but his confidence grew as they flowed from him. "Millions of black people have lived and died as slaves in America. Many of them gave their lives to pave the way for us to be free. My daddy was one of them. The men we lost in battle during the war paid that price as well. We *all* know some of them." He let his words take root in their minds. "They have given us a gift beyond value. You are *free*. Your wives are *free*. Your children are *free*. Every single one of us has a chance to create a life that the slaves before us could only dream about." He stopped, hoping his words were getting through. "What you do right now will determine if the price they paid was worth it."

Silence was the only response as they all looked back at him expectantly.

"When you were a slave, did you dream of never being beaten again? Did you dream of being treated like you were as human as the people who controlled you? Did you dream of living a life where there was no fear?" Passion reverberated through his words. "Did you?" he demanded, taking a moment to gaze at each man standing before him. Most met his eyes squarely, others looked away.

"My question to you this morning is, are you treating every person in your life the way you dreamed of being treated when you were a slave? Or have you become like the slave owners you hated so much and yearned to be free of?" Moses was aware of Simon's startled look, but he wasn't done. "Every single one of you has things to be angry about. There is nothing wrong with anger, because many times it gives you the motivation to change whatever is making you feel that way." He took a deep breath. "It's what you do with the anger that can create a problem. So I ask you again... Are you treating the people in your life the way you dreamed of being treated, or have you become like the slave owners you hated so much?"

Moses watched each man's reaction carefully. He saw thoughtful looks on the faces that registered agreement. He saw caged anger on other faces and knew he was looking at the men who were abusing their families. Pent up anger that intense demanded an outlet. His gut tightened as he thought of the women and children living in fear.

His eyes sought out Morah's husband, Abraham, and he saw what he knew he would. The man was a capable worker, but he carried an intense anger that seemed to radiate off him. Moses tensed even more when he watched as Abraham's eyes sought out Dexter. The two of them together were sure to mean trouble.

Moses understood Morah's fear that direct intervention could make things more difficult for her, but there was only one thing he knew to do. "From this moment forward, I want it known that no man who works on Cromwell Plantation will be abusive to their family. If I hear of anyone hitting or beating their wife or children, I will let them go immediately. I realize many of you are moving on at the end of the season. Some of you have already come to me about writing a letter you can show to the person you work for next. I'm more than happy to do that, but if I find out anyone is not treating their family right, you won't get that letter."

He stopped, searching for what else he needed to say. He could tell by the looks on the faces surrounding him that he had gotten through, but he felt like he was leaving things unfinished. "I know many of you believe your anger is justified. I agree with you. All of us have the right to be outraged about the years that were stolen from us," he said. "What we *don't* have the right to do is take it out on people who had nothing to do with it. The United States government has decided the black man is the head of the household. Maybe you believe that gives you power over your family. What that *really* means is that you have the *responsibility* for your family. You have the responsibility to treat them well and give them a chance to build a life different than anything they have ever lived. You have the responsibility to treat your wife as your equal because *she is*," he said. "Just because the government has decided men are better than women, that doesn't mean it's true."

Moses wished Rose could be present to hear him. He knew she would be cheering. He felt like doing the same thing. He'd had no idea what he was going to say when he began. He couldn't know if his speech would have the impact he hoped for, but he was confident he had been heard, and everything within him told him it had been powerful. He had done what Rose had requested him to do. It would have to be enough for now.

"Very impressive."

Moses turned toward Simon as the men dispersed to their work. "Thank you." He watched Abraham walk away, his face still an angry mask. "Do you think it did any good?"

Simon looked thoughtful. "I hope so, but only time will tell. June told me some of the women are suffering. The important thing is that you told the men the truth."

Moses shook his head. "But if it doesn't do any good..."

Simon interrupted him. "I didn't say that. What I said was that the most important thing was for you to tell them the truth. You're not responsible for what they do with it. You're going to need to understand that as you move forward."

Moses stared at him. "As I what?"

Simon chuckled. "You and I both know you're a born leader, Moses. Didn't you tell me when you got back from the riot in Memphis that you wanted to do more?"

"Yes, but..."

"Now it's your time to do more," Simon continued, not even acknowledging his interruption. "Every man here today was listening to you. I've heard lots of people talk before that weren't never heard. Every one of them heard you just now because you spoke in words they could understand, and you knew how to hit them with what you were saying. Now, I'm not a speaker, but I sure recognize one when I see one."

Moses opened his mouth to interrupt again, but Simon merely kept talking.

"It's time for you to do more than *talk* about being a leader for your people, Moses."

"I'm a tobacco farmer," Moses protested, despite knowing that his days as a farmer were numbered.

"And a good one," Simon agreed. "You've changed things for a bunch of men, but you're meant for something much bigger than this."

Moses turned his head to gaze out over the fields. There was a time when he would have refuted Simon's words, but he couldn't anymore. He also didn't know why he was still resisting. He and Rose had already made plans to go to college. He was already thinking about being a lawyer.

Why was he still so insistent that he was only a tobacco farmer? He knew the answer before he even asked it.

Fear.

The acknowledgement made him both angry and resolute. He was sick and tired of being controlled by fear.

"Boy. You don't neber stop bein' afraid. Fear done grab you when you least expect it, but you can always count on it stickin' its ole head in. Ain't nothin' wrong with fear long as you don't be lettin' it control you. The best thin' you can do is smile at it and then keep right on doin' whatever it is that is makin' you afraid. I reckon them thin's that cause you de most fear be the ones you be most meant to do."

Sarah's words roared into his mind with the force of waves pounding against the shoreline. The sound of them in his head was as strong as the day she had spoken them to him. And like before, the peaceful feeling came instantly. The anger faded away, but his resolute determination was stronger than ever. "You're right," he said.

"Yep," Simon replied, a smile flitting on his lips. "I know you said you and Rose are going off to college next year, but I was waiting for you to decide to accept it. Then I decided I might be an old man before you got around to it."

"I was waiting for it to seem real," Moses answered. "Not acknowledging it made it seem less real."

"You don't want to go?"

"I was *afraid* to go," Moses responded. "I'm not anymore." His decision to face leadership head-on had released an avalanche of feelings within him. Standing on that box and talking to everyone had given him a sense of satisfaction that nothing else ever had. He had been afraid of it, had been certain he wouldn't know what to say, but the feeling of making an impact with his words was one he wanted to experience over and over. Now he could acknowledge that.

"You have to do more speaking," Simon said.

"Yes," Moses replied, surprised when the agreement flowed so easily. "I'm just not sure how."

"You need to do a meeting at the school once a week."

Moses froze. "Excuse me?" Deciding to do something was one thing. Having the venue presented to him was something else.

"The only way to do more speaking is to have folks to talk to," Simon replied as though he was speaking to someone simpleminded.

Moses took a deep breath, pushing away the fear again. "I guess that is true," he managed.

Simon nodded. "I'll send out notice for the first meeting to be next week."

Moses forced another deep breath, his mind racing as he tried to think of a way out of Simon's proposal, while also admitting the idea gave him a thrill nothing else ever had. "Okay," was all he said, "but I think we have to wait until after the Harvest Celebration."

Simon thought for a moment. "That makes sense," he finally said. "But after that...the next Wednesday?"

"Wednesday," Moses agreed, wondering how it was possible to be terrified at the idea of speaking, while also wanting to be heard with all his heart.

Simon turned to walk away, but Moses stopped him. "There's something else I need to talk to you about."

Simon glanced toward the drying barns, about to suggest they talk later. He had a lot of work to do. The men in the barn knew their jobs, but he was proud of the fact he oversaw every barrel of tobacco that left the plantation. It was the only way he could be one hundred percent sure each delivery met Cromwell's quality standards.

"It won't take long," Moses interjected, "but I need to tell you something."

Simon turned back, intrigued by the sudden insistence in his friend's voice. "I'm listening."

"There's a possibility you will take over the management of Blackwell Plantation."

Simon's eyes grew wide. Whatever he had been expecting, it certainly wasn't this. "Come again?" His expression was one of bewildered confusion.

Moses chuckled. "You know Perry and Louisa Appleton are here on the plantation."

"Yes." Simon searched his brain for more information. "I know Louisa's family owned Blackwell Plantation, which makes her and Perry the owners now that her family is dead. I know things weren't going so well for them down in Georgia. I also know Louisa is like a fish out of water around here, because she has no idea what to do with black and white folks treating each other like normal."

Moses nodded. "All that is true." He had known June would tell Simon what was going on. He had been counting on it.

"It's also true that Perry Appleton thinks no nigger will ever be equal to a white man, and he thinks your idea of blacks working his plantation like they do here on Cromwell is crazy," Simon said bluntly. "I'm sure you understand why your statement about me taking over the management of Blackwell Plantation makes me wonder if you got kicked in the head by a horse."

Moses shrugged. "I think Mr. Perry Appleton is going to see the light."

Simon peered at him. "And you're basing this on...?"

"On a feeling," Moses admitted.

"A *feeling*..." Simon was back to thinking his friend had been kicked in the head by a horse.

"I know the look of a man struggling with his beliefs," Moses revealed. "He came out on the porch a few nights ago when I was finishing the report for Thomas. The numbers stunned him."

"They stunned me, too," Simon agreed, "and I was part of every back-breaking hour it took to make them happen. I told June how much money we are going to make, and she about fell over."

"Anyway, Perry might be a bigoted idiot, but he's a smart business man," Moses continued. "He can't argue with the numbers."

Simon considered what he had learned about the Appletons and then slowly but firmly shook his head. "No, thanks."

Moses cocked a brow, waiting quietly for him to say more.

"Me and June are real happy right here."

"You can make even more money over at Blackwell Plantation," Moses argued.

"I'm sure we could, but June wouldn't be around her mama, and little Simon wouldn't be around his grandma and his cousins. It's hard to buy something like that."

"But—"

Simon raised his hand. "It's more than that. I realize Blackwell isn't that far away, and I realize we could visit, so you don't need to throw that argument in the pot. The bigger reason is that I don't have any intention of working for a man who thinks he is better than me just because his skin is white. I've lived with that all my life. I'm done. He may figure out that I know how to make him a lot of money, but that doesn't mean he'll see me as anything but a well-paid slave. I like being somewhere where people see me as human."

"What if Perry changed?"

"I don't see that happening," Simon said.

"Thomas changed. Robert changed. I changed when I quit hating white people," Moses reminded him.

Simon hesitated. "That's true," he admitted.

"Let's wait and see how this plays out," Moses suggested. "If Perry doesn't change, then I will agree it's a crazy idea."

Simon shook his head as a sudden realization hit him. "Are you saying you don't want me to take over Cromwell Plantation when you and Rose leave to go to school?" He tried to push away the hurt feeling that tightened his throat.

"What I'm saying is that Rose and I aren't leaving until next year. What if something happened to delay us? This could be something for you right now. You would be in charge, and you could make a lot of money. I don't want you to miss the opportunity. Think of what you could do to your place with that kind of money. Think about what it would be like if you could buy more land."

Simon had just watched Moses push through his fears about speaking. What if he was hiding behind his own fears by not wanting to leave the comfort of the plantation? "We'll see how things play out," he said. "I'm not saying I will do it, but I'm also not saying for sure I won't." He managed a smile. "I don't even think I'll need to make a decision. Perry Appleton is never going to go for it."

Moses smiled. "I tend to agree with you, but I guess time will tell."

Louisa realized it would be incredibly rude of her not to help with the preparations going on for the Harvest Celebration. She had certainly commandeered enough celebrations at Blackwell Plantation over the years, but she had always been the mistress orchestrating slaves. She knew she had to acknowledge the changes emancipation had brought, but she couldn't find it within herself to be comfortable with them. She also couldn't find a way to be comfortable with strolling in to the kitchen and asking if she could help. She had been stuck in her room all morning as she tried to figure out what to do.

Not that being in her room was a hardship. She had not experienced luxury like this since she and her family had fled the plantation in the first year of the war. When she was in her small cozy home in Georgia, she hadn't missed it, but she could admit it was nice to be back in the world she had grown up in. She gazed around at the flowing white curtains and blue bedspread trimmed in white. Perry had laid a fire in the fireplace before he had gone out to the stables with Robert to go for a ride. Succulent smells were drifting up the stairway. If she closed her eyes, she could almost imagine none of the war had happened...or that she hadn't lost the only life she had ever known. *Almost.*

Nathan's smiling face appeared in the doorway. His blue eyes shimmered with excitement under a thatch of wild blond hair. Louisa had given up on trying to keep him neat. She didn't demand it at home, so why should she demand it here? She pushed away the uncomfortable certainty that it was because she was trying to keep up appearances for the *people*. There were no more *people* in the South.

"Mama!"

"Yes, Nate?' Louisa felt a rush of love as she looked at her son, who was the spitting image of his father. "What are you doing, dear?" Regardless of her own uncertainties, she knew Nathan adored being on the plantation.

"Amber said I could ride Patches, Mama! John said it was all right, too!" Nathan was so excited it seemed he could hardly breathe. "I've never ridden a pony before," he reminded her.

Louisa bit back a smile. "That is true," she agreed.

"So can I, Mama? Pleeasse..." he implored.

Louisa pushed down her feelings of discomfort again. It would have been common for the slaves to teach her son how to ride in the past. Why was she so uncomfortable with Amber doing it? Now, with her son's blue eyes begging, was not the time to analyze her reaction. "Of course, but you must do everything Amber tells you to do," she said.

"I will, Mama!" Nathan cried as he ran from the room.

Louisa smiled as she listened to his small feet pound down the stairs. She had also given up trying to keep her little ball of energy from running in the house. Full speed seemed to be the only tempo he was happy with. Her own mother had been insistent about proper behavior at all times, but she had a houseful of slaves available to enforce her wishes. Now there was just Louisa. She was, quite frankly, exhausted by the life she had suddenly found herself living. In Georgia, she had been able to leave the confinements of her past behind when it was just her, Perry, and Nathan on their farm together. Being back at Cromwell, and having Blackwell Plantation so close as a constant reminder, had placed a weight in her soul that she couldn't seem to shake. She could hear her mother's scolding voice and admonishments in every situation.

Annie appeared in the doorway. "There be a chill in the air this morning, Miss Louisa. Would you like some hot tea and scones?"

Louisa was hungry for just that, but she shook her head. "Thank you, Annie, but I'll come down for it." She longed for her old life of comfort, but she was acutely aware Annie was not a slave. She cringed inside when she realized she simply didn't know how to communicate with her. Annie wasn't a slave, but Louisa couldn't treat her as an equal. She supposed she could figure out a way to treat her as an employee, but Annie was Moses' *mother*. She wasn't an employee. She was simply a member of the household. A household Louisa was living in as a guest. Nothing in her whole life had prepared her for anything like this.

"You just don't know what to do with me, do you?" Annie demanded. Her voice was direct, but her eyes were kind.

Louisa tried to conjure up an adequate response, but she didn't have the energy. Living in this new world, with everything she had ever known ripped away from her, was suddenly more than she could handle. She shook her head. "No," she admitted. "I'm sorry."

"Ain't nothing to be sorry for," Annie replied. "I'm not real sure what to do with you, either."

Louisa blinked. "Excuse me?"

"You look at me and see a slave," Annie continued. "You ain't never had to treat a black person as an equal before. Well, I ain't never had to deal with a white person here in my own home who feels that way."

Louisa stared at her, more at a loss for words than ever. "I see," she finally managed.

"No, I don't reckon you do," Annie replied, only her eyes showing her discomfort. "You don't got no idea what it's like to have lived your whole life as a slave and have white people looking at you like you ain't really human. You don't know what it's like to have your children ripped away from you." She paused. "How you think you would feel if someone came and took Nathan from you?"

Louisa gasped. "I would never let that happen!"

Annie nodded. "You got that choice. I didn't," she said. "Now that I'm back with all my children and all my grandbabies, it's a treasure I don't take lightly. And I don't like someone comin' into *my* home and making me feel less than them."

Louisa stared at her, a small sliver of light forcing its way into her closed mind. "I'm sorry," she murmured, realizing with a feeling of shock that she meant it. "Truly, I'm sorry." She had no idea what to do with the feeling, but it was there just the same.

Annie eyed her closely and nodded. "It's a start," she said with satisfaction. "Now, you been stuck up in this room long enough. Why don't you come down and have some tea and scones with us? And then you can help us."

"Help you?" Louisa asked, feeling a little lost again.

"I know your mama taught you how to run a kitchen," Annie answered. "And I heard you ain't got no slaves down in Georgia, so you must know how to cook. How else do you feed your husband and son?"

"I cook," Louisa admitted, trying desperately to realign her thinking to her new situation. She was at Cromwell as a guest because Blackwell Plantation was not livable. Her old way of life was completely gone. Evidently, it was never going to come back. Certainly, she could swallow her old beliefs and pretend to accept a new way of thinking and living, even if she couldn't feel it. "I'll be happy to help," she said faintly, wondering what she had agreed to as she followed Annie down the stairs.

June and Polly were pouring tea and putting out hot scones when they walked in.

June looked up and gave her a pleasant smile. "I'm glad you could join us, Louisa."

Louisa smiled back, hoping her face didn't reveal her distaste at a black person calling her by her first name. Her slaves had always called her Miss Blackwell, or Miss Louisa. "Thank you for inviting me," she said courteously. She could tell by the flash of anger in June's eyes that the other woman had read her expression, but Louisa simply didn't know how to handle this. She reached for her cup of tea, hoping that having something in her hands would give her a feeling of control, however small.

"You closed the clinic today?" Annie asked.

Polly nodded. "The patient load is very light right now. I left a note saying to send one of the children from school to get us if there is an emergency. I wanted to be right here helping with the cooking."

"Me, too," June added, turning to Louisa. "Carrie told me so much about the annual tournament at Blackwell Plantation. The men have been working hard to get the arena ready for the competition."

Louisa nodded. She sincerely doubted anything could match the splendor of a Blackwell tournament, but she was wondering about something else. "The clinic?"

Polly smiled. "Carrie started a health clinic here before she went off to medical school. She didn't want to leave everyone high and dry, so she trained June and me to handle things while she's away. It's not the same as Carrie being here, but we can handle most things."

Louisa tried to absorb this new information. It had always been the role of the plantation mistress to handle the medical needs of their *people*. She had never even entertained the idea that blacks could offer that kind of care. "I see," she murmured, once again feeling completely lost and out of her depth.

Annie chuckled and handed her a scone slathered with butter. "You ain't got no idea how to live in this new world, do you?"

Louisa shook her head. "I guess I don't." It horrified her to realize how true it was. She knew better than to say it wouldn't be this way for long, but now she was wondering if that were true. All her neighbors back in Georgia insisted the blacks were incapable of caring for themselves. They assured her it was a matter of time before the whites were once more in control of the South, and then things would go back to normal. They had told her of plans all through the South to assure control would return to the whites, and that President Johnson was going to support them in making it happen.

In the time she had been here, she had become aware of how quickly President Johnson was losing any power to make things go his way in the country. She didn't pretend to understand the political side of what was happening, but she was smart enough to realize things were once again not looking good for the old Southern way of living. Perry had told her how profitable Cromwell Plantation was this year. He had come into their room almost bug-eyed with the news of the huge tobacco harvest. Now she was listening to two well-spoken black women talk about running a medical clinic for the community. It both humiliated and enraged her that she simply had no point of reference. She wasn't at all sure she *should* have a point of reference. The blacks here on the plantation must simply be unique. Certainly very few blacks were this capable.

Louisa looked up and saw Annie watching her closely. She flushed, certain the old woman could see inside her head. Rage and humiliation swelled her throat, threatening to choke her. She wished she could run out the door and pretend none of this was happening. The reality of how much the South had changed had not really touched her until now. The only difference for her and Perry when the war ended was that they hadn't had to worry about soldiers destroying their world anymore. She had felt comfortable on their farm, where she seldom thought of her old life. There was really nothing she had missed, because she had the things most important to her right there with her. Perry and Nathan filled her life with so much joy and love. When the cotton crop had been such a dismal failure, Perry had insisted they come to Virginia. She had suddenly yearned to see home again, not realizing every breath she took on Virginia soil was going to throw her old life in her face. She hated how inadequate and confused she felt in the world where she had once reigned.

"It's going to take all of us some time," Polly said.

Louisa stared in amazement as Polly reached out and took her hand. She had never in her life had a black person touch her of their own volition. She bit back a reprimand. She also reluctantly acknowledged that it felt good to be connected with a woman, even if she was a black woman. She let her hand stay where it was as she looked up in wonder.

"Did Robert ever tell you how he changed?" Polly asked.

Louisa shook her head silently. Perry had told her part of what Robert had revealed to him on the porch the first night they were there, but she was certain she only knew a fragment of the story.

"Me and my family saved Robert's life," Polly began quietly. "Moses brought him to us almost dead in the second year of the war. He lived with us until he could come home to Carrie."

Louisa went still, wanting very much to hear the story. "Please tell me," she whispered, not bothering to analyze why she wanted to hear it. The only thing she truly comprehended was that she wanted to find a way to live in this new world. Robert had been raised in the same world she had, and she knew his belief in slavery had kept him and Carrie apart. Something had obviously changed. She had seen Robert's glowing happiness. Now she wanted to understand it.

"Did Robert ever tell you that Moses' father was the one who killed his daddy?"

Louisa gaped at her. She had heard rumors of Robert's father being killed by a runaway slave, but she knew nothing more than that. "You're serious?" Her mind flashed to the close friendship Robert and Moses had. Even she could see it, and Perry had commented on it.

"They've come a long way," June said with a chuckle.

Louisa swung her head toward Moses' sister, drawn to the warm intelligence in the woman's kind eyes. "I want to know the whole story," she said, surprised to discover she wanted that more than anything.

The morning melted away as Polly told the story of how Moses had brought Robert to them after he'd been discovered almost dead on the battlefield. She told of the struggle all of them had faced to overcome their prejudices and fears. Her eyes glowed as she told of Robert taking his first steps, and tears filled her eyes when she spoke of the day he had ridden away. "None of us thought we would ever see him again," she admitted. "It's hard to believe sometimes that we are all living on this plantation together."

"When did Robert find out about Moses' father?" Louisa asked, completely caught up in the drama of the tale.

"A few months after the war ended," June revealed. "Robert almost died of pneumonia, but Carrie brought him back to life. Actually," she corrected, "Carrie kept him alive, but it was Amber who brought him back to life. He loves that little girl with all his heart."

Louisa knew that was true. She had seen the two of them together. She had heard their laughter drifting through the air from the stable.

"They worked it out," Annie said. "Both them men realized they had nothing to do with who their daddies had been or what they had done. They figured out that it don't do no good to live in the past. It will always be a part of who they are, but their lives will be about the choices they make *now*."

Louisa flushed, but she no longer felt rage and humiliation. She got Annie's message loud and clear. She also knew she felt completely at home with these three warm, loving women. They had every right to resent her because of her family and her own beliefs, but they had chosen to embrace her. As she realized what a huge privilege that was, she could almost feel the chains falling from around her heart. But with no words to express her revelation, she knew she still had a ways to go.

"Don't we have work to do now?" was the only thing she could think of to say.

Annie nodded, her eyes bright with approval. "That we do, Miss Louisa. That we do..."

Chapter Seventeen

Carrie was exhausted as she headed toward home. She had lost track of the days she had been going to Moyamensing, but the tide had finally turned. There had been more deaths from the cholera, but there had been many more people snatched back from the brink. People called her name now as Michael, who had become her exclusive driver, ferried her through the neighborhood. Biddy had kept a constant stream of the homeopathic remedies coming. Carrie, Carolyn, and several other of the Homeopathic College students who had offered to help dispensed them as quickly as they arrived. Janie had joined them for a few days, but she had also continued with her classes. Carrie had simply devoted all her time to the Irish of Moyamensing. She knew the day of reckoning would come in regard to medical school, but she didn't have the energy to focus on it.

The cholera hospital was still full, but there were no more from this neighborhood. She and the others had distributed camphor to those who were still vulnerable, but they had found no active cases in their rounds today. They had distributed veratrum to several households where they had trained the women to treat people if they became ill, and they had educated everyone they could talk to about how to avoid cholera in the first place.

If the dropping temperatures were any indication, Philadelphia was not far away from its first frost. Cholera always retreated with the arrival of freezing temperatures. Carrie hated to hasten the arrival of the city's brutal winter, but she realized it would save many people this year. She shuddered and pulled her coat tighter, grateful for the blanket Michael had insisted she put over her lap.

"You did good, Mrs. Borden."

Carrie heard Michael's words through a haze of fatigue. Now that things were under control, she was acutely aware of just how weary she was. She forced herself to look at him and smile. "I couldn't have done it without you, Michael. Without you getting the remedies... Without you picking us up every day..."

Michael nodded. "I told you I would do anything you needed when you saved my sister and nephew. I'm just glad I was there to help."

"It took all of us to save so many people," Carrie murmured. "Thank you." She fought her drooping eyelids, feeling almost desperate to get home, take a hot bath, and crawl into bed. She was quite certain she would be able to sleep for days.

She waved goodbye to Michael when he dropped her off, and then she turned to trudge up the stairs. She felt a vague appreciation for the brightly colored fall leaves dancing on the oak trees that lined the street, knowing they wouldn't be there much longer. In three days, she would go home to the plantation for the Harvest Celebration, and she could hardly wait. She had said she wouldn't go if the cholera wasn't under control, but Carolyn had assured her that she and the others could handle whatever came up. Carrie felt too empty to protest. Every part of her was drained and weary. She had much to deal with when she returned to Philadelphia after the celebration, but she was happy to keep pushing it back. In the meantime, she had done what she had set out to do—help the people of Moyamensing. Her own personal situation would have to wait.

She turned the doorknob and managed a small smile at the scrumptious aromas of fresh bread and soup. Her stomach reminded her how ravenously hungry she was. Delicious heat engulfed her as she took off her winter coat, hung it on the coat tree and stepped into the living room. The day had actually gotten comfortably warm, but a brisk breeze blowing in off the ocean since early afternoon had chased the Indian summer away. Carrie shivered and rubbed her hands together, eager to sit down and eat dinner before she went to bed.

"You're home."

Carrie looked up and smiled at Florence. "I am. Dinner smells wonderful."

Florence gave her a vague smile, but her eyes were shuttered. Carrie hesitated when Elizabeth and Alice both stepped into the living room with hard expressions on their faces. As weary as Carrie was, she was also acutely aware that her dreamed-of, restful evening was not going to become a reality. She had been grateful the last few weeks that no one had pressed her for information. They'd not had a chance. Carrie had returned home late each evening after everyone had already retired, leaving just as quietly early the next morning before the others were awake. Janie had been in her room a few times, but none of the rest of her housemates had sought her out. She had hoped to put off this confrontation a while longer, but it looked like that wouldn't be possible.

Carrie took a deep breath and straightened her shoulders. "Can we talk?"

"That would be a good idea," Alice said, her voice an odd mix of sadness and anger.

Carrie looked around. "Where is Janie?"

"We asked her not to be here tonight," Elizabeth said haughtily. "What we have to say doesn't involve Janie."

"And she agreed?" Carrie wasn't sure if Janie's absence was a relief or a disappointment. She longed for her friend to be here to support her, but she also didn't want to make things harder for Janie. Just because she had made her decision didn't mean anyone else had to follow her. Besides, she didn't know how to interpret Janie's actions the last few weeks. Had she decided to stay at the Female Medical College? Carrie realized they had talked of nothing substantial since the crisis in Moyamensing had begun. There had been neither time nor energy.

Florence shrugged. "We didn't really give her a choice..." Her voice faded off as the door whipped open.

Janie entered the room as Florence was finishing her sentence. "And I find I am no longer willing to let others dictate my actions and decisions," Janie said calmly. She stepped up next to Carrie and took her hand.

Carrie managed to keep from sagging with relief into her friend, but she squeezed Janie's hand to show her gratitude. "Shall we go into the kitchen? I'm happy to talk about whatever you want, but I haven't eaten since morning."

Alice scowled but did as Carrie asked. The rest followed and sat in the chairs around the large oak table.

Even though the atmosphere was stilted and cold, Carrie managed to eat around the lump in her throat, somehow forcing down the hot chicken soup. She knew she would need food to handle whatever was coming, though she took note no one else was making the attempt. She was also aware it would be impossible to force bread down her constricted throat, so she ignored it, her eyes fixed on her bowl while she ate. For a wild moment she wondered if a miracle would make the bowl bottomless so that she wouldn't have to face what was about to happen. She could just eat for the rest of her life. Carrie had known this time was coming, but she had hoped not to face it until she returned from Cromwell Plantation.

Eating the soup not only filled her stomach, it gave her time to think. Surely their friendship was stronger than a philosophical difference. A quick glance up at their faces, however, had her wondering. It had been a ridiculous hope that she could avoid this confrontation until after she returned. The very same women staring at her across the table were accompanying her to the Harvest Celebration. She had a brief thought that they might have decided not to come, but she quickly pushed it aside. All the women loved the plantation and had talked eagerly of returning. They would not be willing to miss the celebration.

Carrie eyed the bowl with sadness as she spooned the last bite of soup into her mouth, swallowed hard, and sat back. She calmly folded her linen napkin and placed it on the table. "I'm ready to talk."

Silence stretched out for several minutes. Still, Carrie waited. She had not asked for this confrontation. She would wait to find out what was on their minds.

"Aren't you going to tell us what you have been doing the last few weeks?" Florence finally demanded, her eyes flashing as brightly as her red hair under the glowing lanterns.

"I have a feeling you already know the answer to that," Carrie said. Weeks of watching people come back from the brink of death had only deepened her commitment to her decision. She would not be bullied, and she would not be intimidated. That sudden realization brought a surge of energy that pulled back the curtains of fatigue.

"Carrie, you've been down in Moyamensing dispensing homeopathic remedies," Alice said almost desperately.

Carrie nodded. "That is true." She could have added much more, but she wanted to see where the conversation was going. Were her housemates open to examining their beliefs, or were they just going to criticize?

"Don't you know that is forbidden by the American Medical Association?" Alice cried. "You'll be kicked out of medical school."

"Only if they do it before I withdraw," Carrie replied. A shocked hush fell over the kitchen. Janie gripped her hand beneath the table and gave it a squeeze. Her touch filled Carrie with courage. "I am planning on withdrawing when I return from the plantation." She could tell that her housemates had not seriously considered this possibility.

She watched them exchange glances as they tried to figure out what to say next.

"You've missed weeks of classes," Elizabeth said, her voice thick with accusation.

"I decided saving the people in Moyamensing was more important than going to class," Carrie answered. "I thought you would understand that since Biddy is so special to your family."

Elizabeth flushed. "Don't make this about Biddy," she said sternly. "What you've done is wrong."

Carrie gazed at her friend, surprised at the formal rigidity in her voice and posture, though she wasn't sure why she would be. Elizabeth's father was a physician. He had been very involved in the founding of the American Medical Association. He was also, though his position was unpopular at times, a champion of the Female Medical College. "How is it wrong?" she asked, forcing her voice to remain gentle.

Elizabeth stared at her. "You know it is forbidden for anyone associated with the American Medical Association to be involved with homeopathy," she said, her voice bordering on pompous.

"Which is a ludicrous position." Carrie realized nothing about this conversation was going to be pleasant, so she might as well dive in headlong. She had a sudden vision of herself as a young girl diving off of a boulder into the James River on a hot summer day. She had always felt it was a leap of faith, and she had always been surprised by the silky feel of the water enveloping her, and the rush of breaking free to frolic in the river. The only way to have that experience was to dive in. The only way to deal with what was in front of her was to do the same thing. "Have you been to the cholera hospital, Elizabeth?"

Elizabeth blinked and shook her head.

"I have," Alice said, sorrow lacing her words. "It's a horrible place."

"How many people have left there well?" Carrie pressed.

Now it was Alice's turn to blink. She thought for a moment and she, too, shook her head. "I don't know of a single person."

"That's because no one comes out of there alive," Carrie said. "The medicine we are taught to practice has no treatment for cholera."

"That's not true!" Florence said.

Carrie, now that she was pushed against the wall, realized she was more than ready for this. "Isn't it?" she asked. "Every remedy being pushed on the poor people of Philadelphia is nothing more than a mixture of high amounts of alcohol and opium. Oh, they throw some herbs in, but they are nothing more than a cover for what is really there." She saw Florence open her mouth in protest, but she kept talking. "The patent medicines being advertising in every newspaper in this city have never been proven to be beneficial, yet it is perfectly legal for people to advertise them and sell them. Have you seen the factory downtown? It's a bottling factory for Parker's Tonic." She paused and stared at Florence. "Do you know Parker's Tonic is over forty percent alcohol? *Any* ingredient, even if lethal or addictive, can be put into a bottle and legally sold without that ingredient being listed on the label. If that's not bad enough, many of these so-called medicines are also full of opium. I found people taking it down in Moyamensing because it is touted as stopping pains in the stomach and bowel complaints. When they started feeling ill from cholera, they were drinking a tonic full of alcohol and opium. No wonder they were dying!"

"I'm not sure what that has to do with anything," Florence said, only her eyes showing her sudden uncertainty. "You have broken the rules of the school."

Carrie stared at her, wondering if she had ever really known her friend. When had free-spirited Florence become controlled by rules? "The people of Moyamensing were *dying*, Florence. The cholera hospital was full of Irish people sent there to *die*." She took a deep breath. "I couldn't help them at the hospital because I wasn't allowed to. I *could* help the remaining people. So I did."

"Did you?" Elizabeth asked, skepticism dripping from her voice.

Carrie met her eyes. "We saved Faith from death. We saved close to two hundred other people who had already fallen ill with cholera. Only five people were too far gone for us to help. Every single one of them had been slated to be transported to the hospital. And we saved many hundreds more from coming down with cholera in the first place." Her resolve strengthened as the words flowed from her mouth. They had done all that. "The homeopathic remedies have been proven to work. *Proven*. I simply used what I read would work. And it did."

"But it was wrong," Alice insisted.

Carrie looked at her with disbelief. "It was wrong to save hundreds of people? How can you possibly say that? You're going to school to be a doctor. Doesn't that mean you want to help people?"

"Yes, but we have to help them with medicines approved by the American Medical Association," Alice responded, her voice sounding wooden and flat.

"Oh, I see," Carrie responded, not bothering to hide her sarcasm. She could feel her anger growing. "I was supposed to save them with medicines that don't exist? What you are really saying is that I should have turned a blind eye and let them die, perhaps taking Biddy and Faith with them. Would that have been better?"

Alice stared back at her with blue eyes full of pain and confusion. "Carrie, it's not that simple," she stammered.

"Turning your back on people and letting them die is never *simple*," Carrie retorted.

"You're putting everything the school is about in jeopardy," Florence said.

"How so?" Carrie asked. She knew the answer, but she was going to let Florence tell her. She hoped letting Florence hear it coming from her own mouth would enable her to realize how ridiculous it was.

"Several of our professors actually believe homeopathy can be effective, but they feel it is more important to gain the support of the American Medical Association if women doctors are ever going to be accepted and taken seriously," Florence answered.

"So being taken seriously is worth the life of hundreds of Irish people in Moyamensing?" Carrie pressed.

"There is sometimes a price to be paid for change," Florence responded. Her voice was weaker this time, but her eyes were just as stubborn.

Carrie felt sick. The fatigue pressed down on her again as she heard the words come from her friend's mouth. She looked around the table. "And the rest of you agree?"

Alice nodded hesitantly. Elizabeth followed with a firm nod of her own, though she couldn't erase the regret in her eyes.

Janie met her eyes squarely. "No, I do not agree with them, Carrie. I believe you did the right thing."

Carrie wished that was enough to ease the ache in her mind and heart, but it wasn't. Still, she was glad not to have to stand completely alone. "I will never agree that letting hundreds of people die a horrible death is worth *anything*. I chose to become a doctor because I want to heal people and help them stay healthy. If it is a requirement to ignore the suffering of people in order to become a doctor under the auspices of the American Medical Association, then all you have done is confirm I am making the right choice." She had come to grips with her decision during her days in Moyamensing. This conversation was doing nothing but confirm what she knew she had to do. She pushed aside her sadness and sense of loss as she looked at Florence, Elizabeth, and Alice. She dearly loved these women who had become close friends, but her integrity demanded she stand for what she knew was right.

"We have to move out," Florence said. "I have spoken with one of my professors about this. Living with you doesn't only put our own acceptance into the medical field in jeopardy. If we were to stay here, it would put the entire school in jeopardy."

Carrie stiffened. She wasn't surprised, but that didn't lessen the sick feeling in her gut. "Are all of you leaving?" she asked. It wasn't as if she needed them there, but she hated the wrenching feeling of losing people special to her.

"Yes," Elizabeth said.

Carrie gazed at her, full of baffled resentment at the medical association that felt it could mandate the beliefs and actions of every member. She had seen Elizabeth fight for equal rights for women. She had seen her endure humiliation to become a doctor. Her ability to do the right thing, however, seemed to have reached its limit.

She looked away from Elizabeth and let her gaze settle on Alice. "And you?"

"I have to go," Alice said, her voice barely more than a whisper. "I'm sorry."

"Sorry?" Carrie asked gently. "Sorry to leave here, or sorry you are making the decision to side with an institution willing to allow hundreds, and possibly thousands, to die because of ignorance and a ridiculous agenda against a legitimate practice, simply because it takes profits from their pockets and won't promote useless and dangerous drugs?"

Alice flushed and looked away.

"You're being arrogant, Carrie," Florence snapped.

"Am I?" Carrie asked, surprised her voice wasn't reflecting the wild pounding of her heart. "I have not said one thing that is not true. If you can prove me wrong, I will be more than happy to listen." She had a sudden flash of Abby talking to her on the streets of Philadelphia when she was struggling with her beliefs about slavery. The older woman hadn't judged her for not being able to let go of all she had learned growing up. Abby had given her time. She had loved her and merely asked questions. *She had given her grace.*

Carrie took a deep breath and spoke into the long silence that followed her challenge. "I'm sorry our differing beliefs and actions have brought us to this point. I am going to deeply miss all of you," she said. "I'm very grateful we had the chance to become friends, and I hope that somehow we can bridge all this and continue to be friends." Elizabeth stared at her with cold eyes, but Florence's face filled with sadness, and Alice made no attempt to hide the tears welling in her eyes.

Elizabeth turned to Janie. "Are you leaving the medical college, too?" she demanded.

Janie nodded. "Yes. I am."

Carrie felt a deep surge of relief that this wasn't going to come between her and Janie, but she could also see from the expression on her friend's face that it had been an agonizing decision.

"Why?" Elizabeth demanded. "You've been going to classes. Why are you going to throw this away?"

Janie took a deep breath and straightened her shoulders. "I almost didn't," she admitted. "I was afraid of taking another unpopular stand. It's not that much fun to be ridiculed and humiliated. When I feel it coming from my closest friends, it makes it even more difficult," she said. "In the end, I simply chose to do what is right for me."

Carrie watched as the impact of her words hit the other three women. Alice looked ashamed. Florence looked even more confused. Elizabeth, though her face remained hard, shifted her eyes away as she blinked back tears. Carrie realized this was just as hard for her housemates as it was for her and Janie. They were also doing what they believed was the right thing to do, but a disagreement didn't have to undo all their months of friendship.

Carrie reached out and grabbed Alice's hand while her gaze settled on the other two. "Just because the American Medical Association has mandated a policy against homeopathy, that doesn't mean they can control friendship. So what if we disagree? We can still be friends, can't we? We'll figure out a way to navigate this," she declared. "We're women. We have to stick together. I understand you have to move out because of the policy, but surely that doesn't mean you can't still come to Cromwell for the Harvest Celebration," she said persuasively. "We'll all have a wonderful time."

Alice and Florence both looked hopeful, but Elizabeth shook her head firmly. "I'm sorry, but I can't do that. I have waited a long time to become a doctor. I won't do anything to put it in jeopardy. My professors would not understand if I joined you."

Alice and Florence sagged with disappointment, but neither refuted her declaration. It was obvious who was in charge.

"So you are going to let the men of the American Medical Association dictate your friendships?" Janie asked. "Is that how you want to live your life? Are you really willing to give up all your rights?"

Elizabeth folded her arms and tightened her lips, but she said no more. Alice and Florence exchanged anxious looks, but they still wouldn't speak up.

A long silence suffused the kitchen. Carrie's heart filled with both compassion and sadness as she realized this might be the last time they would ever sit around this table together. Visions of meals ringing with laughter taunted her. Thoughts of talks late into the night as they learned each other's histories and life stories tightened like a boulder in her heart. She had known there would be a price to pay, but suddenly the price seemed too high. She squeezed Janie's hand and stood. "It's been a very long day. I am going to bed now."

Janie stood with her.

Silence followed them out of the room.

Moses reined Champ to a stop as he waved his arm over the fields. "Our biggest challenge will be keeping the fields fertile."

Perry nodded thoughtfully. "I've been doing some reading in the library. My understanding is that tobacco plants leech almost all the nutrients from the soil. In the past, farmers have had to keep cutting down trees and plowing new fields to continue growing tobacco."

"That's true," Simon agreed, still wondering how Moses had talked him into this tour of the plantation. He had to admit Perry had lost the arrogance that had oozed from him in his first few weeks on the plantation, but he had seen nothing to indicate the man didn't still consider himself far superior to him and Moses simply because he was white.

"So how did you have such a huge harvest?" Perry asked.

"This year was easy," Simon answered when Moses remained silent. He understood Moses was trying to make him carry this conversation. Fine. He would talk, but it wasn't going to do anything to change his mind about working at Blackwell Plantation. "The fields lay fallow throughout the entire war, with the exception of the small number of acres used to grow food crops for Richmond before Carrie had to flee. The land had time to rest and replenish itself. We put in last year's crop very late, so most of the fields were not used. They were ready to produce a hefty harvest."

"What about next year?" Perry asked keenly.

Simon smiled. He was enjoying the conversation, even if he wasn't particularly fond of the person he was talking to. He loved everything about farming. The joy of watching tiny transplanted tobacco seedlings grow into tall, strong plants never grew old to him. He had hated it as a boy, being forced to toil for endless hours without water under a brutal sun and under the constant fear of the whip, but now that he was in charge of the process, it had become pure joy. "We will fertilize the fields with marl," he said.

"Marl?" Perry asked.

"What do you use to fertilize cotton?"

"The cotton seeds are turned into cottonseed oil and meal. We use the meal to fertilize each of the plants." Perry's face held a mixture of anger and pain. "It's all I know how to do," he said as he stared out at the fields, "but that life is gone."

Simon felt an unwanted surge of sympathy. He understood that look of frustrated hopelessness, had experienced it many times himself, but he didn't want to feel anything other than resentment toward Perry. He pushed aside the thought that if he wanted Perry to change, perhaps he needed to be willing to change himself. "Then you have to learn something new," he retorted. He wasn't willing to feel sorry for Perry, but he was willing to give him information. "Marl is a natural fertilizer that consists of clay and calcium carbonate. It counters the depletion of lime, so it neutralizes soil acidity." Simon felt a flash of satisfaction when he saw the stunned surprise on Perry's face. "Marl beds are found all up and down the Virginia coast because it was once covered by the ocean. Marl pits have actually been found more than a hundred miles inland. The marl was formed by the breakdown of rock and the buildup of seashell, animal, and plant remains. It's actually a mixture of sand, clay, azote, magnesium, iron, and limestone."

Perry stared at him. "How do you know all this?"

"I read." Simon tried to temper the sarcasm in his voice, but he knew it was there. Perry flushed and looked away. To his credit, the flash in Perry's eyes seemed to be more embarrassment than anger.

Moses bridged the sudden silence. "Edmund Ruffin was largely responsible for introducing marl to Virginia's tobacco farmers. Ruffin and Thomas were once friends."

Perry looked thoughtful. "I seem to remember Edmund Ruffin being rather staunchly Confederate."

Moses chuckled. "From what Thomas has told me, that would be putting it rather mildly. As time went on, Ruffin and Thomas drifted apart because their views were so radically different. That didn't change the fact, however, that Ruffin's work saved most of the tobacco farming in Virginia."

"Doesn't Ruffin live around here?"

"He did," Simon said. "He found it difficult to live with the changes in the South after the war ended."

"He lost everything," Moses added. "All the fields at his Marlbourne Plantation in Hanover County were salted by Union troops during the war. When the war was over, he had nothing, and he was also sick. He had no money, but mostly he didn't know how to live in the new South."

Simon could tell by the expression on Perry's face that he understood how Ruffin had felt.

"What did he end up doing?" Perry asked.

"He shot himself last year." Simon had no sympathy for a man who had once owned over two hundred slaves, but he had enough compassion to sympathize with Perry's shock.

A long silence fell on the three of them. Simon was happy not to speak. He felt no compulsion to encourage conversation with Perry Appleton. He settled back in his saddle and gazed out over fields bordered with the vivid colors of fall leaves. His favorite were the maple trees showing off their bright red and orange clothes, but the deep yellow of the poplar and oak trees was a close second.

He watched as birds flitted through the dogwood trees to grab the bright red berries. Hawks soared over the empty fields, their keen vision ferreting out any mouse or rabbit foolish enough to venture out in daylight. He was sure Blackwell Plantation was beautiful, but he was also certain nothing could compare with Cromwell.

Perry broke the silence by pointing toward a group of workers in the distance. "What are they doing? I thought the harvest was over."

Simon, knowing Moses was going to remain silent, looked in the direction he was pointing. "They are beginning to apply the marl. The best time to do it is right after the harvest so that it enriches the soil all fall and winter. The ground will be ready to plant next spring."

Perry frowned. "Should we be doing that over at Blackwell?"

Simon shrugged. He would talk about Cromwell, but he wasn't willing to engage in conversation about Blackwell Plantation.

"There is no need," Moses replied. "Your fields have been fallow for almost six years. You won't have to do anything to ensure a good harvest next year. They are in good shape."

"How do you know that?" Perry asked.

"I went over there to find out," Moses said.

Perry looked confused. "Why would you do that?"

"Because Robert asked me to."

Simon heard the unspoken words. *I only did it because Robert asked me to.* He could almost feel sorry for Perry's puzzlement. Simon and June had late night conversations about the changes Louisa was experiencing, but both of these people shared deep-seated prejudices that neither particularly wanted to give up. They might someday be forced to act differently if they wanted to live in the new South, but that didn't mean they would change how they truly felt. Carrie, Thomas, and Robert had had a complete change of heart. He didn't see that happening with Perry and Louisa. His certainty that he would never work for this man grew firmer.

"You really believe Blackwell can be profitable?" Perry asked. He merely glanced at Simon before looking at Moses.

Simon sighed. He had seen Moses play dumb on the battlefield before. It had been his way of forcing Simon into leadership. He didn't really appreciate it any more now than he had then, but he knew they would sit there in silence unless he said something. "Any plantation can be profitable if it is handled correctly," he said, not really caring if he hurt Perry's feelings or offended him. The man was asking a question. He would answer honestly.

Perry stiffened and reluctantly swung his eyes toward Simon. He finally seemed to realize Moses was choosing to remain silent. His expression said he didn't appreciate it any more than Simon did. "And what is *correctly*?" he asked.

Simon shrugged. "Moses has already told you that. I don't see any reason to repeat it." A flash of anger flared in Perry's eyes, but he tightened his lips and remained silent. That was when Simon saw something he didn't necessarily want to see. Vulnerability. It settled in Perry's eyes and twisted his face with something akin to grief before he turned away to stare out over the fields again.

Perry had lost everything when Sherman's Army swept through Georgia. The man had only owned a few slaves, but only because he had no money to buy more—not because he thought it had been wrong. As far as Simon was concerned, Perry was no different than the men who had owned him before the war. Yet he also knew men could change. He had seen it. Who was he to determine who it would or wouldn't?

Moses again broke into the silence. "Those men applying the marl will only be here a few more days," he said.

"Oh?" Perry asked, obviously clueless as to why Moses was telling him about the men.

"Those men all have tobacco farming experience, and they served with me in the army. I wish I could hire them on full time, but there isn't a place for them after the harvest. They will be moving on."

Simon was watching Perry carefully. He knew the minute the Georgian made the connection. Moses was allowing him to discover for himself the men who could help him save Blackwell Plantation.

Perry shaded his eyes for several minutes, watching the men as they worked. Spurts of talk and laughter were carried to them on the breeze. The sun flashed on strong muscles and intense faces. All the men had gained weight during the summer. They were fit, and anyone watching them could tell they were capable. He finally turned to Moses. "You said you would tell them not to work for me."

"I did," Moses agreed. "Can you give me a reason to tell them differently?"

Perry hesitated a long moment and then answered Moses' question with one of his own. "I have to protect my family. If I have a group of men working Blackwell Plantation under the same conditions as Cromwell, will I be putting them in danger from the vigilante groups?"

Moses stiffened. "I suspect you know the answer to that better than I do," he said. "What are their plans?"

"I don't know," Perry answered, "but I've heard rumors they intend to take control of the South again."

Simon watched Perry closely. As far as he could tell, Perry was telling the truth. "What does that mean?"

Perry turned to him, his blue eyes clear, although his face was deeply troubled. "I'm not totally sure, but I've heard talk that they have plans for the freed slaves *and* the white people who help them."

Simon and Moses exchanged a look full of meaning. They had long been hearing the rumors, but having them confirmed by a white man made them much more real and dangerous.

Moses was the one to respond. "Then I guess you have to decide if your family is safer in Georgia where you have no way to make a living, or safer here on Blackwell. You could also sell and take what you get. No one can blame a man for protecting his family."

Simon fought the bitterness rolling in his gut. At least Perry had that choice. There was not a black man in this country who could make a choice that would remove him and his family from danger. It would find them wherever they went.

The Georgian's eyes widened with sudden, shocked understanding. The understanding was followed by a deep look of shame that morphed into pained sympathy. "I'm sorry," Perry said. "Truly."

Simon remained silent, but he felt himself relax a little. It was a beginning.

Chapter Eighteen

Louisa looked around the schoolhouse, more than a little bewildered to find herself there. Earlier that morning, John had proudly announced to Nathan that he was going to school with his mama. Nathan had immediately demanded he be able to join his friend. Rose had agreed but suggested it would be helpful if Louisa came along to help watch the boys while she taught. Nathan had been so excited by the idea of going to school that she hadn't had the heart to say no. So here she was, a lone white woman in a school full of black children. To say she felt like a fish out of water would be putting it mildly. She watched as the school filled with eager-eyed boys and girls. They all looked her way with wide-eyed curiosity. Many of them smiled shyly, but none of them spoke to her. That was just as well, because she had no idea how she would have responded.

Her family's people had never been allowed to read or learn anything. Louisa had believed the explanation that blacks were incapable. She had a quick vision of a time when she could not have been more than six or seven. She had just begun reading lessons with her tutor. Louisa had asked her mother why none of the black children were learning with her. Her mother had carefully explained that blacks were much less intelligent than she was. They weren't capable of learning or of doing anything more than their work on the plantation. That was why white people had to take care of them. Most of the time they could treat them with kindness, but there would be times they would have to discipline them just like they might small children because that's all they really were. Louisa had listened carefully and had certainly had no reason not to believe her.

Louisa shook off the uncomfortable memory and gazed around the simple but well-built schoolhouse. June and Polly had told her about the fire that destroyed the first one. She controlled the shudder that came with the idea of being the target of white vigilantes. She had no desire to be on the receiving end of that kind of anger and hatred. And why should she? She had been born white by no choice of her own. Why should she feel responsible for people who had been born a color that put them in a lower class? It wasn't her fault that she was white. It wasn't her fault that others were born black.

Rose stepped to the front of the room, interrupting her thoughts.

Louisa watched as the children immediately quieted and straightened at their desks.

"We have two guests today," Rose began. "Louisa Appleton and her son, Nathan, are going to be with us at least through lunch."

"And me, Mama!" John yelled, his eyes dancing with excitement.

"And you," Rose agreed, her face soft with love. "We are very glad to have all of you here."

Louisa smiled at the sight of Nathan sitting beside John at a small table next to Rose's desk. He was sitting straight, his eyes locked on her just like the rest of the students. She doubted he would sit still like that for long, but she was grateful for whatever respite she could have from his rambunctious energy.

"In honor of John and Nathan being with us today, I have asked Felicia to start us off with her lesson."

Louisa's eyes widened. Felicia? Rose's ten-year-old daughter? Teaching? She bit back a smile, certain this was an example of the inadequacy of black education.

Felicia stepped to the front of the classroom. "We're less than a month away from the Leonid Meteor Shower," she stated enthusiastically.

Louisa stared at her. What was she talking about?

"Since Mrs. Appleton has just joined us, I'll remind everyone that the Leonid Meteor Shower happens on November thirteenth." She looked directly at Louisa. "Have you ever seen a shooting star, Mrs. Appleton?"

Louisa hid her discomfort and nodded graciously. "Why, yes."

"What you actually saw was a meteor," Felicia explained. "On November thirteenth, you will be able to see hundreds, even thousands of them in one night," she said. "They seem to come down like rain from the night sky. It happens every year, but every thirty-three years it is more intense than ever. This year is the thirty-third year!" Felicia was almost breathless as she delivered this piece of news.

The only thing Louisa could do was nod as she watched the little girl with fascination.

Felicia turned back to the class. "November thirteenth is going to be a very special night, but the entire month of November is known for meteor showers. Just look up every time you are out at night next month. The odds are that you will see a meteor," she said with confidence. "November has more activity than any other month. The last big Leonid Meteor Shower, in 1833, did more to spawn the study of meteors than any other single event. Lots of people saw it and talked about it. Now, more and more people want to know about meteors."

Louisa realized, much to her surprise, that she was one of them. The only thing she couldn't understand was why she was learning it from a little black girl who had watched her parents be murdered. A little girl who was obviously very intelligent and extremely well-spoken. Now, perhaps more than at any other time since she had arrived in Virginia, she felt lost and adrift. There were times she felt like she was getting her bearings, but then something would happen to shift everything again. This was one of those times.

"A few of you have asked me if it is dangerous to watch a meteor shower," Felicia said. "I remember asking my mama that same question when I was little. She didn't have any way of knowing *why* she was telling me the truth, but she told me I had nothing to be afraid of. I believed her. Now that I'm a meteor observer," she said proudly, "I know the why."

Louisa's mouth gaped open. *A meteor observer?* What was that, and how could a little black girl be one?

"I told you last week that shooting stars are really chunks of rock that have broken off from a comet. Now sometimes...there *are* meteors big enough that they don't burn up in the atmosphere, so they crash into the ground." She paused when everyone in the room gasped. "Those are called meteorites, but that is something that hardly ever happens," she said emphatically.

"The meteors that make up a meteor *shower* are actually quite fragile," Felicia continued. "They burn really hot and fast. The most important thing to understand is that none of them will reach Earth. They will burn up long before that happens." She smiled as whispers of relief filled the room. "We'll all be fine as we watch them fall."

"What if it's cloudy?" Louisa burst out, almost appalled when she realized she was asking a black child for information, but she realized she was quite eager to view what Felicia was describing.

Felicia frowned. "I've been praying real hard that it won't be, Mrs. Appleton. If it is, we won't be able to see anything."

"But I want to see it!" one of the children cried. Every other head was nodding vigorously.

"I do, too," Felicia responded, "but we don't always get what we want." Her voice grew very serious, and her eyes darkened with an understanding far beyond her age. "We can hope for the best, and then figure out how to live with what actually comes. I'll be sorry if we don't get to see the Leonid Shower, but I can still choose to be happy. "

Louisa was speechless. Felicia's words resonated in her soul. They gave her courage, but they did far more than that. She could almost see the wall erected around her heart and mind. Her morning with Annie, June, and Polly had started it's dismantle, but her time here was causing the bricks to tumble ever faster.

Felicia turned back to the class. "The Leonid Meteor Shower has the very fastest meteors. That means they are very bright, and when they streak across the sky they have an excessively long tail. I read that some of the ones in 1833 lasted for several minutes!"

Louisa *oohed* with the rest of the class before she caught herself. Falling bricks or not, she still had an image to maintain. She straightened and composed her face, but she caught the knowing smile lurking in Rose's eyes. Louisa stiffened briefly and then forced herself to relax as she realized it was nothing more than an automatic response and not something that she actually felt. Nathan was having a wonderful time and she had learned something new. Without even thinking about it, she smiled at Rose.

Rose's eyes widened with surprise, but the smile she sent in return was warm and genuine.

Louisa stood in the doorway of the school as she watched the children play outside, dashing through the trees in a wild game of tag. Nathan raced freely among them, his wide smile indicating his delight. His laughter was easy to pick out from everyone else's. White children playing with blacks was nothing new to her. There were times she had played with the plantation's slave children when she was growing up, but her parents had been very diligent about letting her know she was better than they were, and as she grew older it was not allowed. What had confused Louisa when she was younger simply became the way things were. She had felt affection for some of their slaves, but she had easily drawn the lines that separated them. It was effortless because she understood they were different.

Louisa watched Nathan thoughtfully. He had never been taught any of those things. Growing up on the farm, he rarely saw other children, and certainly none of them had been black, because there had been no slaves. She had been watching him with John since they had arrived on the plantation. When they became best friends, she had pushed aside her discomfort, thinking she would be able to teach him the truth when they left Cromwell. Now she wasn't sure she knew the truth at all.

"It was good to have you here today, Louisa."

"Thank you, Rose. It's been a very interesting day."

"Interesting in what way?" Rose asked.

Louisa cocked her head, seeing something in Rose's eyes she couldn't quite interpret. Suddenly, she realized all this had been planned. Rose had known seeing Felicia teach would challenge who Louisa thought the little girl was. When Nathan had insisted on coming, Rose had seen her chance. To Louisa's surprise, she didn't feel angry—merely impressed that Rose had found a way to corner her.

Rose seemed to realize she had been discovered. "I did believe you would find school interesting," she said with a quick smile. "I'm sorry if you feel manipulated."

"Managed, perhaps," Louisa murmured, "but I wouldn't say manipulated. You've been talking with Polly and June."

Rose didn't deny it.

"You knew listening to Felicia would show me how wrong my beliefs are," Louisa continued, realizing that it had. It shocked her to see a big pile of the bricks from her wall lying tumbled at her feet.

"I was hoping it would," Rose admitted.

"Why do you care?" Louisa demanded, wanting very much to understand why Rose, Polly, and June weren't treating her the way she certainly would have if the roles had been reversed.

Rose took a deep breath and met her eyes squarely. "Because of our children."

Louisa stared at her. "I'm not sure I understand."

"You and I grew up in a different world. Your family owned slaves. My family *were* the slaves. All of us were taught different things that allowed us to live in the world we were born into. I'm sure you liked your world much more than I did," Rose said, "but the point is that you weren't born with your beliefs. They were *taught* to you. If you hold on to your beliefs and pass them to Nathan, he's going to have a hard time living in the world the way it is now. It's the same with my John. I can't teach him about how to survive as a slave. I have to teach him about how to make the most of his life as a free man." Rose paused. "And, I have to do what I can to change the thinking of white people so that the world John grows up in is better than the one I did."

Louisa listened carefully, struck by Rose's wisdom.

"There were times when I was growing up that I hated everybody in my world who was white," Rose said. "It took me until I was in my late teens to let go of that hate and try to see people just as people. I can't change how most white people see blacks, but I'm hoping I can help *you* change, Louisa. The only way I can do that is to let go of any resentments I still have, and see you as a person who is scared of the future and trying to make the best decisions for her family." She took a deep breath. "Responding to prejudice with prejudice will never do anything to change how things are in our country."

Louisa considered her words. "How did you become so wise?" she asked, still trying to process what she had heard.

"My mama," Rose said, her eyes bright with love. "My mama was the wisest, most loving person I ever knew. She helped me quit hating, and she taught me how to live. I owe everything I am to her. Whatever wisdom I have, it's because of her."

Louisa had loved her mother, but they had never been close. Her mother had taught her how to live in a white world and how to be a capable plantation mistress, but she certainly never taught her about loving and living. In the end, her mother had simply given up on life because she couldn't figure out how to live in the new world that had been dumped on her.

Louisa shifted her eyes to the schoolyard, watching as Nathan disappeared around a tree while a little black boy chased him in wild pursuit. Nathan's laughter made her smile, and it also made her realize the stark truth of what Rose was saying. "Do you hate being black?" she asked.

Rose considered her question for a long moment. "No. I don't hate being black, because this is the way God made me. I'll admit there are many times I think about how much easier it would be if I was white...if Moses was white...if my children were white...but I don't hate being black. That would be like saying God made a big mistake. I guess I don't believe he did." She paused, a funny look crossing her face before she continued. "Besides, I'm only half black."

Louisa gasped. "What?"

Rose nodded. "As long as we're talking honestly, you may as well know that Thomas Cromwell is my half-brother. His father raped my mother. I was the result."

Louisa simply had no words. No idea of what to say. The first thought that flitted into her mind was that a white man could not *rape* a woman who was his property, but just as suddenly she realized how sick the very thought made her feel inside. Looking into Rose's warm, intelligent eyes, she had a clear picture of how terrified her mother must have been when she had been violated. "I'm so sorry," she whispered, perhaps more surprised than anyone to realize she meant it. Then she had another thought. "That's why Moses owns half the plantation," she murmured.

Rose's eyes narrowed. "Moses is half owner of Cromwell Plantation, because he is the best tobacco farmer in Virginia. Thomas knew his profits would increase if he put Moses in charge."

Louisa felt an immediate flash of embarrassment. "I'm sorry! I didn't mean..."

Rose held up her hand. "It's all right. I realize you didn't mean it the way it sounded. And while Moses *is* the best tobacco farmer in Virginia, it's also true that Thomas did such a radical thing because Moses is my husband. He deeply regretted the pain my family suffered because of his father's actions." She smiled. "It's going to take all of us some time not to respond with knee-jerk reactions. White people do not hold the monopoly on prejudice," she admitted with a twitch of her lips.

Louisa nodded. "Being here has turned my whole world upside down," she confessed.

"Even more than the war?" Rose asked.

Louisa considered the question. "Actually, yes. I knew how to think and feel during the war. I was fighting to protect the only way of life I'd ever known. Now, that way of life is gone. The only thing left are the feelings and beliefs..." Her voice trailed off as she struggled to examine her thoughts honestly, shocking herself when she no longer saw it as appalling that she was doing it with a black woman. Somewhere along the way, without even realizing it, Rose had simply become a woman. "Those feelings and beliefs no longer have a place in my life," she said, smiling with relief when she realized her words were true.

Rose gazed at her. "I believe you mean that."

Louisa nodded and grinned. "I believe I mean it, too." A feeling of freedom swept through her as the remaining pieces of her walls crumpled under the weight of her new beliefs. She reached out and took Rose's hand. "Thank you," she said softly.

Rose smiled, grasped her hand, and nodded toward a nearby tree. "Look at them," she said.

Louisa glanced over, her heart melting when she saw Nathan and John, their heads almost touching as they knelt down to examine something they had discovered under the tree. Nathan's blond hair glowed in a stunning contrast to John's curly black hair. The game of tag had ended. The other children were resting in the shade and eating their lunches. Their two boys were off on a new adventure. "We'll help them navigate a new world," Louisa vowed.

A sudden clattering on the road caused Rose to stiffen and turn around. The children all went still—even little John, who stood up and turned to watch.

Louisa watched as a group of horsemen galloped down the road toward them. Her stomach tightened, though she couldn't have explained why, when they began to slow. They craned their necks to glare in the direction of the school, and Louisa saw several of their eyes widen when they caught sight of her. Her stomach clenched even more when their eyes narrowed into angry glares. She didn't recognize any of the men, but that didn't mean they didn't recognize her. She hated the idea that it bothered her.

"Go inside," Rose said.

Louisa, ashamed of herself that she wouldn't stay and stand her ground beside Rose, turned and entered the school. She hurried to a window and peered out as the horsemen pulled to a stop, talking among themselves. Several of them were waving their arms, but she couldn't make out what they were saying. She didn't need words, however, to know they were angry.

Rose remained on the porch, her slim body erect as she gazed out at the road. A simple motion of her hand had all the children filing silently into the school. All of them took their seats except Amber and Felicia.

The two little girls slipped out the narrow door built into the back of the school and broke into a run, the woods swallowing them in seconds. Louisa realized they were running to the plantation for help. The knowledge made her throat go dry. Visions of the school in flames filled her mind, but she pushed them aside. Without knowing how, she was certain the men were angry because of her. The thought terrified her.

The children were all sitting at their desks. Their eyes were wide with fright, but no one made a sound. One of the older boys stood and moved next to the door leading into the woods, his eyes trained on Rose through one of the windows. Louisa was certain he would help evacuate the children if the men took one step toward the school.

Rose continued to stand proudly, her head held high. Louisa took a deep breath, certain Rose shouldn't be alone. Humiliation that she was hiding in the school like a coward swept over her like a wave cresting in a storm. She lifted her head in defiance and moved toward the door.

Just before she stepped out onto the porch, the men turned and galloped off. Louisa watched Rose sag against the column and realized how frightened she must have been. She slipped up next to her and laid her hand on her shoulder. "What was that about?" she whispered.

Rose didn't answer. She glanced toward the children staring out at them and shook her head. "Later," she whispered back.

Rose took several deep breaths and entered the classroom. "Everything is fine," she said to her frightened students in a reassuring voice.

"Them the same men who burnt our school?" one little girl called.

"*Are those* the same men who burned our school," Rose responded.

Louisa was amazed Rose could still think to correct grammar after the fear of the last minutes. She was quite sure she wouldn't be able to, yet she couldn't even identify why she had been so frightened in the first place by a group of her own people riding by the school. There had not seemed to be an obvious threat, but she had a quick understanding that Rose, her children, and every innocent-looking student in the school, must live with fear all the time.

"*Are those* the same men who burned our school?" the little girl demanded with a quavering voice.

Rose walked over to kneel down in front of her and took the little girl's hands. "I don't know, Bonnie," she said honestly. "But I *do* know nothing is going to happen right now."

Rose couldn't possibly know that, but Louisa watched the children gradually relax as they stared at the teacher they trusted. Her respect for Rose jumped by leaps and bounds.

"Why are we hiding in the school?" Nathan asked. "Me and John wanted to play more," he added, his little face set with petulant defiance.

It was John who answered his question. "It's okay, Nathan. There be some people in the world that don't like black people very much."

Nathan looked confused. "I'm not black."

John thought about that for a moment. "But being with black people makes you *almost* black," he explained.

Nathan seemed to accept the answer with no trouble, but the truth of it hit Louisa between the eyes with the same force of the bricks that had crumbled from the wall around her heart and mind. She gasped, stark fear filling her. She wanted to grab Nathan and run from the school so fast and far that no one could be a threat to them ever again. She began to tremble when she realized that wasn't possible. What had she done by coming here today? Had she made herself and her family, including her innocent son, a target?

Rose cast her a sympathetic look and stepped back to the front of the class. "I'm going to end school early today," she said. "I don't believe there is any danger, but all of you are far too precious to me to take a chance. You all know how to slip through the woods to get home safely. Stay off the road today and go straight home. If you hear anything, hide in the woods until you know it is safe. We will have school tomorrow."

Louisa watched as the children nodded solemnly. Their eyes were still fearful, but their faces were set with determination. This was obviously something they had practiced or experienced already. They all lined up at the back door and then slipped through one at a time. Sibling groups joined together, disappearing into the woods quickly. She watched until the last child, except John and Nathan, disappeared. "They have done this before," she said as she turned to Rose.

Rose nodded. "There are times it has been necessary. Sometimes I do it just as a drill to make sure they are prepared when there is a need." She knelt down next to where John and Nathan seemed to be frozen to their desk, both faces a mask of uncertainty and fear. "It's okay, boys." She handed both of them a piece of chalk. "Would you like to draw on the board?"

John brightened immediately. "Really, Mama? Can we draw anything?"

Rose nodded. "Anything," she assured him. "We're going to wait here until your daddy comes."

"Daddy is coming?" John asked in a delighted voice. "Promise?"

"I promise," Rose said.

John nodded, all his fear disappearing at the promise his daddy was on the way. "Come on, Nathan. We can draw anything we want on the board! None of the other kids get to do *that*! We don't have to be afraid. My *daddy* is coming!" Nathan, heartened by John's sudden courage and confidence, nodded happily, grabbed the chalk from him and headed for the board. They chattered and laughed as they drew pictures of the birds, rocks, and trees they had discovered that morning.

Louisa shivered as she looked out the window, praying Moses would appear. Some part of her understood Rose was afraid to walk back through the woods alone, but she tried to push that aside because it only made her more frightened to imagine what Rose might be attempting to avoid. "Are you afraid all the time?" She hated the fear turning her muscles to jelly, but she didn't know how to fight it.

Rose looked her in the eyes. "I wouldn't say I am *afraid* all the time. I would certainly say I am aware every minute of every day that something could happen. I'm not responsible for only myself. I am also responsible for a classroom of children. I can't ever let my guard down."

Louisa appreciated that Rose didn't sugarcoat it. "Was John right? Did I put Nathan and myself in danger by being here today?" Sick fear pulsed through her when Rose hesitated. "Please tell me the truth." She didn't want to hear it, but she knew she must.

"Your family was at risk the moment you decided to stay on Cromwell Plantation," Rose replied, her voice both direct and sympathetic. "You needed a safe place to stay, but I can guarantee you there are people who know you and Perry are living here. In their eyes, it means you support what is happening at Cromwell."

Now was not the time to discuss whether she and Perry supported it or not. "What kind of danger are we in?" Louisa demanded.

Rose shook her head. "I can't tell you that," she admitted. "I know Thomas and Abby have guards. So do Jeremy and Marietta."

"Jeremy is Thomas' brother, too?"

Rose's eyes flashed. "Yes."

"Why do they have guards?" Louisa was afraid to know the answer, but she had to face this squarely if she was to find a way to protect her family.

"Jeremy has been beaten badly by men who don't like his support of blacks. Abby has been threatened, and all of them have received threats in the mail."

"And Marietta?"

Rose sighed. "The same people who hate black teachers seem to hate white ones even more when they come down here to teach the blacks. They see it as a betrayal of their race."

"That's ridiculous," Louisa snorted. She wasn't sure when she had decided she felt that way, but it didn't really matter. She took deep breaths to steady her nerves. "Do you live like this all the time?"

Rose raised a brow. "If you mean do I live with the knowledge that my family is in danger every day, yes. But

I've lived that way all my life," she said. "I lived knowing I could be beaten for learning to read. I knew I could be sold away from my mama. I lived knowing that Carrie would always be considered a better person than me simply because of her skin color." She took a deep breath. "I hoped the end of slavery would mean I could quit being afraid, but in some ways it is worse. When I was a slave, I only worried about what my master or overseer might do to me. Now I have to watch for every white person who is angry because I'm free." Her eyes darkened with grief. "I feel safe on Cromwell most of the time, but I realize trouble is always out there. Our decision to run Cromwell the way we do has only made us more of a target."

Louisa stopped breathing when she had a sudden and illuminating vision of what Rose was describing. "I never understood," she said, a dark anguish burying her fear as she caught a glimpse of Rose's life, and with it, the life of the millions of slaves who were now free.

Rose took her hand. "I am glad you understand, but I want to emphasize that you are in danger, Louisa. I wouldn't have allowed you to come today if I had thought of the possible consequences. I'm sorry."

Louisa gripped her hand and tried to steady her nerves. "Who were those men?"

"I don't know," Rose admitted. "I can usually recognize a few of them, but these were men I had never seen before."

Louisa watched her carefully. "And that worries you."

Rose shrugged, but she couldn't hide the deep concern in her eyes. "They may not be from around here," she said.

"Which means...?" Louisa pressed, trying to hide her impatience.

"I don't know for certain," Rose replied, "but they could be vigilantes." Her voice faltered on the last words.

"Vigilantes?" Louisa's eyes narrowed. "I think I have heard Perry mention something about them, but I also suspect he has been trying to protect me by hiding knowledge of who they are."

"Most of them are Confederate soldiers who still believe they have a war to fight," Rose revealed. "It seems they have decided to do it by fighting against the things they believe are changing the South from the way it used to be."

"Meaning blacks and the whites who don't believe the way they do?" Louisa knew the answer even before she heard it, but speaking the words was giving her a chance to process them.

"Yes."

Louisa turned and stared out the window, relieved when the road remained empty. Her ears strained for the sound of approaching horses, but she heard only the laughter of two small boys. "When is Moses coming?" She was finding it difficult to stay calm. "Why don't we go home through the woods?"

Rose shook her head. "I'm not sure that is a good idea."

"Because you're afraid they are waiting in the woods for us?" Louisa demanded as her throat tightened even more. She fought to keep her voice low so that she didn't scare the boys.

Rose blinked and sighed. "I just don't know, Louisa. If it was just me, I would walk home. I'm not willing to put you, John and Nathan at risk."

"And you believe we're safer here?"

Rose shook her head again. "I don't know," she admitted, her face crumpling for a moment before she composed it again. "I hate being afraid," she said, her voice gruff with anger. "I am so *sick* of being afraid!" she whispered, raw fear shining from her eyes for the first time.

Louisa had a sudden realization. "You're afraid something has happened to Felicia and Amber because it's taking so long."

Rose's shoulders sagged as she stared out the window, but she remained silent.

Chapter Nineteen

Silence echoed through the schoolhouse as the minutes ticked by. John and Nathan, frightened now by their mothers' tense silence, left their chalk and crawled into their laps.

Rose pulled John close to her breast, trying not to frighten him any more than he already was, but her heart was pounding so hard she could barely hear herself think. She certainly wouldn't be able to detect if there were hidden men approaching right that minute. She once again considered dashing out the door and running through the woods, but something held her where she was. She could only hope it was God giving her wisdom instead of fear keeping her from taking action that would save them. She also knew there was a possibility the men had simply ridden off down the road, but she was too afraid to risk finding out. So she sat.

Louisa gazed at her over Nathan's head, but she remained silent, too.

Rose felt a moment's awe that she felt so connected to this woman who had once been Carrie's worst enemy. She had seen the transformation happen in Louisa's eyes while they were talking. While she was glad for that, she also hated the reality of the increased danger it put Louisa and her family in. She hated the danger *all* of them were in. Was there to be no end to the threats and peril? Her thoughts took a different direction. Why was the government simply allowing the South to run rampant over the millions of slaves they had controlled for so long? What had been the purpose of the war? What had been the purpose of all the lives lost? Suddenly, anger pushed back the fear.

Rose drew a deep breath and stood, thankful her legs were no longer quivering. John was almost too big for her to carry anymore, but she held him close against her. "We're going to the plantation," she declared. She wasn't sure if it was wise to let the anger force her fear to the side, but she was quite certain she couldn't sit there one more minute and wait for what may or may not be out there.

"You're sure?" Louisa asked shakily.

Rose was suddenly positive they needed to take action. "Yes," she answered. She wasn't going to voice her fears for the boys to hear. She was simply going to move. She walked toward the door and stepped out. A sudden rustle in the woods made her freeze. The rustling grew louder, but she was too frightened to discern which direction it was coming from. Rose eased back inside, pushing Louisa and Nathan back with her. Fear once again swallowed her courage.

"Quiet!" she hissed, even though no one was making a sound. Louisa and Nathan had frozen into statues, and John was pressed into her so hard she could almost feel him melting into her.

Moses stepped quietly out of the woods on Champ. Rose gasped with relief and sagged against the door of the schoolhouse. She began to tremble when Moses' eyes caught hers across the clearing. He vaulted off Champ and ran to them, grabbing them close in his arms. Moments later the schoolyard swarmed with twenty of his men as they poured from the woods. All of them were armed with pistols or rifles.

Rose pressed her face into his chest as Moses held her and John close. "Thank you," she whispered.

"What happened?" Moses asked.

"Some bad men were here!" John cried. "They scared Mama, but I knew you would save us!"

Before Rose had a chance to explain further, Robert, Perry and Clint burst from the woods on their horses, their guns drawn. Louisa gave a cry of happiness and ran to Perry, reaching him just as he dismounted.

"Thank God," Perry murmured as he pulled his wife and son into his arms.

"What happened?" Moses asked again. "Where are the rest of the children?"

"I sent them home," Rose said as she fought to gain control of her breathing. When she could talk clearly, she explained what had happened.

"You've never seen any of them before?" Robert asked. "Are you sure?"

"I'm sure," Rose replied, her insides settling down as she realized no one was going to attack a large group of armed men. "I watch every white person who passes the school. I've never seen any of those men before." She caught the look Moses sent Robert, but she didn't press for more information. John and Nathan, both clinging to their fathers, were frightened enough. All she could think about was getting them home to safety. "We'll talk later."

Moses understood. He turned and spoke to Simon. "Stay here with at least ten of the men through the night."

He didn't have to say he was afraid the men might come back. Rose was simply glad there would be someone protecting the school. She watched the long look he exchanged with Simon, assuring him without words that Moses would make sure no harm came to June and his son.

Carrie waved goodbye to Michael as he pulled the carriage away from the platform at the Philadelphia train station. She hugged her coat closer and reached for her bag. The colorful, tree-lined streets had melted away into gray industrial development, and the wind whipping up the river had dropped the temperature. Indian summer was clearly something for the history books now. The city still wore its fall wardrobe, but the cold temperatures said winter was on the way. Bright leaves were twirling through the air on their way to forming a blanket that would soon be covered by snow. "I'm so glad to be getting out of this city," she muttered.

"You and me both," Janie agreed as she hoisted her bag.

"You're sure you don't want to wait and come with Matthew later?" Carrie asked for the third time since Janie had told her that morning about Matthew's delay.

"Do I have to write it in blood?" Janie teased.

Carrie smiled, but she was still concerned. "I know you're worried about me, but I will be fine. I *am* fine." Watching their three former housemates have the last of their things moved from the house this morning had been a final, wrenching blow, but there was almost relief in having it finished. At least when she returned, she would not have to look at the ghosts of her former friendships.

"Did you ever consider I'm doing it for me?" Janie asked.

Carrie stopped walking and swung around to look at her. "What?"

"You may have started the ball rolling that resulted in our withdrawal from the Female Medical College, but I made my decision on my own," Janie said, her voice a mixture of patience and frustration.

Carrie cocked her head, not sure she had ever heard Janie sound like this. She had watched her friend change after her disastrous marriage to Clifford. Janie had become stronger and more confident when she decided to go to medical school. Now that she was engaged to Matthew, she seemed to have a strength and power Carrie wasn't sure how to describe.

"You are not responsible for the world, Carrie Cromwell Borden," Janie scolded. "And I am not responsible for *you*. I just happen to want to be with my best female friend while I'm dealing with the fact that the three women I thought were my other closest friends have turned their backs on me because they don't agree with *my* decision." Her voice faltered as sadness darkened her eyes. "I need to be with you, Carrie," she said. "I love Matthew, but he can truly understand only part of what has happened. He's a man—an incredibly sensitive man—but he's still a man. I need to be with the woman who is also my best friend."

Carrie dropped her bag. Mindless of the horde of passengers swarming around them, she swept Janie into a hug. "I'm sorry! As usual, I was only thinking of myself." Remorse flooded her heart. "I am so very glad you insisted on coming that I don't have words to express it. I didn't want to make the trip by myself," she admitted.

Janie dropped her own bag, returned the hug, and then stepped back to examine Carrie's face. "Truly?"

Carrie managed a smile. "The last few days seem to have knocked the wind out of my sails. I'm glad to be going home, but I don't know how to release the pain in my heart right now."

"We'll make it like old times," Janie promised. "We may not have a window seat to curl up on like we did during the war, but we'll have our own room on the train. We'll talk everything through until it doesn't feel like a weight anymore."

Carrie wasn't sure that was possible, but she acknowledged there were many times during the war she had felt even worse than she did now. Their late night talks had always soothed her and given her courage to move forward. She hoped this would not be the exception.

"I can't believe your father got us our own separate seating section," Janie continued. She picked up her bag, waited for Carrie to grab hers, and then began to push through the crowds toward the loading platform.

"Me either," Carrie replied, her gratitude increasing as she saw the masses of people waiting on the platform. The train was going to be full, but instead of having to sit on hard wooden benches crammed in with all these people for the entire trip to Richmond, she and Janie were going to have their own small room. Even if they had the same rigid benches, the unexpected solitude was going to be a luxury. "We should have plenty of space," she said, forcing her voice to sound light. "The room was reserved for six, but there will just be the two of us. I can still hardly believe trains have advanced enough to offer private rooms."

"Are they quite expensive?" Janie asked.

Carrie shrugged. "I imagine they must be, but Father tells me the factory is doing extremely well, and the tobacco crop was the best the plantation has ever had." A surge of joy pushed through her sadness as she thought of what the crop's success would mean to Rose and Moses, as well as all the rest of the workers. She was sure the Harvest Celebration was indeed going to be grand. She wanted to enjoy it, but her heart was still too heavy.

"Do your father and Abby know about what we have done?"

"No. I sent a telegram yesterday, but I didn't explain the situation. I just told them only you and I would be coming." Carrie knew there would be a barrage of questions when they reached Richmond, but she didn't mind. There was nothing she wanted more than a long honest conversation with Abby. She was looking forward to being with her father, too, but Janie was right, there were times you needed another woman.

Janie nodded but said no more as the crush of people pressed around them. The shrill whistles and the sound of trains arriving and departing made it impossible to talk once they reached the platform. Conductors yelled out instructions as metal wheels screeched on the rails. The air was thick with coal soot from the engines, and wood smoke from the heaters blazing in each car to keep them warm. As eager as Carrie was to get home, she wished there was a more pleasant way. Trains were a blessing, but she found the whole experience stifling and suffocating. She kept her thoughts fixed on the fragrant, fresh air waiting for her on the plantation.

Janie had been right. When Carrie stepped off the train in Richmond, most of the weight had been lifted from her heart. She still felt sad over what had happened, but she no longer felt she would be crushed. They had talked through every aspect of the situation. They had laughed together and cried together. They had even made plans, suddenly realizing they had empty rooms for some of the students from the Homeopathic College if they were needed.

Carrie took a deep breath as she walked across the platform. The air had the same coal and wood aroma, but it wasn't as thick and cloying as the atmosphere in Philadelphia. It was also quite a bit warmer. The air was crisp, but it didn't hold the whisper of winter lurking around the corner. She smiled as she glanced up and saw the riot of colors lining the hills of the city. The downtown area was still mostly bare of vegetation after the fire, but she knew the city leaders were busy replanting trees to replace the ones that had been lost. In the meantime, the oaks, maples, and poplars crowded on the hills made it seem as if the city were ringed by fire. "Home..." she whispered.

"I wish we could pick up the school and move it right here to Richmond," Janie said wistfully.

Carrie nodded, her eyes scanning the platform. Her heart leapt with happiness when she saw her father's silver hair bobbing through the crowd. When their eyes met above the throng of people, her own filled with tears. It had only been a month and a half since she had last been home, but it felt like she had lived a lifetime in that span. She waved her arm wildly before she gripped Janie's hand and pulled her through the crowd.

"Carrie!"

"Father..." Carrie's words caught in her throat as she threw her arms around him. She was a married woman in medical school, but at this exact moment, she felt like a little girl who needed her daddy.

Her father held her tightly for a long moment before pushing her back and peering down into her face. "Are you all right, dear?"

Carrie gazed back at him, but the words stuck in her throat. She caught her father's worried glance at Janie over the top of her head. "I'm fine," she managed. She laughed shakily. "I missed you."

Her father's eyes were still worried, but he released her to embrace Janie. "Welcome home, Janie."

"You have no idea how glad we are to be here," Janie replied.

Thomas' expression said he knew something was going on, but all he did was nod. Then he waved to a porter to carry their bags, led them to the carriage and gave them both a hand up to their seat.

"Where is Abby?" Carrie asked. The disappointment pulsing in her heart told her how much she had counted on Abby being there to greet them.

"At home preparing a feast with May." Thomas shook his head. "I should have listened to her. She said she felt she was supposed to come, but I knew how much she had to do before we leave in the morning, so I convinced her to stay."

Carrie could tell how worried her father was. That knowledge gave her the strength to find a genuine smile. "I'm fine, Father. We just have a lot to tell both of you."

"I imagine you do, since we were expecting six and got two," Thomas said dryly.

"You got my telegram?"

"Yes, but all it did was create questions with no answers," he quipped before he turned to Janie. "Where is Matthew? Please don't tell me he's not coming."

"He'll be on the last train in tonight," Janie assured him. "Things are heating up as the election draws closer. His editor asked if he would stay behind to work on some articles. Matthew wouldn't miss the Harvest Celebration for anything in the world."

Thomas snorted. "He wouldn't miss being with you on Cromwell for anything in the world," he corrected her. "Matthew Justin is a smart man."

Carrie chuckled as Janie's face glowed with happiness. "You're right as usual, Father." She could feel herself relaxing as the carriage rolled through the autumn-colored streets. As she leaned back against the cushioned seat she became aware of the lone horseman riding closely behind them, a rifle straddling his lap. "Father...?"

Thomas followed her eyes. "That is Howard. He accompanies me everywhere I go," he said.

"Has something more happened?" Janie asked with a gasp.

"No," Thomas assured her.

Carrie gazed at Howard, liking the calm confidence radiating from his dark eyes. He gave her a solemn nod before his gaze once more scanned the road for any hint of trouble. "Have things gotten worse?" she asked. She held up her hand before her father answered. "And please don't invent something to make me feel better because you're worried about me. I would much prefer the truth."

"Nothing has happened," Thomas stated again. "But...I imagine that is only because of Howard and Burl."

"Burl is Abby's guard?" Carrie asked.

"Yes," Thomas replied. "Jeremy has Mitchell. Either Eddie or Spencer stays close to Marietta." He shook his head. "There are times I believe we are being too cautious, but I am also aware things are becoming increasingly tense as the South realizes they are about to lose President Johnson as their advocate. He'll still be president, but the Republicans are sure to take control of the Congress next month. The South won't be the same after that."

"And the people here blame the blacks, but they also blame the whites who support them," Janie said.

Thomas cocked a brow. "You must be engaged to a reporter," he replied. "You're quite well informed for a medical student."

Carrie could tell the humor in his voice was forced. "Do the vigilantes you are being protected from not realize increased violence will only intensify the consequences for the South when the Republicans take control?"

Thomas sighed. "I'm afraid they're not thinking any more clearly now than they did before the war began." His eyes were dark with trouble.

Carrie was tired of it all. Tired of thinking about what she had left behind in Philadelphia. Tired of what was happening in Richmond. Tired of what may be coming in the South. "No more," she blurted. "I know I started this conversation, but now I'm going to end it. We all know there are bad things happening in the world. I don't want to hear any more of it." She wanted to take back the words as soon as she saw her father's expression. He was watching her *carefully.* Just like he did when she had been a petulant child, or when she had been too overwhelmed with life during the war and thought she would snap under the stress. "I'm sorry," she said contritely as she grasped his hand. She breathed a sigh of relief when she realized the carriage was making the final turn onto his street.

"It's quite all right," Thomas replied carefully.

Carefully. Carrie gritted her teeth as the carriage rolled the last hundred yards.

She was out of the carriage even before it had stopped, laughing as she ran up the stairs to where Abby waited with open arms. Carrie was horrified when her laughter turned to gulping sobs as soon as Abby's arms enfolded her, but there was nothing she could do to stop them. Abby remained silent and held her more tightly, one hand stroking her back. Carrie heard her father and Janie walk up onto the porch, and she heard the squeak of the door as they entered, and the thump of luggage as they deposited it into the hallway for Micah to take to their rooms, but still she held on to Abby.

Finally, the tears abated as calm returned to her heart. Evidently she had not cried enough tears on the train. She lifted her head from Abby's shoulder. "I'm sorry." She knew she didn't need to apologize, but she couldn't think of anything else to say.

"Nonsense," Abby scoffed, though her gray eyes were almost black with concern. "Every mother wants her grown child to cry on her shoulder, especially one as strong as you are. It tells us we are needed."

Carrie smiled. She had loved her mother, but she had always dreamed of the type of relationship she had with Abby. "I love you," she whispered.

May stepped out onto the porch. "You plan on crying all the way through my dinner?" she demanded, her eyes glowing with worry as they stared into Carrie's. She opened her arms wide and enveloped Carrie in a warm embrace. "I swear, I ain't letting you go back to Philadelphia if you gonna come home like this. Don't they know how to treat folks up there? I tell you, them Yankees don't know how to do things right."

Carrie laughed out loud, so glad to be home she could feel it expanding her heart. "Did you make apple cake?" she asked hopefully.

May cocked her head. "I might have."

"Warm apple cake with burnt sugar frosting?"

Thomas eased open the door and poked his head out. He looked relieved when he saw smiles on all their faces.

"Anyone who causes dinner to be late doesn't get apple cake," he teased.

Carrie felt cleansed by her tears. She hoped they were the last ones she would need to shed, though she suspected she would cry again when she felt Robert's arms around her. She would feel like a weakling if Janie had not already told her she had cried buckets of tears with Matthew in the last week. Her overwhelming emotion was gratitude for people who cared about her.

"I wouldn't dream of delaying your dinner, May," Carrie said happily as she wrapped her arms around Abby and May's waists. "Let's eat!"

May grinned. "That's my girl! Mr. Jeremy and Miss Marietta just came in the back. I told them you were having a sob fest on the porch with Miss Abby and gave them some hot biscuits to keep them in the kitchen."

"May!" Carrie wasn't sure whether to laugh or cry again. Did everyone need to know when she was an emotional wreck? She looked up and saw two sets of eyes staring at her from around the corner of the foyer. She decided laughter was the best course of action. "Get out here!" she ordered, laughing harder when Jeremy and Marietta rushed out onto the porch to grab her in a hug. Janie was close behind them.

The sun was setting behind the hills in the distance. Its golden glow imparted an even more brilliant color to the trees. A gentle breeze whispered through the magnolia, the leaves rustling against her shoulder. Her beloved city was coming back to life a little more with each passing day. She heard the laughter of children playing in the streets and the sound of mothers calling them in for dinner. It was the gentle rhythm of a Southern town finding itself again after a brutal war.

Everything important to Carrie was right here in Virginia. She pushed back the knowledge she had to return to Philadelphia in ten days. She had been grateful to discover the new session for the Homeopathic College wasn't going to start until November first, but she dreaded the idea of returning north.

A long silence fell over the dining room table. The dishes had long ago been emptied and cleared. The windows had been closed against the evening chill, a fire had been lit and was now glowing brightly, and the lanterns filled the room with a cheerful light.

"Let me get this straight," Thomas said. "You and Janie have both quit medical school and are now at the Homeopathic College."

Carrie nodded. She knew their long story had been overwhelming. There had been some questions for clarification, but no one had interrupted once they started talking.

"And you're quite sure this is what you want to do?" Thomas pressed.

"I'm quite sure it's what I *have* to do," Carrie said, not certain what the expression on her father's face was communicating.

"As am I," Janie agreed. "I told you how much I disagreed with Carrie in the beginning, but I realize now that I can't practice medicine any other way."

Carrie turned to Abby. "You haven't said a word since we started talking. What do you think?"

Abby smiled. "Do you know of a Dr. Joseph Hobson?"

Puzzled, Carrie shook her head. "No. Should I?"

"Dr. Hobson is a homeopathic doctor here in Richmond."

Carrie stared at her. "That's not possible..." she murmured. "Homeopathy is almost completely contained within Pennsylvania and New York."

"*Almost* would be the operative word there," Abby replied. "Dr. Hobson established his practice here in 1858. He left during the war but returned almost as soon as it ended."

"But how...?"

"How would I know about homeopathic medicine? My dear, I've been involved with the women's rights movement for quite a long time."

"And those are the very women who have caused homeopathy to spread so much through the North," Carrie finished for her. "Elizabeth Cody Stanton?" she guessed.

"She gave me my first homeopathic kit," Abby agreed. "She also sent a letter of introduction to Dr. Hobson. He is quite a remarkable man."

Carrie gasped, her thoughts spinning. "Why didn't you tell me?"

"About homeopathy?" Abby's voice was gentle. "My dear, you had decided you wanted to be a doctor. You seemed quite clear of the direction you wanted to go, and after years of surgery at Chimborazo you were certain you wanted to include that in your practice. There was no room for homeopathy in that course of action. I am well aware of the stance traditional medicine has taken against it."

"Yet surely you believe homeopathy is much more effective," Carrie cried.

Abby remained silent, but her expression was answer enough.

"You should have told me!"

Abby shook her head. "My job is to support your decisions, not try to direct them."

Carrie absorbed her words. Unbidden, visions of her mother trying to force her into the role of a typical plantation wife crowded her mind. She had long ago forgiven her mother for not understanding her, but the memories made her even more grateful for Abby. "Thank you," she whispered.

Thomas had been listening carefully. "And you're both quite sure you realize the consequences of your decision? I'm not saying I don't support you. I just wonder if you know what a difficult path you seem to have chosen."

Carrie laughed. "When have you ever known me to do anything else?" Now that the story was out, she could feel herself relaxing even more. She also felt surer than ever that she had made the right decision.

"And I seem to be becoming quite adept at it," Janie quipped. "We've already paid a high price, Thomas. Losing our housemates was quite a blow. We're still stunned that our decision would cause us to lose them as friends, but it doesn't change what we know is right."

"Losing your friends is one thing," Thomas replied, "but have you really thought through the professional ramifications?"

"Such as our professors not acknowledging us in the hallway when we went to withdraw?" Carrie asked.

"Or other students not willing to even look at us?" Janie added. "Yes, we have thought it all through. If anything, we have decided that something so threatening must be quite powerful. If they didn't think homeopathy makes many of them look bad, they wouldn't be so threatened by it." She frowned, her blue eyes laced with sadness. "I have lost respect for women I once held in high regard," she admitted. "I don't understand how they can refuse to help people they could make well with a different approach."

Carrie sighed. "The most important thing is that I can wake up every day knowing I am doing my best to make patients well."

"And to *keep* them well," Janie added passionately. "Standard medicine—what they call allopathic—focuses on healing people once they get sick. Homeopathy puts its focus on helping them not get sick in the first place."

"For what it's worth, I completely agree with you," Marietta said.

Carrie turned to look at her. "Why?"

Marietta grinned. "Two of my uncles are homeopathic doctors."

"What?" Janie exclaimed.

Marietta nodded. "Two of my cousins became very ill with typhoid in the first year of the war. They both almost died."

"Until someone treated them homeopathically?" Carrie asked with excitement. Now that she was away from the strained atmosphere in Philadelphia, she was free to relish the joy of her new discoveries.

"Yes. One of my uncles had been a pharmacist. The other ran a grocery store. Both of them went to school to become homeopathic doctors because they wanted to help people. They both have thriving practices now."

Jeremy raised a brow. "I learn something new about you every day."

Marietta grinned. "That's just the beginning of my family secrets," she teased. "We'll be married long before you meet any of them. It will be too late for you to run away screaming."

"As if anything would make *that* happen," Thomas scoffed. "I'm afraid you're stuck with this young man, my dear."

"I'm counting on it," Marietta said.

Abby cleared her throat. "I'm still curious about something. I know you were down in Moyamensing helping with the cholera hospital when it was burned down. And I know that is where you met Biddy and Faith, who are both wonderful women, by the way—though you hardly need me to confirm that." She paused, obviously trying to fit the pieces together in her mind.

Carrie tensed, waiting. She had suspected Abby would be the one to press further. She wasn't sure she wanted to delve into this subject now, but she supposed it was as good a time as any.

Abby was watching her closely. "Why were you the one to feel such a compulsion to help the people in Moyamensing? I know you have an incredibly caring heart, but it seems like it was something more than that since you put your entire career at risk to help them."

"I owed it to them," Carrie said.

Abby continued to gaze at her. Carrie felt like the older woman was pulling back the layers of her heart to discover what was really there.

It was Thomas who broke the silence. "I don't understand. How could you owe the people of Moyamensing anything? You didn't know them."

Carrie took a deep breath, certain she wasn't ready for this conversation, but she didn't know how to put it back in the bottle now that it was out. "What do you know about Oliver Cromwell, Father?"

"Oliver Cromwell?" her father echoed in a confused voice.

"Oliver Cromwell, the Lord Protector of England," Carrie answered. "Our ancestor."

Thomas shook his head. "Carrie, I..."

"I didn't know anything either," Carrie responded. "All I knew is what you told me when I was a child, which is what you were told by someone who had probably been told the same thing. I was taught that Lord Oliver Cromwell was a very important man. Someone we should be very proud to have in our heritage."

"That's true," Thomas agreed.

Carrie felt sympathy for what she was about to say to her father. She couldn't imagine he would receive the truth any easier than she had. "Lord Oliver Cromwell was not a good man," she said. "He is *not* someone I am proud to have as an ancestor."

Thomas stiffened. "What have you been told?" he asked. "I assure you..."

Carrie held up her hand. "I heard it first from Biddy and Faith." she admitted. "I believed what they told me, but of course I had to discover the truth for myself. I wasn't just treating cholera patients while I was down in Moyamensing." She glanced at Janie because she hadn't told her friend this part. "I was also researching our family history. Biddy has a library full of history books. I kept digging until I was confident I knew the truth." She paused, understanding all too well the strained look in her father's eyes. "We can talk about all the details another time," she offered. She was aware, though, that Abby's question had not been answered.

"Moyamensing is primarily Irish," Carrie continued.

Abby nodded, her eyes still questioning. "I was aware of that, but..."

Carrie wished even more that she had not started this conversation, but she was aware there was never going to be an easy time. "Lord Oliver Cromwell was largely responsible for sending thousands of Irish to serve as slaves here in the United States before blacks were used," she said. She could probably be communicating this in a more sensitive way, but she was suddenly exhausted. "He single-handedly destroyed almost all of Ireland," she said heavily, the weight pressing on her once again. "Every person I treated was here in some way because of his actions. Philadelphia was going to let them die." She took a deep breath. "I owed them because of what my ancestor did."

"Carrie!" Her father half rose from his seat, his face flushed with anger. "I will not have—"

Carrie stood. "I'm sorry, Father. I know I'm handling this badly. I shouldn't have talked about it when I'm so tired. I've not said anything that isn't the truth, but if I were you, I'm sure I would be feeling the same way you are right now." She held him with her eyes, knowing he was feeling the same angry confusion she had felt when she first discovered the truth. "Biddy gave me permission to bring some of her books with me. You're welcome to read them."

Carrie stepped back from the table. "I'm sorry to ruin a lovely evening. I'm going to my room now."

Silence followed her.

Chapter Twenty

Carrie was waiting on the window seat when Abby knocked. She had known her stepmother would come. As tired as she was, Carrie hadn't been able to sleep because of everything thrashing around in her heart and mind. She'd had a moment of wondering if her father would seek her out, but she innately understood he would need time to process what he had heard. He would also be aware she needed Abby. "Come in," she called as she pulled the blanket around her. The October night was cold, but she was too starved for Virginia air to close herself in. She held up another blanket for Abby and shifted her feet to make room.

Abby snuggled into the blanket and leaned over to gaze up at the stars twinkling in the night sky. "It's beautiful tonight."

"So I didn't totally ruin it?" Carrie asked. "I realize my timing was bad."

"You were answering my question," Abby replied. "I doubt there could have been good timing to share what you have learned about your heritage."

"No..." Carrie said, her head resting back against the wall so she could see the stars dancing between the blowing leaves.

"Your father is downstairs reading."

Carrie straightened. "Really? I'm surprised."

"You think he doesn't want to know the truth?"

"I thought he would have needed more time before he delved in. I certainly did," Carrie confessed. "I felt like my whole world had turned upside down when I learned about Oliver Cromwell."

"Did Biddy know who you were when she told you about him?"

Carrie shook her head. "She knew me as Carrie Borden. The night of the fire was rather chaotic, and we hadn't gotten around to complete introductions yet. We seemed to dive right into intense conversation when we asked her to share her story. Not that my maiden name would have revealed anything. There are plenty of Cromwells in America." She paused, remembering. "More than anything, I think she regretted dumping it on me."

"It was a long time ago," Abby replied, reaching out to touch Carrie's leg. "You seem to be taking it very personally."

"I suppose I am," Carrie admitted. "I've told myself I'm not responsible for what happened hundreds of years ago, and I know that to be true but..."

"But?" Abby prompted.

"I don't feel responsible for the past," Carrie said, "but I do feel I discovered the truth, because I'm meant to do something with the present, and hopefully, impact the future." She had read the *Bregdan Principle* every day she had been in Moyamensing. Every time she read it, her desire to know her life mattered in a positive way intensified.

"That's a rather heavy burden," Abby protested.

"Sometimes," Carrie murmured. "Then I think about all the people I saved in Moyamensing, and it feels like nothing but a privilege. The Irish have suffered so much because of Lord Cromwell. I feel privileged to be able to do *something* to begin to redeem the past."

"I'd say saving hundreds of their lives was more than just s*omething*," Abby observed.

"Not really," Carrie said. "It doesn't begin to undo the harm that was done."

"Tell me," Abby invited. "Thomas is downstairs reading, but I will admit I know nothing about Oliver Cromwell. I remember reading his name somewhere in a book, but I am completely ignorant about the man."

Carrie scowled, grateful the darkness covered her expression. She had come to grips with the things she had learned, but it didn't mean the knowledge didn't still make her stomach queasy. "He was not a nice man," she began. "He was, however, very powerful. He was the effective leader of England from 1653 to 1658. He was also a very devout Puritan."

"So he was extremely religious," Abby murmured.

"That would be putting it mildly. He believed everyone should lead their lives according to what is written in the Bible, but from what I can tell, he had his own interpretations of it," she said. "Puritans believe pointless enjoyment should be frowned upon. The harder you work, the more likely you are to reach heaven. Lord Cromwell took this quite seriously. He shut down all theaters and many of the inns. Most sports were banned. Boys caught playing football on Sunday could be whipped as punishment. Swearing was punished by a fine, and those who kept at it were often sent to prison. You were not allowed to do any work on Sunday. Women were put in stocks if they were discovered doing unnecessary labor. Just going for a Sunday walk, unless you were going to church, resulted in a hefty fine."

"Oh my..." Abby said.

"It gets worse," Carrie continued. "To keep England's mind on religion, instead of having their common feast days to celebrate the saints, one day in every month was a fast day. You couldn't eat all day, though Lord Cromwell certainly did! He divided England into eleven areas. Each one was governed by a trusted major-general who had served under him in battle. He used soldiers to enforce his new laws."

"Seriously?" Abby gasped.

"Women and girls had to dress in a proper manner," Carrie said with disgust. "Make-up of any kind was banned. Colorful dresses were outlawed. Every female had to wear a long black dress that covered her from head to toe."

"I've seen them," Abby confirmed. "They wear white aprons and have their hair bunched under a white headdress. Many Puritans came to America. In fact, it was Puritans who were the first to successfully settle Jamestown."

Carrie snorted. "Only if you use the term *successful* to describe people who were executed if they were not in church two times a day. As bad as it was under Lord Cromwell in England, it was much worse in America for those people. Most of Jamestown settlers weren't Puritans. They were English who had been abducted from the streets and brought here to work the tobacco fields. They lived under very harsh conditions."

"I'm sure that is another story," Abby replied, "but I'm afraid I don't see—even as distasteful as everything you have told me is—how this relates to the Irish."

"I'm getting there," Carrie assured her. "My ancestor had a hatred for all Catholics, but he seemed to reserve a special hatred for the Irish Catholics. He believed they were all potential traitors willing to help any Catholic nation that wanted to attack England, so he vowed to wipe them all out. He considered them less than human, calling them savages to justify their murder."

"No," Abby whispered.

"Yes," Carrie answered. "Lord Cromwell sent an army to Ireland. He demanded surrender, promising he would treat well the ones who did." Her voice trembled as she revealed the next part. "Wexford and Drogheda surrendered. Cromwell had every person slaughtered." Her voice caught. "That was just the beginning."

Abby clapped her hand over her mouth.

"He used terror to tame the Irish. He ordered that all Irish children should be sent to the West Indies to work as slaves in the sugar plantations. Most of them died under the brutal conditions. He counted on that, because it meant they could never grow to adulthood and have more Irish children." Carrie's voice quivered. "He left a very dark stain on Ireland's history. By the time he was done, hundreds of thousands of Irish had been killed or forced into indentured slavery in America or the West Indies. He had destroyed farms, burned buildings and crops, and killed every living animal. Of course, he only *started* the ethnic cleansing in Ireland. The Irish were forced into slavery for at least another hundred years. Most of them came here to America." She couldn't see Abby's face, but she knew her stepmother was staring at her with horror.

Carrie pushed on, wanting to be done with her story. "Famine followed the war. Thousands of people remaining in the country starved to death. The Puritans, led by my ancestor, had only one goal—the total subjugation of Ireland. They were determined to destroy the Irish and replace them with Protestants from England and Scotland. They were quite willing to do whatever it took." A long silence filled the room when she stopped speaking.

"And the English *loved* Oliver Cromwell?" Abby asked, her voice thick with disbelief.

"They did for quite a while," Carrie corrected. "By the end of his life, the English people were sick of his control and strict rules. They hated him," she said, finding some relief in that. What he had done was horrifying enough, but to believe an entire nation had blindly followed him and thought he was a great man had been almost more than she could bear. "At the end of his life in 1660, my sixth great-grandfather was buried with honors in Westminster Abbey. Even though the English people hated him, his soldiers were still quite loyal."

"What happened next?" Abby pressed. "Something tells me you're not done yet."

"My fifth great-grandfather, Lord Cromwell's son Richard, took over England, but it didn't take long before people realized he wasn't up for the task. King Charles had been beheaded in 1649. His son, King Charles II, who had been in exile since his father's death, was asked to return to become king again. The new king was aware Lord Cromwell had been largely responsible for his father's execution. One of his first orders was to have my ancestor"—Carrie couldn't bring herself to identify Cromwell as her grandfather again—"dug up and put his body on trial for treason and regicide. His body was put on trial, found guilty, and symbolically hanged from a gallows. What was left of his body remains a mystery."

"What was *left*?" Abby asked hesitantly.

"His head was put on display in London for many years," Carrie answered in a flat, hard voice.

Abby reached out to grasp her hand. "I know you're angry, but you must have been horrified to learn all this."

Carrie grimaced. "That would be an understatement," she growled. "But it also inspired me to do whatever I could to help the people of Moyamensing. It felt like such a tiny thing—especially as I learned more of who he truly was and what he had done—but it was something I could do. It was a start."

"What you did will reverberate through history," Abby replied. "Just as Lord Cromwell's actions will impact lives for eternity, so will yours. The Irish people you helped save will know that not everyone hates them or believes they are somehow less human. Children will be born for generations to come from the people you saved."

"That is my hope," Carrie said. "I can't change what happened in the past..."

"But you can help redeem it now, and change things for the future," Abby finished.

"Yes." Carrie had known Abby would understand. "Do you think Father will be all right?"

"Your father will be fine," Abby said soothingly. "He will discover the truth, and then he will deal with it just as you have. Not knowing the truth does not change its reality. Knowing it, and accepting it, can change history. Your father has had his world turned upside down quite a bit in the last years. I'm sure he's up to one more."

"I'm glad I found out," Carrie said, wrapping the blanket tighter around her body while enjoying the cold breeze on her face.

"Are you? Why?"

"If I hadn't found out, I wouldn't have cared about the people of Moyamensing," Carrie replied, groping for words as she spoke. "If I hadn't cared, I wouldn't have gone to the cholera hospital and seen what was happening there. If I hadn't witnessed all those people dying, I wouldn't have gone to the Homeopathic College. I wouldn't have discovered the remedies that helped save so many, and I wouldn't have discovered homeopathy. I wouldn't have quit medical school." The truth washed through her in a tidal wave that brought unexpected comfort.

"All the pieces come together in time," Abby said.

"Yes, I'm learning that more and more. There are times I think things that happen are isolated events. But then I discover that each one is simply a piece in a much bigger picture. Sometimes it takes a long time to see it, but everything always fits somewhere."

"Nothing is ever wasted," Abby said gently.

"Exactly!" Carrie said. "Everything I learned with Sarah is part of the picture. Everything I learned at Chimborazo is part of the picture. Everything I learned at the Female Medical College is part of the picture."

"So you don't feel these last months have been wasted?" Abby asked.

Carrie laughed. "Weren't you the one who just told me nothing is ever wasted?"

"I did," Abby agreed. "But you do realize starting over is going to mean more time away from Robert. How are you with that?"

Carrie fell silent, her heart once more feeling like a massive boulder in her chest.

"Carrie?"

"I don't know what to do with how I feel," she admitted. "If I had my way, I would go home to Robert and the plantation and never leave. I miss him so much my heart hurts. I miss the plantation more than I can express. I feel like I'm missing so much, but..." Her voice faltered into silence again.

"But?" Abby prompted.

Carrie shrugged helplessly. "That's the problem. I don't know. I can't be a doctor if I don't go back to school, but the idea of getting on that train and returning to Philadelphia in ten days is almost more than I can bear."

"Then put it out of your mind," Abby advised.

"Easier said than done," Carrie muttered.

"I didn't say it was easy," Abby responded, sounding very much like the mentor who had helped her through so many challenging moments. "You can spend all your time here dreading what will come in ten days, or you can simply choose to make the most of every moment *here*." Her voice softened. "The future is going to come. You will figure it out as it unfolds. You will be given the grace and strength to walk every step you are given to walk."

Carrie listened closely and then leaned forward to wrap Abby in a tight embrace. "How did I ever live my life before I had you?" she whispered.

"It must have been difficult," Abby teased, clasping her close. "I certainly have no idea how I lived without *you* as my daughter. Next to your father, you are the greatest gift I have ever been given. Sometimes I feel woefully inadequate, but then I have to trust my love will be enough."

Carrie sighed as she rested her head on Abby's shoulder. Long minutes passed as the two women sat quietly, letting their hearts speak the love between them.

Abby finally stood. "It's time for you to get some sleep. Tomorrow morning is coming much too quickly. I don't want Robert to think we kept you up all night. I'm sure he would rather you not collapse from exhaustion when you see him." She stood, walked Carrie to the bed, waited until she had crawled under the covers, and then tucked her in. "I've always wanted to do that for a daughter," she said softly. She leaned down and kissed her on the forehead. "I love you, Carrie. Sleep well."

Wrapped in Abby's warm love, Carrie was asleep before her stepmother slipped from the room.

Robert paced back and forth in the woods, his ears straining for the sound of an approaching carriage, but all he heard was the twitter of birds and the rustle of squirrels dashing through the trees. He sighed impatiently, smiling when Granite stomped his foot and snorted his agreement. "She's coming, old man," he promised, his smile turning to a laugh when Granite's response was to toss his head and snort more loudly. Juniper, the mare he had chosen to ride so he could give her more training, just stared at him placidly. She seemed perfectly content to be tied in the middle of the woods on the edge of the road. She stared at Granite for a moment, and then closed her eyes and flicked her tail.

Robert continued his conversation with Granite. "I don't have any way of knowing exactly when Carrie will be here, but in Thomas' last letter he said they would be here in early afternoon." Granite's eyes widened. "Yes, I know that provides rather a large window to wait here in the woods, but it will be worth it when we surprise her. We've already been here two hours. Certainly it can't be that much longer."

Granite suddenly lifted his head to attention, his ears flicking forward as he turned to stare down the road. Robert quit pacing and sprang forward to peer from behind the thick brush. He couldn't hear anything yet, but he trusted Granite. "Be quiet, old man," he whispered as he lay his hand on the big Thoroughbred's neck. Granite remained alert but stayed silent. Robert hoped it was Carrie and the rest, but he also knew it could be anyone, including vigilantes. It had taken him a while to grasp that he was in as much danger—possibly more—than Moses, Rose, and the rest, but they had finally convinced him to be careful. He tightened his grip on his pistol and kept his eyes glued to the road.

When the carriage finally rounded the curve, he let out a relieved laugh, untied both horses, and leapt into Juniper's saddle. He waited until the carriage was less than a hundred feet away before he stepped out onto the road, leading Granite by his bridle. He saw the driver stiffen and reach for his sidearm, but at the exact same moment Carrie's cry split the air.

"Robert! Robert!"

Robert raised his hand and started laughing as Carrie jumped up on the carriage seat, waving wildly as the driver slowed and then stopped the carriage. He vaulted down and was waiting when she ran into his arms. "Carrie," he whispered, crushing her to him. He had missed her every single moment, but having her in his arms made him question how he had survived it. He buried his face in her soft black hair and breathed in her scent. "Welcome home," he murmured.

Carrie leaned back just enough to capture his lips. Robert's blood roared as his wife's body melted into his.

"Are the rest of us needed here?"

Robert chuckled against Carrie's lips when Thomas' voice broke through their passion. "Let's get rid of them," he suggested.

"Please do," Carrie agreed. An impish grin flitted across her lips before she turned and flung her arms around Granite's neck.

Robert smiled up at Thomas and the rest. "Welcome! I'm sure you won't be surprised when I tell you it will be a while before Carrie and I return to the plantation. Everyone is waiting for you at the house. There is quite a feast prepared." He should know. He had a large basket of it hidden away. He'd been busy since early morning.

His eyes narrowed as he inspected the large carriage. "Where are Elizabeth, Alice, and Florence?"

Carrie pulled away from Granite. "It's a long story. I'll tell you later."

Robert nodded. The person he cared most about was staring at him with luminous green eyes. All he wanted was to get her alone.

Thomas gave them a wave. "Have fun," he called as he motioned for the driver to continue on.

Robert watched until the carriage had disappeared around the next bend in the road, and then pulled Carrie close again. The kiss left him weak. If Carrie's sagging body was any indication, she was in the same condition.

Carrie finally pulled back. "Are we going to stand in the road all afternoon?" she teased in an unsteady voice.

Robert laughed. "Follow me," he commanded as he sprang into Juniper's saddle.

"No fair!" Carrie cried, staring down at her green traveling dress.

Robert flicked a glance at the bundle tied behind Granite's saddle.

"Really?" Carrie breathed, a wide smile exploding on her face. She pulled Granite back into the woods. When she emerged a few minutes later, she was clad in breeches and a warm jacket. The air was not cold, but it was crisp enough to relish the thick coat. She had released her hair from its confining bun, and then quickly platted it into a braid that streamed down her back. "I'm ready," she declared.

"Now let's see if you can keep up," Robert taunted her, urging Juniper into a gallop.

He heard Carrie's musical laugh float through the breeze. He didn't have to look to know she had vaulted into Granite's saddle and was now after him in mad pursuit. He had a substantial lead on her, but it was only seconds before Granite streaked past him, Carrie's slender form appearing as one with the horse's muscular, gray body.

Carrie's eyes widened when they broke out into the clearing along the river. She had instinctively known where her husband was taking her, but what was waiting for them almost took her breath away. "Robert!"

Robert remained silent while he removed Juniper's bridle and saddle, and tied her to a tree. When he looked up, Carrie was just turning Granite loose to graze. Granite would never dream of leaving. Robert slipped up behind her and wrapped his arms around her. "Do you like it?" he asked softly.

"It's wonderful," Carrie cried as she took in the square of brightly colored blankets laid on the ground, their corners anchored with large rocks to hold them in place. A picnic basket rested on the edge nearest the river. Off to the side was another pile of blankets. She shivered as Robert stepped up behind her and slowly pulled her coat off her shoulders.

Carrie turned and stared up into his brown eyes. They were glowing with so much love it almost took her breath away. Robert looked wonderful. He was as handsome as the day she had met him, but now his good looks were enhanced by wisdom and experience. The war that had nearly killed him had etched character into his face. All they had been through had done nothing but forge their souls. She reached her hand up and laid it gently on his cheek, her lips trembling with emotion. "I've missed you so much."

Robert sucked in his breath. "How much, Mrs. Borden?"

Carrie smiled as her hand traveled down his cheek to rest on his strong chest. "I'll be happy to show you, Mr. Borden."

Moments later they were buried beneath a mound of thick quilts, their clothes a tangled heap on the side.

Carrie watched Robert as he stood, every part of her satisfied and happy. Her eyes were heavy, but her heart felt light.

Robert glanced back at her. "Ready to eat?"

She raised a brow. "Are we referring to the picnic or to...?"

Robert raised a brow in return, dropped the basket and turned to her with a meaningful look.

"Don't you dare!" Carrie cried as she laughed in surrender. "I'm starving!"

"And I continue to be a neglected husband," Robert said, his eyes dancing with fun as he grabbed the basket, settled down next to her and opened it. "Annie took good care of us," he murmured.

"I'm sure she did," Carrie replied, "but the only way I'm coming out from beneath these blankets is if you hand me my clothes." She shivered as a breeze blew off the water. They still had at least two hours of daylight, but the temperature was dropping.

"Cold front coming in," Robert said casually, his eyes skimming her face appreciatively. He reached in the basket. "Fried chicken. Cole slaw. Potato salad. Biscuits. Pickles. Blueberry cobbler." He smacked his lips as he pulled them out one at a time. "I predict you are going to love this." He laid out the plates on the blanket and loaded them with food. Then he reached for a chicken thigh.

"Robert!"

"Yes, dear?" Robert took a bite, his eyes fixed on her creamy shoulders exposed by the blankets.

"My clothes," she demanded. "It's cold out there."

"I offered to keep you warm," Robert reminded her.

"That's not fair!"

Robert shrugged. "I believe you're the one who told me all is fair in love and war."

"I never..."

"Then you should have," Robert retorted. "Do you know how many nights I have dreamed of having you just like this?"

Carrie's look softened. "I promise I will reward you well if you give me my clothes," she said temptingly.

Robert tilted his head, considering. "How well?"

"You'll be happy," Carrie promised him. "On the other hand," she continued, the playfulness leaving her voice, "if you don't hand me my clothes right now so I can stop shivering and eat, you are going to be very sorry."

Robert smiled. "Ah, there is the fiery woman I know and love." He took another bite of chicken.

"Robert!" Carrie leapt up, grabbed her clothes, and began to dress quickly. She slowed down, suddenly aware Robert was devouring her with his eyes. Relishing in her power to torment him, she ignored her shivering body and drew out the process. "And to think that now I'll have to punish you later," she drawled as she struggled to keep her eyes stern after she had fastened the last button on her coat.

"Punish me?" Robert asked innocently.

"Certainly you don't think you'll be rewarded for this behavior," Carrie scolded.

"And certainly you know I am the King of the Picnic Basket," Robert retorted, pulling back the plates loaded with food. "You may want to rethink your decision, Mrs. Borden."

Carrie laughed and dove for him, wanting to cry with joy as they wrestled on the blanket. How could she possibly leave him again? The very thought swept through her body like a wave crashing onto the shores.

Robert felt the change in her emotions. He sat up, holding her shoulders as he peered into her eyes. "What is it?" he asked.

Carrie struggled for words. Finally she shook her head. "Can we eat first?"

Robert hesitated. "You're all right?"

"I will be," Carrie replied. Looking into Robert's concerned eyes told her everything was going to actually be all right. "I promise. I just don't think I can do one more thing, or say one more word, until I have some food in me."

"Eat." Robert reached behind him and pulled out her plate with a flourish.

Carrie ate slowly, not willing to hurry one moment of this perfect afternoon. Bees and butterflies buzzed and fluttered through the goldenrod spattered with specks of purple aster and Sampson's snakeroot still holding their blooms. The branches covering their sanctuary still had a tight hold on the vivid red, yellow, and orange leaves that seemed to strain against their constraints as the breeze kicked up whitecaps on the James River. The sun sparkling on the water made her catch her breath with the splendor of her home. "I've missed this so much," she murmured, her heart catching again at the thought of returning to Philadelphia for another brutal winter.

Carrie tried to push aside the vision of coal-darkened snow piling up on sidewalks as a vicious wind blew off the coast, but it stood as a sordid contrast to the shimmering white pastures the plantation sported when it snowed. *Don't think about it,* she scolded herself, trying to hold on to what Abby had told her last night. *Just enjoy the moment you have right now.*

"Carrie?"

Carrie knew by the worried sound in her husband's voice that her effort not to think about the looming future was failing miserably. "I quit medical school," she said quietly, not sure if she was disturbed or comforted by the flare of relief she saw in Robert's eyes. Deep concern followed so quickly on its heels that she wondered if she had actually seen it, or simply imagined it.

"What happened?" Robert reached for her hand.

Carrie told him everything. The sun had sunk low in the sky by the time she finished. Robert had not interrupted her once, not even to ask questions. She appreciated that he knew she needed to unburden herself.

There was a long silence when she quit speaking. Robert watched her closely. Even Granite had stopped grazing and was now watching her intently. Carrie waited. She needed to give Robert time to process what he had had heard.

"So you start at the Homeopathic College in two weeks?"

Carrie met his eyes. "That is when the term begins." She couldn't bring herself to say she was going to do it. She just couldn't imagine leaving Robert again. Couldn't imagine leaving the plantation.

"But you're not sure you want to return."

Carrie sighed. "Oh, I'm quite sure I *don't* want to return," she admitted, "but I'm struggling with what I am *meant* to do."

Robert stared out at the river for a long moment before he turned back to her. "I may not be the best person to talk this through with. I know I am probably supposed to convince you to return to Philadelphia and continue your education, but in all honesty I never want to spend another night or day without you again. It is impossible for me to be unbiased."

"I know," Carrie replied. "I realize I have to decide for myself, but I share your feelings. I never want to spend another day or night without you again, either." She gazed at Granite, who was staring at her with knowing eyes. "I don't want to leave the plantation."

"And once all you wanted was to leave here."

"Yes," Carrie agreed. "I've changed. Everything I love and value most is right here on Cromwell Plantation."

"That will change, too," Robert murmured.

Carrie nodded. "I know nothing ever stays the same, but I can't deny that my heart is here."

"Moses and Rose leave in the spring to go to school," Robert said.

"Yes. I received a letter from Rose, and we've already talked about it."

"Simon and June may be leaving, too."

Carrie's eyes widened. "Why? Who will handle the tobacco after Moses leaves?"

"That is still being discussed." Robert paused. "Simon and June may be leaving to oversee Blackwell Plantation."

"What?" Carrie blinked. "Blackwell Plantation has been standing empty since the war started. Has someone bought it?"

"Perry and Louisa are back."

Carrie sat back and stared at him. "Here in Virginia? I thought they lived in Georgia now. Why have they returned?" She wasn't certain why the knowledge was so disconcerting.

"You don't sound pleased."

"I don't know what I think about it," Carrie confessed. "Why have they returned?"

Robert shrugged. "General Sherman was quite successful in his march across Georgia. He set out to destroy a way of life. He succeeded. Perry and Louisa lost everything during the war. Perry tried to rebuild, but this year's cotton crop was dismal. He brought his family here to start over."

"When did they arrive?"

"About a month ago."

"A month?" Carrie tried to absorb this information as she watched Robert. "You never liked Louisa."

"There was not much to like," Robert replied, "but she has changed."

Carrie's eyes widened. "You like her now?"

"I like both of them," he said easily. "It took some time, though. We offered to let them stay here on the plantation when it was obvious Blackwell wasn't livable."

Carrie's brain was swimming. Though she and Louisa had reached a peace, she had never considered having her for a neighbor again. "She was quite the Southern plantation mistress," she murmured. "I can understand their returning, but are you sure Simon and June should work for them? I'm afraid it won't be anything like Cromwell."

"Actually it will be *just* like Cromwell Plantation," Robert replied, a smile dancing on his lips. "Simon had refused to even entertain the idea, and Perry was acting like a prejudiced, entitled Southerner for a long time. Moses made it clear he would not encourage any of his men to work there unless it was run the same way. Perry wouldn't even consider it at first."

"And yet it's the only way for Blackwell to become profitable again," Carrie said.

"He knows that now," Robert agreed.

"He has to change for more than money," Carrie replied.

"Protective?" Robert teased.

"Of course I am! Simon and June are my family. I won't have anyone treat them the way most Southerners treat blacks," she said, her eyes flashing. "They've both dealt with too much already."

Robert laughed. "Relax. Perry and Louisa have truly changed. Their time here worked something of a miracle in them. I'll admit neither Moses nor I thought they could change, but they have. You're going to be surprised."

Carrie gazed at him, knowing it was her painful history with Louisa that was making her skeptical. They had found peace in Richmond, but she had many humiliating memories of Louisa when they were growing up. Having her on the plantation was reviving them in her mind.

"Give them a chance," Robert urged. "Especially Louisa."

Carrie sighed. As usual, Robert was reading her mind. "They'll be there when we get back to the house?"

Robert nodded.

Carrie, not wanting to think about Louisa anymore, returned to their earlier conversation. "I don't know what to do about school."

"You don't have to know right this second," Robert responded. "Neither one of us does, though I don't really have much to do with this decision."

"You have *everything* to do with this decision!" Carrie cried.

Robert smiled. "I knew, almost from the day I met you, that you wanted to be a doctor. I decided that day that I would never stand in your way. I have told you honestly that I never want to spend another day or night without you, but I will also never try to dictate your decision. My job is to support whatever you decide. I have a beautiful and brilliant wife. You will make the right decision."

"I wish I believed the same thing," Carrie muttered, feeling comforted in spite of her lingering confusion. Just being there with Robert almost convinced her she truly would know what to do.

"I repeat that you don't have to know right now. You're not due to return to Philadelphia for nine more days. So much can happen in that period of time. Just wait and see what happens."

Carrie gazed at him for what seemed an eternity. "I hope you're right." She began to repack the picnic basket. "I know this plantation like the back of my hand, whether the sun is shining or it is pitch-black dark, but I'm afraid if we're not home soon, the others will begin to worry."

"They probably will," Robert agreed.

Carrie couldn't identify what was in his voice that made her tense, but she felt sudden anxiety course through her body. "What is it?"

"I'll tell you on the way home," Robert replied.

Carrie wanted to demand answers right then, but she knew they couldn't afford the time it would take for him to give them. She tightened her lips and packed faster.

They picked their way through the darkening woods. Granite's calm steadiness and Robert's reassuring hand on Juniper's neck were the only things keeping the mare from bolting as a strong breeze brought down small limbs from the trees. "Good boy," Carrie murmured to her steady gelding. She turned to Robert as soon as they broke free from the woods onto the road leading back to the house. "Tell me what is going on around here," she demanded.

Chapter Twenty-One

"There is something else I need to tell you first," Robert responded.

Even with dusk shrouding the plantation, Carrie could see Robert's eyes were deeply troubled. She waited quietly, her gaze fixed on him.

"No one will buy the horses, Carrie."

Carrie was astonished. "Why ever not? Eclipse has sired some of the most amazing colts and fillies I have ever seen. Surely people will realize that soon. We just have to get the word out more."

"It's not that," Robert broke in. "Plenty of people know."

The truth hit Carrie as soon as the words were out of his mouth. "They won't buy them because of how Cromwell is being managed," she said, anger beginning to boil in her.

"That's the gist of it," Robert answered.

Carrie reached out and grabbed his hand, stricken by the look in his eyes. She pushed aside her anger. "Why didn't you tell me when I was here in August?"

"I wanted to. When you were called back early, I didn't want to dump it on you right before you left."

Carrie could understand that, but her heart ached for her husband. Her anger melted beneath the weight of her sorrow. He had lost everything during the war except his burning passion for horses. His great hope had been to start over and raise the finest horses in Virginia. "Someone will buy them," she said. "It's not possible that every horseman in this state is a bigoted idiot," she snapped, her anger surging back as she talked.

"It might be," Robert muttered.

Carrie stared down the road, her mind racing. "What have you been doing with this year's crop of babies?"

Robert shrugged. "Training them. If a miracle happens and someone actually buys them, they are going to be more than pleased. Clint is truly gifted, and Amber has a natural ability I've never seen in anyone else but you. All of the colts and fillies are coming along incredibly well."

"And the mares?"

"I bought more in the spring before I realized no one would buy their offspring. All of them are bred and due in the spring. Come March and April, there will be twice as many that no one wants to buy," he said ruefully.

"What does Polly say?" Carrie asked.

Robert shifted in his seat to look at her better. "What does *Polly* say? What difference would that make?"

Carrie smiled and shrugged. "She seems to know things. Just like Sarah did." She saw a smile begin to form in Robert's eyes. "So what did Polly say?" she repeated.

"She said somebody with sense in their head is gonna come buy these fine horses."

Relief flowed into Carrie. "Then someone will," she said with confidence.

"And if she isn't right?"

"Have you ever known her to be wrong?"

"Well, no, but…"

"If I were you, I would keep on training those babies. When the right person finally shows up to buy them, they are going to be so thrilled they'll spread the word like wildfire. You probably won't even have enough in the spring to fill the demand. You'll have to start a waiting list for the following year."

"Time will tell," Robert muttered, but his eyes were more hopeful.

Carrie remained silent for several minutes, the pieces clicking together in her mind as they cantered down the road. When the final piece had snapped into place, she slowed to a walk, motioning for Robert to move closer. "So people are displeased with what is happening at Cromwell. That means everyone is in danger, and all of you have to be extra careful. The vigilantes are becoming bolder as the elections draw nearer because they know the South is soon to be without support from President Johnson."

Robert stared at her, and then a bemused smile spread across his face. "That would be the issue in a nutshell," he replied. He told her quickly about the last incident at the school.

"They didn't return?"

"No, but it's just a matter of time," he said. "I think things are rather chaotic right now because of the elections. There is a last ditch effort being made to strengthen President Johnson, but I don't believe it will work."

"It will fail. Matthew has been keeping us abreast of the news. Things are about to change radically."

"For the better?"

Carrie hesitated. "I hope so. It will take some time to implement the changes the Republicans vow to initiate, but it will take even longer to truly change the *attitudes* in the South. It's going to require great courage and persistence from both whites and blacks to make that happen."

When Robert didn't reply, she looked up and was surprised to see they were almost back to the house. She put all the troublesome talk behind her as she saw the crowd of people waiting on the porch. "Rose!" she yelled, pushing Granite into a gallop for the last hundred yards. Rose laughed joyfully as Carrie leapt from her saddle and hurled herself into her arms.

"I missed you," Rose cried.

Carrie gazed up at the ring of faces on the porch and knew she was truly home. She always enjoyed returning to the plantation, but never had she felt the connection so strongly. Never had she feared her heart would rend in two if she dared to leave. The feeling both thrilled her and confused her. She believed so strongly she was meant to be a doctor. What could this mean? She caught Abby's eyes as she peered up at the porch. The message was loud and clear. *You don't have to know now.* The words, silently whispered on the breeze, released the vise around her heart.

"I missed you, too," Carrie whispered. "Oh, how I missed you." Only she needed to know that the missing encompassed everything she could see, hear, and smell.

A loud whinny attracted her attention. She grinned when she looked over and saw Amber clinging to the pasture fence, a horse's head resting on her leg. Robert had told her about Amber's reaction to their gift. "That's a fine looking filly you have there, Amber."

"The best in the world," Amber declared, her eyes glowing with warm happiness. "Thank you," she said shyly, her expression expressing her gratitude far more than her words ever could.

Carrie smiled as she walked over to stroke All My Heart's silky head. "The two of you belong together. Just like Granite and I did."

Amber sucked in her breath. "That's what I thought," she whispered. "Did you know right from the first moment?"

"Right from the first moment," Carrie confirmed. She laughed when Granite, his reins hanging free, trotted over to nuzzle her shoulder and then touched his nose to the filly's.

"Granite is helping me train All My Heart," Amber confided. "She adores him. She copies everything he does."

"She couldn't have a better teacher," Carrie replied. She felt a fierce desire not to miss one moment of it, but now was not the time to ponder what she was feeling.

A movement on the porch caught her attention. She felt herself tense, but saw Amber's surprised look and forced herself to relax as she turned around. "Hello, Louisa," she called, glad when her voice came out warmly welcoming.

"Carrie!" Louisa called. She ran down the steps and across the yard.

Carrie watched her with surprise. She had never seen Louisa move any faster than a sophisticated Southern woman's stroll.

"It's so wonderful to have you home," Louisa said as she wrapped her in a big hug.

Carrie saw the wide grin on Robert's face over Louisa's shoulder. Stunned, she returned the hug and then stepped back to peer into Louisa's face. "It's so good to see you."

"Oh, you probably don't mean that right this minute," Louisa said blithely, "but I hope you will soon."

Carrie searched for a response but came up empty. Her mouth almost dropped open when Rose strolled up next to Louisa and wrapped her arm around her waist.

Louisa laughed. "I told you she wouldn't know what to think."

"It takes time to undo the past," Rose said, sounding exactly like her mama. "I predict it won't take too long, though."

The sound of squealing children broke through Carrie's shock. She watched as Simon, Jr., John, and a bright-haired boy that could be no one but Louisa's son raced across the yard, chasing the last fireflies of the season. It was easy to tell they were the best of friends. She shot a look at Louisa, mesmerized when she saw easy affection on her face as she watched the boys play.

Carrie let out a long breath. "Well..." she managed. Rose and Louisa stepped up next to her, wrapped their arms around her waist, and pulled her toward the porch. Carrie smiled when she saw Moses, Simon, and Perry sitting together on the porch talking easily. Jeremy was pushing Marietta in the swing that hung from the branch of the oak tree positioned outside her childhood bedroom. Thomas and Abby reclined on the porch swing as Annie stepped out with a new tray loaded high with cookies. June's voice, calling from the kitchen, floated out into the night air.

Suddenly she knew, truly knew, that she was home. More importantly, she was looking at proof that miracles really did happen.

"Robert! Robert!" John dashed from behind a tree, Nathan close by his side. "You can't catch us!"

Robert leapt off the porch to give chase. "I'll get you!" he called. His laughter rang through the still evening as he ran after them, making sure to let them remain just out of reach.

Carrie's step faltered as she watched her husband cavorting with the boys. She summoned a bright smile when Rose squeezed her waist more tightly, but she suspected her best friend was not fooled.

Carrie knew Rose would be waiting for her as she slipped out onto the porch bundled in breeches and an even thicker coat than she had worn that afternoon to ward off the chilly evening air. Both of them should be sleeping, but neither could wait another moment to be alone. The evening of nonstop talk and laughter with everyone had been wonderful, but now she wanted nothing more than to talk with her best friend.

They linked arms but remained silent as they walked out into the night, illuminated by a moon that was just shy of full. The cold fall air had silenced the frogs, but the hooting owls and coyote yips more than made up for them. Carrie shivered as the house disappeared around a curve. "Are we safe?" She hated to ask the question, but she had been sensitive to the unspoken tension all night. She peered around, searching the shadows for any unexpected movement.

Rose shrugged. "We all listen and watch carefully."

Her simple statement alarmed Carrie. She had wanted Rose, even *expected* her, to deny there was any reason for concern. "Are you really afraid?"

Rose turned to look at her. "Every day," she admitted. Her beautiful face tightened with a frown. "I abhor feeling this way, but it's the only way I know to take care of everyone. I feel if I relax for even one minute that somebody might sneak past my guard and harm those I love." Her voice was a mixture of bitterness and pain.

"Robert told me about the latest incident at the school." Carrie was horrified by the fear she saw shining from Rose's eyes. She had so hoped the end of slavery would mean the end of this kind of terror.

Rose sighed. "Talking about it won't change it. Just for tonight I'm going to pretend all is well because my best friend is back where she belongs."

Carrie stared at her. "Is this *really* where I belong?" Her heart surged with longing and hope at the same time her mind protested what she was thinking.

Rose stopped walking and turned to look at her. "Talk to me, Carrie. What is going on?"

Carrie sighed. She was growing weary of telling her story, but Rose deserved to hear it all. She pushed sleep from her mind as she filled her best friend in on all that had happened.

"Well..." Rose murmured when she finished. "That's a lot."

Carrie laughed. "Leave it to you to encapsulate almost two months of life-changing experiences into three words." She hooked her arm through Rose's and kept walking. Just being with her, strolling through the moonlight, made her feel better. Even though she was tired of talking about all that had happened, each time she did it seemed to shave a little more of the heavy weight from the burden.

"You're not sure you should go back to Philadelphia."

"Yes," Carrie admitted, wondering if the moonlight was working some type of enchantment on her. The angst in her heart seemed to lift and disappear. "I haven't changed my mind about being a doctor, but for some reason my soul can't imagine leaving the plantation again right now."

"Your gut is telling you to stay," Rose stated calmly.

In the clarifying gleam of the moon, it all seemed so simple. Carrie suddenly realized it was true. No matter what her mind was telling her, her instincts were telling her to stay. She drew a quick breath.

"You don't have to know why, Carrie."

Carrie stopped again and swung Rose around to face her. She inspected her friend's eyes in the light of the moon, envying the peace she saw radiating there now. "How can you say that? All I've ever wanted to do was be a doctor. Now I'm walking away. I want to know *why*."

Rose shrugged, a smile playing across her lips. "And I'm saying you don't have to know why. I've learned God works in very mysterious ways. I couldn't believe I was coming back to the plantation after the war. I thought it was going to keep me from accomplishing what I was meant to do."

"And you don't feel that way anymore?" As much as Carrie's heart was urging her to stay, her mind was shouting at her that she could be making a decision that would be fatal to her future.

"No," Rose answered. "I wouldn't have been able to say goodbye to Sam if I had left. I wouldn't be a mother to Felicia. I wouldn't have seen Perry and Louisa change before my eyes, and I wouldn't have the joy of watching John ride out into the fields with his daddy every day." She took a breath. "Even though I'm frightened, I love teaching my students. I realize if I had left when I wanted to, that I would have missed so much that is actually preparing me for the future. I don't know what is going to happen between now and next spring, but I'm quite certain I don't want to miss any of it."

"Well..." Carrie murmured, struck by the intense certainty in Rose's eyes. "That's a lot."

Rose laughed and tightly gripped Carrie's hand. "You don't have to know why, Carrie. You simply have to listen to God the best you can and follow your heart. At some point in time you will understand, but you can't expect to understand when you *make* your decision."

Carrie turned her eyes up to gaze at the moon, wishing a shooting star would streak across the sky as a sign. The few glimmering stars bright enough to be seen in the moonlit sky remained stubbornly in place. She sighed and lowered her head. "And what if I'm wrong?"

"Then you're wrong," Rose replied.

"But..."

"Oh, for heaven's sake, Carrie," Rose said in an exasperated voice. "We're going to make decisions for the rest of our lives without knowing if they are right or wrong. All we can do is make the very best decision we can at the moment and then live with the consequences that come from it."

Carrie stared at her. "Your mama..."

"What's my mama got to do with this?" Rose asked in a puzzled voice.

"Nothing." Carrie chuckled. "You sound just like your mama. There have been other times when you repeated things your mama said, but this is different. You were speaking with your own words, but you sounded like your mama."

Rose smiled. "Nothing could make me happier. I doubt I'll ever be as wise as that woman, but I sure hope I come close some day."

"I think that day is coming sooner than you think," Carrie said, staring at her with admiration.

Rose smiled again but remained silent. The two friends walked on through the night, their frosty breath weaving a white mist that floated up to the sky.

Carrie gasped as the moon began to reflect off dancing crystals on the ground, grasses, and remaining flowers. "The first frost of the year," she whispered, not wanting to break the reverent feeling the silence had wrapped around her.

"Just in time for the Harvest Celebration," Rose whispered back, her eyes gleaming with delight.

Carrie stood and watched as the glistening frost seemed to float down from the sky to lay glittering diamonds on everything it touched. She was always sad at the end of harvest when the fields lay bare and empty, but the shining frost beckoned her forward. She caught her breath as she realized she was being pulled into a new season of her life. It was impossible for her to understand why she was supposed to stay on the plantation, but the peace that claimed her heart as soon as she uttered the words said she was making the right decision.

"I don't have to know why," she whispered.

Rose remained silent but reached down to grip her hand. Carrie had lost track of time when Rose finally let go. The beauty of her world glistening beneath the moon while honking geese split the sky with their V formations had her mesmerized.

"We should go back," Rose said reluctantly. "The others are probably already worrying."

Carrie was loath to leave the magical night, but they still had a long walk home. "All right," she sighed as she began to retrace their steps.

"So are you going to tell me what else is bothering you?" Rose asked.

Carrie blinked. "I don't know what you're talking about." So much peace was pulsing through her heart that she honestly couldn't feel anything else.

Rose grunted. "Did you think I wouldn't notice how you tensed up when you saw Robert playing with the boys?"

Carrie felt her newfound peace evaporate. "I had hoped you wouldn't," she admitted. She truly didn't know how to talk about her suspicions. More accurately, her fears.

Rose remained silent.

Carrie struggled with what to actually say, but she felt a hint of relief that Rose was pushing her to give words to the thing that had sat tightly in her heart for months. "Robert was very sick after the war," she began, her words slow and halting. "He had a high fever for a long time."

"I remember."

"No one knows for sure what a high fever for that long can do," Carrie continued. She fell silent, suddenly unable to voice the fear she had been trying to ignore.

"You're afraid Robert can't produce children," Rose said gently.

"I don't know anything," Carrie cried. Hearing the words spoken out loud was suddenly more than she could bear. "I could be completely wrong!"

Rose stopped and turned Carrie to face her. "But that is what you are afraid of?"

Carrie stared into her eyes for several moments before she nodded. "Yes. That is what I'm afraid of." She had hoped saying the words would offer some reprieve from the haunting suspicions, but they seemed to only mold them more firmly in her heart where they now lay like a sodden weight. "I never thought much about children," she admitted. "I knew I wanted them someday, but medical school was always what pulled me forward."

"And it had to be one or the other?" Rose asked.

"I thought so," Carrie murmured. "Until I met several women at school who had children. They came to medical school anyway. They decided the two years away from their children wouldn't harm them, and they hoped their decision to become doctors would encourage their children to follow their own desires."

"Have you been trying?" Rose asked.

Carrie hesitated again. She suspected she should be talking to Robert about this, but she couldn't imagine voicing words that might make him feel less adequate as a man. "He was so wonderful with the children tonight," she whispered.

"He is all the time," Rose responded. "He would be a fabulous father."

The simple statement tightened the band around Carrie's heart so strongly she feared she would explode. "I know."

"And you would be a wonderful mother," Rose said.

Carrie nodded. "I would like to think so..." Her voice trailed off. "I'm not sure I'll ever get the chance to find out. We have been trying," she admitted, unable to stop the rush of tears.

"You certainly couldn't have had much time to try," Rose replied, her concerned voice laced with amusement. "You're not here very much."

Carrie knew Rose was teasing, but the words sliced her heart into ribbons. The tears pooling in her eyes began to stream down her face.

"Carrie! I'm so sorry," Rose cried. "That was a terrible thing to say!"

Carrie shook her head. "It's the truth," she managed. Then she felt a surge of hope. "Maybe that's one of the reasons I feel I have to stay. Perhaps if I am here more, Robert and I will be able to conceive a child." Speaking the words planted a fragile seed of belief in her heart.

"I hope so," Rose whispered.

Carrie thought back to the afternoon's passion by the river. *Perhaps...*

Chapter Twenty-Two

Carrie could feel the excitement in the air when she stumbled downstairs the next morning. When she pushed through the kitchen door, Annie held out a steaming cup of coffee without a word. "Thank you," she mumbled, sighing with relief as she sipped the hot brew.

"You and Rose talk out everything you needed to?" Annie asked as she began to scoop a tray full of perfectly browned biscuits into a large wooden bowl.

Carrie nodded, quite sure she couldn't form coherent words yet.

Annie finished the tray and then stepped back to look at her, one sturdy fist planted on her hip. "You don't look much like a woman who gonna ride in that tournament this afternoon," she scolded.

Carrie gasped as she sucked in too much hot coffee. Coughing, she reached for a glass of water. Once she had cooled her throat and mouth she stared at Annie. "How do you know?"

"That you gonna ride in that tournament? You think everybody here don't know you're gonna prove what a woman can do?"

Carrie grinned. She heard nothing but warm approval in Annie's voice. "Tired or not, I'm going to win," she announced.

"You've got some stiff competition," Annie warned.

Carrie shrugged. "Robert, Clint, and Moses are good horsemen, but they don't have Granite. Are any of the other men riding?"

Annie shook her head, a smile dancing across her lips.

Carrie's mind was waking up as the coffee worked its magic. She took another sip and leaned against the counter. "Out with it," she ordered. "Who else is riding? I don't know of any men who could begin to compete with the rest of us."

"Nope. You be right about that..." Annie let her voice trail off as she watched Carrie closely.

"Then who?" Carrie's eyes widened. "Amber? Is Amber riding?"

Annie chuckled. "Yep. I done put my wager money on Amber," she revealed.

"Amber? She's a little girl, Annie!"

"A little girl who done been practicing more than anyone else around here," Annie retorted. "She's out there every evening until it's too dark to even see them rings she be trying to catch."

Carrie smiled with delight. She wasn't worried about a ten-year-old child beating her, but she loved the fact that society had changed enough to allow it to happen. This was the first time for a woman to ride in a tournament, and now she was going to be joined by a child. "I love it!"

Annie eyed her. "You don't seem to be too worried."

"She doesn't have Granite," Carrie replied. She was confident no one could beat her horse. The only horse that could come close was...

"Amber be riding Eclipse."

Carrie lowered her cup and stared. "Eclipse? Amber is riding Eclipse?" She tried to envision the little girl on the towering Thoroughbred, but her mind wouldn't form the image.

"Sho 'nuff." Annie's voice was gruff with pride.

"He's too much for her to handle," Carrie cried, pushing aside the thought that Eclipse was the only horse on the plantation that would provide competition for Granite. "Robert will never let her ride him."

Robert entered the kitchen just then, his face glowing from the cold. He had clearly been up for hours before her. "Amber is riding Eclipse," he informed her.

Carrie was eager to tell Robert the knowledge she was hugging close to her heart, but now was not the time. "And you believe she can handle him?"

Robert hesitated. "I wouldn't let her ride him if I thought it wasn't safe," he replied, though his eyes said he was concerned.

Carrie's eyes narrowed. "I thought you would ride Eclipse."

"I did, too," Robert admitted.

"Little Amber is a smart girl," Annie chortled as she pulled out another tray of cookies from the oven.

Carrie turned to Robert for an explanation. She was surprised to see a red flush creeping up his neck. "Robert?"

Robert grinned. "Amber made a wager with me. She bet me she could learn how to vault onto Eclipse before today."

"That's impossible!" Carrie cried. "She's too small."

"That's what I thought," he responded dryly. "Now I've decided Amber is not just a little girl. She is clearly part bird. You should have seen her flying through the air to land on Eclipse's back."

Carrie gaped at him. "And Eclipse let her?" She had seen how the spirited stallion fidgeted when anyone approached him to mount.

Robert laughed. "My rebellious stud turns into a prissy mare when Amber is around. I swear he would kneel down to make himself lower if she needed him to." He shook his head, his eyes glowing with pride and admiration. "She showed me yesterday. Amber walked right up to Eclipse, took one little jump, and soared straight onto his back. She reached for his mane halfway into the air, but the only reason she needed it was to keep herself from flying right over the top of him. I swear that horse looked as proud as she did."

Carrie laughed, trying to envision what he was describing. "You said she was a natural. I'm quite sure I couldn't have done that at her age."

"You didn't have to," Robert replied. "I'm quite sure you *could* have done the same thing if you had equal motivation."

Carrie smiled. "To win the tournament," she murmured. She was duly impressed but still not concerned. "Who are you going to ride now that Amber has claimed your horse?" Her lips twitched with amusement. "I don't see a repeat of six years ago in your future," she teased.

Robert grinned. "Time will tell, wife. Time will tell."

Carrie stared at him, running through all the horses in her mind. Not one of them could offer competition to

Granite or Eclipse. She took another sip of coffee, more confident than ever that she was going to win.

Robert read her thoughts. "Victory is not based solely on the speed of the horse," he said calmly.

"Exactly," Carrie agreed. "Which makes me all the more confident. Women are far more patient and focused than men."

Robert laughed. "We'll see, my dear."

Carrie felt a rush of happiness so strong she thought she might take flight just like Amber had. Being in the fragrant kitchen... Teasing with Robert... Seeing Annie's indulgent smile... Hearing the plantation come to life... To know she wasn't going to be leaving caused her entire body to vibrate with joy. The future would take care of itself. The *now* was quite sufficient to keep her from thinking about it.

"You two can keep on thinkin' one of you gonna win," Annie said. "I'm keepin' my wager right on little Amber."

Carrie leapt up and twirled in a circle. "It's a beautiful day!" she cried. Laughing at the surprised looks on Robert and Annie's faces, she sprang forward and gave both of them a hug. "Bring on the competition," she declared. Ducking away from Annie, she grabbed two biscuits stuffed with ham, stuck her tongue out at Robert, and strolled from the kitchen. "I have a tournament to prepare for."

Carrie found Amber brushing Eclipse in the aisle. She had to stand on a wooden box to reach his back, but Eclipse was as still as a docile cow. Carrie chuckled. Robert was right—the spirited stallion had been enchanted by a little girl.

Amber looked up as Carrie approached. "Robert tell you?"

Carrie grinned. "That you are going to be my stiffest competition?" She nodded. "I welcome the challenge." She reached up to pat Eclipse's gleaming neck. "I'm also very proud of you. Robert told me about the bet you won."

Amber grinned back at her. "My mama and Rose keep telling me I can do anything a boy can do," she confided. "I reckon I'm out to prove it."

Carrie looked up when Granite hung his head out of the stall and snorted. "We're both going to prove just what females are capable of, young lady. May the best woman win!"

Amber bobbed her head. "May the best woman win!" she shouted. "Or girl," she added with a grin.

Carrie laughed and settled down to the business of getting her horse ready. She knew she wasn't needed in the kitchen. Annie, Polly, June, and all the workers' wives had created mountains of food so large it would probably take the entire state of Virginia to eat it all. Of course, she knew there would be throngs of people pouring toward the house soon. All the workers and their families were going to be joined by all of Rose's students, as well as their parents. Carrie knew invitations had gone out to most of the white plantation families in the area, but no one had accepted. Her lips tightened as she thought about it, but she pushed it out of her mind. Today was going to be a celebration of the best harvest in Cromwell Plantation history. She wasn't going to let anything spoil it.

Carrie hummed as she groomed Granite. She inhaled deep breaths of the barn air, her heart once again bursting with happiness. She wasn't going to return to the sooty, snow-clogged, Philadelphia streets. A vision of Moyamensing thrust its way into her joy, but she pushed it back resolutely. She knew she had given the residents what they needed to thwart almost any sickness that could invade that winter. Carolyn would keep watch on them. Biddy and Faith also knew how to reach Janie.

Carrie's hand froze. *Janie!* What was Janie going to think when she realized Carrie wouldn't be returning with her? She had been so thrilled with her decision that she hadn't stopped to think how it would impact Janie. She was certain nothing could change her mind, but she just hoped her friend and housemate would understand.

Pushing the uncertainty from her mind, she focused on the tournament. It had been two years since she had even played around on Granite to capture the rings, but she had practiced it in her heart and mind so many times she was quite confident her body would respond. She could hear Sarah's voice in her head. *"The mind be a real powerful thin', girl. You fix somethin' real hard in your mind, and your body gonna do it."*

Carrie focused her mind as she brushed Granite's coat. She also remembered...

Robert looked splendid astride Granite at the Blackwell Tournament. She had begun to lose her heart to him the night before. When she saw his dark good looks on top of her horse and watched him ride to victory, she had known she could love him. It seemed like an entire lifetime had passed since that sunny afternoon six years ago. And, indeed, it had. They had fallen in love, married, survived a horrible war, and were now forging a life together. Carrie could hardly even remember the carefree girl she had been, but she was comfortable with the woman she had become.

"Carrie!"

Amber was tugging at her arm. She jolted back from the past and stared down at her. "Amber? What's wrong?"

Amber was staring out the barn door. "I didn't think there were any other white people coming," she said anxiously. "Who are those people?"

Carrie stiffened, certain Amber was worried about whites making trouble for them. She put down her brush, moved to the barn door, and looked out. What she saw made her laugh with surprised delight. "They are friends!" she called over her shoulder as she ran for the wagon rolling down the road.

"Carrie!"

Carrie was still laughing when the wagon pulled to a stop. "What in the world are you two doing here?"

Thomas appeared on the porch. "Hello, Captain Jones! Welcome, Susan!"

Carrie stared at her father. "You knew these two were coming?"

"I invited them," her father answered with a grin that made him look years younger. Carrie could almost forget the war had aged him before her eyes.

Susan jumped out of the wagon and embraced Carrie warmly. "It's wonderful to see you again, Carrie."

"And you," Carrie replied, as drawn as ever to Susan's bright blue eyes and dark hair. She was a female replica of her brother. "What a wonderful surprise! How did you get your brother away from Oak Meadows?"

Captain Jones looked at Thomas. "No one knew we were coming?"

"Only Abby," Thomas admitted.

Carrie didn't understand the flash in her father's eyes, but she knew she wasn't imagining it. What did he have up his sleeve? She began to get an inkling when she saw Mark and Susan turn to look at the pasture. Their eyes widened with appreciation when they saw the colts and fillies roaming the fields, prancing and playing in the early morning chill.

"Oh my," Susan whispered as she raised her hand to her mouth.

"That's quite a crop of babies," Mark said, his voice almost reverent.

Carrie shot a look at her father. He smiled back at her with wide-eyed innocence. Then he winked and turned away. She laughed and hooked her arm through Susan's. "I bet you would like to see their sire."

"I would," Susan murmured as Mark fell in beside her.

Carrie was suddenly very glad everyone was busy somewhere else on the plantation.

Mark stopped short when he entered the barn, his eyes locked on Eclipse. He walked forward slowly, his gaze devouring the perfectly formed Thoroughbred.

"He's stunning," Susan said as she stepped forward to stroke his neck.

"He's the second best horse in the world!" Amber stepped forward and jumped onto the box. She laid a protective hand on Eclipse's neck. "You can't have him."

Carrie smiled. "You have nothing to worry about, Amber. Eclipse will never leave Cromwell Plantation."

Amber relaxed and then eyed the two strangers. "Are you the two that bought Oak Meadows?"

"We are," Mark replied as he continued to gaze at Eclipse. Finally he turned his attention to Amber. "And you must be Amber. Robert told us about you."

Amber lost her suspicious look. "I'm one of Robert's trainers," she announced. "My brother, Clint, is the other one. He's down helping to get the arena ready for the tournament."

"I bet you're excited to watch it," Susan said.

Amber grinned. "I'm not watching. I'm riding!"

Carrie understood when Susan and Mark gaped at her.

Susan was the first to recover. "And who are you going to ride?" she asked.

Amber laid a proud hand on the Thoroughbred's neck. "Eclipse," she answered firmly.

Carrie finally took pity on Mark and Susan when their silence continued to stretch out. "Amber can handle Eclipse," she assured them. "This horse would do anything for her."

Susan smiled. "It's about time this ridiculous sport was open to women," she declared.

"And to girls!" Amber added seriously.

"And to girls!'" Susan agreed. Her attention turned back to the pasture. "You helped train the colts and fillies?"

"Yes, ma'am," Amber said. "Are you the ones my mama said was going to come buy them?"

Carrie tensed, but relaxed again when Susan and Mark merely smiled.

"We're in the market," Mark murmured. His eyes caught Carrie's over Amber's head.

Carrie shrugged. "No one other than my father and Abby had any idea you were coming. Polly is Amber's mother. She has been telling Robert all summer that someone was coming to buy the horses."

Mark nodded. "No one will buy them because you choose to treat blacks equally?"

"That's about it," Carrie agreed, not wanting to say any more until Robert had returned. She could hardly wait to see his face when he spied his friends.

Mark nodded, seeming to know she wouldn't say anymore. He turned back to Amber. "Will you tell us about the ones you have been training?"

Amber nodded and hopped down off the box. She unsnapped Eclipse's lines and led him into his stall, her slim, small form making him look even more massive. She reached up to pat his neck, murmured something to him that made him duck his head, and then pulled the door shut. Eclipse stuck his head out immediately and blew softly into her hair. Amber giggled and reached up to pat his nose. "Right this way," she called.

Carrie watched, a sense of something close to awe flooding her as she watched Amber's face fill with determined purpose. She joined Mark and Susan at the fence as Amber clambered up to perch on top.

"That is Eclipse's Sparkling Lady," she began, pointing out a powerful sorrel filly with an etched, refined head. "She was the first to learn to lead. She's already used to the halter and bridle, and I've been putting the saddle pad on her for several weeks now. She's spirited but friendly. She's got her sire's fire, but she is also as gentle as her dam."

Amber shifted to point toward a prancing bay with two white stockings on his front legs. "That's Eclipse's Jim Dandy." She launched into her explanation of where he was in the training process, her voice confident and smooth.

"And that one?" Susan asked when Amber finished.

Carrie hid her grin as her eyes followed Susan's pointing finger.

"That's All My Heart," Amber said.

"She's beautiful," Susan murmured, her eyes taking in the filly's perfect conformation with hungry eyes.

"And she's mine," Amber added. "Robert gave her to me." Her voice was thick with pride and love.

Susan turned to gaze into Amber's eyes. "You are a very lucky little girl."

"Luck had nothing to do with it." Robert strode up and put his hand on Amber's shoulder. "I owe this little girl more than I can ever repay, and All My Heart is in the best hands possible."

Amber grinned and ducked her head, but not before Carrie saw the sheer adoration she had for Robert on her face. Once again she battled her fear they may never be able to have children. Her husband should have the chance to be a father.

Robert turned to shake hands with Mark. "What a surprise!" He embraced Susan. "To what do we owe this pleasure?"

Susan exchanged a glance with Mark. "Should we tell him now?"

A clatter of wagon wheels and the pealing laughter of children filled the air.

Amber slid down off the fence, her face glowing with excitement. "Everyone is here!" she cried. "The Harvest Celebration is beginning!"

Carrie watched as a steady stream of people, laughing and talking, poured into the yard. Their arms were full of blankets to sit on. "The Harvest Celebration has begun," she agreed. She understood the look on Robert's face. "You can stay here and talk to Mark and Susan while I go greet everyone."

Robert hesitated, his expression saying that was exactly what he wanted to do, but he shook his head. "This day is too important." He turned to Mark. "We can talk afterwards?"

"Absolutely," Mark agreed. "Thomas told me this is the best tobacco harvest he has ever had."

Robert nodded. "And all these people are the ones who made it possible. We're going to give them the party of their life!" He turned to Carrie. "Finish getting Granite ready. Thomas, Abby, and I will greet everyone. Moses and Rose will be here in just a minute. They are finishing up down at the tournament arena."

"I'll come with you," Mark said. "I'm eager to see Moses."

Robert grinned. "He is going to be thrilled you are here, *Captain* Jones."

Susan waved as Robert and Mark left the barn, and then she turned to Carrie. "Can I stay here with you?"

"I would love it!"

"Me, too," Amber said shyly.

Susan put a hand on Amber's shoulder. "Will you introduce me to All My Heart?"

"Yes, ma'am!"

Carrie smiled, knowing Susan had made a friend for life. She suddenly couldn't wait another moment. "If I promise not to say anything to Robert, will you tell me why you're here?"

"And me, too?" Amber cried. "My mama was right, wasn't she?"

Susan smiled. "When we got your father's invitation, we were intrigued. We became more intrigued when we learned Eclipse's lineage."

"He's out of Lexington," Amber boasted. "My brother, Clint, had Abby buy him when Robert was still real sick."

Susan looked at Carrie with surprise. "Is that right?"

Carrie nodded. "Clint is a very gifted horseman. He spent the years during the war studying everything he could get his hands on about horses so he would be prepared. He fell in love with horses when Robert taught him how to ride. He never gave up hope that someday he would work with Robert."

"And now he is," Susan murmured before she turned to Amber. "Your brother made a very wise choice."

"Yep."

Susan grinned. "As I said, we were intrigued enough to make the trip down. We recently decided to expand. Thomas' letter came at the perfect time."

"What did my father say?"

Susan shrugged. "Just that the folks around here were too stupid to recognize the best horseflesh he had ever seen."

Carrie laughed. She could hardly wait to tell her father she wasn't going back to Philadelphia. She wouldn't be in Richmond, but she would see him far more often. "He does know how to encapsulate an issue," she said.

Susan turned back around to stare into the pasture. "He was right."

Amber stepped up to tug on her arm. "Miss Jones?"

Susan looked down. "Yes, Amber?"

"You can't have All My Heart because she's mine. And you can't have Pegasus, either. He belongs to my brother," she explained earnestly.

Susan nodded. "Which one is Pegasus?"

Amber pointed toward the tree where a bay colt rested in the shade, his head lifted to attention as he watched everyone arrive. "That one!"

Susan chuckled. "Why am I not surprised the two of you chose the best ones of the bunch?"

"They're all fine colts and fillies," Amber promised. "Any one of them would be a fine addition to your stable."

Carrie's heart swelled with love. "You are absolutely right, Amber." She turned to Susan. "Do you have any idea how many you want?" She could hardly wait for Robert to discover some of them were going to have a home. Perhaps that would open the gate for other buyers.

Susan hesitated. "I should probably wait for Mark..."

"Or just tell us since we're all women here," Amber broke in. "We have to stick together, you know!"

Carrie laughed. "She listens to Rose and me."

"And to June, and Annie, and my mama," Amber added. "Are they right?" she demanded.

"They're right," Susan chuckled. "I really *should* wait for Mark, but I already know we are in agreement."

"So how many?" Amber pressed, her eyes fixed intently on Susan's face.

"All of them."

A long silence fell on the barn as more people streamed into the yard. Carrie finally found her voice. "Did you say *all* of them?"

"*All* of them?" Amber echoed in a whisper.

"Well, all of them except All My Heart and Pegasus," Susan responded. "Unless you decide to change your mind and sell her to us, Amber," she teased.

"No, ma'am," Amber said, but a wide grin was spreading across her face. "Robert is sure going to be happy!"

Carrie had dozens of questions swarming through her mind, but Thomas, Abby, Matthew, and Janie were walking out onto the porch. It was important to be with them. Granite was ready for the tournament. Now that she wasn't going back to Philadelphia, she wanted to take a more active role on the plantation. "You'll have to excuse me," she said quickly. She wrapped Susan in a hug. "Thank you," she whispered. Then she turned and hurried across the yard.

Chapter Twenty-Three

Granite snorted and pranced as the crowds pressed closer to the arena. Carrie couldn't hold back her grin as she felt him move beneath her. After years of dreaming about it, she was finally going to compete in a tournament. She knew Granite was as excited as she was.

It was a perfect day for the Harvest Celebration. The early morning chill had retreated with the sun, but the air was still crisp and cool. The aroma of roasting pigs seemed to fill every inch of the plantation. The men had dug pits for four huge hogs, to make sure there was enough for everyone. The long tables groaned under the weight of all the food, but the feasting would not begin until someone had been crowned the winner of the tournament.

She watched as the crowd talked and laughed. She couldn't help comparing the spectators to those from the Blackwell Tournaments of years past. The Blackwell Tournament and Ball had always been an event where every woman from surrounding plantations strove to outdo the others who would attend. They chose their resplendent gowns carefully, always wore hats to protect their delicate complexions, and would never be seen without a frilly parasol. Men wore elegant suits and chatted with friends they saw only a few times a year.

Carrie chuckled. What a difference six years could make. The dresses surrounding the arena were just as colorful, but there were no fancy gowns, and not one woman wore a hat or carried a parasol to protect their ebony skin. The look of happiness on their faces was the only adornment they needed. The men, forged by months of working together under brutal conditions, wore justified expressions of pride as they laughed and talked.

Carrie looked over and saw Clint talking earnestly to Amber. The expression on her little face was as intense as Carrie had ever seen, but she couldn't detect even a trace of nervousness. Amber was ready. She sat easily on Eclipse, probably not even aware that people were discussing how such a small girl could handle such an enormous horse.

Carrie's gaze swung to Robert. He was mounted on a black gelding named Mischief. In spite of his name, the gelding was calm and well-mannered. She admired her husband's dark looks on the stunning horse but had no concerns that Mischief could outpace Granite or Eclipse. She was sure Robert was disappointed he couldn't ride his stallion, but she knew he was equally proud of the fact that Amber had won the honor.

Moses was astride Champ. The powerful horse easily handled Moses' size but was not going to be competition for Granite. She smiled at him and continued scanning the field of competition.

There were several of Moses' men on their horses. They would have fun, but they did not present a challenge. She glanced at them and looked around until her eyes settled on the last minute competitor.

Susan, inspired by the fact that both Carrie and Amber were riding, had accepted the offer of a Cromwell horse for the Tournament. She looked magnificent on Lucky Lady, a towering gray Thoroughbred that looked like a feminine version of Granite. Carrie inspected the mare carefully. Out of all the horses, this was the one she knew the least about, but she knew Susan was savvy enough to pick a mount that would give her the best advantage. The mare's legs were powerful, and her wide chest spoke of speed, but Carrie's examination brought her to the conclusion that Lucky Lady would not be as fast as Granite, and she knew Susan had never practiced capturing the rings. She would not be a threat.

Granite snorted again and shied a little as a piece of cloth went flying by. Carrie quit inspecting the field of competitors and turned all her attention to her horse. Granite had almost lost the competition six years ago when he had been frightened by a loose handkerchief. It was up to her to keep him calm and focused. Blocking out everyone else around her, Carrie soothed Granite and murmured softly to him, her hand stroking his neck as her father mounted the platform built next to the arena.

Carrie, completely immersed in her horse, was surprised when she heard the horn blow. She knew Louisa had found the old tournament horn in a hiding place on Blackwell Plantation that the Union soldiers had not discovered. Perry flashed her a grin when he lowered the horn from his lips. He had been practicing for days to make sure he could do more than make the horn sputter. Carrie grinned back at him and turned toward her father as he climbed the stairs to the platform. The boisterous crowd fell completely silent.

Thomas, resplendent in a black suit that marked the importance of the occasion, smiled as he gazed out over the crowd. Carrie felt a surge of pride but pushed aside any thoughts other than the tournament as he began to speak.

"Ladies and gentlemen. It is now time for the *Charge of the Knights.*" Thomas' deep voice rang out through the still air. The quiet seemed to grow even deeper as everyone listened intently. Not so long ago, the closest any of the people in this crowd could have gotten to a tournament was in their role as slave. To simply be part of the spectators was a momentous occasion. Not one person was taking it lightly.

Carrie straightened as her father turned to gaze at the group of competitors gathered below the platform. His eyes rested on her for a moment, warming her with pride and love, and then he smiled at all of them. Out of the corner of her eye she saw Amber flash him a big grin.

"Ladies and gentlemen, you are gathered here today to participate in the most chivalrous and gallant sport known. It has been called the sport of kings, and well it should. It has come down to us from the Crusades, being at that time a very hazardous undertaking," Thomas said solemnly.

Carrie shivered as she felt the years melt away. Her father was speaking the exact same words that Colonel James Benton had spoken every year of the Blackwell

Tournament. It was as if no time at all had passed, but yet it also felt as if several lifetimes had been lived. She glanced over and caught Robert's eye. She knew he was thinking the same thing she was—reliving the day they had begun to fall in love. She smiled at him lovingly and then turned her attention back to her father.

"The knights of that day rode in full armor, charging down the lists at each other with the intent that the best man would knock his opponent from his horse. It was a rough and dangerous pastime. Many were seriously hurt. Some were killed. But we, in this day, have gotten soft and tender—as well as much smarter, I believe—and have eliminated the danger and roughness of the sport." Laughter rippled through the crowd, but as in years past, no one spoke up to mar the seriousness of the charge.

Thomas sobered as he leaned forward to address the riders. "But with all that, it is still a challenging and fascinating sport. One that tests the horsemanship, dexterity, skill, quickness of eye, and steadiness and control of the rider, and the speed, smoothness of gait, and training of the horse. It is an honorable sport, and I do not need to mention that a knight taking any undue advantage of his opponents will be ruled out of the tournament." His eyes bored into each competitor's until he seemed confident he had made his point. "Now, for the rules."

Carrie knew the rules by heart, even after all these years, but she listened attentively, still hardly believing she was actually going to ride.

"The three ring hangers are spaced twenty yards apart. The start is twenty yards from the first ring—making the total length of the list sixty yards. Any rider taking more than seven seconds from the start to the last ring will be ruled out. Should anything untoward happen during the tilt that would prevent the rider from having a fair try at the rings, he will so indicate by lowering his lance and making no try at the rings. The judges will decide whether he is entitled to another tilt."

Carrie glanced over to where Matthew, Perry, June, Louisa, and Abby sat, their solemn faces communicating they were aware of the importance of their role as judges.

"All rings must be taken off the lances by the judges," Thomas continued. "No others will be counted. The rings on the first tilt will be two inches in diameter; on the second tilt, one and a half; on the third tilt, one; on the fourth tilt, three quarters; and on the fifth and last tilt—if there are any competitors left—one half inch."

Carrie listened closely, allowing her mind to envision her capturing all of the rings on every tilt.

Thomas smiled and swept his arm grandly. "All of you are riding not only to win, but to gain the coveted honor of crowning the lady of your choice the Queen of Love and Beauty at the ball later tonight."

Carrie cleared her throat loudly.

Thomas looked down with a grimace. "I'm sorry. Old habits die hard," he said ruefully. "I should have said all of you are riding not only to win, but to gain the coveted honor of crowning the lady, or man," he hesitated as he looked at Amber, "or *boy* of your choice the Queen or King of Love and Beauty at the ball later tonight."

Everyone laughed but quieted quickly to hear the rest of the instructions. A sense of competition had charged the air as Thomas had been talking. The crowd, here for a celebration, suddenly seemed to realize the importance of what was about to happen.

Thomas continued. "The next seven riders will have the privilege of honoring the person of their choice as royalty-in-waiting for the queen or king. Only the members of the court will participate in the opening dance at the ball tonight. Good luck to you," Thomas finished. "May the best *person* win!"

Another mighty blow on the horn announced the beginning of the competition. A rousing cheer rose from the crowd along with a whoop from all the riders as they galloped their horses toward the start line.

Carrie felt a flurry of nervousness and tamped it down firmly. Granite's confidence and steadiness would come from her. She gripped her lance tightly, ignoring everyone else around her as she stared down the list at the rings that already seemed impossibly small at two inches. Had they really been so tiny six years ago? She straightened in her saddle and pulled her shoulders back. She had waited all her life for this moment. She was going to compete, and she was going to win. She looked over to find Robert's eyes fixed on her. "*Good luck*," he mouthed.

Carrie smiled, blew him a kiss, and then touched the handkerchief he had given her the night before as her token. He touched his pocket lightly, his eyes sparkling with laughter. Carrie's focus melted as her own laughter bubbled in her throat. In memory of the first tournament six years earlier, she had cut a lock of her hair and left it for him on his pillow before she joined Rose. He had been holding it tightly in his sleep when she had gotten in late.

"Ladies and gentleman, our first contestant is Knight Moses Samuels."

Carrie's full attention was pulled back to the arena. It was just as she had imagined it would be. The crowd and every other competitor seemed to melt away. The only thing that remained real was the list stretched out before her. She was aware of Moses finishing his run, but she was too focused to hear the results. It didn't matter what anyone else did. Her only real competition was the rings dangling from their clasps. She imagined herself capturing them time and again until Thomas' voice broke through her concentration.

"Our next contestant is Knight Carrie Borden," Thomas said, not bothering to hide the pride in his voice.

Carrie moved forward, a steadying hand on Granite's neck. He was excited, but there was no nervousness in him as he waited for her signal. Out of the corner of her eye she saw the wave of the flag. As she leaned forward slightly, Granite shot down the list. Carrie brought her lance up, her eyes focused on the first ring. It was hers! The second ring was captured just as easily. Pushing down a sense of triumph, she concentrated on the third ring, allowing a smile to split her lips when it slid easily onto her lance. Granite thundered to the end of the list and then settled into an easy trot toward the judges' table. Before they got there, the next contestant was off.

Only then did Carrie realize Amber was right after her. She watched closely as Amber captured all three rings easily. Both she and Eclipse gazed out over the crowd with triumphant expressions as they trotted over to join Carrie.

"Well done!" Carrie called to Amber as Matthew counted her rings and then waved her over to join the next round of competition.

"You, too!" Amber called back, her face glowing with happiness.

No one in the crowd moved as the competition continued. Carrie remembered that the Blackwell crowd had all melted away after the first list, only returning for the last few tilts when the competition had been narrowed down. Not today. It was clear no one wanted to miss a second of the fun.

There had been an initial field of fifteen knights. Only ten had been able to capture all three rings. They lined up for the next tilt. Carrie smiled at Robert, Moses, Susan, and Amber, and then put her entire focus on the list again. She had expected all four of them to make it through the first tilt, but now she had to prepare. She knew the rings were only a half inch smaller, but they seemed much tinier. She forced herself to breathe evenly, murmuring to Granite while she waited her turn. This time she was fifth in line.

Once again, Granite ran like lightning. Once again, she captured all three rings.

Carrie felt a thrill of accomplishment, but her attention was already on the next tilt as she cantered over to the starting line after Abby had counted her rings. Only when she was lined up did she realize there were only five of them left. In the past, tournaments had been prepared for with months of practice. None of the knights, with the exception of Amber, had been able to do that. They had ridden for fun. Now those who had failed in their quest were lined up along the arena fence, cheering on the remaining competitors.

Carrie allowed her focus to diminish just long enough to identify the remaining riders—Robert, Susan, Amber, and Bob, one of Moses' seasonal field hands. Bob looked surprised to still be in the field, but he was clearly eager to win.

"Ladies and gentlemen, the third tilt is about to begin. The rings have been reduced to one inch in size," Thomas called out. "You have before you five very talented knights."

The start flag waved, and Susan tore down the list on Lucky Lady. Carrie couldn't be sure, but it looked like she only got two rings. She pushed aside all thoughts of anyone else and let her entire attention settle on the list.

"Knight Carrie Borden!" her father called.

Granite and Carrie, linked as a single unit, thundered down the list again. Carrie, her mind calm and focused, watched as all three rings slid easily onto her lance. She trotted to the judges' table, nodded her acceptance of their congratulations, and then returned to the starting line. Her father's voice broke through her concentration.

"What you are seeing here today is the reason women were banned from competition for so long," Thomas said, his face wreathed in a proud smile.

The crowd laughed loudly and clapped. Only then did Carrie look around. Susan and Amber were the only other knights still with her. Her eyes widened with both surprise and delight. "May the best female win!"

"May the best female win!" Amber laughed.

"May the best female win!" Susan echoed.

Then all three of them shut out the crowd and focused.

Carrie was not happy to be first in line. She had no way of knowing if the other two knights would miss any of the rings. All she could do to insure her continuation was to capture all three rings again. She cleared her mind and settled deeper into her saddle. "Good boy, Granite," she said softly. His ears flicked to show he was listening, but his entire concentration was on the list stretched out before them, his muscles bunched tightly in anticipation.

Not waiting for her signal, he surged forward the instant the flag started down, giving them a precious advantage. Carrie caught her breath, ignored the fatigue in her arm from holding the lance, and set her eyes on the first ring. She could no longer afford to watch to see the results. She simply had to ride as fast as she could. They raced to the end of the tilt before Granite slowed and turned toward the judges' table with no urging from her. Carrie threw back her head with a joyful laugh when she realized all three rings were on her lance.

"Congratulations!" Robert called.

Carrie grinned at him, nodded to the cheering crowd, and then rode over to have her rings counted. When she returned to the starting gate for the final tilt, only Amber was still in the competition.

"It's just you and me!" Amber crowed.

"That it is," Carrie acknowledged, feeling a twinge of nervousness for the first time. Amber was completely confident in her ability to capture rings of any size, and Eclipse seemed to have a smug look on his face. Granite snorted and bobbed his head. Carrie felt the nervousness dissipate as her horse assured her they could handle whatever was waiting for them. She flexed her right arm to relieve muscles tired from holding the lance, and took deep breaths.

When Carrie lined up for the fifth and final tilt, she reflected that the finish was just what she had dreamed of for years. The only part that hadn't figured in her fantasies was the fact that she was competing against a ten-year-old black girl. The reality made it even more special, but it did nothing to diminish her determination to win.

The crowd's noise had died away to a silent hush as the new rings—just one half inch in diameter—were placed on the tilt. Everyone seemed to hold their breath collectively. Carrie felt herself tighten but forced herself to try to relax. "Good luck," she murmured to Amber as her father waved for the little girl to advance.

"You, too," Amber replied, her eyes staring forward. The flag waved. Eclipse seemed to float down the list.

Carrie was being waved forward before there was time to hear Amber's results. She gripped the lance tightly but kept her touch on the reins very light. "We can do this, Granite," she said confidently.

Again, he surged forward with no signal from her. Carrie honed in on the rings but honestly couldn't tell if she had captured any of them at all. Even when Granite reached the end and turned to trot over to the judges' table, she couldn't see the tiny rings on the end of her lance. Her heart sank as she realized she must have missed all of them.

"Two rings!" she heard Matthew sing out as Amber trotted away from the table, a frown on her face as she looked back over her shoulder.

Carrie opened her mouth to call out her congratulations but closed it in surprise when Louisa stepped forward and pulled two rings off her lance.

"Two rings!" Louisa called out, holding them up triumphantly. She leaned close to Carrie and whispered. "My bet is on you and Granite."

Carrie laughed with both relief and incredulity as she saw the two glimmering rings in Louisa's hand. It seemed somehow incredibly fitting that there was a Blackwell judging the tournament.

"Now this is what I call competition!" Thomas yelled out, his voice tight with excitement. "I don't believe I've ever seen tighter competition than this." He raised his hand. "May the best female win!"

"May the best female win!" the crowd roared back.

Carrie looked at Amber. The little girl's face was flushed with pride and happiness. For just a moment she considered deliberately missing a ring, but then pushed the thought aside. She was too much of a competitor for that, but she also knew Amber would suspect if she didn't win fairly. She moved up close to Amber. "You're amazing," she said quietly. "May the best female win." The simple statement had become the mantra of the day.

"May the best female win," Amber replied. "Thank you, Carrie." Her voice was husky with emotion.

Carrie tore her eyes from the list. "For what?"

"If it hadn't been for you, Moses would never have brought Robert to us. None of this would be happening."

Carrie blinked her eyes, her thoughts spinning to Biddy's Bregdan Principle. Truly, nothing happened in a vacuum. "You're welcome," she said, suddenly realizing that no matter who won, they were *both* the winners. The knowledge completely relaxed her. "Go out there and have fun," she said.

Amber grinned and nodded, moving forward when she was called to the starting line. Once again, Eclipse seemed to float, not merely run, down the list. Amber looked to be just a small speck carrying a very large lance.

Still relaxed, Carrie advanced to the line. "Show them what you can do, Granite," she called, letting out a whoop as they sprang forward. Her arm held steady as they flew toward the first ring, but as they reached the second ring, she felt her grip slip on the lance for just a moment. She didn't have time to bemoan the fact before the third ring was rushing toward them. She tightened her grip, eyed the ring, and then flew down the rest of the list.

All the judges were standing quietly beside the table as Carrie rode forward. Again, she couldn't tell what was on the end of her lance. Suddenly, after years of wanting nothing more than to win the tournament, it no longer mattered. She smiled as she approached Matthew. Only then did she realize Louisa was just walking up to Amber. They had waited for her to finish her tilt before they counted either of their rings.

Matthew reached for her lance. "Two rings!"

The crowd held its breath as Louisa reached for Amber's lance. A look of astonished admiration filled her face. "Three rings!" she called as she held them to the sky triumphantly.

The crowd exploded with applause and cheers.

Amber's face burst into a grin. She caught Carrie's eye just a second before Clint ran up to Eclipse and pulled her down into a long hug. "I won!" Amber cried. "I won!"

"That you did!" Clint told her. "You deserved it, little sister. I'm proud of you."

If possible, Amber beamed even more brightly as she wrapped her arms around her brother tightly.

Carrie joined in the cheering, her heart swelling as she looked around at the mass of faces, both black and white, celebrating an extraordinary accomplishment.

Moses had never felt such a deep sense of satisfaction as he gazed around the plantation grounds.

Rose walked up and slid her hand in his. "Look at them. They are so excited."

Moses nodded. "They should be. These men have never earned anything other than what the army paid some of them." He didn't add that many of them had left the army being owed money for work done. Now was not the time to look backward. He would only look forward. He had just told his workers the final numbers for the harvest and handed out slips of paper letting each of them know how much they had earned. It had been pure joy to watch their faces. Now all the men were huddled with their wives and children, excitedly talking about the future. As his gaze continued to rove, he suddenly tightened.

"What's wrong?" Rose asked, and then she sucked in her breath when her eyes followed his. "Morah..."

"I thought I got through to Abraham," Moses said through clenched teeth as he saw the fear on Morah's face. Abraham was clutching his piece of paper with fierce pride, but there was no joy in his eyes. He was staring at his wife with a look full of angry power. Morah seemed to shrink away from him, clutching her children to her tightly. They watched their daddy with wide eyes, sadness etched on their faces as the other families celebrated together.

"She's terrified," Rose whispered.

Moses searched his mind for what to do.

Rose read his expression. "Don't do anything right now," she whispered. "If you draw attention to him, he will take it out on them later."

Moses ground his teeth, but stayed where he was because he knew she was right. He thought about the letter of recommendation he had written Abraham just a few days earlier, after the man assured him all was well in his home. He realized now that it had been a blatant lie. He had not given him the letter yet, but he had planned to. Now he didn't know what to do.

Rose continued to read his mind. "If you don't give him the letter, he will be angrier and more desperate. He will take it out on Morah and the children."

"So I do nothing?" Moses growled.

"We offer Morah and the children the opportunity to stay here."

"Without Abraham?"

"Without Abraham," Rose said firmly. "He must be told to leave."

Moses looked at Morah. "Do you think she will do it? Stay here without him?"

Rose sighed heavily. "I don't know. She's become so much more confident in school, but she'll be terrified by what we're proposing."

"Perhaps Janie could talk to her," Moses suggested.

Rose smiled at him. "That's a very good idea. Janie has been through what she is experiencing. Perhaps that will give her the courage to make another choice."

A voice broke into their conversation. "I knew you would make me proud, Moses!"

Moses spun around and accepted Captain Jones' firm handshake. "Thank you, sir."

Mark grimaced. "Are you ever going to lose the *sir*?"

Moses grinned. "It was rather ingrained for a few years. It may take a while." Somehow it seemed wrong not to address him as Captain Jones or show the proper respect.

"Work on it!"

"Yes, sir!" Moses responded automatically. Both Rose and Mark started laughing.

"You've done a remarkable thing here," Mark commented, his eyes sweeping the men. "You were a natural leader in the army, but you have created something here that I wish the rest of the country would emulate."

"You and me both," Moses said. "Most of the problems in the South would disappear right now if everyone were treated fairly. The whites are terrified because they have lost what they consider the only way of life they have ever known and they have no idea how to live any differently. The blacks are terrified because they have no idea how to live in this new world that the white folks don't want them in. The terrors are colliding into each other." He couldn't hold back the scowl that accompanied his words. More reports had been coming in, but so far he had kept the knowledge to himself.

Mark looked at him closely. "You believe it's going to get worse."

Rose held up a hand. "It doesn't matter what he believes. Not tonight. Tonight is about celebration. The problems in America will wait for just one night."

Moses laughed and nodded easily. He wasn't convinced, but now was not the time to say so. Something in his gut said trouble was coming, but he pushed it back with effort. He would deal with it if it came.

Carrie looked around the yard, mesmerized by all the lanterns glowing as the sun sank below the horizon. Their radiance formed pools of soft light beneath the trees they hung from. A chill was beginning to invade the air, but she knew no one would feel it once the dancing began. The tables had been relieved of their heavy burden of food. After the tournament had ended and the awards were distributed, the feasting had begun. Felicia and Rose had led games for the children while the women huddled together on blankets, talking and laughing. The men had played a rousing game of baseball, thrilled by the equipment Thomas and Abby had brought with them. None of them had ever played before, but that didn't keep them from a fierce competition. All in all, the day had been a complete success. And it was far from over. She knew every person there had been waiting for the dancing.

She had seen Polly, Annie, and June disappear upstairs with Amber an hour or so ago. She watched as several of Moses' men picked up guitars, banjos, and fiddles. They moved to an area under the tree and began to play. The sound of their music caused everyone to quit talking.

Thomas, dressed once more in his black suit after shucking it to join in the baseball game, stepped forward to announce the beginning of the Cromwell Ball. The lantern light shimmering on his white hair seemed also to swallow his wrinkles. Carrie had a flash of the very young-looking blond man who had entered the Civil War years. The death of her mother and four years of conflict had stolen his youthful appearance, but it hadn't stolen his vibrancy, and they had also given him a maturity and elegance that almost took her breath away.

"The Cromwell Ball is about to begin," he called. There was to be no similarity to the carefully cultivated elegance of the Blackwell Ball, but Abby had insisted they give it the same importance. "We will start by welcoming our conquering knight."

Chapter Twenty-Four

The music swelled louder as everyone watched the back door of the plantation house. The door opened slowly. Amber stepped out onto the stairs, pausing to look around, her head raised regally.

Carrie caught her breath. The three women had worked wonders. Little Amber had truly been turned into a female conquering knight. Her hair, normally pulled back into a tight braid, had been piled on top of her head with wisps floating around her narrow face. Her eyes seemed huge as they sparkled in the lantern light. Her breeches and shirt had been replaced by a creamy white, flowing dress that reached to her ankles. It danced around her as the breeze stirred brightly colored leaves that framed her like a painting.

Robert stepped out of the crowd and held out his hand. "May I accompany you, my knight?"

Amber giggled as she nodded. "But of course," she managed to say demurely. "I would be honored."

Carrie choked back a laugh. The preparation committee had been very thorough in prepping Amber for the evening.

Amber seemed to nearly glide as Robert tucked her hand through his arm and led her to Thomas. Thomas smiled warmly as he took Amber's hand and turned her to face everyone. Other than a collective gasp when she had walked out, everyone had remained silent. Carrie felt as if someone had cast a spell on the evening.

"Ladies and gentleman, I present to you Amber, the Conquering Knight of the Cromwell Tournament."

Carrie pushed aside the thought that Gabe and Polly needed to take a last name as she joined in the warm applause and cheering. Thomas reached into a box behind him and pulled out a crown woven of tobacco leaves, interspersed with bright yellow and white flowers.

He held it high and placed it in Amber's hands. "Madame Conquering Knight," he said solemnly, "you are now to choose the King of Love and Handsomeness for the evening's festivities."

Carrie chuckled, knowing just how appalled Southern aristocracy would be with their rendering of the tournament and ball.

Robert edged up beside her. "Do you think the Blackwells are turning in their graves?" he whispered, his voice laced with humor.

"Absolutely," Carrie whispered back as she saw Amber's eyes sweep the crowd before she held the crown high in a display of sheer triumph. "The whole day has been perfect."

"You were amazing on Granite," Robert whispered. "Should I tell you that my money was on you?"

"At the very least, you should *not* tell me if your money was actually on Amber," Carrie teased, stretching up to kiss Robert on his cheek. "That little girl deserved to win. She was truly amazing."

"She was, wasn't she?" Robert replied, love and pride coating his words.

Amber's voice stopped their talking. "I was planning on winning the tournament," she began, pausing to wait for the laughter to die down, "so I've had a lot of time to decide who would be my king. Robert told me choosing my king should not be taken lightly if I won." Her eyes sought out Robert. "I thought about Robert because he's taught me almost everything I know, and he let me ride Eclipse..."

"I didn't *let* you ride him," Robert called. "You won the right in a bet."

"Well, yes, that's true," Amber responded. "But you were a good loser!"

Laughter rolled through the crowd again, but Amber raised her hand to silence them, looking every inch the Conquering Knight. "I thought about some boys at school because there are a couple I'm watching real close." She had to pause again when mirth interrupted her. "Anyway, after I thought about that a while, I realized who I wanted to crown king. Next to Robert, my brother, Clint, has taught me everything I know. I know most people believed Carrie would win, but my brother kept telling me I could do it. After a while, I guess I started believing him."

She held the crown high in the air. "I guess this crown is going to look funny on my brother, but I can't think of anyone I would rather crown the King of the Cromwell Ball!" she said loudly.

Clint was laughing, but he had a look of deep pride and love on his face as he strode forward. He stepped in front of Amber, bowed deeply, and then knelt in front of her so she could place the crown on his head. "I am honored to be your King, O Conquering Knight."

Amber placed the crown on his head, her eyes glowing with happiness, and then she held out her hand. "May I have the honor of the first dance?" she said sweetly.

Carrie knew this ball wasn't going to resemble any she had been to, but she was still startled when the musicians broke into a lively rendition of the Juba, instead of the waltz she had danced with Robert when he won. She glanced at Louisa standing on the other side of the clearing with Perry, both surprised and pleased to see both of them smiling as they watched the proceedings.

"Not so fast," Thomas called, waving to the musicians to stop playing as he moved back into the center of the circle. "We still have to select the kings and queens-in-waiting."

Amber dropped her eyes. "Sorry, I forgot about that part."

"I can understand why when you have such a perfect king waiting to dance with you," Thomas responded. "Will you call the top five competing knights up here, Amber? Do you remember the last five you vanquished on your way to victory?"

Amber's eyes lost their embarrassed look as she nodded confidently. "Carrie. Susan. Robert. Moses. Bob. Will all of you please come join me?" She smiled mischievously. "You might not have won, but you still get to be with me."

A fresh wave of amusement swept through the waiting crowd.

"Gloat this year, Amber," Carrie said as she walked forward with Robert. "But next year is coming. I will be ready." And she would be. She could hardly believe she had held her secret in all day. She had enjoyed every minute of the Harvest Celebration, but she was eager for the day to end so she could tell Robert she wasn't leaving. Yes, Amber was definitely going to have competition next fall.

Carrie watched as Robert chose Abby to be his lady-in-waiting. Moses pulled Rose out of the crowd. Susan selected Mark. Bob solemnly announced his wife, Cassie Lou, was to be his lady-in-waiting. Carrie walked forward as Thomas beckoned to her. "I can think of no one I would rather have as my King tonight than you, Father."

Thomas smiled proudly and held out his hand. "I am honored," he replied. He bent down to talk softly. "I'm not sure I'm your best choice for the Juba, however."

Carrie laughed as the musicians burst into loud music. "We'll both do the best we can," she murmured, watching Moses and Rose closely as they began to move around the floor. The Juba Dance was originally from West Africa, but it had become a plantation dance during the slave gatherings when no rhythm instruments were allowed due to fear of secret codes hidden in the drumming. "Watch Rose and Moses, and Bob and Cassie Lou. Do what they do."

She and her father laughed their way through the first dance. They exchanged helpless looks as Rose and Moses circled them, stomping their feet and slapping their arms, legs, chests, and cheeks.

"Come on," Moses teased. "You're not too white to pick up the Juba!"

Carrie rolled her eyes, but by the third dance, when everyone had joined in the celebration, she and her father had fallen into the rhythm. "This is fun!" she cried.

Robert and Abby moved closer. "Speak for yourself," Robert muttered. "How in the world are you making your feet and arms do that?"

"My question exactly," Abby cried with exasperation.

Carrie released her father and grabbed Robert's hand. "Father, you teach Abby. I'll take care of my clumsy husband."

"Clumsy?" Robert sputtered. "You'll regret that!"

"Only if you can figure out how to make your hands and feet work at the same time," Carrie teased. By the time two more dances had been played, Robert was keeping up with her.

Robert was laughing as the music swelled around them. "Well, I wouldn't say I'm graceful, but at least I look like I know how to dance!" He looked at her with sudden suspicion. "How did you learn how to do that so quickly?"

"You mean other than the fact that I'm a natural dancer?" Carrie asked demurely. She chuckled when she saw the threatening look in her husband's eyes. "I had the privilege of seeing Master Juba in action while I was in Philadelphia."

"Master Juba?"

"His real name is William Henry Lane. He is actually one of the first black performers in the country. His show was amazing." She paused as she remembered. "I had seen the Juba Dance on the plantation for years, though of course my mother wouldn't let me dance it. When I saw Master Juba, I went home and practiced what I had seen until I didn't feel totally awkward. Having the music with it makes it much easier."

"I knew you had a secret advantage!" Robert crowed as he stomped around her and slapped his legs.

"That's not the only secret I have," Carrie teased.

"Oh, really?" Robert murmured in her ear. "Don't you know you shouldn't keep secrets from your husband?"

Suddenly Carrie couldn't stand it another second. "Come with me!"

Carrie pulled Robert away from the dancing until they were encompassed in darkness, but the beat of the music still pulsed around them. She remained silent as she continued to make her way down the path she knew like the back of her hand. Robert followed willingly. She began to relax as the music faded behind them. By the time they reached her intended destination, the music was only a faint hum in the distance. She stopped on the banks of the river, breathing in deeply as she listened to the swish of the water against the shore and gazed up at the stars forming a gleaming canopy overhead. Robert wrapped his arm around her waist and pulled her close, but he seemed content to remain quiet.

"I have something to tell you," Carrie finally said after the river and the night had worked its magic on her.

"I have something to tell you, too," Robert replied, his voice thick with satisfaction.

"You first," Carrie said, curious to know what he was hiding, although she was fairly sure she knew what it was.

"Oh no," he said. "You were the one who pulled me away from the dance. You have to talk first."

"But I am next in line to the Conquering Knight," Carrie protested. "You must do my bidding."

"Nice try," Robert shot back, "but you only came in second. Now that we have left the circle of the Cromwell Ball, you are nothing but a lowly wife. You must speak first."

Carrie laughed, joy almost bursting her heart. She threw her arms around her husband. "I love you!"

"That's your secret?" Robert asked, puzzled. "I'm pretty sure I knew that. I'll hold it close to my heart, however. It will help when you leave."

Carrie heard his teasing voice, but she also felt the pain hidden behind his light words. She was suddenly more aware than ever how much he missed her. "And what if I was here to tell you every day?"

Robert went still and stepped back to peer into her face. "What are you saying, Carrie?"

Carrie gazed up at him, wishing it wasn't too dark for him to see all the love in her eyes. She could only hope it was coating every word she spoke. "I'm not going back to school, Robert. At least not now. I'm staying here on the plantation." She couldn't see the expression on his face, but she felt him remain very still.

"Why?"

Carrie recognized the sound of reluctant hope in his voice. She needed to give him an answer he could hold onto, but she wasn't ready to talk about the possibility he couldn't have children. "I know I want to be a doctor, Robert, but my heart is telling me to stay here on the plantation for now. I love being in school, but I miss you and the plantation every single day I am away from here."

She could feel Robert staring down at her, and she could almost see the questions in his eyes. "I am going to run the clinic and learn as much as I can about homeopathy. Abby knows a homeopathic physician in Richmond. I'm sure she'll set up a meeting."

"Does she know you're staying?"

"I've told no one but you," Carrie said. "Well, Rose...she was with me last night when I decided."

Robert drew a deep breath. "You're sure? Might you change your mind?"

Carrie knew he was protecting his heart from possible disappointment. She laughed and pressed close to him. "I'm not changing my mind," she assured him. "I'll send a letter to Philadelphia tomorrow and let them know my decision. And then I'm going to go riding with you every day and wait for the first snowfall. Though I must warn you, I may never get out of bed that day. I spent all last winter dreaming of being snuggled up with my husband on a snowy day!"

Robert clutched her close to him for a long moment and then threw his head back with a joyous laugh. He picked her up and swung her in a circle around him before lowering her to the ground to claim her lips in a passionate kiss. When he finally released her, he continued to hold her close. "Carrie..." he whispered.

"So may I take this as a sign of approval?"

"You've made me the happiest man alive," Robert assured her. "I've been dreading the day you were going to leave again."

Carrie felt a twinge of discomfort. "The day will come..."

Robert held a finger to her lips. "Of course the day will come," he said. "I want you to be a doctor almost as much as you want to be one. I will support you when you decide it is time to move forward, but for now I'm simply going to celebrate having my wife with me."

Carrie sighed and pulled his head down for another long kiss. "I love you," she whispered. Then she pulled away, her hands still on his face as she remembered. "What do you have to tell me?" She could feel Robert's face split into a wide smile.

"Do you know why Mark and Susan are here?" he asked.

Carrie hesitated for a split second before deciding not to let him know she knew the reason for their visit. She wanted him to have the joy of revealing it. "I assumed my father invited them for the Harvest Celebration."

Robert laughed. "You, my darling wife, are a horrible liar."

"What?" Carrie protested. She soon joined him in laughter. "I don't know why I even try. I suppose it is a good thing that I can't hide anything from you," she said, hoping she would do a better job of hiding her suspicions from him. She needed to make sure they never had a conversation about having children.

"So you know they came to see the crop of foals..."

"And they are going to buy all of them!" Carrie cried. "*All* of them!" She pulled away from him, grabbed his hand, and began to dance on the beach. Robert laughed and joined her, spinning her in circles until she was gasping for breath. "I can't breathe," she finally cried, dropping onto the closest boulder on the shoreline.

"*All* of them," Robert said slowly. He turned to stare out over the river as a fish splashed in the distance. "I guess Polly was right. I should have listened to her and the rest of them who kept insisting someone would buy the horses."

Carrie didn't need to see his face to know his eyes were gleaming with happiness and satisfaction. "You're on your way," she said. "Other buyers are going to see them, and they are going to realize their prejudices are only making them miss out." She knew Robert was watching his greatest dream come true. She pushed away the thought that she was letting *go* of her greatest dream. She wasn't letting go, only setting it aside for a time to do what she believed her heart was telling her to do. She would understand why at some point, but right now she was willing to trust the pieces would fall into place at the exact right time. And she was going to hold close the joy of being exactly where she wanted to be.

Robert pulled her to him and pressed his lips against her hair. "Do we have to go back to the dance?"

Carrie pretended to consider the question. "I doubt they will miss us," she finally said. "Do you have something else in mind?"

"The house is probably empty," Robert answered as he ran a hand down her cheek.

Carrie jumped up from the rock. "What are we still doing down by the river then?"

"My thoughts exactly," Robert said, throwing his head back in another joyful laugh.

Rose sensed the trouble before she could identify it. She stopped dancing and turned slowly, looking for what she was feeling.

Moses cocked his head. "What is it?"

Rose shook her head. "I'm not sure, but something doesn't feel right."

"I've been feeling trouble all night," Moses admitted reluctantly. "I was hoping nothing would come of it."

Rose took a deep breath and continued to scan the crowd. Her stomach tightened when she saw a small group of four women sitting beneath a tree, their heads close in intense concentration. Morah was in the middle of them, her face a mask of pained frustration and fear.

Moses' eyes followed hers. "What is going on?"

"I'll find out," she replied as she stepped away.

"Wait," Moses said tersely.

It was Rose's turn to follow his gaze. Her stomach clenched even more as she recognized the husbands of the four women standing together. She could tell by the expressions on their faces that they were angry. Their eyes were full of a dangerous fury that made her nervous. "You watch the men," she said. "I'll go talk to the women."

"What are you going to say?"

"I have absolutely no idea," Rose admitted. She walked around the edge of the clearing and settled down on the blankets the women were sharing. "Good evening."

Morah looked at her with desperate hope. "Hello, Rose." Her voice was quiet and unsteady.

"What's going on here?" Rose asked, relieved when she saw Moses step closer to the men. Their faces tightened with belligerence, but she was sure they wouldn't do anything. They were all seasonal workers who were counting on Moses for a reference letter the next day, and they were also surrounded by people who would do anything for her husband.

"Oh, our men are pouting because we won't dance with them," one of the women replied.

Rose eyed the men again. They weren't pouting. They were obviously trying to contain their anger in the midst of so many people. "Why won't you dance with them?"

"Because they ain't treating us right!" Morah said defiantly. "We thought about what you said at that meeting. We all decided we would make our stand here at the dance. We're letting them know that if they don't treat us right, we ain't going to just keep being dutiful wives."

Rose took a deep breath. Something told her they weren't taking the wisest course of action, but she honestly didn't know that she could come up with something better. Maybe being shunned by their wives in public would make the men rethink their actions. "And you believe this will work?"

Morah sighed. "I don't reckon I believe anything will work, but things can't get worse than they are," she said bitterly.

Rose's heart sank at the look of futility clouding the eyes of the beautiful young woman. She looked at the rest of them. "All of you are being beaten?"

The other three shook their heads. Della, a stout woman in her forties, had evidently been chosen as the spokeswoman. "Our men ain't beating us," she said. "At least not like Abraham is doing to Morah. They hit on us a little, but mostly they just do a lot of yelling. I think Moses must have said something to get through to them." She shook her head with disgust. "What I learned from being in school is that I'm just as smart as any man. I didn't live all them years in slavery just to have my man hit on me and yell at me and my children. I want my girls to know they can do anything they want now that they be free. I see the light in their eyes die a little more every day." She scowled. "I ain't gonna let it happen."

The other two women murmured their agreement.

Rose was mystified as to what to do or say. She desperately wished her mama was there to give her advice, though she wasn't even sure Sarah would have the answer. Everyone had been equal in the days of slavery. They feared being beaten, but not by each other. Slavery had been abolished, but new problems were raising their heads. She prayed quietly for wisdom. "No man has the right to hit you or demean you," she said. She looked at Della. "What are you planning on doing?"

The defiance on Della's face melted into confused fear. "I don't got no idea," she admitted. She glanced over at the men. "My man, Dexter, looks real angry," she murmured. She glanced at Morah, who seemed to be pulling into herself as Abraham glared at her. The woman's fear was palpable. "What you think we ought to do, Rose? I'm real sorry I ain't talking right, but I just can't seem to think clear."

Rose knew now was not the time to worry about correct grammar. There were far more important things at stake. She stared at the women, knowing that whatever she said would impact their children—her students. The responsibility she felt was like a heavy stone around her heart. "You're going to do nothing," she said.

"Huh?" Della stammered.

"You're going to do nothing. You're staying right here at the end of the dance. We'll put all of you up in one of the rooms in the house." Rose was suddenly very certain the women should not return to the cabins where their husbands would probably be waiting. Nothing good would come from it.

Della was already shaking her head. "I can't be leaving my children with Dexter," she protested. "If I ain't there for him to take his anger out on, he will take it out on the children. I won't let that happen."

"Della is right," a young-looking woman in her thirties said. "Not dancing with our men seemed like a good idea when we had it." She glanced toward the knot of men and then jerked her gaze back. "We may have done nothing but made it worse." She bit her lip. "I hope not," she muttered. "Stan can get real mad."

"I ain't leaving my kids either," the last woman said, speaking up for the first time. Her twenty-year-old eyes were far too old, and the lines on her face spoke of years of suffering in slavery.

Rose continued to beg silently for wisdom. "Moses and I will walk back with you," she said. She was confident the men would not do anything if the women weren't alone. Perhaps Moses could talk some sense into them. She had thought about having the children stay in the house as well, but she suspected taking their children would enrage the men even more. She desperately wished she knew the right thing to do, but she felt like she was casting around in the dark.

"That won't work," Morah whispered.

"How do you know?" Rose demanded, suddenly exasperated. "You're saying all my ideas are bad, but you don't have any of your own. Surely it won't make things better for you to infuriate your husbands by not dancing with them, and then merely walk home with them hoping there won't be consequences. I wish I could say they would all change and start treating you right, but you and I both know that isn't true." She took a deep breath, not questioning where the words were coming from. "Your husbands rule by fear. They do what they want because you are afraid of them. You are afraid to stay away from your home because of what they will do to your children. You are afraid to return home because of what they will do to you. They feel powerful, but they are really nothing but cowards," she said angrily.

The four women stared at her, shocked into silence. They had never seen their teacher angry before.

"It's time they learned they are not all powerful. Moses is their boss. They may have just finished the harvest, but they are still counting on Moses to give them a recommendation letter so they can find more work further south, and they are not being paid until tomorrow. It's time they realize there are consequences for their actions," Rose added. Her eyes swung toward Morah. "Moses and I have already talked about you. I believe that no matter what the other women choose to do, you should stay here tonight with your children. In fact, I believe you should leave Abraham and stay here permanently. Once he is gone from the plantation, you and your children can have your own cabin."

Morah was already shaking her head, her eyes wide with panic. "Leave him? Stay here?" she whispered. "He'll kill me if I do that, Rose. That idea is just plumb crazy."

"What's crazy is thinking you can go back there and have him treat you any differently. The other women have already said their husbands don't treat them as badly as Abraham treats you. He beats you, Morah. He's going to beat you if you go home tonight. You know he is!" Rose wanted to take the woman and shake her, but she knew that wouldn't do any good. The abuse she had suffered had stolen every shred of self-confidence. She could only pray her words were getting through.

Della groaned and buried her face in her hands. "I thought the end of slavery was going to mean a better life. In some ways it be worse than when we was on the plantation."

Rose took a deep breath. "Everything has changed, Della. For everyone. That means everyone is trying to figure out how to live their life. Men are trying to figure out how to live as free men. Women are trying to figure out how to live as free women. All the hatred and prejudice is making that harder. Just trying to figure out how to be free would be challenging enough. Now we have to add in that plantation owners aren't willing to accept us as free, and they are making it very difficult to find work and fair pay. The men are angry and frustrated." She shook her head. "That doesn't mean they have any right to do what they are doing, but it does mean things aren't going to change for them very fast. It's not realistic to think they are going to just change into nice people. That means each of you are the ones who have to make the right decision for yourself and your children."

Rose thought quickly. "Each of you can stay here on the plantation with your children where you will be safe. We'll figure things out as we go." She gritted her teeth as they all stared at her, shaking their heads in refusal. She knew she was speaking the truth, but she also knew their fear was too great for them to believe there was an answer. She stood reluctantly as she realized she was not getting through to them. "Let me know if there is a way I can help. Until then, I will be praying." She bit back a scream of frustration when she walked away. There seemed to be no way she could help these women. It went against everything inside her to walk away, but she couldn't help someone not willing to be helped.

Moses was waiting for her on the far side of the clearing, a questioning look on his face. Rose filled him in quickly. "What did the men say?"

"Not much," he admitted, his eyes filled with angry worry. "I don't know that I have much control over them anymore."

"But they haven't gotten their letter of recommendation yet," Rose protested. "Surely that is worth something."

"I'm hoping so," Moses said. "The other men may consider that, but Abraham is infuriated by the humiliation of Morah refusing to dance with him. I don't know that he can control the rage brewing in him right now, even if he wanted to."

Rose said nothing, very much afraid he was right, and knowing that neither of them could do anything if Morah refused to let them help her. She stared across the clearing where the four women were still huddled together, her mind racing to find a solution.

Moses was relieved when the night finally wound down. The Harvest Celebration had been a huge success, but he was exhausted, and he was also worried about Rose. He had seen the look in her eyes when she was watching the four women. His beautiful wife had something planned, and his instincts told him it was going to mean trouble. He chatted easily with everyone as they left, most of them carrying their sleeping children as they walked away, but he also kept an eye on Morah and the others. He knew the instant they stood up, and he was not surprised when he saw Rose step up to join them. He couldn't hear anything they were saying, but he knew they were arguing with her. She merely shook her head and fell into step with them when they started to walk away, their children in tow.

Moses smiled and nodded at a few more people, and then he slipped into the woods, grabbed what he had sequestered there, and quietly followed the women on a trail that ran almost parallel to the road down to the quarters. He had already decided his presence might be more intimidating than helpful, but he was not willing to let Rose go by herself. He was quite sure she had decided to walk the women back to their cabins with the hope that her presence would offer them protection. His eyes cast around for their husbands, but they were nowhere in sight. He wasn't sure what that meant, but he was positive it was nothing good.

The women walked quietly, their children stumbling along almost half-asleep. Morah clutched her baby close to her breast and gripped her son tightly by the hand. Her frightened look said she was expecting Abraham to come for her at any moment.

Moses was surprised when they were left alone to walk home, but he realized the men would hardly accost them when there were so many people around. His skin prickled as he searched his mind to figure out what they were likely to do. He knew Rose had tried to convince the women to stay behind at the house. All of them had refused. His only job now was to protect his wife.

He watched as Rose stood at the door of each cabin with the women. The cabins were all dark, but it was impossible to know if they were empty. She hugged them all briefly and then turned to walk back home when the last woman was in her cabin. She waved to others drifting into the quarters, but she didn't tarry to talk. Moses could tell by the stiffness of her posture that she was nervous, but she held her head high as she started back home.

Rose was grateful for the half-moon that illuminated the road. She was already berating herself for not telling Moses where she was going, but it was too late to change her actions now. She straightened her shoulders and walked briskly, fighting the urge to break into a run. She also scolded herself for her fear. These men were Moses' workers. Surely they would do nothing to harm his wife. Besides the fact that he partially controlled their future, surely they knew his wrath would fall on them if they dared to harm her. Her fear faded a little as the certainty restored her courage.

She was halfway home when she looked up and saw three men blocking the road.

Chapter Twenty-Five

Rose faltered, and then continued to walk forward, acutely aware all the families had made their way home. She was alone with three of the husbands who had been publicly humiliated by their wives—the same women she had walked home with. A quick glance told her Abraham was not with them. The instant of relief was followed by the terrible realization he was probably with Morah. She tightened with anger, reminding herself these men were nothing but cowards who abused their wives. She lifted her head high and cast them a withering look, and then reached slowly for her pocket, glad for the pistol Moses had insisted she carry. She prayed she wouldn't have to use it, but she was certain she would if she had to.

The men remained silent as she got closer, but she could feel the anger coming off them in waves. Rose considered walking around them, but she was quite sure they wouldn't allow that, and it would also indicate she was afraid. These men operated off fear. Her best strategy was to not show them any. She stopped in the middle of the road about five feet from them, grateful for the light from the moon, and regarded the men steadily. "Hello, gentlemen. What can I do for you?"

Dexter had evidently been designated the spokesman for the group. He edged forward, his eyes glinting angrily. "You can leave our wives alone, Mrs. Samuels. We don't appreciate you turning them against us."

Rose stared at him. "You three men turned your wives against you all by yourselves. I had nothing to do with it."

Dexter shook his head. "Our wives were just fine until they started going to your school," he growled.

"The same school where I taught *you* how to read?" Rose asked him, striving to remember Dexter's eager excitement when he had finally learned to make sense of the letters. Beneath the anger suffusing his face, there was a good man. At least there was once a good man. She remembered Moses telling her that sometimes men couldn't come back from the anger and bitterness.

"That ain't got nothing to do with our wives," Dexter shot back, taking a step closer.

Rose tensed, but she remained where she was. She was determined not to show her fear because she knew men like this thrived off of it. She was glad they couldn't hear her pounding heart. She fought to keep her voice steady. "Why are you doing it?"

Dexter eyed her. "Doing it?"

"Why are you hitting Della? Why are you yelling at her and your children?"

"They are *my* wife and children. I can do whatever I want."

The other men nodded their agreement, though they continued to let Dexter do the talking.

Rose saw her chance. "So you have the right to treat your family any way you want to?"

"That's what I said," Dexter replied, his expression saying he was glad to finally be getting through.

"So it's all right for you to treat your family the way the slave owners treated you for all your years of slavery?" Rose didn't wait for an answer. "Have you decided it was all right for you to be beaten during your years as a slave? Maybe you would rather go back to slavery."

Dexter looked confused for a moment and then shook his head. "Ain't nobody got the right to beat a man."

"But it's okay to beat a woman?" Rose asked, trying to keep her voice calm.

"Women are our property," Dexter sputtered.

"Like you were the slave owners' property? If that's true, then the slave owners were right in doing whatever they wanted to." She paused, sensing she had the advantage. She didn't know if her words would have any long-term impact, but since she had the opportunity to talk to them, she wasn't going to pass it up. "Who told you that your wives are your property?"

"That paper from the Freedmen's Bureau," Dexter said quickly, looking relieved to have an answer. "They said we done be the head of the household. That means we're in charge of the women."

"So you believe that means you can hit your wives and terrify your family? Is that what being the head of the household means to you?" Rose paused, but pressed on as she realized Dexter was listening. She prayed she was getting through to the other two as well. "Don't you know that most of the men aren't abusing their families? Isn't it possible that you've got so much anger inside of you that you don't know what to do with it other than to take it out on your family?"

Dexter stared at her, obviously at a loss for words. Emboldened, Rose took a step forward, grateful when each of the men edged back. "Don't you know most of the other men think less of you because of what you're doing?" Rose wondered if she had gone too far when Dexter's eyes tightened with anger again.

"I don't reckon any man going to tell me what to do with my own wife and children," Dexter shot back. "Why should I care what they think?

Another man stepped forward. "I reckon Abraham done be teaching Morah what happens when she do something foolish. The rest of us gonna do the same thing when we get home. Our women are going to know they got off easy till now." He glanced around to make sure they were still alone and then stepped close to Rose. "I know you be Moses' wife," he said in a low, deadly voice, "but that don't mean nothing to me. Me and my family gonna be out of here tomorrow. I ain't sure Moses' letter gonna do nothing to help me get a job. Since he ain't man enough to teach you your place, I reckon I'm gonna be the one to do it."

Rose stiffened, her mind racing to figure out a way of escape, but she was certain she couldn't outrun these men in her long dress. Unbidden, a flashback from six years ago shot through her mind. She had been standing in almost the same spot when Ike Adams pulled her into the bushes and tried to rape her. Back then she had been terrified. She was wise enough to be afraid now, but she was also boiling with anger. "I don't think so," she snapped, yet she knew she couldn't fend off three men. Her pistol might take down one of them, but she couldn't shoot all three of them before they could reach her. She fought to control her trembling as she stared the man in the eyes. She pulled out the pistol and leveled it at him. "If you do something stupid, I'm afraid you will regret it," she snapped.

Dexter edged between them. "Don't be stupid. You know as well as I do that if we lay a hand on this woman, Moses will hunt us down. Besides, she is just crazy enough to shoot you. She might not be able to get us all, but someone will hear the shot and then Moses will find us for sure. You know he will! He may not be man enough to teach his wife her place, but we ain't the ones to do it. Not if we want to live."

Rose managed to hide the relief pouring through her as she held her head erect, her hand steady as she gripped the pistol. "I'm glad one of you has some sense," she said calmly. She wondered if the men would simply let her walk home if she were to show fear and let them think they had succeeded with their scare tactics, but she stubbornly refused to give them that power over her. She also suspected any show of weakness would trigger violence in them whether they feared the pistol or not.

"The two of you can act like cowards if you want," the last man snarled, "but things can't get no worse for me. My wife and my two babies are all I got. That wife of mine thinks 'cause she got some learning that she can act like she's somebody. I'm gonna keep right on teaching her what her place is."

"She doesn't have to be able to read to *be* somebody," Rose shot back. Her heart was pounding in her chest, but she was angry enough now to throw all caution to the wind. "The four women you cowards are beating are far better people than any of you will ever hope to be," she said furiously. "You want to think you are big, strong men. You are nothing but cowards who thrive off of fear." When the three men went rigid, Rose knew she had gone too far, but she was too angry to care. Whether or not she survived whatever they were going to do to her, at least she would have spoken the truth, and she was certain she could shoot one or more of them before they reached her.

"You shouldn't have said that," Dexter hissed as he reached for her. The other men surged forward, as well.

Rose took a deep breath and prepared to squeeze the trigger. Before she could shoot, the sound of gunfire exploded in the woods. The whistle of a bullet whizzing through the air above their heads caused the men to freeze in place.

Moses stepped from the woods. "If any of you lays a hand on my wife, I will shoot you where you stand." His deep voice, taut with anger, seemed to vibrate in the still air.

Rose allowed herself to sag with relief as Moses strode up to stand beside her. One hand reached down to grasp hers, while the other held the pistol firmly.

Moses had chosen to listen for a while, hoping he wouldn't have to step in because he knew his presence would make the men feel even more trapped. Trapped men, the same as animals, tended to be more dangerous. He had listened with admiration as Rose spoke, praying the men would be able to hear her. He suspected they had, but their pride had not allowed them to admit it. None of them wanted to look weak before the others. Individually, he suspected she would have had a powerful impact on each of them.

When Dexter had reached for Rose, he took action, careful to make sure the bullet went over their heads, but still close enough to get their attention. "Which one of you would like to be the first to die?" Moses asked. His voice was even, but he could feel the rage pulsating through every part of him. "I figure I can shoot two of you. Rose can take care of the other of you cowards. Step forward if you want to be first," he invited coldly.

The three men remained frozen in place, their eyes searching for a way to escape.

"The first one of you to move is going to be the first to be shot," Moses snapped, his thoughts searching for an answer of what to do next. He knew the sound of the gunshot was bound to draw attention. He wanted a plan in place before anyone arrived, but short of shooting all three of them to make sure their wives and children remained safe, he didn't have a clue what to do. And he didn't really want to kill the men.

Rose sensed his quandary. "We're not going to be alone for long," she observed. "I imagine it won't take but a few minutes for the gunshot to call in reinforcements. Unfortunately for all of you, anyone who comes to find us is going to be on our side."

Moses watched Dexter shift his feet as all their eyes widened with frightened comprehension. Suddenly, he had a plan. "I figure you've got three or four minutes to make sure you are never seen or heard from again." He nodded toward the woods. "I can tell anyone who comes that I was scaring off a coyote that got too close to Rose. Of course, if they see any of you, they are probably going to know the truth. Every person there tonight saw your wives huddled in terror under that tree," he snapped.

The men jumped as Moses' voice tightened and grew louder.

"We can't just leave," Dexter whined. "Della and the children won't know where I am."

"That would be the point," Moses said grimly. He kept the pistol trained on all of them. "Your wives are too frightened to leave you, so you're going to do them the favor of leaving them. I can guarantee you your families will be taken care of."

"Which is more than you ever did for them," Rose added. She turned to look down the road. "I think I hear horses in the distance," she said pointedly.

Moses couldn't hear anything yet, but he was sure the other men's hearts were beating far too loudly to know if anyone was coming. "Yep," he agreed. "I reckon these fellows have about two minutes before this window of opportunity closes."

"Where are we going to go?" Dexter asked, his voice edged with defeat.

Moses shrugged. "You were leaving tomorrow anyway. I suggest you go wherever you were going. Only now you are going to do it alone." He heard the first sound of hoofbeats in the distance. "And just to make sure we are clear, I never want to see you again. Neither do the rest of the men who work for me. I'm going to give them clear instruction of what to do if any of the three of you show your faces on Cromwell Plantation again." He pulled the trigger back on the pistol to make his point clear.

"I won't forget this," one man growled as he turned and ran toward the woods.

"Watch your back," another threatened.

Dexter held his ground, his eyes flaring with rage, until the drum of horse hooves sounded through the still air. He tensed and then began to flee.

Moses let them go but aimed another shot over their heads, smiling with grim satisfaction when they ducked and ran faster. Then he turned and gathered Rose close in his arms. "You scared me to death," he groaned.

"I'm so sorry," Rose murmured as he crushed her to his chest with trembling arms. "I know now that I should have never gone down there without you. I've been happy to see you a lot of times in my life, but never more than tonight." She pressed into him for long moments before she pushed back and peered toward the woods. "Will they come back?"

Moses considered the question and then shook his head. "I don't believe they will. Men who beat their wives are exactly what you said—cowards who thrive off of fear. They have no more power now, and they know we will be watching for them. We'll watch Morah and the others very carefully."

"Morah!" Rose cried, her stomach clenching with panic. "Abraham must have been waiting in the cabin when she got home. We have to get to her!"

Moses thought about what he had heard the men say just as a group of horses rounded the curve at a gallop. He knew Rose was right. He was relieved when Robert, Matthew, Perry, and Mark rode up and slid to a halt.

"What happened?" Robert asked, his eyes searching the area.

"I'll explain later," Moses responded. "I need you to get to Morah in the quarters as quickly as you can."

Robert didn't press for an explanation. He had seen what was going on that evening just like everyone else had before he and Carrie had disappeared. He reached down a hand to Rose. "Swing up behind me. Morah will need you."

Rose accepted his hand as Moses stepped forward to boost her up.

Mark dismounted from his gelding. "Take my horse, Moses. I'll start walking back to let everyone know you and Rose are all right."

Moses nodded his appreciation as he mounted. "Let's go."

"Wait!" Rose cried. She reached out to put a hand on Matthew's shoulder. "Please go get Carrie and Janie. And Mark shouldn't walk home alone." She shuddered as she realized the men might be in the woods plotting their revenge.

Matthew nodded, understanding instantly why she was making the request. "I'll have them back as soon as I can." He pulled Mark up behind him and then turned and galloped off.

"Let's go!" Rose cried.

People, their faces filled with confusion and fear, were milling about in the quarters when they galloped up. Rose knew they were afraid the gunshots meant vigilantes were on the prowl. The fear melted from their faces as they identified the riders, but the confusion didn't lessen.

Della stepped forward. "What is going on?"

Rose saw Della's children huddled in the doorway. She felt a surge of relief that they were going to be safe, but she also grieved for the loss of their father. She pushed the thoughts from her mind. There were more pressing things at the moment. "Where is Morah?"

Della stiffened. "She went into her cabin."

"You didn't hear anything?"

Della shook her head. "No, but that don't mean nothing," she said. "Some of the men kept playing their instruments when we got back. Folks weren't quite done dancing yet."

Rose swallowed her groan as Moses reached up and pulled her off Robert's horse. She turned and ran toward the cabin, hearing the sound of soft weeping as soon as she reached the door. Moses grabbed her arm to hold her back while he stepped through the door, his pistol held steady.

Della boldly stepped in behind him with a brightly lit lantern to illuminate the cabin.

Rose gave a cry as she sprang forward. Morah and her son lay battered on the floor, both of them crying and whimpering. The baby lay motionless on a blanket in the corner.

Della rushed over to the baby and scooped her up. A single sad look was all it took to confirm what Rose already knew.

Rose knelt down next to Morah and touched her arm gently. "We're here, Morah. You're safe now."

Morah managed to open one swollen eye enough to peer up at her. Her face had been beaten almost beyond recognition and both her arms dangled brokenly at her sides. "Rose... I..."

Rose held a finger to her lips, anger and grief making her voice shake. "Shh... We'll talk later. Right now we're just going to take care of you."

"Dwane..." Morah whispered. She tried to push herself up from the floor but collapsed back with a cry of pain.

"He's going to be all right," Moses assured her.

Rose looked over, breathing a sigh of gratitude when six-year-old Dwane managed to give her a very weak smile. He had been badly beaten, but obviously Abraham had taken most of his rage out on his wife.

Morah nodded weakly but forced her eye open again. "Shirley?" she whispered.

Rose could tell she already knew the truth, but was desperately holding on to hope. She held back her tears as she gripped Morah's hand. "I'm so sorry," she murmured.

Morah began to weep again as the meaning of Rose's words seeped in. "My baby," she whimpered, suddenly finding the strength to sit up without the use of her arms. Her head swiveled as she tried to find her daughter.

Rose, no longer able to hold back the tears, nodded to Della. Della, her own tears rolling down her cheeks, carried Shirley forward tenderly and knelt down to hold her where Morah could see her daughter.

"Shirley..." Morah groaned. Her voice softened into a raspy whisper. "I'm so...sorry, baby..." Her voice trembled with pain and grief. "My fault... My fault..."

"It's not your fault," Rose said. "Abraham did this."

Morah swiveled her one eye before she fixed it back on her dead child. "Shouldn't...have...come... home," she gasped as her face twisted with pain. "He's...coming...back..."

"No," Moses said firmly. He stepped forward and knelt down to make sure Morah could see him. "He's not ever coming back, Morah. You have my word on that. You and Dwane are safe here on the plantation."

Morah stared up at him beseechingly for a long moment and then sagged back, unconscious. Rose caught her and lowered her gently to the floor.

"Mama," Dwane moaned. "Mama..." He remained huddled on the floor as he looked up. "She gonna die, Miss Rose?"

"No," Rose replied, hoping it wasn't a lie. She got up and moved over to him, stroking his head while she prayed Carrie and Janie would arrive soon.

Carrie, Janie and Matthew pounded down the road, the moonlight casting a bright enough glow for them to see easily as the first layer of frost sparkled up at them. She had watched the men respond to the gunfire, and then she had sprung into action. Certain they would be needed soon, Carrie had her father tack up Granite and Juniper while she and Janie made sure their medical bags were complete. They had just tied the equipped bags onto the saddles when Matthew had galloped back into the yard. Carrie and Janie had mounted as Mark slid down from behind Matthew. There had been no time for explanations. It was not necessary. Answers would come in time. It was enough to know they were needed.

Carrie thought through the supplies they carried. It was a mixture of Sarah's potions that June and Polly had made over the summer and the homeopathic remedies she had brought home with her. She was grateful for whatever force had compelled her to stock up on every remedy the homeopathic pharmacy in Philadelphia carried. She whispered a prayer of gratitude that she had done as much reading as possible on how they were used. Now she could only hope she and Janie possessed the knowledge that was needed for whatever was waiting for them. She banished the images that kept pressing into her mind. It would do no good to make things up. They would simply deal with whatever they found.

The quarters were deathly silent as they rode in and dismounted. That, perhaps more than anything, told Carrie how serious the situation was. Every face, tight with worry and fear, looked back at her, but no one said a word. Children were pulled tightly against their mothers. Tiny eyes peered at her, but none of them called out. Carrie exchanged a somber look with Janie as Moses stepped out of one of the cabins.

"Over here," he called, his words echoing through the clearing before they wrapped around the branches that seemed to draw closer to offer protection.

Carrie took a deep breath, locked eyes with Janie again, and then stepped into the cabin. It took her only moments to assess the situation. "You check out the boy," she murmured as she stepped toward where Morah lay on the wooden floor. She locked eyes with Rose. "Is she...?"

"She's alive," Rose whispered.

Carrie knew what Rose wasn't saying—it might not be for long. She took note of the broken arms and battered face before she began a gentle examination of Morah's body to see if she could detect more damage. "Her husband?"

Rose nodded, her face set in grim lines. "Her husband."

Carrie glanced over at Janie, glad to see the little boy was conscious and talking to her. "He beat his son, too?"

"His name is Dwane. He just started school this year," Rose answered, her voice trembling now. "Yes. He beat him, too, but not as badly."

Carrie's eyes swept through the cabin as she continued to probe Morah's body, glad she was unconscious. Suddenly she stiffened when her eyes landed on one corner of the room. "The baby?"

Rose choked back a sob. "Shirley is dead."

Carrie set her lips, her heart constricting with sorrow, but said no more. Janie would treat Dwane. It was her job to take care of Morah.

Polly suddenly appeared beside her. "We just heard. They sent someone down for us. Can I help?"

Carrie gave a sigh of relief. "Yes. I'll need your assistance setting her arms."

Janie appeared at her side. "Do you have a homeopathic treatment for the results of a beating?" she whispered angrily, obviously trying to keep Dwane from hearing.

Carrie knew the whole situation was bringing up terrible memories for Janie, but she also knew her friend could handle it. They would talk it through later, and she knew Matthew would give Janie the support she needed. She nodded and reached into her bag. "Rose, I want you to boil some water to make a tea from these arnica blooms. You'll need four cups of water for this amount. As soon as the water boils, add these blooms and let them simmer for ten minutes." She held up her hand as Rose started to move. "Be very careful with this. Arnica is extremely poisonous. Don't get any on your skin until it has been diluted, and make sure no one puts any of it into their mouth."

She turned to Janie as Rose hurried to the fire someone already had blazing to warm the cabin. She held out a small bottle. "This is a homeopathic dose of arnica. It will help with the swelling and bruising from the beating. Put three drops into a glass of water for Dwane to drink. He should have the same dose every three hours for the next twenty-four hours. Have you found any other injuries?"

Janie shook her head. "Dwane said Morah stepped in between him and Abraham when he was being beaten." Her eyes deepened with pain. "Morah took the brunt of things."

Carrie nodded, unwilling to visualize what she was hearing. Though she knew the horror would come, she had to focus on her patients. "Once Rose has made the arnica tea, I want you to bathe all of Dwane's body that has been beaten. Make sure, though, that you don't put it on broken skin. It will help reduce the swelling and bruises, and it will take away the pain much more quickly." She paused. "We're only going to do this for them twice tonight. Arnica is quite effective, but it can damage the skin if used too often. Once you have finished bathing him, make sure you wash your hands carefully."

Done with her instructions, Carrie turned back to Morah, glad to see she was still unconscious. She wanted to set her broken arms before she woke up. She managed a smile when she saw Polly re-enter the cabin with a handful of quickly made wooden splints. She was sure there were enough people gathered around the cabin to take care of any needs they had.

Feeling gratitude for all she had learned treating soldiers during the war, Carrie set Morah's arms while Polly held the unconscious woman still. She put the splints in place and wrapped them carefully with the strips of sheeting that seemed to appear from nowhere. She knew there must be women outside ripping up clothing and cutting it into strips. Morah moaned once, but other than that she didn't make a sound, and there was no movement.

Carrie prayed she would remain unconscious for a long time. The pain from her injuries—combined with the grief of losing her daughter—was not something Morah would be able to face right now.

"The arnica tea is ready," Rose said as she appeared by her side.

Carrie carefully pulled away Morah's clothing, wincing at the dark areas of swelling all over her body. Abraham had been quite thorough in his beating, though closer examination told her some of the bruises were not fresh. She tightened her lips and went to work, carefully bathing every inch of her. Rose and Polly lifted Morah's slack body to a sitting position so that Carrie could bathe her back, but the battered woman's broken arms made it impossible to turn her over. Morah was still going to hurt when she woke up, but she fervently hoped the arnica would eliminate the worst of it. While she was propped up, Carrie held a small container of water with the arnica treatment to Morah's lips, massaging her throat to make sure she swallowed it.

When she was done, she realized some of the women had slipped in and made a soft bed of blankets on the floor next to where Morah lay. Carrie was not ready to move her into bed yet, but she signaled for them to lift the unconscious woman onto the makeshift pad. She turned back to her bag, searching for the yarrow tincture she had taught Polly and June to make. She mixed it quickly and had Polly and Rose lift Morah again so she could drink it. There was no way of knowing yet if the woman had suffered any internal injury, but the yarrow tincture would help stop any internal bleeding. She sat back and took a deep breath. "All we can do now is wait for her to wake up."

"I hope it takes a long time," Rose murmured.

Carrie nodded her agreement, battling the fatigue that came from a very long day. She saw Robert come to the door, but he only glanced inside and met her eyes for a moment before he turned away. She knew from the expression on his face that something else had happened, but she had her hands full right where she was. She could hear about it later.

Janie stood and walked over to join her. "We put Dwane in bed. The poor little boy is exhausted. The arnica tea seemed to help him so much." She shook her head with amazement. "It never ceases to amaze me that God has given us every single plant we need to take care of ourselves. I don't understand why everyone isn't taught this."

Carrie scowled. "The going price for arnica plants that grow wild is not very profitable."

"Did Sarah teach you about arnica?" Janie asked

Carrie shook her head. "Arnica grows mostly in the northern and western parts of America. Sarah had never seen it. I learned about it through my reading."

"How did you get it?"

Carrie shrugged. "I ordered it from a company in Vermont. They have a variety that is quite effective. I made a mixture while I was at school, but I sent most of it to June and Polly for use in the clinic. They keep a box of supplies in the stable in case of emergencies. I was able to grab it before we came. I suspected it would come in handy."

Janie shook her head. "You're amazing. The Homeopathic College is going to believe they have nothing to teach you when you start school next month."

Carrie simply nodded and turned back to Morah, careful not to look at her friend. She knew Janie would see the truth in her eyes. Now was hardly the time to reveal she would not be returning to school.

Rose laid a hand on her shoulder. "How long do you think Morah will be unconscious?"

Carrie was grateful the conversation was being steered away from medical school. "I don't really know, but I hope it will be most of the night. I'm going to stay here with her."

"No you're not," Janie said. "You're going home."

Carrie opened her mouth to protest, but Janie continued talking.

"Carrie, you know as well as I do that Morah is going to need more than medical care when she finally wakes up. I have everything I need to care for her, and I'm also the only one here who has been beaten and abused by my husband," she said bluntly. "I suspect Morah will need me more for that than anything else. Her bones will heal and her bruises will go away, but her heart is an entirely different matter—especially since she watched her husband kill her baby daughter." Janie's voice caught on the last words. "I feel totally inadequate, but I can at least share some degree of the experience with her."

"You're right," Carrie admitted, hating that Janie could relate to *any* degree, but she wasn't sure she was willing to leave her. "I don't know that you're safe here, though."

"Surely you don't think Abraham will come back tonight?"

Carrie shrugged. "I have no idea what he will do. I'm just not willing to take the chance."

"The cabin is surrounded by people."

"Right now it is, but they will eventually go to bed. He could be out there waiting." Carrie hated the fear she saw tighten Janie's face, but she would hate it far more if something were to happen to her. She needed to know the reality of the situation.

"We'll all stay," Rose announced. She stepped to the door, but Moses' frame filled the doorway before she reached it.

"Abraham is gone," he said.

Carrie looked up, but the flickering light in the cabin made it impossible to read the expression in his eyes. "You mean he has left? How do you know? How do you know he won't come back?"

"He won't come back," Moses stated firmly, looking somberly toward Morah.

"She's still unconscious," Carrie assured him. "And little Dwane is sound asleep. You can talk."

Moses nodded, but kept his voice very low. "Abraham tried to come back. Some of the men found him in the woods with a pistol."

All four women gasped and looked toward the window.

"You don't have to worry," Moses said. "My men were ready. When he pulled out his pistol, they shot him."

"He's dead?" Carrie asked.

Moses nodded again. "It's for the best. My men said he was acting crazy when he came back. I think he knew he had killed his little girl. Something must have snapped." He shook his head heavily. "Sometimes people can't come back from things they have experienced. Abraham's years in slavery were harsh. His time in the army was just as harsh in many ways. He couldn't let go of his bitterness and anger. It ate him up from the inside."

Carrie knew he was right, not just about the blacks who had fought for the Union, but about everyone who had served in the war. She had read reports of how many Civil War veterans were now alcoholics or addicted to the morphine given to them for pain. The divorce rate had skyrocketed as women ran from their abusive husbands. "It's just another reminder that the war isn't really over," she said sadly. "The ramifications are going to continue for a very long time."

"I'm afraid you're right," Moses agreed. He reached for Rose's hand. "I'm taking you home," he said.

Rose hesitated, and then smiled. "And I'm going to let you." She looked at Carrie. "Janie is right. You should come home, too. If Morah wakes up, Janie will be here. You can come back in the morning after you have had some sleep." She turned toward the door but jolted to a stop. "What about the other three men? They could come back." She glanced at Carrie and Janie. "I'll fill you in on that story later."

"I'm going to have men around all four cabins all night," Moses replied. "No one will get through them."

Matthew entered the cabin and assessed the situation quickly. "I'll be right here with Janie," he said. "If someone manages to get through the guard, I promise you they will not get through me." He laid a hand on Janie's shoulder. "It won't come to that. The guards are prepared."

Carrie shuddered, understanding he was saying all of them would be armed. They were all former soldiers trained in combat, but she couldn't believe this had come to the plantation. The festivities and joy of the Harvest Celebration seemed to be eons ago, not just a few hours. The celebration had melted into violence and death. "They are all frightened of vigilantes, but it is one of their own that has done this," she murmured.

"Yes," Moses replied, his voice thick with regret. "And it's going to continue. All of us hoped the end of slavery would mean a chance to rebuild our lives with dignity and respect, the way we dreamed of for years. Instead, the South is fighting our freedom as hard as they fought to keep us slaves, and there are too many people in the North who agree with them. The bitterness and resentment are going to build in people who are being forced to feel helpless. The freed slaves hoped for a hand up into their new life. What they have received is a boot stomping on their neck." He held up a hand. "I'm not saying any of them have a right to do what Abraham or the rest have done, but I can sympathize with how they feel."

Rose laid her head on his chest. "We have to do everything we can to help them. They may feel helpless, but *we* are not helpless. You've already done so much to help the families who work on the plantation. We are going to do more."

Moses' eyes remained heavy with grief as he looked toward the corner where Shirley still lay, looking like what she should have been—a sleeping baby.

Janie and Matthew waved to them as they mounted and headed back toward the house.

They rode in silence, each consumed with their own thoughts.

Chapter Twenty-Six

Carrie and Robert rode into the quarters early the next morning. The quiet that lay over the cabins was natural this time. Almost all the residents were fast asleep after their long night. There were four men standing guard around each of the cabins where the abusers had lived. They nodded their assurance to Carrie and Robert when they arrived. All was well.

Janie and Matthew appeared at the door of the cabin. Their eyes were heavy with fatigue, but they both had peaceful looks on their faces. Carrie caught her breath with relief. They wouldn't look that way if either Morah or Dwane had passed away during the night. She swung down from Granite and tied him to a post in the clearing.

"I'll be back in a few minutes," Robert said. "I have a message to deliver for Moses."

"What message?" Carrie asked, puzzled.

Robert smiled. "I'll tell you about it on the way home. I knew your mind was too occupied with Morah and the other women to think about anything else."

"More trouble?" Carrie asked with a frown.

Robert shook his head. "Definitely not. Nothing but good news from my end." He nodded toward Morah's cabin. "Go. I'll answer all your questions on the way home."

Carrie watched him head toward the cabin occupied by the men from Moses' old unit before she turned to wave at Janie and Matthew. "Good morning," she called.

"Good morning," Janie replied.

Carrie stepped into the cabin, disappointed to see Morah was still sleeping. "She hasn't regained consciousness?" She wracked her brain for what to do next.

Janie smiled. "She woke up a few hours ago."

Carrie smiled in return and stepped closer to examine the beaten woman. Her eyes widened with amazement. "The swelling on her face is almost all gone!" She knelt down to look at her more closely, her smile morphing into a grin. "I've never seen anything like it." In spite of what she had read about arnica, experience told her she should expect to find Morah's eyes swollen shut and the rest of her face looking like a watermelon.

"I thought you were the one who told me the arnica would work," Janie teased.

"I told you I had *read* it would work," Carrie corrected as she sat back on her heels and continued to stare. "I've never had an opportunity to put it to the test." She shook her head. "This makes me want to learn even more."

"Which is going to be challenging here on the plantation," Janie observed.

Carrie nodded her head in agreement and then stiffened. "What did you say?"

"I said your learning is going to be more of a challenge here on the plantation," Janie repeated. "When are you going to learn I can always tell when you are hiding something? When you wouldn't look at me last night, I knew you were trying to keep a secret from me. I had all night to think about what it could be." She gazed at Carrie. "You're not going back to Philadelphia are you?"

Carrie sighed. "I wasn't trying to keep a secret. I had just told Robert, and I didn't think the middle of a medical emergency was the time to talk about it. But, no, I'm not returning to Philadelphia, at least not for this term. I don't know what the future holds, but I believe I'm supposed to stay on the plantation for now."

"Do you know why?"

Carrie loved Janie for asking the question. She loved her even more for the fact that she would understand her answer. "No," she replied, managing a smile. "Oh, I have some ideas of what will happen in the next few months, but I already know that things I couldn't begin to anticipate are going to happen. I figure I'm just going to have to take one day at a time and see what comes."

"That's the only way to live life," Matthew agreed.

Carrie grasped Janie's hand. "Are you angry with me?"

Janie chuckled. "For doing what you believe you are meant to do? What kind of friend would I be if I resented that?"

"But you're going to be in Philadelphia all by yourself," Carrie pressed. "All our housemates are gone. I can't stand to think of you in that big house all by yourself." She peered into Janie's eyes, almost puzzled when she could detect nothing but peaceful acceptance.

Janie nodded. "Abby seemed to handle it just fine, but I thought about that during the night, too. I'll admit I don't want to live by myself."

"Do you have a solution?"

"I offered one," Matthew said, "but she turned it down."

Carrie glanced at him, hearing nothing but love in his voice. She knew how much he wanted to marry Janie. She also understood why Janie wasn't ready yet, though it would make her feel better about staying home at the plantation if her friend were married to Matthew and living with him.

"I'm going to fill the rooms with students from the Homeopathic College. We talked about it before. There's no reason not to do it. It will work out well for everyone."

"Don't give my room away," Carrie said, her mind filled with images of housemates schooled in the miracle of the homeopathic remedies. "I don't know how long it will be before I return."

Janie looked at her closely. "So you're still committed to becoming a homeopathic physician?"

"More than ever. I don't pretend to understand all the reasons I'm staying. I'm thrilled not to leave Robert or the plantation right now, but I know the day will come when I have my own practice." She reached out and grabbed Janie's hand. "My greatest dream is that we will share a practice someday."

Janie smiled as she squeezed Carrie's hand. "Nothing would make me happier." She glanced at Morah. "There might just be three of us."

Carrie blinked in confusion. "Three of us? What do you mean?"

Janie nodded toward Morah. "We had a long talk when she woke up. It's going to take her a while to get over what has happened, but she admitted her relief that Abraham is dead. She was weary of being terrified all the time, and I don't know if Morah would have had a minute's rest if she knew he was still out there somewhere." She scowled. "The story she told me was horrifying."

Carrie shivered as she thought of what Morah had been through. "You told her about Clifford?"

"I did, though what I went through was nothing compared to what she has experienced. She seemed grateful to hear my story."

"What you went through was not *nothing*," Matthew said as he laid a hand on her shoulder. "You understand Morah's pain and terror. People need to know they are not alone. You let her know that."

Janie nodded thoughtfully. "The memories lost a little more of their power as I talked." She quickly changed the subject. "Morah was mystified as to why she wasn't in more pain than she was. She had far too many experiences of his beatings in the past. She knows exactly how terrible she should be feeling. Even her arms don't hurt as badly as she thought they would."

"The arnica is even more effective than I hoped it would be," Carrie murmured.

"I told her all about it." Janie grinned. "Now Morah wants us to teach her the things Sarah taught you. By the time we finished talking, she was having thoughts of going to the Homeopathic College, too. I swear, it was like I watched her become a new woman when she realized Abraham could truly never hurt her again. She will grieve Shirley, and have to deal with her feelings of grief, but I believe she will be fine."

Carrie shuddered as she thought of Abraham trying to creep back to the cabin before he was shot. She wondered what his last thoughts were before he died. She hated the fact that a man had been killed, but she understood Morah's relief. "Rose says she is extremely bright. She learned how to read in record time, and she has been absorbing everything she can, even though Abraham beat her if he caught her reading. She came to pick up Dwane from school every chance she got so that she could read more. It wasn't safe to bring books into the house."

"Miss Rose said that about me?" Morah whispered.

Carrie reached down and put a hand on the woman's shoulder, glad to see that her eyes were clear. There was nothing there to indicate any kind of permanent injury. "Good morning, Morah," she said gently. "Rose did indeed say that. She is very proud of you."

"That's good," Morah responded, a smile flitting across her lips before she reached up to feel her eyes and cheeks. "My face feels better."

"The swelling is almost gone," Carrie assured her, "though we're going to put cold rags on it through the day to help with any remaining pain. I'm afraid you're going to have two black eyes, however."

Morah gave a weak chuckle. "I guess there are times when being black is an advantage," she murmured. "These black eyes won't look near as bad on me as they would on you."

Carrie laughed, astounded the woman still had a sense of humor.

"Will you teach me, Mrs. Borden? About the plants?" Morah asked.

Carrie had to lean close to hear her words as fatigue grabbed hold of Morah again. The arnica had worked wonders, but to truly heal, the woman needed sleep more than she needed anything else. "I'll teach you," she promised. "But only on two conditions."

Morah managed to open her eyes a little wider. "What?" she whispered.

"You have to call me Carrie, and you have to quit talking and get some rest," she said firmly. Morah smiled, gave an almost imperceptible nod, and slipped back into a healing sleep.

Minutes later, a little voice, thick with fatigue, broke the stillness. "Mama?"

Janie stood and walked over to Dwane. "Good morning!" she whispered brightly. "Your mama is sleeping right now, but I bet you are a hungry little boy."

Dwane nodded. "Shirley be gone?" he asked, looking over at the corner. Shirley had been buried during the night.

"Yes, honey," Janie said. "Shirley is gone. Somewhere up in heaven there is a new little angel dancing on the clouds."

Dwane frowned as he thought about that. "You reckon that be true?"

"I do."

"I sure wish Shirley were still down here," Dwane said plaintively.

"I know, Dwane. I do, too."

Dwane looked away from the corner and sought out his mother. "Is Mama going to heaven, too?" he asked.

"Absolutely not," Janie said. "Your mama is going to be fine."

Dwane regarded Janie suspiciously. He was used to being lied to by both his father and his mother, who had tried to hide what was going on.

Carrie walked over to join them. "She's right, Dwane. Your mama is going to be fine. She was talking to us just a minute ago, but now she's sleeping again."

Dwane stared at her, but finally seemed to accept what she was saying as the truth. "I'm hungry," he announced.

Matthew was already at the fire, stirring a pot of porridge. "I figured you would be," he said. He ladled up a bowl and carried it to the little boy.

Dwane ate quickly, his eyes locked on Morah. "Can I sleep some more with Mama?" he asked when he was done.

Carrie smiled. "I think that is a grand idea. I know there is nothing that your mama would love more than to have you snuggled up next to her. Just take care not to knock her arms. She will want to hold you very badly, but it will be a while before she can do that."

Dwane smiled for the first time. "She must sure be still alive if you gonna let me sleep next to her," he stated.

Carrie understood why the little boy needed solid proof. He had asked nothing about his father. She wondered if he had heard something about his death during the night, or if he was simply relieved to not see him there. Morah would tell him about Abraham when the time was right.

Within minutes, Dwane was cuddled up to Morah and sound asleep, his breathing steady and even.

Thomas settled down on the porch with a steaming cup of coffee. He had heard Carrie and Robert leave earlier, but he knew he would have been notified if there had been more trouble in the quarters. Abby, exhausted from the late hours, was still sleeping soundly. He had crept out of bed so he wouldn't disturb her and stumbled down into the kitchen, reaching blindly for the coffee Annie had held out to him, before making his way outside. He sipped the brew gratefully as he watched the sun melt away the early morning frost. The leaves still gleamed with brilliant color, but he knew they would begin to fall in the next two weeks.

"Do you miss it?"

Thomas looked up when Moses walked out onto the porch. "I will always love the plantation," he replied, "and I will always be glad to return, but I'm surprised to find it is Richmond I miss. My home is there now." He took another sip of coffee as he stared east. "I'm already thinking about what I want to do with the factory when we get home."

"Are things safer there now?" Moses asked. "We haven't had time to talk about it, but I'm imagining Jeremy and Marietta stayed behind because you didn't want to leave the factory without someone in charge."

Thomas nodded. "It's true that I felt better leaving Jeremy there, but it's equally true we couldn't afford for him to leave now. We had several big orders come in right before we left. Since Jeremy will be coming out for two weeks around Christmas..."

"And then taking a week for his honeymoon," Moses added with a grin.

"Yes. He felt better about staying in Richmond and getting a strong start on the new orders. We have a good floor manager, but things are just volatile enough for us to not feel comfortable about all three of us being gone at the same time." Thomas glanced toward the house. "I have some things I would like to discuss with you. Do you want to get some coffee?"

Moses shook his head. "Mama is bringing some out to me, along with a plate of ham biscuits for both of us."

Thomas almost moaned with pleasure. "Your mama is an angel."

"And don't you never forget it," Annie said as she pushed through the door. "Both of you look like you been run over by a horse."

"That bad?" Thomas muttered, knowing she was right. His eyes felt like sandpaper. "I guess I'm getting too old for nights with very little sleep."

"Age has nothing to do with it," Moses grumbled as he reached for the coffee and took a drink. "I keep telling myself, though, that I feel a lot better than Morah and Dwane do."

A somber silence filled the porch.

"What did they do with that sweet little Shirley?" Annie asked. "I declare, that little girl was pure sunshine. I'm glad Abraham can't lay another hand on them."

"They buried her in the cemetery," Moses assured her. "It was the middle of the night, but everyone was there." He knew what his mama was really asking. In the early years of slavery, it had been illegal for slaves to gather together for a funeral because the owners feared revolt. When his daddy had been hanged, his body was taken away and shoved in the ground somewhere on non-crop-producing land. They had never been told where—never had a chance to say goodbye. "It's not like before, Mama," he reassured her. "They gave Shirley a proper burial."

Annie stared at him. "With singing?"

"With singing," Moses confirmed.

"I'm glad that little baby girl ain't knowing no more pain," Annie said. "I reckon God done grabbed her up in his arms and just hugged her close when she got there. The way I figure it, she couldn't even remember what made her end up there." Her voice was deep with satisfaction. "Little Shirley was happy to be home."

Moses nodded, hoping fervently that she was right. It had broken his heart to see the little girl crumpled like a rag doll in the corner. When he had gotten home last night, he picked Hope up and cuddled her to his chest for a long time before he had been able to go to bed. If possible, it had given him even more determination to make things different. He wanted John and Hope to always feel safe.

"When you gonna start them meetings, Moses?" Annie asked. "You gots to do all you can to make things right for people."

"I know, Mama." And he did. The knowledge had kept him awake during the few hours he could have been sleeping. "I had to wait until the harvest was finished, but I told Simon this morning that he could set up the first one at the schoolhouse next week."

Annie grunted her approval and turned around. "I'll leave you two men to it." Just as she opened the door to step through it, Perry appeared. "I reckon you be wanting some coffee, too," she said briskly.

"If it's not too much to ask, ma'am," Perry responded.

Annie barked a laugh of approval. "You done come a long way, Mr. Perry Appleton. That's the proper way to talk to a woman old enough to be your mama, no matter whether I be black or white."

Perry laughed. "I may be a little thick, but once I start learning something, I pick it up pretty quickly." He crossed the porch and sat down as the door slapped shut behind him. "Am I interrupting anything?"

"No," Moses assured him. Then he looked at Thomas, suddenly remembering there were things Thomas wanted to discuss with him. "Unless..."

"Not at all," Thomas said. "In fact, I would like to talk with both of you."

"About?" Moses asked.

"I'll get to that," Thomas replied. "First, I would like to hear about the changes over at Blackwell Plantation."

Perry grinned. "So you've heard that I've finally seen the light?"

"I've heard you made a smart business decision," Thomas responded. "It's up to you to convince me you have seen the light." His voice was casual, but his eyes were locked on the younger man.

Perry's grin disappeared. "I understand, sir."

"Do you?" Thomas pressed. "It wouldn't take a genius to realize what Moses has created here is phenomenally successful. It's much harder for a man to change what he has known all his life."

"I understand it was hard for you, sir," Perry said evenly.

Thomas smiled. "More difficult than you can imagine," he agreed. "I had many more years of thoughts and beliefs I had to undo."

"And have you, Thomas?" Perry asked. "Have you undone all of them?"

Thomas considered his question as he stared out into the pasture. "I would like to give you an unequivocal yes," he said honestly. "Most of the time I know I am completely different from the man I used to be. I would like to tell you I have released all my prejudices and beliefs that I am superior." He spoke slowly, determined to be completely forthright. He was uncomfortably aware of Moses' presence, but he wouldn't let it stop him from telling the truth. It was too important to help Perry navigate this time in his life. "Just when I'm sure I am who I believe myself to be, something will happen that will call up those old beliefs and feelings. Then I'm right back to fighting them just like before. In many ways it is a constant battle, but one I am determined to wage."

"I know exactly what you mean," Moses replied, not giving Perry time to respond. "Prejudice and hatred do not belong only to the white race. Most of the time I just look at you and see a man I have grown to love and admire, Thomas. I see my business partner in the plantation. I see Rose's half-brother." He paused as he searched for words. "Then there are moments I look at you and I see the memories of all my beatings... I remember you used to own me... I remember my daddy hanging from a tree..." His voice trailed off. "I have to continually let go of those old feelings."

Thomas stared at Moses, relieved to know he fought the same kind of inner battles. The long gaze they exchanged gave him confidence they would both persevere until the reality of their lives and thoughts matched what they wanted them to be.

Perry nodded his thanks to Annie as she stepped out with a cup of hot coffee and then marched back into the house. He took several sips before he responded. "I've decided it is like an onion," he announced.

Thomas and Moses exchanged an amused glance. "An onion?" Thomas asked with a cocked brow.

"Yes. An onion," Perry said. "Have you ever peeled one? The layers keep coming and coming. It seems there is no end to them. Annie told me the only way you can discover whether the onion has a sweet heart or a rotten core is to peel away all the layers."

"So you're an onion?" Thomas asked, completely understanding the analogy now.

"Yes," Perry agreed. "My time here has peeled away a lot of the layers of my prejudice and beliefs, but I would be foolish to believe I have completely reached the core of all that created them in me. I have decided I need to keep peeling the layers back, and at some point I will reach the real truth."

Thomas nodded. "You're a bright young man."

Perry shrugged. "I wish I could take credit for my transformation, but Moses and Simon are the bright ones. They knew they had to force me to examine my beliefs before either of them would agree to be involved with Blackwell Plantation. The need for an answer to my financial situation forced me to take an honest look. The reality of what I found there gave me the motivation to change."

"And what did you find?" Thomas asked, impressed by the frankness of Perry's answer.

"I discovered I was the result of my culture, not of my own beliefs."

"The result of your culture..." Thomas murmured.

"Yes," Perry replied. "I've been told all my life that whites are better than blacks. I've been told it is our job and responsibility to be in control of them. I've been told that if we lost control of the blacks, I would lose the only way of life I've ever known." He cast an apologetic look at Moses.

Moses lifted a shoulder. "You're not telling me anything I don't already know."

Thomas watched Perry closely. "You no longer believe those things?"

"No. I'm sure there are still more layers to the onion," Perry said quickly, "but my time here has shown me how blatantly false those beliefs are. They were formed by people who knew they would benefit if they could make an entire race believe them. I suppose it was easy to convince whites that blacks are inferior because whites had so much to gain from that belief."

"Teaching them to believe something else is going to be more difficult," Thomas murmured.

"Yes," Perry agreed. "It is going to be *much* more difficult."

Thomas reached for a ham biscuit, took a bite, and chewed while he thought things through. Finally he swallowed and turned to Perry. "You know you are putting yourself and your family in danger?"

Perry gazed at him for a moment. "I know Jeremy has been beaten, and both you and Abby have been threatened. I know you travel everywhere with armed guards now. I know Robert couldn't sell his horses for a very long time, and I know he goes nowhere without his pistol. So, yes, I'm aware I will be in danger."

"And you're all right with that?"

His question elicited a scowl from Perry. "Who could ever be all right with having their family in danger? Are you all right with it?"

"Absolutely not," Thomas assured him.

"Yet you continue to live your life the way you believe you should."

Thomas grinned in appreciation. "Nice job. You turned the tables on me quite skillfully, young man."

Perry smiled, but his eyes lost none of their intensity. "Once I got past my own prejudices and beliefs, it took many long conversations with Louisa before we made this decision."

"So you made it together?"

Perry laughed. "When Louisa left Virginia, she was still a spoiled, pampered plantation daughter," he admitted. "That is something she would tell you herself," he added quickly. "She is now quite a strong-willed woman who would never tolerate me making decisions without her."

"But the same culture that taught you what to believe about blacks also taught you your beliefs about the proper place of women," Moses said. "How did you—"

"How did I change my beliefs about women?" Perry interrupted. "That was simple. I'd always been taught women were incapable of doing hard things and that they would never be the equal of men. Then I saw Carrie in action." He paused, his eyes serious. "Don't forget she saved my life. I'm quite sure I wouldn't be sitting here if she had not been my doctor at Chimborazo. And if Janie had not been my nurse. If that experience wasn't enough to teach me just how capable women are, then there is no hope for me!" He took several more sips of coffee. "I believe the war changed our country more than most of us have probably realized. Women were forced into roles they never envisioned. It changed them. Now the men have to change *with* them."

Thomas was more impressed than ever with the young man sitting before him. The war had robbed him of his leg, but he was sure Perry's mind and heart were much stronger than before the conflict. "Is Louisa truly aware of the dangers?" he pressed, not sure why he was pushing the issue so much. In some ways, he supposed he felt an obligation to Louisa's father to make sure his daughter was aware of the risks. No one would judge her harshly if she sold the plantation, took what money she could get, and returned to Georgia. He realized that marriage had mandated Perry was now the legal owner of Blackwell Plantation, but their conversation made him confident Perry would follow Louisa's wishes.

"*Truly* aware?" Perry asked. "Can one ever be truly aware of a situation before they are in it? I know Louisa has spoken in depth to Abby. Evidently, Abby was very direct."

Thomas smiled. "That would be Abby," he agreed. His admiration for his beautiful wife increased every day.

"Louisa has talked to Robert, and she has had very long discussions with Rose, June, Polly, and Annie. She is quite clear that anyone who doesn't adhere to the Southern Code of Aristocracy is setting themselves up for trouble, but she has the benefit of having watched Carrie do it her whole life, and she rather loves who Carrie has become." Perry chuckled. "Though I'm not sure I'm comfortable with her attitude, I think she is rather looking forward to the opportunity to rock the boat."

Thomas frowned. "You definitely should not be comfortable with her attitude," he said. "All of you are in danger the moment the area plantation owners discover you are planning to emulate Cromwell policies. It's important she understands that."

Perry sobered. "I believe she does," he said. "But then, Carrie also knows her beliefs put her in danger. From what I have observed, she has a part of her that welcomes the challenge even though she understands the possible consequences."

Thomas relaxed. "You're right." He had lost track of the times Carrie's independence and strong will had put her into situations that terrified him, but he also knew it was what made her who she was, and he would not want her to ever change. If Louisa was becoming the same kind of woman, he must simply support her. "I'm not trying to frighten you."

"No," Perry responded. "I don't believe you are. I believe you are trying to ensure we go into this situation with our eyes wide open." He paused. "I also believe you want to make sure her father doesn't come back from his grave and haunt you for not stopping his daughter from taking this foolish course of action." His eyes twinkled with amusement.

It was Thomas' turn to chuckle. "I'm afraid you're more right than I care to admit." He decided it was time to change the topic of conversation. It was clear Perry and Louisa were making the decision they believed was right for them. He would be nothing but glad they had found a way to save Blackwell. Only time would show the results. He turned to Moses. "Have you been staying up to date on current events?"

Moses nodded. "Yes, thanks to Felicia, and thanks to all the papers and journals you send. She gives us our current events briefing every night at dinner." His eyes were bright with pride.

Thomas smiled fondly, remembering Felicia's excitement when he had insisted she call him Uncle Thomas from now on. "That little girl is quite something. She drilled me with questions yesterday morning before everyone arrived for the Harvest Celebration. It is hard to remember sometimes that I am talking to an almost eleven year old little girl. I find she has a better grasp of the political situation in this country than most adults I know."

"She has reason to," Moses said somberly.

"Very true," Thomas agreed. "You're aware of the election coming up?"

"The one that will happen in exactly ten days?" Moses asked. "The one that, if all goes well, will strip President Johnson of his power and give it to the Radical Republicans? The one that will hopefully change things in our country so that blacks can actually have an opportunity to create a life?"

"That would be the one. I'm sorry if I implied you wouldn't know about it," Thomas said. "There were so many times when I was running the plantation that I was completely oblivious to what was going on in the government. The pressures of harvest time made that even more true."

Moses nodded. "I wish I could have that luxury. The reality in our country demands that every black person have complete knowledge of what is happening." He took another drink of coffee before he continued. "If Felicia wasn't keeping us informed every night, I would be adding time to my day to make sure I stayed current with the news. If everything I've heard is correct, President Johnson is about to become a president with absolutely no power."

"I believe that is true." Thomas searched for the best way to say what he needed to say. "I don't believe things are going to change immediately, though." There was so much more that needed to be said, but he was feeling his way forward carefully. Fear could prepare a man, or it could paralyze him. He wanted nothing more than to prepare the two men sitting in front of him.

"I don't believe they are, either," Moses said. "The South has been pretty much getting its way from President Johnson since the war ended, and things are still bad for the freed slaves. Once they lose that advantage, I believe they are going to take out their anger and frustration the same way they always have—on the blacks."

Thomas frowned. "I wish I could dispute that."

"I wish you could, too," Moses replied, his voice suddenly weary, "but we both know it would be a lie."

"Things won't just remain unchanged," Thomas continued. "They will probably get—"

"Get worse?" Moses finished. "I expect they will. The old Confederate soldiers who have now become vigilantes are going to think they have to fight even harder to hold on to their way of life."

"Our way of life is gone," Perry said. "They have nothing left to hang on to. It's time everyone understood that."

"That may be true," Thomas said, "but they have plans to hang on anyway. Or perhaps they have plans to build it again."

"It will never happen," Perry snorted. "The Old South is dead. If any of us expect to build a new life, we have to think and behave differently."

"I wish everyone felt the way you do," Thomas replied, "but I know that is not true."

"Will the new government not take action to stop the vigilante groups?" Moses asked with a frown. "It sounds as if you expect the vigilantes to have a free rein."

Thomas shook his head. "I believe the government will work to stop them, but it is going to take time. President Johnson will lose any hope of power or influence when the Congress shifts to a Republican majority after the election, but it is going to take time to pass new bills and strip the southern states of the power they believe our president has given them."

"So now the government will once more have to take military action," Moses said. "The North won the war, but now they are going to have to send troops into every southern state to fulfill what winning the war meant."

Thomas nodded heavily. "I believe that is the gist of it."

A long silence fell on the porch. Thomas watched as Amber ran from the barn with All My Heart prancing by her side, unaware of the violence in the quarters the night before. She had been sound asleep when Polly had been called out, and Polly had been sleeping in her bed when Amber awoke to come to the barn. He smiled as her laughter rang through the morning air. He fervently wished the entire country could experience the peace of the plantation. Even more than that, he wished he could protect everyone he loved from the violence he was sure was going to continue. He had hoped the end of the war meant the end to all the fighting and fear, but it seemed to have just morphed into a different form of it. What would Amber have to deal with in the future?

"I'll fight to protect what we have here," Moses said finally, his voice almost harsh. "I won't go looking for a fight, but if one comes here, I believe the vigilantes will regret it."

Thomas had no doubt of that, but he was less confident of Perry and Louisa's safety.

Perry seemed to read his mind. "Simon has agreed to manage the tobacco production on the plantation. Twelve of Moses' seasonal workers have been offered the chance to join him."

Thomas nodded. "I know about that. Robert took the letters to them this morning."

"Yes," Perry acknowledged. "They know I have nothing to pay them right now, but the men who have received the letters have enough to hold them until the profits from next year's crop. The details have been laid out clearly. Each family will have a cabin that they can expand if they wish. Each man who works through the end of next season, and who does a good job, will be given forty acres of Blackwell land. The profits from the crop should give them enough to build their homes and take care of themselves through the end of the next season. We will continue to build from there. They all served with Moses," Perry continued. "They will all be armed, and they all know the risk they are taking."

"No more risk than they would be taking if they worked on *any* plantation in the South," Moses said grimly. "At least now they are taking a risk while they are building a life for themselves, instead of having to endure sharecropping situations that are nothing more than white-washed slavery."

"They know they may be targeted first because the whites will consider our plantations a greater threat to the life they are trying to protect?" Thomas asked. He was sure he knew the answer, but he still felt the need to press. It was Moses who read his mind this time.

"You're not responsible for what happens," Moses said. "Every man here knows the war isn't really over. We may not have uniforms on anymore, but that doesn't mean we're not completely ready to protect what needs protecting. When it comes to protecting their wives and children, and their homes, I can assure you they are prepared to do so."

"How did they handle last night?" Thomas asked.

"Many of the women and children were scared and confused, but they had good reason to be. No one expected the threat to come from within," Moses said. "The men had already spread into the woods to fight off whatever threat was out there. When they realized it was one of their own, they still didn't hesitate to do what needed to be done." He reached over and put a hand on Thomas' shoulder. "Thomas, you didn't create slavery. You didn't start this war. You didn't have anything to do with the formation of the Ku Klux Klan and the other vigilante groups." He paused, his eyes lit with gentle humor. "At the risk of being offensive, you need to understand you're not actually powerful enough to take on the responsibility for the reality of our lives."

Thomas chuckled, feeling a huge weight lift from his chest. "I do believe you're right," he said, realizing another layer of the onion had just been peeled away. "Thank you for reminding me."

Moses smiled. "How long are you and Abby staying?"

"Just a few more days. We'll head out in time to take Carrie and Janie to the train station to return to school." Thomas was surprised by the flash in Moses' eyes. He opened his mouth to question him, but a noise in the distance pulled his attention away. A glance down the road revealed Carrie and Robert returning home. "Thank you for the conversation, gentlemen. I have an overdue talk with my daughter to take care of now."

Chapter Twenty-Seven

Carrie felt the fatigue of too few hours of sleep, but she was too exhilarated to care. She smiled up at the three men on the porch as she and Robert rode up. "Good morning!" she called.

"How is Morah?" Moses asked.

"Remarkably well," Carrie said. "The arnica seems to have worked a miracle."

Rose walked out on the porch holding Hope just in time to hear the news. "Aren't you used to my mama's miracles by now?" she teased.

"Oh, I'm used to hers," Carrie said, "but this is one I learned about through my homeopathic books." She explained the situation to the men quickly.

Moses gazed at her as if he couldn't believe what he was hearing. "There is no swelling?" He shook his head. "I saw her last night."

"Me, too," Rose murmured. "She was so badly beaten."

"The books I read about arnica said that the sooner you get it into someone who has been injured, the more quickly it will work." Carrie grinned. "They were right."

"And Dwane?" Rose asked.

"He's fine," Carrie said. "I don't pretend there won't be consequences from what his father did, but he is fine physically. He ate a good breakfast. When I left, he was snuggled up to his mama sound asleep."

Rose smiled, but her eyes were still heavy. "Shirley..." she whispered, pulling Hope closer to her. "That sweet little girl."

The reminder was enough to deflate Carrie's exhilaration. "Yes," she said sadly.

Robert sensed it was time to change the subject. "I gave the letters to all the men," he told Moses and Perry.

Perry tensed. "And?"

Robert grinned. "Simon and all twelve men are on the way over to the plantation to check things out. They were thrilled with the opportunity. They have seen what happened here this season."

Moses grinned. "I told you there was no reason to worry."

Perry sagged against the porch column. "So we may actually pull this off?" He raised his eyes to his and Louisa's bedroom. "Excuse me, everyone. I want to go tell my wife."

"I heard." Louisa stepped out onto the porch with a plate full of hot scones. She gave Perry a brilliant smile. "I'm going home," she said, her eyes trained on the horizon. "My mother would probably throw up her hands and shriek, but my father is somewhere beaming with pride. He used to tell me I could be more than Mother told me I could be." Her face twisted with something like sorrow.

Carrie watched her closely, reminded anew how far her childhood friend had come. "You didn't believe him?"

"I didn't *want* to believe him," Louisa admitted. "I was rather fond of the idea of simply being a wealthy plantation wife. I never wanted to have to be involved in all the tedious details of making the money. I just wanted to manage the benefits," she said with a smile.

Carrie laughed. "I admire your honesty. You no longer feel that way?"

Louisa shook her head, pulling her shoulders back as she stood up taller. "I will never again give someone control of my life. Perry and I will rebuild the plantation *together.*"

Perry reached out and grasped her hand, both of them looking into the distance. "I say we have something to eat and then take Nathan home," he announced.

Louisa nodded happily as she passed around the plate of scones. "Annie said the rest of breakfast would be ready soon."

Moses lifted his hand to stop everyone from standing. "I understand Morah wasn't the only miracle that happened yesterday." Everyone turned their eyes toward him. He grinned and nodded toward the pasture. "I hear the drought on horse buying is over." Then he turned his eyes toward Robert. "I believe this is also my cue to say '*I told you so*'," he said smugly.

"That it is," Robert agreed willingly.

Thomas took a breath. "I haven't had a chance to talk to Mark and Susan since they arrived. The Harvest Celebration kept me busy all day and night, and then with Morah…"

Robert grinned happily as he stepped forward and shook Thomas' hand. "I have you to thank for this miracle," he stated. "Thank you for the letter you wrote to Mark and Susan."

"They are buying some of them?" Thomas asked gladly.

"All of them."

Thomas stared at his son-in-law, quite certain he hadn't heard correctly. "Come again?"

Robert laughed loudly. "They are buying *all* of them."

Mark strode out onto the porch with a cup of coffee in his hand. "Susan and I were out in the barn this morning before it was even light. We had to at least touch every one of those fine colts and fillies to convince ourselves they are actually ours." He slapped Robert on the back. "You will have a waiting list in the spring. I'm just glad we have the boasting rights of purchasing the *first* Cromwell horses."

Thomas shook his head, his heart soaring with happiness. "Now this is the way to start a Cromwell Plantation morning!" He glanced around the porch filled with people who had come to mean so much to him. "It truly does feel like a miracle."

Carrie gazed around the table as Annie brought out platters of scrambled eggs and bacon. Her exhilaration had returned. Everyone would mourn Shirley, but Morah and Dwane were now free to live a new life, and…

"What are you thinking about, Carrie?" Abby asked with amusement. "You are positively glowing."

Carrie exchanged a glance with Robert. He grinned at her and nodded. "It's easy to glow when you're as happy as I am," she replied. "Now is as good a time as any to tell everyone." She paused as she gazed at the faces of everyone she loved best.

"Tell us what?" her father demanded. "I'm too tired to be left hanging in suspense, my dear."

Carrie laughed. "You haven't learned by now that I like to extend the drama?"

Thomas shook his head. "Do all of you see what I was forced to endure while she was growing up?"

"Just while she was growing up?" Abby asked. "I don't believe that's changed since I've known her."

Thomas grasped her hand. "I'm so glad I have someone who takes sympathy on my plight."

Abby laughed and pulled her hand away. "Sympathy? I rather admire her technique."

Carrie laughed when Thomas groaned and shook his head. "Thank you, Abby. Now, if I may be allowed to continue..." She paused as everyone laughed, and then she reached over to take Robert's hand. "I've decided not to return to school this term."

A complete silence filled the room.

Thomas was the first to break it. "Has something happened, Carrie? What is wrong?"

Carrie shook her head. "Nothing is wrong, Father." She explained what she had been feeling, and why she had made the decision. "I want to be a homeopathic doctor more than ever," she finished, "but I feel quite strongly that I'm to remain on the plantation right now. I don't know why, but I am beyond thrilled to be here with Robert and the rest of you." Her eyes shifted to her father. "Richmond is much closer than Philadelphia, so I know I'll see you more often." Then she looked at Abby, wondering if she was disappointed in her. "You haven't said anything," she murmured.

Abby smiled. "I wanted to give everyone else a chance before I told you how absolutely joyful I am to have my daughter so close. I learned a long time ago that it is impossible to understand the decisions we make sometimes, but I also know you well enough to know you would only make this decision if you were completely confident of it. I'll let you deal with what it all means. I'll just be happy to have you on the plantation, and I will look forward to regular visits."

Carrie grinned as everyone else chorused their agreement. Thomas stood and pulled her into a strong embrace. "I know the time is coming when I may lose the ability to even have you close enough to visit as often as you do. I would be nothing but a fool if I didn't rejoice in your decision. I prefer to believe I am not a fool," he said. Then he threw his head back with a laugh. "Welcome back to Cromwell Plantation, my dear!"

Carrie sat down in the rocking chair after a late lunch, glad to have the porch to herself. So much had happened in such a short period that she was suddenly desperate to have time alone to process it all. She thought briefly about riding Granite to her special place on the river, but her tired body resisted. Pulling her coat closely around her, she rested her head on the back of the chair and gazed up at the brilliant yellow leaves of the oak tree that shaded the house. She thought of all the times she had climbed the tree as a girl. She had seen it grow from a large tree into a truly giant guardian that would forever hold the secret of how many times she had climbed down its sheltering limbs from her window to escape her mother's attempts to turn her into a proper plantation mistress.

"I'm back home, Mama," she whispered, and then chuckled as she imagined the look on her mother's face if she could see her clothed in breeches, boots, and her father's heavy coat. Mama probably would have fainted away with horror. Just being late for meals seemed to have triggered anxiety attacks in her fragile parent. Yet, in the end, she had encouraged Carrie to follow her dream of being a doctor. She would always treasure the last conversation they had shared.

Carrie relished the cool, crisp air. All signs pointed to a snowy, cold winter, but she didn't mind. They would most assuredly have less snow than Philadelphia, and it would not be covered with black soot before it turned into a foul, gray slush on the streets. It would simply drape the plantation with a luxuriant blanket of white. A surge of peace spread through her body so strongly it elicited a quiet laugh.

"You sound happy."

Carrie bit back her disappointment at being interrupted. "Hello, Father."

"Do you need some time alone?"

Carrie loved him for asking because it revealed how well he knew her, but she shook her head. "Never from you."

Thomas smiled and settled down in the chair next to her. "I would say there were certainly some times when you were frustrated with your old father and would have relished time away from me."

"Certainly no more than you were frustrated by me through the years," Carrie said playfully. "I happen to know just how many times you protected me from Mother's displeasure."

"Oh, I'm sure you don't know them *all*," Thomas responded. He sobered then. "I'm glad we have reached the stage of our relationship where we are now friends."

"Me, too," Carrie agreed as she reached out to take his hand. She felt the peace encompass her again as her father's strong fingers enveloped hers.

They sat that way for several minutes before Thomas cleared his throat. "I'd like to talk to you about something."

Carrie straightened in her chair as she heard the seriousness in her father's voice. "Is anything wrong?"

"No…" her father said. "I've merely been trying to come to grips with something. I believe I'm ready to talk about it now."

Carrie suddenly knew where the conversation was headed, but she waited for him to say what he needed to.

"Your revelation the night before we left to come here was rather disturbing."

Carrie nodded. "I felt the same way," she replied. Another long silence fell on the porch, but it was one Carrie was comfortable with. She was content to let her father discuss Lord Oliver Cromwell in the way that worked best for him.

"Did you feel as responsible as I do?" Thomas finally asked.

"I did."

"You don't anymore?"

Carrie considered the question. "Not in the way you might be thinking."

"Could you illuminate me? I have spent hours in the past few days studying the history of England and Ireland during Lord Cromwell's time. I find it sickening." He paused, his eyes deeply troubled.

Carrie watched him closely. She knew she had seen little of her father since they arrived, and now she understood why. She was happy to answer his question, but she sensed he had more to say first.

"Since we were here, I decided to go through the records from the beginning of the plantation," Thomas revealed.

"And...?" Carrie prompted after another long silence.

Thomas sighed. "The first Cromwells had many indentured servants."

Carrie remained silent. She was not hearing anything she had not already learned and come to grips with.

"You're not going to remind me they were actually slaves?" Thomas asked ruefully.

"Would you like me to?" Carrie was unsure how to proceed. She was relieved when her father laughed.

"You have turned into a diplomat as you have matured," he murmured, his voice filled with both surprise and pride.

"I couldn't stay a child forever," Carrie reminded him.

"No, but you also didn't have to become such a magnificent woman. I am very proud of you."

Carrie glowed with delight as she squeezed his hand tightly. "Thank you, Father. That means the world to me."

Thomas nodded absently, buried in his thoughts again. "I found the records about the indentured servants," he continued after a long silence. He took a deep breath. "They were nothing more than slaves."

"I know," Carrie replied.

"I knew some of them when I was very young. My grandfather had at least ten white indentured servants, as well as black slaves."

Carrie didn't see the need to repeat that *all* of them were slaves. Her father had accepted the truth. How he communicated it was his business.

"As I said, I was quite young, so I don't remember what happened to them. I do remember, though, that by the time I was eight or nine, there were only black slaves working Cromwell." His voice was reminiscent.

Carrie nodded and continued to rock when another long silence filled the porch.

"You're very much like Abby," Thomas said suddenly, his voice laced with humor. "She lets me sit with my own thoughts for as long as I need to figure out how to communicate them."

Carrie smiled. Nothing could make her happier than being compared to the woman who was equal parts mother and mentor to her.

"You're really just going to let me squirm until I say something about Lord Oliver Cromwell?" her father asked, his voice almost petulant.

Carrie couldn't contain her chuckle. "You seem to have done just that."

Thomas grimaced. "I suppose I have," he said. "Our ancestor was quite a barbaric fellow," he growled.

Carrie nodded, so glad to know they were in agreement. "I wish I could dispute that, but history is quite clear."

"And you don't feel responsible?" Thomas pressed.

"Do you?" Carrie turned the question back to him.

This time her father groaned and pressed his face into his hands. "My God. You truly are just like Abby. Did she teach you to never answer a question with anything but a question?"

Carrie was flooded with memories. "Actually, it was Sarah. I used to go to her with questions all the time. I can't remember a time when she just answered one straight out. She always told me I would appreciate my own answers the most. She just asked questions until I figured out what I really felt or believed."

"Did you resent her?"

Carrie couldn't control her grin. "Are you resenting me?"

Thomas laughed loudly and began to pace the porch. "I have felt so many emotions since I learned all this that I hardly know where to start. I've felt angry because I have been lied to all my life. I've felt intense shame, because I can't believe I'm related to someone who would do what that man did, and then the shame has been multiplied by the fact that I owned slaves until you set them all free. And I've felt like a complete fraud because I always believed I was someone special because of the family I came from. I never dreamed that knowledge would end up being something I wished I could pretend had never happened."

Carrie listened quietly, empathizing as he uttered all the things she had felt. "I understand," she said. There was so much more she wanted to say, but she wanted her father to have all the time he needed to sort through his own feelings.

Thomas stopped and looked down at her. "Yes, I'm sure you do. Yet somehow you've managed to take all this knowledge and figure out a way to deal with it."

"It took me some time," Carrie replied.

Thomas sat down and took both her hands. "Please tell me how you did that," he pleaded.

Carrie looked into his eyes and knew it was time for a straight answer. "I felt all the things you did, until Biddy helped me understand I could consider it a weighty responsibility, or..." her voice softened even more as she remembered Biddy's compassionate eyes staring into hers. Her heart caught at the idea she might not see the elderly woman again, but she pushed it away. Biddy might be ninety-seven, but she was strong and healthy. "She helped me realize I could view it simply as a privilege."

"How?" Thomas asked. "I'm not feeling privileged."

"Neither did I," Carrie admitted. She thought about all she had done down in Moyamensing. "I couldn't go back and change anything that had happened," she said, "but I could do something about now, and I could help create a different future with my actions. When cholera struck Moyamensing, I knew it was my opportunity to begin to do that." She gazed out over the plantation, watching the horses playing in the field. "I don't know if I would have felt the same compulsion to help if I hadn't also felt the weight of the responsibility. I truly believe I was granted the privilege of making a difference for the people who have suffered so much because of our ancestor."

Thomas gazed into her eyes for a long moment before he nodded. "You said something like that the other night, but I didn't have a point of reference to understand it."

"You reacted exactly like I did when I first heard it," Carrie answered. "I would suspect no one would be thrilled to learn what we have."

Her father looked thoughtful. "So the question becomes, how can I redeem some of what Lord Cromwell has done."

"Is that what you want to do?" Carrie asked.

Thomas stared at her. "I'm not even going to say anything about you answering a question with a question," he teased before he grew serious again. He peered at her closely. "Why do I get the feeling you have a suggestion for me?"

Carrie blushed. "Am I that transparent?"

"Only to me," Thomas answered. "And perhaps Robert... And then, I imagine Rose would see right through you." He cocked his head. "And probably Abby..."

Carrie laughed and held up her hands. "All right! I'm transparent. Is that terrible?"

"Not as long as you tell me what it is you are trying so unsuccessfully to hide," Thomas replied.

Carrie couldn't believe she was having the opportunity to share her idea so soon. She had thought it would take months for her father to process what she had told him. There were so many moments in her life that she had been proud of him, but perhaps never more so than she was right at that moment. "The Irish find it very difficult to get good jobs because of the image people hold of them," she began.

"Isn't a lot of that justified?" Thomas asked with a frown. "I remember that it was primarily the Irish police who led the riots in Memphis and New Orleans."

"That's true," Carrie acknowledged, "but is it really fair to paint an entire group of people as all being the same? That's like saying everyone who originated in England is the same."

"I suppose it's not fair," Thomas agreed. "You are a wonderful judge of character, daughter, and I can tell you care deeply for the Irish in Moyamensing. I am open to having my perception changed." He sat forward. "Tell me what you have in mind."

Abby stepped out onto the porch then, hesitating when she saw them in intense conversation. "Am I interrupting something?"

"No," Carrie said, thrilled to see her. "I was just getting ready to share an idea with Father that you need to hear. It will take both of you to make the decision."

"Oh?" Abby asked, an intrigued look in her eyes. She walked over and settled down in the chair next to them. "What is this about?"

"It's about me coming to grips with our scandalous relative," Thomas answered.

"And your idea is about that, Carrie?"

Carrie nodded. "You already know what motivated me to help the cholera patients in Moyamensing." She took a deep breath as she tried to choose her words carefully. Abby had a heart bigger than anyone she knew, but she was also a very successful businesswoman. She had not become that way by making careless decisions. "I believe there is a way to help them even more."

Abby regarded her steadily for a long moment. "You want us to build a factory down there."

Carrie gaped at her. "How did you know?" she finally gasped.

"I didn't," Abby admitted. "I've just thought so much about what you told us back in Richmond. I thought about Biddy giving her whole life to make things better for her people. I knew that your wonderful father, once he had come to grips with his heritage, would want to do something about it." She paused. "I'm assuming the reason poverty is so rampant in Moyamensing is because there are very few jobs."

"That's true," Carrie agreed. Her mind was spinning with possibilities. "I love you!" she cried.

Abby laughed and reached out to squeeze her hand. "I love you, too. Now let's see if there is a way to do this that makes financial sense. It won't do any good to build a factory if we can't make it profitable. If we can't make money, we'll have to shut it down, and that will hurt everyone."

Carrie nodded earnestly. "I've thought a lot about it," she said.

"Have you?" her father asked with surprise. "I didn't realize you knew much about clothing factories."

Carrie smiled. "I may not care to be involved in the factory, but that doesn't mean I don't listen carefully," she said.

Abby laughed. "That's my girl! Tell us what you have in mind."

"Real estate in Moyamensing is very inexpensive. Most of the area is covered with shabby tenement houses, but while I was making my rounds helping patients, I saw a few large buildings that I believe could be transformed into a factory. They must have been left over from the days when Biddy's husband was attempting to build industry down there. He failed back then because he didn't have enough money to use as capital, but I think at least two of the buildings could be perfect. One of them is almost the same size as your factory in Richmond," Carrie said. "I don't know this for sure, but I suspect Biddy owns the buildings. I believe the price would be quite reasonable if she knew you were doing it to provide employment for her people."

"And what do you consider reasonable?" Thomas pressed.

Carrie shrugged. "It's not my job to know that," she replied. "I'm trusting your business negotiating skills will enable you to acquire it at a price that would produce a profit."

Abby laughed. "Well played, Carrie!"

Thomas smiled, but his eyes were serious. "And you really believe the Irish in Moyamensing would make capable employees?"

Carrie realized he was trying to hide his skepticism, but it came through in both his voice and his eyes. It was up to her to convince him her idea would work. "I do," she said firmly. It was important she help both of them believe what she was saying. "My time caring for the people down there taught me so much. The government may have outlawed indentured servants and slaves, but that doesn't mean many of the Irish are not still being forced to live in slave-like conditions. They have been treated horribly in this country, just as the blacks have, but they dream of being given a chance to show what they are capable of." She took a deep breath. "Biddy is paying for every single child in Moyamensing to go to school," she revealed.

"Every *one* of them?" Thomas echoed with disbelief. "That must cost a small fortune."

"Evidently she has a small fortune to spend," Carrie replied. She could tell the moment her father's eyes shifted from automatic resistance to cautious interest. "The children are going home and teaching their parents. Every household I was in had books, and everyone was reading at some level. I realize reading is not critical to factory work, but I believe it is a clear indicator of how committed they are to changing their lives."

"I would have to agree with you," Abby said, "but we wouldn't be able to do anything before next spring if we determine it is feasible," she cautioned.

"Of course not," Carrie agreed. "It would be impossible to move forward in the middle of a Philadelphia winter, but the need is not going away. There will be plenty of people eager to work for you next spring or summer. Just the knowledge of the opportunity will give them the hope they need to make it through another harsh winter."

She watched as Abby and Thomas exchanged a long look. She was thrilled when she saw nothing but thoughtful consideration. She knew they would talk it through. She also knew Abby would send a letter to her plant manager in Philadelphia. "I'm sure Biddy will be happy to show the property to your manager at any time."

Abby chuckled. "You know you have us interested."

Carrie smiled demurely. "I do know both of you fairly well." She then threw all pretenses aside as she jumped up and did a little jig around the porch before settling back down in her chair. "I realize nothing has been decided, but I'm confident that once you examine the situation you will agree with me!"

Abby eyed her for a long moment. "Confident enough to travel back up to Philadelphia to tell Dr. Strikener of your plans in person, and then take me to visit Biddy and Faith?"

Carrie stared at her as she searched for words. She had absolutely no desire to return to Philadelphia.

Abby reached for her hand. "I understand why you have chosen to stay on the plantation, my dear, and I completely support you, but I believe you might be leaving some things unfinished. In my experience, unfinished things can sometimes cause problems and regrets we would never have anticipated," she said gently. "I was planning a trip to Philadelphia this fall anyway. It would give us a wonderful time together, and when you returned, you could feel confident in your course of action. It's just a suggestion," she added quickly. "You are a grown woman who is fully capable of making her own decisions."

Carrie met Abby's eyes evenly as she thought through her words. She felt like the eighteen-year-old girl who had been challenged about her beliefs concerning slavery. She didn't really enjoy the challenge any more now than she had then, but she had matured enough to know it deserved to be considered carefully. She swung her eyes out to the pasture when she heard Granite give a loud snort. Smiling, she watched as he kicked up his heels and raced around the field, his head and tail held high. There was no part of her that wanted to leave the plantation and board a train for Philadelphia, but there was a very quiet voice murmuring that Abby was right.

Her last conversation with Dr. Strikener had ended with her assuring him she would be back in two weeks to start school. She had promised Biddy and Faith the same thing. She knew they would all understand if they were to receive a letter of explanation, but she wondered if they would be hurt. There was another tiny voice asking how she would feel if she never saw Biddy again. She thought of Janie going back home alone and suddenly knew it would be much easier for her friend if she had help choosing new housemates.

Carrie took a deep breath. "I guess I did make a rather abrupt decision," she said ruefully, as she continued to stare out into the pasture.

Abby shook her head. "You followed your heart, Carrie. It's one of the things I love the most about you. I just happen to have done something many years ago that was very similar to what you are planning on doing. I don't regret my decision, but I do regret some of the ramifications of how I did it."

Carrie swung around to meet her eyes again. "When are you thinking about making the trip?" She had made a promise to Felicia that she had no intention of breaking.

"I had already planned on returning with you and Janie," Abby admitted. "I want to go, and then return home, before the first snows come. Your father assures me winter is coming early this year, though I have never seen a wooly caterpillar talk!"

Carrie and Thomas both laughed.

"I don't know that we'll ever turn our city woman into a farmer," Thomas said affectionately.

"Probably not," Carrie agreed, "but I'm not sure either of us will ever be as wise as she is. I'd say having the benefit of her wisdom is much more important than turning her into a farmer." She smiled when she saw relief fill Abby's eyes. "You're right, Abby. As usual," she sighed.

Abby shook her head. "There are plenty of times when I'm wrong," she insisted.

"Perhaps," Carrie replied. "But I have yet to see them." The moment she decided to return, she knew she was making the right choice. She was also quite sure she and Abby would have a wonderful time, and then she would come home to spend the winter right where she wanted to be.

Four days later, Carrie stood next to the wagon already pointed toward Richmond. She wrapped her arms around Robert. "I'll miss you," she murmured.

Robert smiled as he leaned down to kiss her. "You'll be back in two weeks. You're not leaving, Carrie, you're going on vacation. I hope you have a wonderful time."

Carrie grinned. "You're right." She was very much looking forward to her time with Abby and Janie. Matthew had left two days earlier to cover the elections in Washington, DC. Janie would start school almost immediately upon their arrival, while she and Abby would have time to enjoy the city. She knew Abby had some business obligations, but she had already been assured they would not take much time.

Felicia ran out onto the porch. "Don't forget you promised you would be back, Carrie."

Carrie gave the girl a firm nod. "I wouldn't miss the Leonid Shower for anything," she assured her. "I know I could see it in Philadelphia, but I also know the street lights would diminish it, and I want to have you there to explain everything to me. I'll be here, Felicia," she promised again.

Felicia, obviously satisfied, nodded and then ran forward to hug Thomas one more time. "Thank you for everything, Uncle Thomas."

Thomas knelt down so he would be at eye level and took her in his arms again. "I'm proud of you, Felicia."

Felicia looked startled for a moment, and then her smile beamed out. "You'll send me everything about the election as soon as you get it?"

Thomas smiled back. "I'm sending a special courier just for you as soon as we have the results," he told her.

Felicia stared at him, wide-eyed with wonder. "By special courier," she gasped. "Really?"

"I promise. This election will probably mean more to your people than any other election in history. I won't leave you in suspense."

"It is important that black men get the vote," Felicia said. "That won't happen until Congress is held by enough Republicans to veto anything President Johnson comes up with."

Abby cocked her head. "Just black *men*, Felicia?"

"Yes, ma'am," Felicia said in a solemn tone. "I wish women would get the vote at the same time, but it's not going to happen."

"And why is that?" Abby pressed.

Felicia frowned. "Partly because I don't believe our country is ready for it, but everything I have read also tells me that women are not united enough to make it happen. There are too many women who don't understand the necessity of having a voice."

Abby was the one to frown now. "I'm afraid you're right, my dear."

"It won't be long before I will be able to help, Aunt Abby," Felicia said fervently. "I'll be eleven years old soon, and then I will just keep getting older. I believe this will be a long battle, but there are a lot of us growing up who will be able to make sure it happens. I believe it will happen in my lifetime."

Abby seemed at a loss for words as she gazed at Felicia.

"I told you she's not your average ten-year-old," Thomas said.

"I'm almost eleven," Felicia protested.

"When is your birthday?" Carrie asked.

Felicia grinned. "The same day as the Leonid Meteor Shower," she revealed. "It will be the best birthday present ever!"

Thomas smiled. "You're almost eleven," he agreed. "But you're still not an average *eleven*-year-old."

"You're absolutely right." Abby knelt down beside Thomas. "You are a remarkable girl, Felicia Samuels."

"Not a remarkable *little* girl? So many people tell me I shouldn't worry so much about these things because I'm just a little girl."

"You are definitely not a little girl," Abby said. "You are a very intelligent young lady on the verge of becoming a powerful woman. Age should never make a difference." She reached out and grasped Felicia's hand. "Keep learning. I predict people will be listening to what you have to say very soon. In fact, I'm going to make quite sure they do."

Felicia straightened as her eyes snapped with a determined confidence. "I'll keep learning, Aunt Abby. I'll be ready when the time is right."

Abby met her eyes squarely, woman to woman. "I know you will be, Felicia. *I know you will be.*"

Robert grinned as Mark and Susan emerged from the barn. "Did you get your goodbyes all said?" he called teasingly.

Susan laughed. "I can hardly bear to leave them," she murmured. "I know all those babies are in the best hands possible, but I'm heartbroken that I won't see them again until spring."

Amber, walking at their side, piped in. "They aren't even going to look the same, Miss Susan. They'll be almost all grown."

"Great..." Susan groaned. "Just rub it in." Then she brightened. "Those colts and fillies are going to put our stable on the map, just like they are going to do for you."

Amber nodded. "Yes, ma'am. I reckon that is true. Me and Clint will work real hard with them over the winter."

"Clint and *I* will work with them." Rose corrected as she gazed down from the porch, Hope asleep on her shoulder.

Amber shook her head sadly, but her eyes danced with fun. "You see what it's like, Miss Susan? All I want to do is work with horses, and instead I have my teacher hounding me about how to talk. I just can't ever seem to get away from it."

Susan patted her shoulder. "You'll be glad for it one day," she promised. "Most people, rightly or wrongly, judge others by how they speak. You don't want anything to stand in your way of being seen as exactly what you are—a smart girl who is also an amazing horse trainer."

Amber lifted her head proudly. "Yes, ma'am," she replied. "Clint and *I* will work with your colts and fillies all winter long. I promise you and Mr. Mark will be thrilled with them."

"That I'm sure of," Mark agreed as he pulled Amber into his arms to hug her tightly. "It has been an honor meeting you, Amber."

Amber ducked her head shyly, but her eyes shone with delight. "Thank you, Mr. Mark. Will I see you in the spring?"

"That you will, young lady. We had discussed Robert shipping them up to us, but we feel better about taking the entire journey with them. We'll be back in April or May, depending on the road conditions, to take all of them home."

A sharp whinny sounding from the pasture made all of them laugh.

"Not you, All My Heart!" Amber called. "No one will ever take *you* away from me."

The laughter increased as All My Heart stared at her young mistress and bobbed her head several times to confirm the promise.

Chapter Twenty-Eight

Matthew gazed up at the Capitol Building in Washington, DC, his heart pounding as he envisioned what must be happening within Congress. He had lived through many exciting and intense times in American history, but he was quite certain none of them could exceed the impact the next months and years would have. The war had changed the canvas of the country. What happened in the next months and years would determine what was painted on that canvas.

"Wouldn't you like to be inside those walls today?"

Matthew nodded as Peter Wilcher joined him on the bench. He had been thrilled to run into his friend the day he had arrived in the city. They had secured a hotel room together, sharing the exhilaration of the election returns as they had come in. "I would give just about anything to be in there," he admitted.

Peter leaned his lanky frame back against the wooden slats. "There's never been an election like this," he said, satisfaction dripping from his voice.

Matthew smiled. "It's the first time a midterm election has swung so far from the typical results," he mused, creating his next article in his mind as he spoke. Political experience said this election should have resulted in the Republican Party losing influence. Instead, the party that had taken power with Lincoln's election had just swept the midterm elections as well, giving them enough members in Congress to gain the two-thirds majority required to override any of President Johnson's vetoes.

Peter chuckled. "The most amazing thing is that the Democrats seem to be actually shocked by the results. Surely they knew what was coming."

Matthew lifted a brow as he stared up at Lady Liberty reigning over the city from her perch atop the Capitol Building. "I think they actually believed the possibility of black suffrage would sway enough people from the Radical Republican stance to change the outcome of the election."

Peter scowled. "In spite of the Democrats' insistence on making the entire election about black rights, the country is smart enough to recognize this election actually determined whether the war had any true meaning or not. The last months have made it obvious that President Johnson's policies are doing nothing but allowing the South to recreate the same society that led us into the war in the first place. The country has paid too high of a price to allow that to happen." He glanced over at Matthew. "The articles you wrote after the riots in Memphis and New Orleans played a large role in making people realize the truth."

"Thank you," Matthew replied, wishing he could believe that, but too frustrated with the reality for Peter's statement to make him feel better. "We still have a long way to go, though. While the Republicans have regained Congress, the situation in Memphis and New Orleans is still ridiculous. It's not going to change," he added. He watched the wind catch the flag flying over the Capitol. The breeze caught it and made it stand out strongly against the blue sky. The sight caused a mixture of pride and a despair he was doing his best to battle.

Peter turned to look at him more fully. "I'm afraid the election has taken all my attention," he said apologetically. "I've lost track of what has happened in the aftermath of the riots."

"You and the rest of the country," Matthew said wearily. "I'm sorry. I know the elections have taken up the majority of everyone's time and attention, but the people of Memphis have received nothing in the way of justice."

Peter stared at him. "Nothing?" he asked with disbelief. "I know I've been preoccupied, but I should know this."

Matthew shrugged, his frustration deepening as he thought about what he had learned regarding the aftermath of the riot. He had written articles, but they had been buried in the crush of news about the election. "It gained the attention of Congress long enough for them to use it to malign Johnson's policies. They set up investigations that clearly revealed the truth about the murders that took place during the riots, but our government ultimately left it up to Tennessee and Memphis to mete out justice." He clenched his fists as he thought about the horror he had witnessed during those days. "Of course, they did nothing. There have been no indictments, and Memphis has refused to pay to rebuild anything that was destroyed."

"And the government let them get away with that?" Peter gasped.

"General Grant tried to change the outcome. When he sent the findings of the committee, he included a letter recommending the army arrest and hold the rioters until the Memphis civil authorities agreed to prosecute them, and he also urged that the government force the city to pay restitution."

"That sounds right," Peter said. "What happened?"

"Nothing," Matthew growled. "General Grant sent it on to Secretary of State Stanton. Stanton promptly passed it off to President Johnson. Instead of making a decision, our president sent it on to Attorney General Speed."

"So he could avoid responsibility," Peter snapped.

"Or at least try to," Matthew responded. "Speed's reaction was predictable. He said he found the actions against the blacks reprehensible, but that he saw no legal basis for army intervention, and no legal basis to force Memphis to pay restitution. He sent the papers back to Johnson, who had Stanton file them."

"In a very dark place, most likely."

Matthew sighed. "That's the crux of it." He shook his head. "Men who were there during the riot have either resigned or been reassigned to get them out of Memphis. There is virtually no one left who was there during those terrible days. It just all seems to have disappeared," he said bitterly. He knew those days would never leave the minds of those who had been attacked.

Peter joined him in a long silence. "What happened to the little girl Moses took home?" he finally asked.

The question elicited a smile from Matthew. "Felicia is one of the brightest little girls I have ever had the privilege to know. Her parents were murdered, but I believe Felicia will be a powerful voice in black rights when she grows up."

"Dare I ask what is happening in New Orleans after the riots?"

Matthew gritted his teeth. He wished he could push the terrible memories of the New Orleans violence from his mind, but they still haunted him at night. The nightmares were diminishing, but he didn't think he would ever lose the vivid images of coldblooded murder all around him. "It's worse."

"Worse?" Peter echoed hollowly. "Is that possible?"

"A grand jury was called just two days after the riot. They indicted every man, white and black, who was a leader in the convention for the black vote. That is, those who were still alive after the massacre," Matthew seethed. "None of the police, nor one white citizen, was charged." He understood Peter's total silence. What could you possibly say in response to such blatant injustice? "On top of it, the Republican congressmen who encouraged the leaders of the convention to move forward all denied doing so, and most of them denied having any knowledge of it at all." He couldn't control the shudder that rippled through him in the wake of the raw memories this conversation was unearthing.

"I'm sorry," Peter said numbly.

Matthew forced himself to shake off the sense of futility that had almost made him walk away from journalism entirely. "It wasn't all for naught," he managed. "The riots, and all the articles that were written, painted a clear picture that the South was willing to take any measures necessary to make sure the former slaves would be denied freedom and equality."

"All the articles in the Southern papers after the New Orleans riots only confirmed that truth," Peter observed.

"Yes," Matthew replied, biting back his anger. "There was a barrage of editorials making it very clear that the riot was a *'salutary warning that the South would never submit to Yankee rule.'* " He drawled the words in a very passable imitation of a New Orleans accent, and then scowled. "The editorials convinced northern voters that the South has refused to accept the verdict of their defeat in the war."

"And now we have a new Congress. Would it be crass to say that perhaps the riots were not in vain?"

"I suspect it would be to those who lost loved ones and have seen no justice," Matthew said, "but I am objective enough to acknowledge that President Johnson may have succeeded if the riots had not jolted the American public awake." He continued to gaze at the Capitol. "It was a terrible price to pay, but I am doing my best to focus on the possibility of change, because I know it's impossible to rewrite the past." He was grateful for Peter's silence. It was taking every bit of his mental energy not to fall back into the horrors of that day in New Orleans.

Peter finally broke the silence. "Things will be different now. The South may have attempted to restore slavery in substance, if not in name, but everything has changed. This election has ensured Congress can override any vetoes that Johnson might impose. I have spoken with many Congress members. They are moving forward with the Reconstruction Acts that will bring control back to the government. The South is to be divided into five military districts. Each state will be required to accept the Thirteenth and Fourteenth Amendments."

Matthew nodded. He was thrilled the South would be forced to grant freedom and political rights to the blacks, but he had seen too much during the riots to believe it would be a simple process. The government could force a political mandate, but they could not change attitudes. His earlier exhilaration had been swallowed by searing memories of the unreasoning hatred he had seen on white faces during the riots.

"What are you thinking?" Peter finally asked after it became obvious Matthew wasn't going to respond.

"I'm thinking," Matthew said, "that things will not change as long as people don't have to bear the consequences of their actions. The country can pass laws, but they can't change hearts." He continued to speak slowly, his words taking shape as he spoke. "The police in both Memphis and New Orleans have faced no consequences for what they did. That reality is going to embolden others who want to use their same tactics. The government has practically said that they will squawk about the riots, but they will take no action to punish those who participated." He shrugged. "If every one of those police who murdered blacks was sitting in jail, others would at least stop to think before doing the same thing."

"It's going to be different," Peter insisted. "The new Reconstruction Acts will ensure that."

Matthew wished he could be as certain as his friend, but he knew how difficult it was to mitigate hatred. Still, he would allow Peter his hope. Maybe someday he would share it.

"Can I change the subject?" Peter asked.

"Please," Matthew said, eager to think of something else.

"When are you going to marry Janie?"

Matthew stiffened. He didn't really want to talk about that either, but he had opened the door to the conversation. "When she'll have me," he finally said. He could tell Peter was staring at him, but he didn't take his gaze away from Lady Liberty.

"Is there a problem?" Peter pressed after a long silence.

Matthew sighed and forced himself to relax. Peter knew about the abuse Janie had suffered during her marriage to Clifford. "No," he said. "She just isn't ready." Most of the time he understood that, but there were moments when his loneliness was so intense he didn't think he could stand it. Being out of town was almost easier than being two doors down from her. The realization she was so close, but still not his, was sometimes more than he could bear. He knew they had only been engaged for less than three months, but he had waited so long for the right woman that he was impatient to have her by his side all the time. By his side, and in his bed.

"Living through the war and surviving prison makes you long for the nicer things in life," Peter murmured.

"Yes." Matthew was grateful for Peter's understanding. His friend was the only one who could come close to comprehending what he had endured during his two stays in Libby Prison. "I promised her I would be patient," he muttered. "I will continue to try—however much I am failing."

Carrie couldn't resist bouncing on the seat as the carriage navigated the heavy traffic clogging the streets leading to Moyamensing. "We're almost there!"

Michael glanced back at her with an indulgent smile. "Let me guess. You would rather get out and walk."

Carrie grinned back at her friend. She had been so happy to discover Michael was free for the two weeks she and Abby were in town. They had hired him to be their driver during the whole period. Long conversations between the three of them had deepened their friendship and helped Abby gain a greater understanding of the neighborhood they were about to enter.

Michael looked to Abby for help. "Has she always been like this?"

"Ever since I've known her," Abby replied, "and her father assures me she was always this impulsive and impatient and *wonderful*," she said warmly.

Carrie stuck her tongue out at Michael. "Can't you drive this thing any faster?"

Michael laughed. "Sure, I can drive it as fast as you would like, but first you'll have to get out and make all the traffic and people disappear."

Carrie heaved a heavy sigh and sank back against the cushions. She knew Michael was right. They had been in Philadelphia a week. This had been their first opportunity to drive into Moyamensing.

While Abby had taken care of business in her factories, Carrie had met with Dr. Strikener, who had asked her why she chose not to simply send a letter explaining the circumstances. He had laughed heartily when she shared Abby's challenge and told her she had a very wise stepmother—something she couldn't agree with more. He understood her decision completely and had loaded her down with books and materials she could study over the winter, teasing her that she might be ready to be on the faculty when she returned. Her situation treating Morah with arnica was discussed at length, and Dr. Strikener took pages of notes while they talked, explaining he would use the experience in one of his classes that winter. He had also written her a letter of introduction to Dr. Hobson, the homeopathic physician in Richmond, assuring her Dr. Hobson would be honored to offer any assistance he could. The two men had been friends for years.

When Carrie had returned to the house, she thanked Abby profusely for challenging her to come back to Philadelphia. Staying on the plantation would not have harmed her application to the homeopathic college, but she certainly would have missed out on so many opportunities, and she sensed she had gained a deeper respect from Dr. Strikener.

Meanwhile, Carolyn Blakely and two other homeopathic students had eagerly accepted Janie's offer of housing. They had moved in the night before. It was wonderful to have the house full of laughter and talk again, and knowing Janie would not be alone in the house had done much to ease Carrie's mind about her decision to stay on the plantation.

"Mrs. Carrie! Mrs. Carrie!"

Carrie, deep in her own thoughts, had not even realized they had entered Moyamensing. She laughed as two children ran up to the carriage, their faces split with wide grins. "How are you?" Carrie called.

"We're doing real good. There ain't anybody sick from cholera at all!"

Carrie felt a surge of satisfaction. "I'm so glad," she said. "Are you two in school?"

"Yes, ma'am. We been studying hard just like you told us to. Does Miss Biddy and Miss Faith know you're coming? They ain't said nothing about it. I was real surprised to see you."

Carrie shook her head, giving them a conspiratorial wink. "It's a surprise," she said as she put a finger to her lips. "Can you keep it for me?"

"Sure, we can keep it, but I don't know about everybody else."

"Everybody else?" Carrie asked as she gazed around. For the first time she noticed the group of children clustered on the side of the road keeping pace with the wagon as it inched forward. She waved, laughing with joy when they erupted into wild waving of their own. She was so glad she had come.

"There was a whole bunch of us seen you drive in," the little boy confessed. "We drew the long straws for the right to come welcome you back. Miss Biddy would have had our hides if we had all run out into the street at the same time." His brown eyes danced with mischief. "I don't reckon I know *what* the others are doing. There is some of them that aren't on the side of the road anymore, though."

Carrie laughed, certain their arrival was no longer a secret, but she didn't care. Just being back there was enough joy. "I've missed you all."

"We've missed you, too."

Carrie's determination to make sure the factory was built was stronger than ever. A glance at Abby's face told her she felt the same way.

Carrie motioned for Michael to stop the carriage that had been barely inching forward. She patted the seat next to her. "Why don't you two join us for the last part of the ride?"

They scrambled up as soon as she issued the invitation, snuggling close in the blankets. Suddenly, Carrie knew how she was going to spend her last week in Philadelphia.

The traffic cleared for a few minutes, allowing Michael the chance to navigate the last few blocks. Carrie was not surprised when she saw both Biddy and Faith peering out the windows. She waved wildly, climbing down after the children leapt to the street flashing triumphant grins as they ran over to join their friends.

"They are going to be the heroes today," Abby said with a chuckle. She stepped down from the carriage with Michael's assistance. "I'm sure every one of them would have given up all their marbles to ride in the carriage with you."

"That they would," Michael agreed. "Almost all of them had someone in their family who would have died without Carrie or Carolyn."

Carrie glowed with satisfaction, but she was eager to get inside and visit with Biddy and Faith. "Will you be down at the pub?"

"Aye, that I will," Michael answered. "I'll be keeping warm until you're ready to be going home. Send someone down to get me."

Carrie nodded, tucked her hand in Abby's arm, and walked up the steps. The door opened almost immediately, a warm blast of air reaching out to grab them. She knew Biddy must pay dearly for wood and oil to keep the house warm. She was glad it was not a problem.

Faith stood in the doorway, a wide smile on her face as she reached out to grab Carrie's hand, and then reached over to grip one of Abby's. "If the two of you aren't a sight for sore eyes!" she exclaimed. She pulled both of them into the foyer and quickly closed the door to shut out the chilling cold.

"Don't you say another word until you have those two women back in this parlor," Biddy called.

Faith shrugged her shoulders as she lifted her eyebrows. "She made me promise."

Carrie laughed and hurried down the hallway. She felt a surge of relief as she took in the woman grinning up at her, her snapping blue eyes as alert as ever. "Biddy!"

"It's about time you got back here," Biddy said, her voice gruff with emotion as she grasped Carrie's hands.

Carrie felt another surge of gratitude for Abby urging her to return. It was important she explain her reasons for staying on the plantation in person—at least as much as she understood them. "I missed you, Biddy," she said as she encircled the tiny lady with her arms.

"I missed you too, girl," Biddy murmured as she patted Carrie's shoulder. "Now, am I really seeing Abby Livingston in my parlor? I mean Abby Cromwell," she corrected. "I was certain I would never see you again."

"I was so excited when Carrie told me who her new friends were," Abby said as she moved forward to take Biddy's hand, her other hand reaching out to grasp Faith's. "I've never forgotten you and Faith. How are you?"

"Better than most ninety-seven-year-olds can say," Biddy quipped.

"That's because most ninety-seven-year-olds are in the grave," Faith observed.

Carrie grinned as laughter rang through the parlor.

"So you're a Rebel now, are you?" Biddy asked Abby.

"I prefer to say I'm a transplanted liberal woman," Abby responded. "I've learned it's better not to apply labels like 'Rebel' and 'Yankee' to people."

Faith snorted. "Calling yourself a liberal woman might just be the most dangerous label of them all."

Abby nodded. "Perhaps, but at least it doesn't bring up discussions of the war. Most of my neighbors seem to have either forgotten where I've come from, or they have simply chosen to forgive me for my Yankee ways."

"That would be wise," Biddy said. "Carrie has told us your factory is the most successful in Richmond. I imagine most of your neighbors have someone in their family benefitting from the factory. That seems to promote forgiveness," she added.

"There is that," Abby agreed, smiling when laughter erupted again.

Carrie caught her eye, but Abby shook her head slightly. Obviously, she wasn't yet ready to talk about the other reason for their visit. Carrie was happy to allow her to decide the timing. She was impatient to tell Biddy, but she had to give Abby the lead in the conversation since it was her factory that was being built. There were plenty of other things to talk about.

"So you're going to keep it to yourself for now?" Biddy asked, her eyes glinting with humor.

Carrie was not surprised Biddy had noticed their exchange. Her eyes didn't miss much.

"If you don't mind," Abby replied.

Biddy nodded. "It's not a problem. Michael is probably down at the pub, but I figure I won't be sending one of the children down to call for him until I know all the reasons for your visit."

Abby laughed. "That's a deal." She lifted her nose. "I do believe I smell oatmeal cookies," she said hopefully. "Annie and May have learned to make them since Carrie sent the recipe home, but I suspect yours are even better, Faith."

"They'd better be," Faith sniffed. "I don't believe it's possible for a Southerner to cook Irish oatmeal cookies as well as I do."

"Sometimes she forgets she's black," Biddy whispered dramatically. "I've decided it's best not to remind her if I want the cookies to keep coming."

Faith laughed along with them before she disappeared into the kitchen. She returned moments later with a large platter that held a basket of warm cookies and tea service for four. "It helped that the children provided advance notice of your arrival," she said. "I had everything ready before you got here."

Carrie sighed happily as she bit into the cookie. "I'll never tell Annie your cookies are better than hers, but..."

"It's best not to compare one woman's cooking to another," Faith agreed. "It will be our little secret."

Carrie grinned and sipped her tea, relishing the companionable silence that fell over the room for a few minutes. Then she decided that if they weren't going to talk about the factory, it was high time she heard the rest of Faith's story. "Faith, in the midst of the cholera epidemic, we never had a chance to talk about *your* story. I've wanted to hear it so badly. Abby knows Biddy's story because I told her about it, but I would dearly love for us to hear yours."

"I guess since you saved my life, the least I can do is tell you my story. It's not one I'm proud of, but all of us have learned we are given the privilege of knowing so that we can make a difference with the knowledge. I've made peace with it."

Biddy smiled. "Arden came in and added wood to the fire right before you arrived. We're good for a while." She settled back against her chair and pulled the thick quilt wrapped around her a little closer. "It's time you learned some more of the truth about what has happened in this country."

Faith poured herself another cup of tea and took a bite of her cookie, chewing thoughtfully as she sat back and gazed at the flickering flames. When she had swallowed her bite, she began. "Sometime back in 1619, the Portuguese ship *Sao Jogo Bautista* set sail from the colony of Angola with three hundred fifty African slaves destined for Veracruz, New Spain."

Carrie had no idea what she was talking about. "I'm lost already. New Spain? Slaves in 1619?"

"New Spain gained its independence in 1821. It is now known as Mexico," Faith explained.

"But slaves?" Carrie asked.

"Slavery did not originate in America," Faith said. "Let me tell my story. I believe it will answer your questions."

"Of course," Carrie said quickly. "I promise to not interrupt again."

Biddy snorted. "I think you told me the same thing."

"It didn't work out that way?" Abby guessed.

Carrie laughed when Biddy shrugged. "I'm not old enough to have learned all the patience the rest of *you* have."

Abby raised a brow. "I do believe Carrie just called us all *old.*"

Carrie held up her hands in defeat as Biddy and Faith nodded solemn agreement. "Not another word, I promise. I don't stand a chance against the three of you."

Biddy looked at Abby. "The child is gaining wisdom. I believe there is hope for her yet."

"There just might be," Abby responded playfully.

Carrie opened her mouth to respond, but snapped it shut and looked at Faith meaningfully.

Faith smiled and continued. "Back to the slave ship. It turns out that when they arrived in New Spain, they were short about fifty slaves. History tells us that English privateers attacked and plundered the boats. The boat's captain, John Colyn Jope, had a letter of marque that gave him permission from the Dutch government to attack and plunder Spanish ships."

Carrie's eyes widened as she envisioned the battle at sea and the terror the slaves must have felt as they were helplessly shackled in the hold. Her heart felt heavy as she was reminded of how many humans were seen as nothing more than property. She had so many questions, but she was determined to keep her promise to just listen.

"One of the English ships was called the *White Lion.* They carried about twenty of the slaves they had stolen. They immediately set sail for Virginia, landing at Point Comfort. We know it now as Fort Monroe. The crew aboard the *White Lion* was low on supplies, so they sold the slaves for enough food to continue their journey." Faith paused, remembering. "One of the men sold as a servant was called Antonio. He was one of my great-grandfathers."

Carrie gaped at her but remembered to stay silent.

"Antonio was sent to work for a very devout Puritan named Edward Bennett, who was also a very wealthy ship owner," Faith continued. "Antonio worked the tobacco fields, but in February of 1622, he and fifty other servants were sent to clear the woods for a plantation that was to be called Bennett's Welcome. One month later, before a palisade could be built, the Powhatan Confederacy launched what we now know as the Good Friday Massacre. Antonio was one of only twelve who survived the attack by the Opechancanough Indians. Twelve years later, he was given his freedom. He married a woman named Mary, and they began calling themselves Anthony and Mary Johnson. They moved to Northampton County on the Eastern Shore, where they raised four children and accumulated two hundred fifty acres of land. By the time their boys were grown and had bought land of their own, they had over a thousand acres."

So far, Carrie had heard nothing that should give Faith anything but intense pride in her heritage. Anthony Johnson had survived against incredible odds and had managed to create a life of freedom for himself and his family. She leaned forward, certain there was more to the story.

Faith rewarded her with a warm smile before she went on. "My grandfather Anthony became successful enough to start buying servants of his own," she said sadly. "He bought several slaves—both black and white."

Carrie was shocked, but she remembered that Sam had told her if he had the opportunity, he would probably own slaves himself. Sam had insisted owning slaves had nothing to do with color. It was about power.

Faith nodded. "Grandfather Anthony completely adopted the ways of Virginia planters. Perhaps the only thing that made him stand out was that his holdings were eventually given the name Angola—a tribute to his true heritage. Anyway, the story doesn't end there. Up to that point, in spite of the reality of the situation, it was at least stated that all indentured servants would have the opportunity for freedom at some point in their lives. My grandfather helped change that."

Carrie and Abby caught their breath at the same time.

"About thirty years after Grandfather Anthony was brought to America as a slave, he got into a dispute with one of his servants. The servant was a fellow African named John Castor who was demanding his freedom after many years of labor. He claimed his time of servitude had run out years before. I imagine it had. John ran away and took refuge with a sympathetic neighboring plantation owner who was white. Grandfather Anthony went to court to get his property back. I've learned the court case went on for almost two years." Faith paused again, her eyes heavy with regret.

Carrie struggled to envision the bewildering sight of a white planter fighting a black planter to save a black servant from perpetual slavery. She desperately wanted this story to end well, but she was already certain she was going to be disappointed.

"My grandfather resolved it by persuading the courts to enslave John Castor for life. It was one of the first cases of lifetime slavery being imposed in America," Faith revealed in a soft voice. "And certainly the first time the sentence of lifetime slavery was imposed on a black man by another black man. My grandfather helped change the face of slavery for over two hundred years."

Carrie stared at Faith, stunned into silence. "No wonder you understand how I feel about Lord Oliver Cromwell," she finally said.

Faith laughed. "Yes. I am just as appalled by my ancestry as you are."

"I can only imagine how you feel," Abby murmured. "Were your people always free?"

"Yes," Faith answered. "Things began to change in America even before the court case. Massachusetts had already legalized slavery. The other colonies followed rather quickly. The new laws mandated that people like Grandfather Anthony and his children would remain free, but they were no longer treated the same. They could still buy black servants, but they could no longer buy white servants because they were considered too low-class to buy whites. Grandfather Anthony's children lived in a different America, but it continued to change rapidly. For a long time, there were more white slaves than black. The numbers began to even out by the end of the 1600s, until eventually all the slaves were black."

"Because of money?" Carrie asked, knowing the answer already.

"What else?" Faith asked ruefully. "Too many of the decisions that shape any society are mandated by finances. The shift from the supposed time-limited servitude of whites to the lifetime slavery of Africans was prompted by economics as much as racism. The Caribbean plantations showed that larger profits could be made from an openly enslaved workforce. American planters took notice. They decided black slavery was a much better long-term investment, especially when the death rates continued to fall. For most of the 1600s, at least half of the workforce died within five years because of the brutal conditions. It just wasn't good business to purchase men for a life term at twice the price of a time-limited white servant. When the blacks began to live longer, and when Virginia passed the first law that the children of slaves were also slaves for life, it began to make financial sense."

Another long silence fell on the room. Faith served more tea while she allowed everyone time to process what they had heard.

"None of it makes any sense," Carrie muttered. "How can people live with themselves?"

"Slavery never makes sense," Abby said, "but societies throughout all of written time have done it. People with power find it remarkably easy to bury any inherent moral objection to slavery when it means they can use it to line their pockets."

"And now slavery has been abolished in America," Biddy reminded them. "It took time, but when enough good people find the courage to raise their voice time and time again about a wrong, it can be changed."

Carrie was glad for the reminder. "You're right." She cocked her head. "Faith, were you involved in the Abolition Movement?"

Faith smiled. "My mama and daddy took me to a revival meeting led by Reverend Charles Finney when I was a teenager back in 1825. I had heard them talking about how bad slavery was, but it didn't impact me, so I didn't think about it very much. I was astounded when I found close to one thousand people crowded into a big white tent to hear Reverend Finney preach. The things he said that night changed me and my family forever. Reverend Finney believed your faith should be lived out in your daily life.

He helped launch the Abolitionist Movement *and* the Women's Rights Movement." She smiled as she remembered. "Reverend Finney was a teacher at Oberlin College where I went to school. I made sure to take every class he taught."

Carrie gasped. "You went to college?" She so wanted Rose to meet this remarkable woman.

"Yes," Faith assured her. "Oberlin was the first college to accept both genders and all races. My parents made many sacrifices to make sure I could attend. It was while I was there that I learned the truth about my heritage. I went to school to become a teacher, but I was far too busy after I finished school to teach. My time there did nothing but fire my commitment to bring about change."

Biddy chuckled. "Faith was one of the first people in Philadelphia to provide assistance to blacks escaping through the Underground Railroad. She started helping people back around 1840."

"More than twenty-five years ago?" Abby asked with deep admiration.

"That's why you were too busy to teach," Carrie added. "That's remarkable!"

Faith shrugged. "It was an honor to do what I could."

Biddy snorted. "Do what you *could*?" She looked at Carrie and Abby. "Faith is too modest to reveal that she helped more than one thousand slaves escape."

Abby's eyes widened. "One thousand...?"

Faith shrugged. "I found a way to help."

"And it's how you met Biddy?" Carrie murmured, stunned by what she was learning. She couldn't believe she might have missed knowing exactly how extraordinary Faith was if she hadn't returned and asked to hear her story.

"Yes. It was becoming quite a challenge to find enough houses to hide all the escaping slaves on their way north. The logistics were becoming something of a nightmare. I went looking for an unused building large enough to hide them until they were ready to head on." She glanced at Biddy.

"Faith found one of my buildings," Biddy continued. "When she came to talk to me—my husband was already dead—we became instant friends."

"I moved in just a few weeks later," Faith revealed. "We've been together ever since."

"Faith had the same passion to help her people as I did to help the Irish," Biddy said. "That huge empty building wasn't doing anything but sitting there. I was thrilled for it to be put to good use. They never caught even one slave who stayed there. Not even after the Fugitive Slave Act passed in 1850." She chuckled with satisfaction. "Folks never thought about coming down here to Moyamensing to look for runaway slaves."

Carrie sat in silent amazement. For the first time, she had a clear picture of just how extraordinary these two women were. To sit in the same room with Biddy, Faith and Abby reminded her of how much impact a woman could have if she was determined to do so. "What a story..." she finally said.

Faith smiled. "Every person is a story, Carrie. You just have to care enough to ask questions and hear it. You are surrounded every day by extraordinary people. Most of us miss that fact entirely."

"What's happening with the building now?" Abby asked after another long silence.

Biddy shrugged. "It's sitting there. It was used almost to the end of the war, though certainly there were far fewer runaway slaves once the war started. It wasn't too far into the war before they all knew they could just head for a contraband camp. That was much easier than long trips north."

"Where is it?" Abby asked.

Chapter Twenty-Nine

"The building is down on Carlton Avenue," Biddy replied, her eyes revealing she knew Abby was asking more than a casual question.

"At the intersection of Jamison Street?" Abby asked, her voice sparkling with excitement.

Biddy cocked her head. "Now why would you be knowing that, Abby Cromwell? What's going on inside that head of yours? Why do I get the feeling we're about to get to what you didn't want to talk about earlier?"

Abby smiled. "You've always been a smart woman, Biddy."

"What in the world are you two talking about?" Faith demanded. She cast a suspicious look at Carrie. "If *you're* not popping in with questions, it's only because you already know the answer."

Carrie laughed. "Perhaps some of the answer, though I will admit I think I've been left out of something." She couldn't help the twinge of hurt she felt, but she pushed it aside.

Abby reached out and touched her leg. "I just got the information I needed this morning right before Michael picked us up, Carrie. I didn't want to talk about it in front of anyone else because I didn't want to risk any of this getting out before I talked to Biddy."

"Well, I'm sitting here," Biddy said bluntly, "and I'm getting just as impatient as Carrie gets. Talk!"

Abby grinned. "I know about your building because I had one of my factory managers go down to check it out yesterday." She leaned forward. "Thomas and I would like to start a clothing factory in that building. Now that I know the history of the building, I can't think of a more perfect place."

Biddy gazed at her. Her face was calm, but her eyes were avidly curious. "And why would you be wanting to start a factory there? Surely there are better locations."

"Probably," Abby agreed. "But it seems the best location for the people of Moyamensing to get to work easily."

Carrie watched Biddy and Faith as they both froze. Abby's words hung in the air for several long moments.

"What are you saying?" Biddy finally asked. Her expression was both cautious and hopeful.

"Carrie is not the only one who had to come to grips with her heritage," Abby answered. "Thomas was also horrified by what he discovered. He understood Carrie had dealt with the discovery by making a commitment to help the people down here. He wanted to do the same thing, but he wasn't sure *what* to do." She smiled proudly at Carrie. "My wonderful daughter suggested we start a clothing factory down here to employ as many people as we can." She held up a hand before either woman could say anything. "We'll be able to start out with about seventy-five employees, but within a year, I believe we could expand it to several hundred. Both men and women will have an opportunity for work." She paused. "If we are successful in proving the people here are good workers, I believe other factory owners will follow. I saw at least three other buildings that could be converted for industry." She stopped and waited for their reaction.

Biddy and Faith stared at each other again, and then Faith leapt up from her chair laughing, and did a little jig around the parlor.

Biddy joined her in the laughter. "I'd get up and dance with her, but I'm afraid I'd collapse." She reached over and grabbed Abby and Carrie's hands. "Carrie, thank you from the bottom of my heart. The people of Moyamensing will be forever in your debt."

Carrie shook her head. "It's not enough to make up for what has been done, but at least it's something."

"It's more than something," Biddy said. "Changing the financial situation for a family will echo down through countless generations to come." She squeezed Abby's hand tightly. "I know you realize what this means," she said softly. "It will change everything down here."

Abby nodded. "I know. I wanted to make sure the building could be made profitable before I made the offer.

Of course," she added, "it will depend some upon the asking price for the building."

Biddy threw back her head with a laugh. "And so the negotiating begins," she chortled. She became serious again, her eyes fired with certainty. "I don't need the money. The title will be transferred to you and your husband this week. That building is sitting there empty. It served a vitally important role for the last twenty-five years, and it will serve just as important a role now. Nothing could make me happier."

Abby grinned. "It's such a pleasure doing business with you, Biddy."

The afternoon wore away as they made plans.

Biddy finally turned to Carrie. "Enough factory talk. I believe you are starting school tomorrow?"

Carrie shook her head. "No."

Biddy cocked her head at the same time Faith did. "Tell me," she ordered.

"I'm going back to the plantation," Carrie said. She explained the situation as best as she could while Biddy and Faith listened. For the first time they heard about the split with their other three housemates and Janie's decision to attend the Homeopathic College, as well. She saw both sadness and acceptance creep into Biddy's eyes as she told her story. Carrie's stomach clenched as she talked. Biddy had become like a grandmother to her. She couldn't bear the thought she might not see her again. But Biddy was healthy, and certainly she wouldn't allow herself to die before the factory was up and running. She would want to see the results of so many in Moyamensing having a steady income.

When Carrie finished there was a long silence.

"I know you're doing what you believe is the right thing," Biddy finally murmured, "but I won't pretend it doesn't make me sad."

"And me," Faith said. "We'll miss you." She peered at Carrie. "You're sure this is what you want?"

Carrie was grateful to be confident in her decision, but no matter what she did, someone was going to be sad. Her heart ached as she saw the disappointment in her friend's eyes, but the ache was tempered by the memory of the unrestrained joy on Robert's and Rose's faces when she had told them. "I'm sure."

"When do you figure you'll be coming back to school?" Biddy pressed.

Carrie shook her head. "I don't know," she admitted. "I know I'm making the right choice, but I don't have any idea when the next thing is supposed to happen. I am one hundred percent sure I will be a doctor, so I know I'll return, but I don't know when."

"You'll write?" Biddy asked.

"Every week," Carrie promised. "You'll take care of yourself?"

Biddy blinked. "I'll be here when you get back," she replied.

"I'm holding you to that," Carrie said huskily.

Moses watched as the schoolhouse filled with people. Workers, neighbors, students, parents... The seats all filled rapidly, and people pressed against the walls. Still they came. He exchanged a look with Rose as he swallowed a heavy lump of nervousness. He had not expected so many. He hadn't even known there were so many black people in the area who could attend. He wondered how many had left their plantations without permission. That thought led to the concern that the plantation owners would come after them. He pushed that away because all it did was make him more nervous.

Simon spoke to him through the open window Moses was standing next to. "Everyone is in place," he said.

Moses resented his calm tone. "One of them going to come speak for me?" He tried to not sound desperate.

Simon chuckled. "You're going to be fine, Moses. You'll get used to it."

"And you know this how?" Moses knew Simon had never stood in front of anyone and said more than five words, but he obviously knew how to spread news about a meeting.

"I read it in a book," Simon answered as he chuckled again. "You're going to be fine," he repeated. "You're meant for this."

Moses tried to believe him, but the pounding of his heart made it difficult for his brain to engage. He stood silently as the last of the people pushed their way in. Simon and ten of the men had formed an armed ring around the schoolhouse. They knew better than to be careless. Moses had made him promise his men would not fire the first shot if they had visitors, but he also gave them permission to do whatever was necessary if they came under attack. He would never lose the memories of the police and other rioters surrounding and opening fire on the blacks in Memphis.

When Rose nodded her head, smiling at him brightly, he took a deep breath and stepped onto the small stage hastily constructed for the meeting. "Good evening, everyone," he called.

"Good evening, Moses," came the ready reply from what had to be over one hundred people.

Moses took another deep breath as he fought to calm his nerves, praying for the ability to speak to this crowd. Talking to his men had been one thing—this was something else entirely. He caught Rose's eyes again. The strong confidence and pride radiating from them helped him relax enough to open his mouth. "I'm here tonight to share some exciting news," he began. "I realize most of you are unable to get news as quickly as we do, but I'm confident all of you are aware a very important election took place." Most of the heads nodded, but no one interrupted. They were waiting.

"The Republicans won a landslide victory," he announced. "I'm here to explain what that is going to mean to all of us—at least the part we can hope to anticipate. The most important thing to understand is that the policies that President Johnson allowed the South to put in place that have caused so much pain and suffering are about to be reversed!"

Moses smiled as cheering broke out in the schoolhouse. He also relaxed even more as he looked at the faces full of hope and determination. These were people who had survived slavery and four years of brutal war, many of them fighting to make sure their freedoms would be secure. Nothing would stop them from moving forward. It would not be easy, and they would probably have many setbacks, but they would continue to move forward. *Always forward...*

Moses held up his hand for quiet. "I'm as excited as all of you are, but I want to make sure you know this is really only the beginning of all we have worked and fought for. Nothing is going to change overnight, and we need to accept that," he said, his strong voice ringing through the building. He felt the thrill of influence as he realized every eye was riveted to him. He also felt the sudden weight of responsibility. These people were listening to him. They seemed to trust him. He could never take that lightly. He swallowed as he realized the fate of these people, as well as the generations of their families that would follow, could well rest on how he led them over the months to come. He and Rose would be leaving sometime in the spring. He would make the most of every moment he had now.

"President Johnson's policies have created a country that is unsafe for every black person. We cannot afford to forget that as we fight for change. We need to be bold, but we also need to be careful. We must assume that most of the white people around us are committed to maintaining white supremacy." He saw the scowls mixed with blatant fear.

"Every person in here is strong and resilient," Moses continued. "You have lived through slavery. You have lived through a long war. Now you are fighting to rebuild your life in the midst of continuing racism. We are going to take big steps forward, but sometimes we will crash into walls. Sometimes we will fall back." He paused and looked around the room. "But we will never quit moving forward." His heart pounded with the certainty that he was telling the truth. "We will never quit moving forward!"

"Amen!" one woman called.

"We'll never quit," a man hollered, raising his hand for emphasis.

The call went up around the schoolhouse. "*We will never quit moving forward!*"

Moses held up his hand again until silence allowed him to continue. "Each of you is the only person in charge of your future. Yes, the government plays a role, and yes, things are about to change, but that doesn't mean it's not up to you. If you don't know how to read yet, you need to get yourself into this school and let my wife, Rose, teach you." His voice rang out with authority. Suddenly, he was no longer nervous. He felt strong and confident. He knew he could help his people. Whether it was here on the plantation or on a larger scale as an attorney, he was going to do whatever it took. *As a politician?* Moses stiffened for a moment as the thought flitted through his mind, but he pushed it aside.

"If you already know how to read, my guess is that you aren't using that knowledge. You should be reading every book you can get your hands on. White people believe we are ignorant. It's up to you to prove they are wrong. You need to learn everything you can so that you can take control of your own life. No one else should do it for you." Moses paused. "We already know there are people eager to step up and take control of everything about your life. It's up to *you* to make sure they don't do it again."

He gazed around for a moment, letting his words sink in. "I already know you all have a long list of excuses as to why you can't learn more. You think knowing how to read should be enough. You think you're too tired after a long day of work in the fields. You think you have too much to do to take care of your families. You believe learning more won't make a difference." He stopped and watched everyone's faces. He could tell many of the crowd did indeed believe the excuses he was listing. "I have some questions for you. What percentage of the crop would it be reasonable to ask a plantation owner to pay you at the end of a long year of work? Can you do the math to make sure you are being paid fairly?" He spoke slowly, letting the questions burn into his listener's minds "Can you read a legal contract and understand it enough to make sure you are not being taken advantage of? Can you help your children with their homework so they have a good chance at a better life?"

A thick silence filled the schoolhouse as most of his listeners either lowered their eyes or shifted to stare out the window into the darkness. "I already know the answers to those questions," Moses continued. "The answer is no. How do you expect to create a new life if you simply let the whites continue to control how you make a living? How do you expect to demand respect when you aren't doing the things to *deserve* that respect?" His voice filled the room. "I don't care how tired you are at the end of the day. Read. Learn. I don't care how much you have to do to take care of your families. *Read. Learn.* I don't care if you believe what I'm saying or not, though if you're smart you will..." He allowed his voice to trail off with a hint of humor.

A ripple of laughter relaxed the audience a little but didn't diminish how avidly they were listening. "Read. Learn," Moses repeated once again. "There are books here in the school. Borrow them. We'll keep adding more." He fell silent and let his words take hold. Then he said it again. "Read. Learn. It's the only way you can take control of your life. *Your* life."

Moses correctly interpreted the looks on some of the faces. "I know slavery robbed you of so many things. It stole years of your life. It means the rest of your life is going to be a struggle to undo the things done to you." He watched as many people nodded, a look of something like relief flitting across their faces. They thought he was giving them a way out of taking responsibility. "So what?" he continued, watching as the looks of relief wilted as quickly as they had appeared. "You can't go back and undo the past. Making your choices today based on the past won't get you anywhere. Whites believe blacks are stupid and incapable of being educated. It's up to you to prove them wrong. Whites believe blacks are incapable of caring for themselves. It's up to you to prove them wrong," he thundered as his passion took hold.

"You can spend the rest of your life feeling sorry for yourself for what you experienced, or you can allow your anger to fuel your determination to change your life. I would be the first to agree that the whites in this country owe the freed slaves many things, but I'm certainly not waiting around for it to happen. I'm going to fight to make that happen, but I'm certainly not going to wait for it."

Moses let silence fill the schoolhouse for several moments. "You shouldn't wait around either. I encourage you to keep moving forward."

"Keep moving forward," several people called back to him.

Moses was thrilled by the looks of determination firing the faces all around him.

"We will never quit moving forward," an elderly woman sang out. "I might have had most my life stole from me, but I still got breath inside me. As long as I do, I plan on moving forward!"

"Yes!" a man from a neighboring plantation yelled. "I'm gonna be in here every week to claim some of them books. I'm gonna prove I ain't stupid!"

Moses grinned as the comments continued to ring out around the room. He exchanged a look with Rose, thrilled with the pride he saw in her eyes. "*I love you*," she mouthed, her eyes glistening with tears.

"We gots to keep having these meetings." The elderly woman who had ignited the outburst peered at him intently as the voices quieted.

"What's your name?" Moses asked. He had never seen her before, but he was drawn by her enthusiasm.

"Corabelle," she responded, emotion radiating from the black eyes set deeply into her wrinkled face.

Moses gazed at her. She could be eighty or fifty. Slavery had a way of aging people far past their actual years. "Where are you from, Corabelle?"

"I came from down in Florida," she answered.

Moses stared at her. He couldn't imagine making a trip like that at her age. "And what are you doing now?"

Corabelle smiled. "Nothing, thanks to you. My boy, Jamison, worked for you this summer. Because of you we got enough money to make it through the winter if we be real careful. I know most of the men be moving on to look for new jobs, but my Jamison is staying right here because he knows I ain't got another move left in me," she confided. "He figures he'll work for you again next year."

Moses nodded as his eyes roamed the crowd. He smiled when he found Jamison standing back against the wall. The man had worked hard for him all season. "Jamison will have a job," he promised Corabelle, not mentioning he would not have to wait until next spring. He was going to make sure her son was added onto the crew at Blackwell Plantation.

"That's real good," Corabelle said with an even warmer smile, "but I still want to know if you gonna keep having these meetings. It gets to where folks think they all alone sometimes. The fight to make a better life seems to be more than folks believe they can handle. We need to be reminded just like you did tonight. It would be nice if folks needed to hear things once to really get them, but that ain't the way people work, Moses."

"I believe you are right, Corabelle. We are going to keep having these meetings every two weeks." He smiled as applause broke out from the crowd. "Here's the thing, though. It's not enough for me to come up here and get you excited about what you can do with your life. It's up to you to go home and actually do something with it. As long as I see changes in people, I will keep doing these meetings. If there comes a time when I think I'm wasting my breath, I'm going to stop," he cautioned.

"You ain't gonna have to stop, Moses," Corabelle replied in a firm voice. "You do your part. We'll do ours."

More applause filled the room. "We will never quit moving forward," a man called out. Within moments, it was a unified call bursting from every throat. "*We will never quit moving forward!*"

Moses reached for Rose as soon as she crawled under the covers. She sighed and snuggled up to him, relishing his warmth after settling John and Felicia in for the night. Moses had rocked Hope for almost an hour when they arrived home. Their daughter had been asleep in just a few minutes, but Rose knew Moses loved to simply hold her. She never tired of watching the two of them together. She had longed for a daddy the whole time she was growing up. To know Hope had Moses was sheer joy.

Rose cuddled close, relaxing as she warmed. She reached up to caress Moses' face. "I was so very proud of you tonight," she said, careful to keep her voice low so she wouldn't wake Hope. John had been such a heavy sleeper, but his little sister seemed to awaken at just about any unexpected sound.

"I would have been too terrified to say a word if you hadn't been there," Moses admitted.

Rose cocked her head and gazed up at him. "No one would have ever guessed," she assured him. "You looked like you were meant to be up there."

"It felt that way once I got over my terror," Moses agreed, a small smile playing across his lips. "I liked the way it made me feel, but I liked the looks on people's faces even more."

Rose smiled. "Most of them stopped on their way out to tell me they would be back for books this week. I'm sending a letter to have Abby bring back more books from Philadelphia if she can. If it doesn't reach her in time, I know more will arrive from her friends soon. I predict our little school will have the best stocked library in Virginia." She reached for Moses' hand and squeezed it tightly. "They all heard what you said, Moses. Because of you, they will be more prepared for the future."

Moses shook his head. "Because of *us*. I can give them the determination to learn, but you're the one who will teach them."

"Well, me and your lovely daughter, Felicia," she said with a chuckle. "She was talking to me on the way home about her plans to help the girls and women prepare to fight for equal rights. That is, when she is not teaching them about astronomy." Rose shook her head. "That little girl never ceases to amaze me."

Moses smiled. "Felicia had her first mama to give her a hunger for knowledge. Now she has a mama that can help her learn everything she needs to know. She is a lucky little girl."

Rose shook her head. "I appreciate that, but Felicia is learning so quickly that I'm close to feeling behind her. All I can do is say yes every time she asks if she has played outside enough to earn library time." She smiled, feeling a fierce pride. "I'm so glad you brought that little girl home." She paused. "I didn't want you to at first," she said hesitantly. She had never confessed this to her husband. She wasn't sure why she was now. Moses lifted a brow, waiting for her to continue.

"I thought Felicia would be something else to hold me back from doing what I wanted to do," Rose admitted, the words coming easier when she realized how completely she didn't feel that way now. "I couldn't imagine being able to go to college if I had three children." Her gaze strayed to where Hope slept peacefully, her thumb tucked securely in her mouth as the dim flicker of a lone candle on the nightstand next to the bed played across her face.

"And now?"

Rose shrugged. "You could bring another one home," she said. She slapped her hand over her mouth when she forgot to speak softly, but the continued silence said Hope was sleeping soundly for once. "I realize nothing is going to stop us from going to college," she whispered. "There will be more things to juggle with three children, but between both of us, we can handle it."

Moses eyed her. "I do believe you mean that."

"Of course I mean it. Why wouldn't I?"

"The part about having another child?"

Rose smiled, recognizing the look in her husband's eyes. "I don't need the possibility of another child to make me want to love my husband." She ran her hand down his chest and then rolled over to blow out the candle.

Robert knew he should be sleeping, but something was calling him to go outside. Since he couldn't sleep anyway, he rolled out of bed, reached blindly for his clothes in the dark, dressed quickly, and then slipped out of the house. Nothing but frosty silence met him as he looked toward the barn. He thought about checking on the horses, but there was no indication of a problem, so he turned and began to walk slowly down the road. The night wrapped around him like an icy blanket and the stars seemed to merge with the diamonds littering the ground as the temperature dropped. Winter was here, but they had not had their first snowfall yet. He glanced at the sky, comforted by the glimmering stars. He was eager for the snow this winter, but he didn't want it to come until Carrie was home again.

Her train would be chugging into Richmond in just two days. She would arrive on the plantation the following day. He had been dreading the long, cold days in a lonely bed. Now he had nothing but sheer anticipation of the winter. It would be fine with him if they were snowed in for days at a time. He smiled as he envisioned it.

Robert strolled along, relishing the realization that he was free from worry. Mark and Susan's check for the colts and fillies had arrived the day before. They had paid half of the agreed upon amount. The balance would be paid in the spring when they picked them up. Even the half was more than Robert had hoped to earn in his first year. In spite of his willingness to negotiate, Mark had insisted on paying top dollar. Robert had protested but had given in easily, because he knew the quality of horses Mark was getting. They were worth every penny.

The hooting of several owls broke the stillness as they called back and forth. Robert listened closely, wishing he could interpret what they were saying. Perhaps they were doing nothing but heralding the arrival of a new season. He wondered how many of them were watching him right now. When he heard a very quiet whooshing sound over his head, he knew an owl had just flown by. Felicia had explained to him, after emerging from the library one day for her mandatory ride, that owls have specialized feathers with varying degrees of softness that help muffle sound when they fly. Their broad wings and light bodies make them nearly silent fliers, which means they can stalk prey more easily.

She had also told him that the flattened facial disk of an owl funnels sounds to the bird's ears and magnifies it as much as ten times to help the owl hear noises mere humans can't detect. Felicia's eyes had been wide with the excitement of discovery when she told him what she had learned. In truth, it was as fascinating to him as it was to her. It also made him want to spend more time in the library over the winter so he could learn more. He had ordered many new horse publications, but Felicia's hunger for information had ignited an answering passion in him to learn about more than just horses.

Robert smiled as he peered at the sky. For the first time in his life he felt settled and truly content. Carrie's decision to stay on the plantation that winter had solidified that for him. When she went back to school, he would support her, but he also intended to savor every moment they had together.

A thought crept in that brought a frown to his face. Being with Amber, Felicia, John, and Hope had given him a hunger to have children of his own. The war had kept him from thinking about it, and then the pressures of starting the breeding program had kept him preoccupied, but now that things had settled down, he spent a lot of time imagining what having children would be like. He and Carrie had never talked about it, other than a conversation early in their relationship that revealed both of them wanted to have children one day. His frown deepened as he thought about the reality that *one day* kept being pushed back by circumstances. It would have been folly to have children during the war, in spite of the fact that many soldiers had done just that, but now there were new things to delay the *one day*. He was beyond thrilled that Carrie had decided to stay on the plantation, but her delay in becoming a doctor would surely postpone any plans for children.

He continued to peer into the sky. He knew it was silly to expect to find an answer there, but still he could hope. He thought about Felicia's explanation of a shooting star. He had seen many of them growing up, but knowing what he was looking at now made them seem almost more mystical, not less. His neck was getting stiff from gazing at the sky, but he remembered Felicia saying the Leonid Shower on November thirteenth would be bracketed by more meteors than usual on the days surrounding it. It was still four days away, but... His eyes widened as a bright gleam shot across the sky, followed almost immediately by another one, and then another, before the stars went back to their random twinkling.

Robert took a deep breath. He had asked for a sign, but he had not defined what it would mean. Was it too late to do that? After a moment's thought he decided the wonder of seeing three shooting stars almost simultaneously meant he could determine what the sign meant. "I will be a father," he murmured into the glittering sky. "*I will be a father.*"

Chapter Thirty

Carrie had watched the sky anxiously all day. The morning had started out with thick gray clouds pillowing across the sky. As excited as she was for the first snowfall, this was not the day for it. The cumulus mass had cleared away under a weak, cold sun, but the afternoon winds had blown more in.

Felicia walked out on the porch and joined her on the edge to peer upward. "It can't be cloudy tonight," she cried. "It just can't."

"It won't be," Carrie said. "We are going to see the Leonid Shower. It's your birthday present, honey."

Felicia peered at her with cautious hope. "And how do you know that?"

Carrie smiled. "There is more than one way of knowing something my young scientist friend."

Felicia looked at her appraisingly. "You mean like magic?" Her voice was thick with disappointment.

Carrie laughed. "You don't believe in magic?"

Felicia shrugged. "I don't know enough to deny that it may have a place somewhere in the world," she admitted, "but I don't believe magic will make the clouds go away."

"I see," Carrie murmured as she continued to watch the sky.

"So what makes you so sure the skies will clear tonight?" Felicia demanded again. "Everyone will be here as soon as it gets dark. That's not so far away." Her voice held a hint of panic.

Carrie knew how important this night was to the little girl. If it hadn't been, she would have stayed in Philadelphia a few extra days. As it was, she and Abby had worked with other women in the city to send close to five hundred warm coats and pairs of gloves to the children of Moyamensing. Michael took a wagon down the day Carrie had left. She would have loved to see the expressions on the faces of the children, but it was enough to know they would be warm this winter. Abby had chosen to remain in the city a few extra days so she could send another wagon, but Carrie's promise to Felicia had brought her home.

Carrie smiled. "You spend so much time studying the night sky, Felicia, that you haven't learned how to read the daytime sky."

"Huh?" Felicia was clearly confused. "What's to study? There is a sun."

Carrie chuckled as she took Felicia's chin and turned it so she could look toward the east. "What do you see?"

"Clouds," Felicia said morosely.

"Beyond the clouds," Carrie prompted.

Felicia stopped fixating on the clouds and trained her eyes on the farther horizon. "I see a patch of blue."

"Right. Now, what way is the wind blowing?"

Felicia frowned, but answered. "From the east."

"So what is the wind blowing toward us?" Carrie watched as Felicia's frown melted away into a hopeful look.

"The blue patch," she whispered as understanding dawned on her face. "The wind is blowing clear skies toward us." Then another frown puckered her brows. "How do you know the clear skies will get to us in time?"

"Ah..." Carrie started. "That's where the magic comes in for one eleven-year-old birthday girl who dreams of seeing the Leonid Shower more than anything else."

Felicia's face fell. "So you don't really know?"

Carrie reached down and lifted her chin so their eyes could meet. "I told you there was more than one way of knowing," she reminded her. "Trust me. Your skies will be clear tonight."

Felicia still looked doubtful, but she nodded her head. "If you say so," she said, her eyes fixed on the clear band of sky that seemed so achingly far away.

"I tell you what," Carrie said. "Let's go in and help Annie in the kitchen. Staring at the sky isn't going to make the clouds disappear any faster."

"Is it like watching a pot will keep it from boiling?"

"Well, from a scientific perspective, that is not really true," Carrie observed. "Given enough time, a pot will boil whether you are watching it or not." She reached down and grabbed Felicia's hand. "Come on. Even a scientist likes sugar cookies."

Felicia's frown disappeared immediately. "*Sugar* cookies? I thought Annie was making oatmeal cookies."

"That's just what she told you," Carrie whispered, glad she had found a way to erase the troubled worry from Felicia's eyes. "It's supposed to be a birthday surprise. I'm going to *forget* that I'm not supposed to take you into the kitchen. Make sure you look *very* surprised."

"Okay," Felicia whispered back as she hurried into the house.

Carrie drew a sigh of relief and followed her, praying the wind would blow all the clouds away before the meteor shower was supposed to begin.

Felicia edged up to Carrie as everyone arrived laden with armfuls of quilts and looking like they were wearing everything they owned. "You were right, Carrie!"

Carrie smiled up at the sparkling clear sky, breathing a sigh of relief that the wind had blown the clouds away in time. She had seen another band of clouds tucked far away on the horizon just as the sun was setting, but since the breeze had died down completely, they should still be far away. She was praying they would stay away long enough for everyone to experience the historic event that was about to happen.

Felicia darted away to welcome everyone. It looked like every student in the school had come, almost all of them accompanied by both parents. Evidently, the picture the children had painted for their parents of what they had learned from Felicia was enticing enough to make them leave their warm fires on a bitterly cold night.

Thirty minutes later, when everyone was settled on top of a thick mattress of quilts, with more quilts wrapped snugly around their bodies, Felicia stepped up to stand in the middle of the circle that had been created. She had mandated no fires be built because she wanted nothing to mar the brightness of the meteor shower. The darkness was almost complete, but there was just enough light from the stars and the half-moon hanging above the treetops to outline her lithe body.

"We are all here tonight for the Leonid Meteor Shower," Felicia said. The crowd quieted instantly, seeming to sense they were about to experience something very momentous. "The last Leonid Meteor Shower was in 1833. It actually marks the discovery of the shower, but it also marks the actual birth of meteor astronomy. Pretty soon you are going to see a lot of meteors falling from the sky, but the sky will really light up in the last four hours or so preceding dawn," she announced. "I don't know how many of you will make it that long, but I can promise I will be out here the whole time."

Carrie wondered if she could last the night. Robert reached for her hand under the layer of quilts and squeezed it gently. "I'm up for it if you are," he whispered.

"If I don't turn into an ice statue," Carrie murmured.

"I can keep you warm," Robert promised as he blew warm air gently into her ear.

Carrie shivered, but not from the cold. She snuggled closer to her husband as she listened to Felicia.

"People reacted in different ways to the 1833 meteor shower," Felicia continued. "Some people were hysterical because they believed the Judgment Day was at hand. Scientists, though, were wildly excited by the thousand meteors a minute emanating from the constellation Leo. Just about everyone knew about it back then. They were either awakened by the cries of their excited neighbors, or they were jolted awake by flashes of light from the fireballs." Her voice was high with excitement.

Carrie could feel both excitement and trepidation radiating from the people around her. The students had learned there was nothing to fear, but she wondered if they had passed the knowledge on to their parents. "Is there any reason to be afraid?" she asked.

"No," Felicia answered. "Meteors like the ones we are about to see tonight are very small and not very dense. They are moving very fast so they will look very bright when they enter the atmosphere, but they will burn up long before they reach earth." She understood the reason for Carrie's question. "We are in absolutely no danger."

Carrie heard the sighs of relief from many of those around her.

"Where did you say the meteors are coming from?" another person, unable to be identified in the darkness, asked.

"From the constellation Leo," Felicia answered. "Leo means 'lion.' It's called that because if you drew a line and connected all the stars, you can see a lion in the sky."

"Really?" one of the children asked with a gasp. "Where is it?"

"If you look toward the north you'll see it. It's one of the largest constellations in the sky. In fact, it's the twelfth largest one," Felicia added.

"I don't see no lion," a little boy protested. "Ain't nothing but a bunch of stars."

"Come up here with me," Felicia invited. A little boy scrambled quickly to her side. "Now, kneel down with me." He quickly obeyed. "See that tallest tree out there at the edge of the pasture?"

"I do," the boy said solemnly.

"Now look straight up until you see a star that looks brighter than any of the others around it."

"I see it!" the boy cried as murmurs of agreement rose from the watchers.

"That star is called Regulus," Felicia announced. "It means 'little king' or 'prince' in Latin. It's also the star that is right in the heart of the lion."

"Really?" the little boy breathed. "Where is the rest of the lion?"

Felicia chuckled. "You have to use your imagination a little."

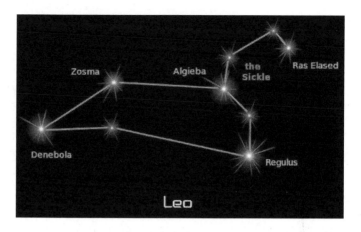

Rose moved forward at that moment and passed out a basket of candles, as well as a sheath of papers. "This will help everyone find Leo," she called.

Carrie reached for her paper eagerly. She was about to discover what Felicia had been hunched over for the last two days. She had witnessed her drawing something, but the little girl wouldn't let her see it. When she lit her candle and examined the sheet of paper, she realized she was looking at a star chart for the constellation Leo. "Felicia is amazing," she murmured.

"It's a good thing she did this," Robert muttered. "I'm as lost as that little boy."

Felicia patiently pointed out the stars on the sheet of paper that formed the lion's chest, the ones that defined the lion's head, and then the ones for Leo's body. "Now," she instructed. "I want you to close your eyes and think about seeing the shape of a lion."

Carrie knew Felicia had brought pictures of a lion in for all the children to see at school, and she had told all of them to make sure their parents saw them before tonight. Carrie hoped they had. She also wondered briefly what it had been like to see the picture of such a magnificent animal that was from the continent their ancestors had come from.

"You really think I can see a lion?" The little boy's voice dripped with skepticism. "I sure don't see nothing like that up there."

"Trust me," Felicia urged. "I never thought I would see the constellations either, but I do now. I want everyone to blow out your candle and close your eyes until I tell you to open them. I want you to think about seeing a lion." She waited for all the candles to be extinguished. "Now close your eyes, but keep looking toward where you saw the stars," she ordered.

Carrie did as she was told, but she had her own serious doubts about seeing anything but stars when she opened them again.

"Now I want you to imagine a big lion in your mind," Felicia commanded. "Imagine it standing tall and proud in the sky. I would tell you to hear it roar, but since none of us have *ever* heard that, it probably won't help."

Carrie chuckled as she pressed her eyes together tightly. She so wanted to see what Felicia was describing. She kept them closed for at least two minutes, amazed how completely silent everyone was. They must want to see it as badly as she did.

"Now open them," Felicia ordered.

Carrie gasped as she gazed into the sky, actually seeing what seemed to be the shape of a lion. As she continued to peer at it, the stars seemed to wrap around the picture she had in her mind. "I see it," she cried excitedly.

"Me, too!" the little boy cried. "There really *is* a lion in the sky."

There were some cries of disappointment, but most were able to see the lion.

A little girl ran forward and tugged at Felicia's arm. "I can't see no lion," she said sadly. "Does that mean I won't be seeing the meteor shower either?"

Felicia laughed. "Not at all. I wanted to teach everyone about the Leo Constellation, but I promise you that every person here is going to see the meteor shower."

"How do you know when it is coming?" a woman called out. "How do you know it is tonight?"

"That's a great question," Felicia responded. "After the last one in 1833, a lot of people started going back into history trying to figure out if it had happened before. They were able to find accounts of it all the way back to the year 585."

Carrie gaped at this new information. She was quite certain everyone else's mouths were hanging open too. "They kept records that far back?" she murmured.

Felicia heard her quiet comment. "I wouldn't go so far as to say there were actual records, but they were able to find accounts in people's journals and notebooks. It was clear they were describing the same thing," she said. "This research is the reason we are out here tonight. They found accounts of ten different significant showers. It allowed them to calculate that the showers appear every thirty-three and a quarter years. The Leonids actually happen every year in November, but once every thirty-three years, it is spectacular." Her voice trembled with anticipation. "Calculations tell us the shower will be tonight." Her voice was almost reverent as she finished, her gaze fixed to the sky.

Carrie knew Felicia was desperately hoping all the calculations had been correct. If not, people would get a great astronomy lesson, but they would go home cold and sorely disappointed.

"Look!" a man suddenly hollered.

Everybody's eyes shot to the sky in time to see a blazing meteor streak across the sky, its long tail suspended for several seconds.

"Pretty," one girl cooed.

"And you're sure we're safe?" a woman cried anxiously.

"Perfectly safe," Felicia confirmed. "Everyone lay down on your blankets. You'll get the best view that way!" She hurried over to lay down with Moses, Rose, John, and Hope.

Carrie smiled as she watched Moses pull his daughter close, wrapping a quilt around her snugly. It seemed as if Felicia had always been their daughter. It was hard to remember the terrified, thin-faced girl who had arrived on the plantation after her parents were murdered. As she gazed at them she had a sudden thought that if Robert couldn't have children, surely there were scores of children in need of a home. She had heard of orphanages, even if she knew nothing about them.

"There's another one!" a child yelled.

"And another!"

Carrie laid back as the skies erupted into a display so magnificent it took her breath away. As soon as one fireball faded away, another one seemed to take its place, streaking across the sky in a blaze of glory before it was swallowed by the darkness. In the beginning, there was a steady stream of meteors lighting up the night, but she knew they weren't yet seeing what Felicia had described. She glanced toward the horizon, relieved to see nothing but clear sky.

No one moved through the long night. Every person there knew they were seeing something so special there were no words to adequately express it. The older ones knew they would probably not live long enough to see a repeat. The younger ones were simply mesmerized by the beauty. Carrie completely forgot about being cold.

"I never dreamed of seeing something like this," Robert said quietly.

"Nor I," Carrie murmured as she squeezed his hand.

It was past midnight when it happened. Carrie gasped with awe as the skies seemed to open up. A veritable rain of meteors blazed across the sky. It looked as if the entire heavens had exploded into the most amazing fireworks display she had ever seen.

"The entire sky is falling!" a woman screamed, clearly on the verge of panic.

"It's the shower!" Felicia cried out as she sprang up from the blanket, raised her arms and began to dance under the bright light. "Look at it! I've never seen anything so beautiful! Just look at it!"

Carrie laughed and jumped up to join her, holding her head back to watch the meteors as she danced. "It's beautiful!" she yelled. "Absolutely beautiful!" She was so glad she had learned the truth of the meteor shower from Felicia. Otherwise, she would have been terrified. As it was, she knew this was a moment she would remember her entire life.

Suddenly people were throwing their blankets aside, joining in the dance as the skies opened to pour an endless treasure of gleaming diamonds toward them.

Carrie knew it was a night she would never forget.

Chapter Thirty-One

Abby shivered, not from the cold buffeting her as a brisk wind assaulted the carriage, but from sheer excitement. After being on her own for so long, she could hardly believe she was part of such a big, vibrant family.

"Are you cold?" Thomas asked solicitously, reaching for another blanket to tuck around her. "It's brutal out here," he muttered.

"It's wonderful!" Abby cried. "I'm not cold at all. I can hardly believe Jeremy and Marietta are getting married next week. And it's almost Christmas. And we're going to the plantation."

Thomas grinned. "You sound like you are about four years old."

Abby stuck her tongue out at him.

Thomas laughed harder. "Now you are acting *exactly* like your daughter!"

Abby bounced on the seat, grinning up at Spencer as he turned back to look at her, his broad face spread in a wide grin.

"Sure does a heart good to see you so happy," Spencer drawled.

"I could say the same thing for you," Abby answered. "Carrie was insistent in her letter a couple weeks ago that you would stay on the plantation for Christmas. I have a feeling, though, that she'll understand your desire to get back to your new bride."

Spencer ducked his head with embarrassment, but his smile still beamed. "I can't believe May agreed to marry me," he said, his voice thick with wonder. "She's something, that woman is."

"Both of you are," Abby replied warmly. "I could not be happier for both of you."

"You're certainly going to eat better," Thomas joked.

Spencer threw his head back with a loud laugh. "Yes, sir. That be right for certain!" He patted his stomach. "I think I'm already gaining weight."

Abby settled back against the carriage cushion as she laid her head on Thomas' shoulder. She suspected it was a lull before the storm, but she was determined to simply relish the last four weeks of peace that had covered Richmond. Perhaps it was because the cold had snuffed out any fires of passion, but she didn't care—she was simply going to enjoy it. They had experienced such a successful year in the factory that they had decided to simply pay everyone their full wages and shut it down for the two weeks they would be gone. Their employees had gaped at them with disbelief when they had made the announcement the night before, and then had erupted into excited talk before they disappeared into the night toward their homes to create their own celebrations.

"I know we promised no business talk once we got to the plantation, but we're not there yet," Thomas observed. "May I ask you a question?"

Abby nodded. "Ask away, my dear."

"I saw you reading a letter after we got home last night, but we were too busy with last minute packing for me to ask you about it."

Abby nodded. If it was possible to be any happier, the letter she had received had made her that way. "It was from our plant manager in Philadelphia." In spite of the brutal cold, they had decided to move forward with preparing the Moyamensing building for production. "Things are going smoothly. There have been some delays because of weather, but the people of Moyamensing have kept the streets amazingly clear of snow around the building, and they keep the workers provided with hot food. Biddy is providing the money for the food, but the residents are cooking it."

Thomas nodded his approval. "So you still believe it will open in April?"

"Definitely," Abby said with a grin. It thrilled her heart to have so much to grin about. "We may even have it ready in March. We'll start small, but we should be up to full production by the end of April, expanding the workforce during the summer." She shook her head. "I knew Biddy was a powerful woman, but I didn't realize she has so many connections. Things that should have taken weeks to accomplish are happening in mere days. Our decision to put the factory in Moyamensing has already garnered interest from other factory owners."

"Of course it has," Thomas replied. "When the most successful businesswoman in Philadelphia does something so radical, it was sure to make them take notice. They also don't want to miss out on a good thing," he said dryly.

Abby supposed she should respond modestly, but she was too thrilled with what was happening. "That's true."

Thomas laughed and pulled her closer. "I have had a lot of wonderful Christmases on the plantation, but I am quite sure none of them will hold a candle to the one we are about to experience."

Carrie beamed with delight as Moses and Robert wrestled the towering cedar tree across the porch and into the house. It had taken ten of them, all on horseback, to find the right tree. Their laughter had echoed through the woods for hours as they discussed, and eliminated, all the trees they examined. It wasn't until Amber came cantering up with news of the perfect tree tucked into the woods beside a hidden pond that the search had ended.

Amber jumped up and down and clapped her hands as the cedar entered the foyer. "My tree is perfect!" she cried.

"If we raise the ceiling," Robert muttered as he and Moses finished pushing it into the parlor.

"It will fit, Robert," Felicia said. "I measured it."

Robert eyed her. "You measured it from a shadow."

Rose laughed. "You haven't yet learned not to question our resident genius?" she asked.

Robert smiled, but still looked unconvinced as he gazed up at the twelve-foot ceiling. "I only want to put this thing up once."

Felicia looked at with something like disdain, but her eyes sparkled with fun. "It's really quite simple," she said, her tone indicating she was speaking slowly because she doubted his ability to understand her. "The secret is in the sun's rays. They fall on both me and the tree from the same direction. That means the rays are parallel. Both me and the tree are straight, so that means we are parallel, too. Since the ground was flat around the tree that made both of our shadows parallel." Excited now, she pulled out a sheet of paper and drew a quick picture. "See, the shadows the tree and I cast look like a triangle. The top of the tree is joined to the shadow of the top of the tree by a line that points back up to the sun." She drew a straight line connecting the two to demonstrate. "My shadow can be drawn the same way."

"So?" Robert asked, his face saying he was already confused as he stared down at the drawing.

"So even though the triangles are different sizes, they are the exact same proportion," Felicia said earnestly.

Carrie hid her smile. Robert, exhausted from his struggle with the tree was clearly not understanding Felicia's explanation, but he was at least trying to listen. She loved him for it.

"It was easy to figure out *my* shadow," Felicia continued. "I'm five feet tall. My shadow is two and a half feet long, or half as long as my height. The ceiling is twelve feet tall. That meant our tree had to have a shadow no longer than six feet. When Amber found this tree I was able to calculate its height."

Moses chuckled when he looked at Robert's face. "It's best not to question her," he advised as he finished hammering the stand onto the bottom of the luxuriant tree. "When it comes to things like this, she is always right."

John, standing close to his daddy, nodded wisely. "Fe-Fe is real smart."

Dwane nodded, too. "Fe-Fe be real smart," he echoed, his eyes shining as he stared at the tree with complete wonder.

Robert stared at Felicia with admiration and then helped Moses hoist the tree. He knew this was the first time Dwane had ever seen a Christmas tree. The resilient little boy seemed to have completely forgotten the beating that had taken his little sister and almost killed him. Morah and Dwane had moved into the room Perry and

Louisa had occupied as soon as they had left for Cromwell Plantation. Dwane had erased John's sadness at seeing Nathan ride away in the carriage. Morah was helping Annie in the kitchen and devouring every book she could get her hands on. Felicia spent time helping her every night.

As Felicia had predicted, the tree fit perfectly, its top within two inches of the ceiling.

"Well done," Carrie exclaimed as she applauded. "All of you!" She inhaled deeply as the aroma of the cedar filled the room, her skin tingling with the wonder of another Christmas on the plantation.

Annie appeared with a platter heaped tall with cookies. Polly and Morah were right behind her, their hands full of trays of coffee and hot chocolate. Just as they set them down on the table, the door opened and allowed in a rush of cold air. Clint and Gabe stomped in, their arms full of cedar boughs to decorate the mantels and doorways.

Clint sniffed appreciatively. "I can smell my mama's gingerbread cookies from a mile away." He eyed the platter. "Is it time?"

Carrie laughed. "It's time." She showed him where she wanted them to deposit the cedar boughs and then pointed them toward the table. Soon the laughter and talk had been replaced with complete silence as the cookies and hot drinks disappeared into a memory.

Robert wiped his mouth with a napkin and gazed up at the tree. "It seems strange not to have it decorated before your father and Abby get here."

"I know," Carrie agreed, "but Abby insisted she didn't want to miss out this year, and Marietta said she wasn't going to have her first real Southern Christmas messed up by not being able to help decorate." She glanced at the four children. "How are the decorations coming?"

"Real good," Amber assured her. "Mama and Annie pulled all the boxes out of the attic for us, and we've been making new ones all week. Morah has been helping us!"

Carrie smiled, her mind spinning back to all the Christmases she had enjoyed on the plantation. She had always led the group of children from the quarters when they went into the woods scavenging for pinecones, mistletoe, and wispy moss to make hordes of decorations. There were fewer children now, but the excitement was just as strong.

The quarters stood empty, waiting for the next round of seasonal workers to arrive in the spring. The other families, snug in their own homes, were busy creating their own Christmas celebrations.

Felicia stared up at the tree with huge round eyes. Carrie exchanged a meaningful look with Rose. Felicia might be a child prodigy, but she was still just a little girl who had never seen such a huge Christmas tree in her life.

"This is the first Christmas tree I've ever seen," Felicia said quietly, reaching out to touch the fragrant boughs.

Moses stepped closer. "The first one, honey? What about the plantation you lived on?"

Felicia shrugged, her eyes never leaving the tree. "I heard the house slaves talking about one a couple times, but I've never seen one. It's beautiful," she murmured in a reverent voice.

"As beautiful as the Leonid Meteor Shower?" Carrie teased. She could hardly wait to see Felicia's face when the little girl experienced the tree decorated with ornaments and glimmering candlelight.

Felicia shook her head quickly. "Nothing will ever be as beautiful as that!" she exclaimed.

"I agree with you completely," Carrie replied.

"What time are Uncle Thomas and Aunt Abby getting here?" Felicia asked as she stepped away from the tree to stare out the window.

"This afternoon," Carrie answered, glancing at the tall grandfather clock in the corner. "They should actually be here any minute," she said with surprise. "Where did the morning go?"

"What about Jeremy and Marietta?" Amber asked.

"They will be here tomorrow," Rose said. "Matthew and Janie will be with them."

"Marietta told me I could help her get ready for the wedding," Amber announced proudly. She danced a quick jig. "I can hardly wait. I ain't never seen a real wedding," she proclaimed.

Rose cleared her throat.

Amber clapped a hand over her mouth. "I meant to say that I have never seen a real wedding," she said hastily, giggling when Rose nodded her approval. She went back to dancing around the room.

Robert smiled as he stepped forward and held out his hand. "May I have this dance?"

Amber giggled harder. "There is no music, Robert!"

"That has never stopped me yet," Robert assured her. He began to hum softly as he held out his arms. Amber's eyes widened, but she let him take her hand before he put the other one on her waist. "Have you ever waltzed?"

Amber shook her head. "I've heard about it, though." Her eyes were bright with anticipation.

"Just follow my lead," Robert told her. "You'll catch on in no time."

Carrie watched, her heart swelling with love as her tall husband carefully led Amber around the room in her first dance, his humming filling the air.

Moses held out a hand to Felicia who reached for it with a grin. They imitated Robert and Amber.

John sidled up to Carrie. "What about me, Carrie? Don't I get to dance, too?"

Carrie smiled down at him. "Of course you do," she assured him. "You're never too young to learn how to dance." She led him out into the parlor and began to instruct him in the simplest moves of the waltz. He giggled helplessly, but did his best to follow her directions.

"Mama?" Clint asked. "I don't really know how to waltz, but we can at least move to Robert's humming."

Polly grinned and reached for his hand. "I would be honored."

Gabe moved out onto the floor with Annie at the same time that Morah glided past with her son.

Rose rocked peacefully as Hope snuggled to her breast.

Flames flickered as a huge fire roared in the fireplace.

Carrie looked around the room certain her heart would burst with happiness.

"Any regrets?" Janie asked as she and Carrie strolled down a path toward the river. The skies were threatening snow, but so far, the threat had not been realized. The frozen, bare ground crunched beneath their feet as the wind rattled the limbs over their heads. They had asked if others wanted to join them, but their incredulous looks made it plain everyone else wanted to hunker down around the fireplace and wait for the first flakes to fall.

"About coming on the walk?" Carrie asked.

"About staying home from school," Janie clarified.

"None," Carrie said, thrilled when she realized how completely she meant it. "Every minute of my time here has been so special."

Janie smiled. "Have you gotten any studying done?"

"Not even one little bit," Carrie admitted. "Granite loves our long rides around the plantation, and Robert and I have talked about so many things." She was uncomfortably aware that she had so far avoided talking to her husband about the topic she wasn't ready to discuss, but she pushed that thought aside. "I've had wonderful times with Rose, I beat Moses in a horse race..."

"Like he ever stood a chance," Janie snorted.

"I tried to tell him," Carrie said with a shrug. "He insisted."

"What was his payment for losing?" Janie asked with a grin.

"I made him agree to get up when Hope cried for the four nights after the race so Rose could get some sleep."

Janie laughed, the sound ringing through the trees and settling down on them like a blanket.

Carrie grinned. "It's only fair. The harvest is long done, but Rose was still getting up every day to teach school."

"Did he protest loudly?" Janie asked with anticipation.

Carrie gave a mock frown. "He didn't protest at all, which somewhat diminished the victory, but Rose definitely looked more rested after the four days, and she was deeply grateful." Her frown was captured by another smile. "I declare, Moses absolutely dotes on that little girl. I think he was glad for a reason to spend more time with her, even if it meant doing it in the middle of a cold winter night."

Janie smiled wistfully.

Carrie raised a brow. "What is that smile about?"

Janie hesitated and looked away.

Carrie felt a twinge of alarm. "Janie, is something wrong?"

"No," Janie said quickly. "I'm sorry, I've just been thinking quite a bit about having children lately," she said.

"Is that a bad thing?" Carrie asked.

"Not at all, but first I have to get married."

"And you're still afraid."

Janie looked away again before she swung her eyes back. "I know it's silly."

"It's not silly."

"But it is," Janie cried. "Matthew is the most wonderful man I know. He loves me so much, and I know without a doubt that he would never hurt me. He also encourages my independence. I know he would never try to take it away from me." Her voice trembled as she added, "He's perfect for me."

"Then why won't you marry him?" Carrie asked.

They broke out of the woods and onto the bank of the James River. Carrie smiled as she watched chunks of ice bob along in the gray waters, the sluggishly moving river seeming to blend seamlessly into the clouds hovering low over its surface. Janie walked up to the edge of the river and stared out over the water.

Carrie could tell her friend's fists were clenched in her mittens. "Janie?" She reached out to put a hand on her shoulder.

"I'm scared," Janie admitted in a low voice, every word coated with pain. "I hate it, but I'm scared."

Carrie thought about the many times she had heard Janie give the same excuse for her refusal to marry the man she loved. She thought about the aching desire she saw in Matthew's eyes when he looked at his fiancée. She knew he was willing to be patient, but she also knew how hard this was for him. The time for sympathy was over. "So Clifford wins after all," she said.

Janie spun around to stare at her. "I thought you said you understood." Anger laced her voice.

"I did," Carrie agreed. "And then I realized my understanding was simply allowing you to keep living in your fear." She wondered if she was doing the right thing when she saw Janie flinch, but she forged ahead, her instincts telling her to keep talking. "Clifford's abuse left you with fear, but it is your own choices that are *keeping* you in fear."

"How would you know?" Janie snapped.

Janie's anger made Carrie realize just how close she must be to the truth. "Fear is fear," she said. "You are letting your fears keep you from something absolutely wonderful. So even though Clifford is no longer in your life, he is still controlling you every day because you are letting him. Is that really what you want, Janie?"

Janie gasped and turned away, her rigid shoulders revealing her fury.

Carrie waited quietly, thinking of all the times Janie had helped her work through her own fears. It was natural to be angry if you were challenged to let go of something you believed was keeping you safe. She knew she couldn't really understand what Janie had been through, but she completely understood what her friend was missing by holding Matthew at arm's length. She began to shiver as the wind picked up on the river, kicking the calm surface up into whitecaps that blended with the ice chunks, but still she waited.

When Janie finally turned to look at her, her eyes were swarming with tears. "I want to stop being afraid," she whispered.

Carrie moved forward and clasped Janie's hand firmly. "Then do it."

Janie blinked and looked away. "How?" Her whisper was a cry for help that was picked up by the wind and whisked into the clouds.

Carrie was glad the waiting had given her time to think about what her answer would be. "Change the story."

Janie turned her eyes back. "Change the story?"

"Yes," Carrie said. "You have allowed the memories of Clifford to become the only story playing through your mind. Every time you think about marriage, you think about his anger and abuse. Of course it scares you." She took a deep breath, praying she would say the right thing. "Every time that story starts, you need to stop it and tell yourself another one. The new story should center on how wonderful your marriage to Matthew will be. You're going to tell yourself the story of what it will be like to crawl into bed with him every night."

Janie blinked again, but the tears had disappeared in the wake of a new light in her eyes.

"You're going to tell yourself the story of what it will be like to bear Matthew's children... to watch him hold your babies... to hear the laughter of your family in your home."

Janie held her free hand up to her heart. "Oh, Carrie... that is what I want more than anything."

"Then go get it," Carrie said. As she watched, she saw the shadow of fear begin to creep back into her friend's eyes. "Tell yourself a different story right now," she commanded. The shadow retreated as Janie obeyed. "It will take some time," Carrie continued, "but it won't take long."

Janie's eyes sought hers. "It won't?"

"It won't." Carrie's voice was loving, but firm.

Janie stared at her. "How do you know?" Her voice trembled with hope.

Carrie chuckled. "I've lost count of the times I have let fear stop me from doing something. You have helped me so many times. It was Abby who taught me the power of telling myself a different story. When I keep telling it to myself, the new story becomes my reality, and it washes away the fear so that I can move forward."

Janie listened intently. "I will do it," she promised.

"Starting now?" Carrie pressed.

"Starting now," Janie said, her eyes glowing with determination.

Carrie eyed the smoke coming from the chimney.

"We could be inside where it's warm if you want to change your mind," Marietta offered.

Carrie smiled. "Too soft for a little winter weather?"

"Certainly not!" Marietta retorted, her blue eyes flashing with fun. "Where are we going?"

Carrie nodded toward the barn.

Marietta narrowed her eyes. "You made me put all these clothes on and come out into this cold just for a stroll to the barn?"

Carrie felt a flash of remorse, but it was quickly followed by the excitement of her idea. "I did, but you'll understand why in a few minutes."

The barn, protected from the wind by sturdy walls, felt almost warm in contrast when they walked in. The horses snuffled a greeting, but quickly turned back to their feed. Carrie had seen Clint leave the stable just minutes before she invited Marietta for a walk, so she knew they would have some privacy.

Marietta turned on her as soon as they walked inside. "Out with it," she ordered. "Why are we here?"

Carrie spoke quickly, not at all certain someone wouldn't choose to follow them.

When she finished talking, Marietta was already bobbing her head up and down. "Absolutely. Yes!"

"It might not happen," Carrie reminded her again.

"But if it does..." Marietta murmured. She clapped her hands with delight.

Smiling, they clasped hands and walked back to the house.

An Invitation

Before you read the last chapter of Shifted By The Winds, I would like to invite you to join my mailing list so that you are never left wondering what is going to happen next. ☺

Join my Email list so you can:

- Receive notice of all new books & audio releases.
- Be a part of my Launch celebrations. I give away lots of ~~Free~~ gifts! ☺
- Read my weekly blog while you're waiting for a new book.
- Be part of The Bregdan Chronicles Family!
- Learn about all the other books I write.

Just go to www.BregdanChronicles.net and fill out the form.

I look forward to having you become part of The Bregdan Chronicles Family!

Blessings,
Ginny Dye

Chapter Thirty-Two

Marietta took a deep breath and turned toward the mirror in Carrie's room. She gasped as she saw her reflection in the gleaming glass. "Oh, my..." she murmured.

"'*Oh, my*' is correct," Abby breathed. "You look absolutely stunning, Marietta."

"You're the most beautiful thing I've ever seen," Amber cried with wonder.

"I'm so glad I didn't let my mother send me a dress," Marietta whispered as she twirled slowly, letting the wispy softness of the ivory-colored dress float around her, soft lace whispering a song through the room. Flames from the fire sparkled off glass beads, making the dress seem alive. "Abby, I don't know how to thank you for letting me wear your wedding dress. Jeremy wanted to buy me one, and I know he can afford it, but having something from the family is so much more special."

Tears gleamed in Abby's eyes. "You have no idea what that means to me. I always dreamed of having a large family. Howard and I couldn't have children, but the dream never died. Now I suddenly have a huge family. I felt silly keeping that dress all these years. Now I know why I did." She walked forward to clasp Marietta's hands. "You're stunning, my dear. Jeremy isn't going to know how to feel when he sees you."

"On the contrary," Carrie chuckled. "I think he's going to know *exactly* how to feel."

Marietta blushed but met her eyes squarely. "Is it wonderful, Carrie?"

Carrie nodded, aware Amber was in the room. "It's more than wonderful." She locked eyes with Abby. "Wouldn't you agree?"

Abby laughed. "Though it feels a little odd to confirm that in front of my husband's daughter, yes, it is wonderful!"

"I know what you're talking about," Amber proclaimed. "Don't you know I learned all about sex when Eclipse took care of the mares this spring? Isn't that what you're talking about? I'm not a little girl," she added. "You don't have to talk in riddles to hide things from me."

Carrie managed a small laugh as she nodded her head, completely at a loss for what to say.

Abby took care of it for her. "Come here, Amber." Amber walked over and stood beside her. "You are most definitely not a little girl. You are a very smart young woman, but sex between a man and a woman is much more special than what you see Eclipse doing to the mares. It is something to be cherished, and you will always deserve to have a man treat you very special. I know your mama would tell you the same thing."

Amber was quiet for a long moment. "I reckon you are right," she said thoughtfully. She looked at Marietta. "Does Jeremy feel that way about you?"

"He does," Marietta confirmed, her face glowing with a warm smile.

Amber cocked her head as she stared at the bride-to-be. "I want that, too," she declared with a grin. "I wasn't really looking forward to what Eclipse does."

Carrie couldn't help laughing.

Marietta laughed along with her and then turned to twirl in front of the mirror again. Lantern light caught her reflection and sent it spinning back toward her. She quit spinning and walked forward slowly to caress the mirror. "Your mirror is extraordinary. Did I hear you say one day that this treasure has been passed down from your family?"

Carrie nodded as she exchanged a glance with Abby. "Yes, it came over from England. My great-great-grandmother refused to leave it behind when they came to America. She received it as a wedding gift from her parents."

Marietta examined it more closely. "This mirror is quite valuable," she murmured, gazing at Carrie with a curious expression. "Excuse me if this seems rude, but your bedroom seems a rather strange place for it to be. It seems as if it should be downstairs where everyone can see it."

"My mother quite agreed with you," Carrie replied. "I'm certain my grandmother felt the same way."

"Then..."

"The Cromwell *men* refused to have it moved from this room." Carrie grinned as Marietta's expression grew more confused. "I suppose now that you're going to be a member of the family it is time for you to know the secret."

Marietta shook her head. "The secret?"

"There's a secret?" Amber cried.

Carrie had almost forgotten Amber was in the room when Marietta was asking about the mirror. "You're family, too, Amber. You should also know the secret."

Amber's eyes widened. "I'm family?" Her expression was a mixture of longing and disbelief.

"You are," Carrie said. "You may be someone else's daughter, but Robert and I love you just like you were our own."

Carrie smiled as Amber's face glowed a little more brightly, and then she strode forward, reached for the hidden handle she knew so well now, and tugged it gently. The heavy mirror swung open soundlessly, revealing the gaping corridor hidden behind it.

"A tunnel!" Marietta cried, moving forward to peer into the darkness.

Amber jumped up and ran to stare into it. "Where does it go?" she breathed.

"To the river. My great-great-grandparents built it when they built the house. The original idea was to protect them from Indian attacks, but it has served many more purposes than that," Carrie said with a smile.

"Will you tell me the stories?" Marietta asked eagerly.

"Me, too!" Amber echoed. "I want to know all the stories!"

"Perhaps *after* the wedding?" Abby asked in an amused voice.

Marietta grinned. "Definitely after the wedding," she answered. "Quite a few *days* after the wedding," she added, batting her eyelashes.

Rose found Jeremy out on the porch, bundled heavily against the cold. "Hello, brother."

Jeremy glanced around with a smile and drew her close with his strong arm. "Hello, sister. I thought you would be upstairs with the women."

"I was for a while, but then all I wanted to do was come find my twin brother."

Jeremy smiled and continued to stare out over the plantation. "It's funny how life has come full circle," he murmured.

Rose could feel the depth of emotion in him. She stood silently, waiting for him to continue.

"Do you think our mama knows?"

"That her baby boy who she lost when he was only a day old is back on the plantation getting ready to be married to a beautiful woman who is perfect for him?" Rose asked. "Yes, I believe she knows."

"How?"

Rose shrugged. "I won't even pretend to know the answer to *that* question. There have been so many times when I needed Mama since she died." Her voice trailed off as the memories flooded her. "Whether I simply saw her in my mind, or whether God opened a veil to the universe to let me see her, I don't know. I just know that sometimes I can see her, and that I can hear her."

"Do you see her now?" Jeremy asked eagerly.

Rose shook her head. "I'm not the one who *needs* to see her," she said. She reached up and laid her hand on Jeremy's cheek. "I do know that Mama would be so very proud of you. I believe she knows we're together again, and I believe she knows how much our world is changing."

Jeremy nodded. "There are still times I feel like I'm being selfish to marry Marietta."

"Then you're not as smart as I thought you were," Rose said.

Jeremy stiffened, but relaxed just as quickly. "You sound like Marietta."

"Good," Rose said crisply. "I suspect it will take two strong women to keep you from thinking ridiculous things like that." She interpreted the look of protest in her twin's eyes. "I already know you and Marietta have had many conversations about your marriage putting her, and the children who will follow, at risk."

"Did she tell you about them?"

"She didn't have to. You're not the kind of man who would not be concerned about what could happen to a white woman who marries a mulatto."

Jeremy sighed. "I hate that word."

"I do, too," Rose agreed. "We're just people. You happen to look white. I happen to look black. Either of us could have children that look completely different from us. You would be careless if you didn't at least consider it."

"Did you?" Jeremy asked.

"Certainly. Right before John was born I was terrified he would come out looking white. I didn't know how Moses would handle it, and I was scared for what it would mean for my baby as he grew up."

"And now?" Jeremy's eyes blazed with intensity.

"And now I simply rejoice when a child is born. It's not that I don't think about it," she added. "Hope could have been born looking more white." She considered her next words. "It just doesn't matter anymore. I figure if God wants my baby to be born looking different than Moses and I, that I don't have the right to question it or be upset about it. I will love that child as equally as I love my other two. I will treat them the same, and I will do everything I can to raise them to be good, loving people."

Jeremy was silent for several minutes. Rose continued to stand quietly, letting him think through her words.

"My sister is a very wise woman," Jeremy finally said.

"I am," Rose agreed, chuckling almost as soon as the words escaped her mouth. "You're going to be an amazing husband and father, Jeremy. You and Marietta will deal with whatever comes because you love each other."

Jeremy nodded. "Thank you." He glanced at the house, his smile suddenly eager. "Isn't it almost time?"

"I believe it is. Perhaps you would like to come out of the cold so that your cheeks aren't bright red when your bride comes down the stairs. That's not a problem for me, but you white people are different..."

Jeremy exploded into laughter and pulled her into the house.

Carrie found Felicia staring up at the Christmas tree. She laid her hand on her shoulder. "Does it meet your approval?"

Felicia grinned. "Next to the Leonid Meteor Shower, it is the most beautiful thing I have ever seen," she whispered.

The twelve-foot-tall Christmas cedar was indeed beautiful. The children had started by using everything in the attic to decorate the tree. It was dressed with cotton balls, gilded nuts and berries, paper garlands, colored pieces of glass, and white lace. But then they had taken it from beautiful to spectacular by adding tiny sculptures the children had created from pine cones and nuts. Swatches of pink, white, and blue dried flowers nestled in the branches. To finish it off, they had directed the placement of hundreds of tiny white candles that were gleaming and twinkling in preparation for the wedding that was about to take place.

All the women had worked together, laughing the entire time, to weave long strands of cedar garlands that now framed every doorway and window. Sprigs of red holly berries had been tucked in to add splashes of vibrant color, and the children had added leftover decorations to make them even more beautiful. Candles glowed on every table and along the fireplace mantle.

"Marietta is going to have the most perfect wedding ever," Felicia breathed. "Someday I hope I can get married in this exact same spot."

"I hope that, too," Carrie said as, for a moment, she looked into the future a decade or more away. What would their country be like then? What kind of world would young Felicia be living in? Her thoughts were interrupted when her father walked into the room, resplendent in his black tuxedo.

"Uncle Thomas!" Felicia cried. "You look so handsome."

"Why, thank you, my dear," Thomas said as he pulled her into a hug. "Your yellow dress makes you look like a ray of sunshine."

Felicia suddenly frowned. "Not sunshine," she cried. "Marietta said she wants it to snow tonight."

"Then it will snow tonight," Thomas said.

Felicia cocked her head. "Do you really think so?"

"I do," he assured her, exchanging a look with Carrie over her head.

Felicia caught the look and grinned. "It could have something to do with the fact that the temperature has dropped and the clouds look much heavier with moisture."

Thomas laughed. "It could," he agreed as he shook his head. "You're getting too smart for me, young lady."

"But will it snow in time for the wedding?" Felicia persisted. "That is the important part!"

"You'll have to ask Carrie about *that*," Thomas said.

Felicia flicked a glance at Carrie before she turned back to Thomas. "Why would Carrie know?"

Thomas shrugged. "I gave up trying to figure it out years ago. She just seems to know."

Felicia turned and gave Carrie her full attention. "Do you know the same way you knew the clouds wouldn't cover the Leonid Meteor Shower?"

Carrie nodded. "The same way."

"Magic?"

Carrie hid her smile when she heard the disappointment in Felicia's voice. "I prefer to call it women's intuition."

Felicia gazed at her. "Why can't I feel it?"

"Because you're not a woman yet," Carrie said with a smile.

"But I'll know then?"

"Perhaps," she allowed.

Felicia frowned. "Why *perhaps*?"

Carrie laughed. "Because you want everything to be proven scientifically, my dear. Not all of life works that way."

Felicia stared at her and then turned to look out the window hopefully.

Rose walked into the room. Carrie could tell by the relieved look on her face that Hope was sound asleep.

"Carrie is right, you know. Not everything can be proven scientifically," Rose said.

"But most things can, Mama," Felicia insisted.

"Most things are not *all* things," Rose replied. "You will spend your whole life frustrated if you choose to only believe the things you can see and prove."

Felicia considered her statement for a long moment. "I'm glad I have women in my life that will help me not do that," she said finally.

Carrie caught her breath but remained silent. She sensed there was more Felicia wanted to say.

Felicia walked back over to stare at the tree. "My mama believed in that thing you call women's intuition," she murmured thoughtfully.

"She did?" Rose asked gently as she joined Felicia beside the tree.

"Yes. The night before she was killed she tucked me into bed." Felicia's voice caught at the memory, but she continued. "She did that every night, and then she made me read to her because she never learned how to read." Her voice wavered, but she took a deep breath and continued. "She told me I was going to be a very important woman someday. She told me I was going to help black women everywhere." Felicia tipped her head back so she could see all the way to the top of the tree. "I asked her how she knew. She just smiled and told me she knew. I asked her again how she *knew*." She fell silent. "Mama gave me a big hug and told me there are things you can only know with your heart." She peered up at Rose, her eyes glistening in the candlelight. "Is that how you know?"

Rose laid a hand on the little girl's cheek softly. "That's how you know."

Felicia thought for a moment. "Then my mama might be right? I might be an important woman one day?"

Thomas stepped over to lay a hand on her shoulder. "I don't need to have women's intuition to know that is going to be true, Felicia. You are going to be important to women everywhere one day soon."

When Carrie walked downstairs an hour before the wedding was to begin, she saw Janie standing out on the porch, bundled tightly against the cold. She knew Matthew had gone upstairs to change clothes. She grabbed her father's thick coat and pulled it around her scarlet red dress. She wasn't dressed for the cold, but Janie's rigid stance told her that her friend needed her.

Janie looked up as she walked out on the porch. "Hello," she said softly.

"Are you all right?"

Janie didn't answer for a long moment. "I always dreamed of getting married on Christmas Eve," she finally revealed. She shook her head impatiently. "I know it's my own fault, and I know it's not possible anyway because this is Jeremy and Marietta's night, but I can't help feeling sad, which only makes me feel stupid."

"Nonsense!" Carrie cried, happiness soaring through her. "I didn't think you would *ever* come to your senses."

Janie stared at Carrie as if she had gone completely mad. "What in the world are you talking about?"

Carrie ignored her. "You're not afraid anymore?"

Janie considered the question. "I can't say I don't feel twinges of fear, but I have new stories I tell myself as soon as they try to creep in."

"Have you told Matthew yet?" Carrie pressed.

Janie shook her head. "I thought perhaps I would tell him tonight after the wedding," she murmured, her eyes growing soft as she thought about it.

Carrie grinned. "I have a better idea." Not allowing Janie to ask any questions, she grabbed her hand and pulled her back into the house. "We don't have much time."

Matthew dressed carefully. He was truly happy for Jeremy and Marietta, but the reality of the wedding taking place tonight was bittersweet for him. He hated that he couldn't feel open-hearted joy for them, but he was too aware of the intense loneliness choking him at times. Being here around Robert and Carrie, Thomas and Abby, and Moses and Rose only magnified it. He hated that he found himself wishing he had remained in Philadelphia for Christmas, but it would have been easier.

He moved to stare out the window into the dark night. He was quite sure it was going to snow. The knowledge only made him feel worse. Janie had long ago confided her wish of marrying on a snowy Christmas Eve. He blamed himself that he hadn't been able to move her beyond her fears. He hated the thought that he might not be the right man for her. With that thought came the memory of all the years he had longed for Carrie. He shoved those aside certain his love for her was never meant to be more than friendship, but he also wondered if he was destined to spend his life alone. Perhaps he would never marry.

The sound of pounding hooves made him smile even through his misery. The horses were reveling in the brittle, cold night. He could see shadows racing around the pasture. He flung his window open, suddenly desperate for cold air to clear his thoughts. He leaned against the windowsill and took deep, steadying breaths as the frigid air enveloped him.

Janie loved him. He knew she did. Someday, perhaps she would move beyond her fears. Until then, he had to be willing to content himself with their love and the time they had together.

A light tap on the door made him turn around.

Robert slipped into the room. He stared in astonishment and walked closer to the fire. "Are you trying to freeze to death, or simply attempting to warm the outdoors?"

Matthew shook his head and shut the window. "I needed some air," he muttered.

Robert eyed him. "You're glad for Jeremy and Marietta, but you're wishing it was your wedding tonight."

Matthew didn't bother to refute his obviously true statement. "I'm alright now." He expected Robert to say something to make him feel better, but his friend only nodded his head briefly. "Let's go. They are waiting for us."

Matthew sighed, straightened his jacket, and followed Robert from the room.

Carrie walked into the parlor, fighting to keep her breathing even. A quick glance told her everything was ready. The minister had arrived, and Abby was seated at the piano. The candles filled the room with soft light, and the tree was radiant in all its glory. She closed her eyes and took a deep breath. The aroma of cedar made her feel as if she were standing in an enchanted wooden glen. "It's perfect," she breathed, her heart pounding with excitement and happiness.

She exchanged a look with Robert and smiled briefly at Jeremy before she slipped from the room, careful not to look in Matthew's direction.

"Are we ready?" Thomas asked.

Carrie nodded and pulled his head down for a whispered conversation.

Thomas' eyes widened. "Let's get on with it," he whispered back with a grin.

Carrie ran back to the parlor door, nodded to Abby, and listened for a moment as Abby broke into the opening notes of Mendelssohn's "Wedding March." With the music ringing in her ears, she turned and ran back up the stairs to where Marietta was waiting. "It's time," she said.

Marietta smiled radiantly, took a deep breath, and walked slowly down the stairs. As soon as she reached the bottom, she took the arm Thomas offered, her heart pounding wildly.

She caught her breath as she entered the room, but the only thing she saw was Jeremy standing tall next to the Christmas tree, his blond hair gleaming in the candlelight, and his eyes full of love as he watched her move toward him. She had waited for this moment for so long. She never could have dreamed she would find someone as wonderful as the man who stood before her. She knew their future held many question marks, but the certainty of their love would see them through whatever awaited.

Thomas put her hand in Jeremy's and then turned and nodded to Abby again. Abby smiled and broke once more into the wedding march.

Marietta tore her eyes away from Jeremy just long enough to peek at Matthew's face. His smile faded into a look of confusion. Marietta blinked back tears. This night was going to be even more perfect than she had envisioned.

Matthew swung his head to look at Abby. Why was she playing the march again? Why was Thomas leaving the room again, and why was the minister not stepping up to begin to speak? He gazed around the room. They all seemed to be waiting for something.

He caught a glimpse of Carrie's grinning face at the door, but it disappeared as fast as it had appeared. Wasn't she coming in for the wedding?

Robert appeared at his side. "Care to join me?"

Matthew stared at him. "Join you where?"

Robert gripped his arm and pulled him from his seat. "Follow me, old man."

Matthew shook his head and obeyed, completely perplexed as to why they were moving up to stand beside the tree. He looked at Abby again. She was gazing back at him with a look of so much love and happiness that it caused his heart to swell, even though he had no idea why. Then she tilted her head as the music faded away.

Matthew gasped when his eyes turned toward the parlor door. Janie was standing in the arch, her arm tucked through Thomas', glowing in the most beautiful wedding gown he had ever seen. He stared at her dumbly, his brain refusing to process what he was seeing.

"Ready to get married?" Robert said.

Matthew swung his head to stare at his friend. The calm assurance radiating from Robert's face told him he wasn't just imagining this. When he looked toward the door again, Janie was moving toward him, her eyes bright with so much love that he could suddenly hardly breathe. He felt his face explode into a wide grin, but he was still uncertain that some part of what was happening wasn't actually fantasy.

Matthew watched as Thomas released Janie's arm and slid it through his own. Her touch broke through his shocked stupor. He released the breath he had been holding ever since he had seen her at the door.

"Marry me?" Janie whispered up to him.

"Oh, yes," Matthew murmured as the fog of fantasy lifted and swirled from the room.

The minister cleared his throat. "Now that we're all here..."

Laughter swelled through the room before silence draped it once more. The only sound was the crackling of the fireplace.

Suddenly Amber started waving her arm wildly. She had insisted on standing beside the window. "It's snowing! You got your wish, Marietta. You, too, Janie! It's snowing!"

Matthew threw his head back in a joyful laugh as both Janie and Marietta gave a cry of delight.

The minister grinned. "Now that we're all here, and now that the snow has arrived..."

Carrie caught Felicia's eyes from across the room. "I told you," she mouthed.

The minister's voice filled the room. "Jeremy, wilt thou have this woman to be thy wedded wife, to live together after God's ordinance in the holy estate of matrimony? Wilt thou love her, comfort her, honor and keep her in sickness and in health; and, forsaking all others, keep thee only unto her, so long as ye both shall live?"

"I will," Jeremy replied, his voice thick with emotion.

Then the minister turned to Matthew. "Matthew, wilt thou have this woman to be thy wedded wife, to live together after God's ordinance in the holy estate of matrimony? Wilt thou love her, comfort her, honor and keep her in sickness and in health; and, forsaking all others, keep thee only unto her, so long as ye both shall live?"

Matthew smiled down at Janie. "I will." His voice rang through the room with complete joy.

Carrie stood back and gazed around the room. These people were her family. Every single one of them—whether related or not—they were family.

Her eyes rested on Matthew and Janie first. She didn't think she had ever seen more joy on anyone's face than she saw on Matthew's. Until she had talked to Janie on the porch, she had given up hope of her surprise becoming a reality. It was amazing how fast someone could be prepared to be married. Janie had laughed with delight when Carrie had pulled out her wedding dress—the same one they had chosen together for her and Robert's wedding. Rose had fixed her hair, while Amber and Felicia hastily constructed a ring of greenery for the headpiece Carrie had found in a trunk in the attic. She didn't know how far it went back in her family, but the delicate lace had looked ethereal on Janie's soft brown hair.

Jeremy and Marietta glowed just as brightly. Their eyes never left each other as they waltzed around the room Abby was filling with music. Carrie's thoughts were interrupted when Amber came running into the room.

"It's snowing real hard, everybody. Come look!"

Felicia laughed and dashed from the room. "Come on, everybody! The first snowfall came just for the wedding. Come look!"

Everyone moved out onto the porch, grabbing coats as they pushed forward to catch the first snowfall of the year. The early snowflakes had been tiny. Now, huge flakes were falling. Within minutes, the ground was blanketed with a layer of white. The snow would be deep before this storm was over. The minister, determined to be with his family for Christmas, had already left. Carrie knew there was plenty of time for him to arrive home safely. He was probably already hunkered down around his fire.

Amber, Felicia, Dwane, and John ran down the stairs, grabbed hands, and began to twirl around in the snow, their heads lifted so their tongues could catch the flakes.

Robert moved up next to her and wrapped an arm around her waist. "What are you thinking?" he asked.

"I'm thinking I am the luckiest, most blessed woman in the whole world," Carrie replied around the huge lump of joy in her throat. "And I believe 1867 is going to be a remarkable year."

Rose and Moses stepped up beside them.

Moses nodded, his face content as he watched the children play. "It is going to be a remarkable year," he agreed. "We will keep moving forward."

Rose nodded. "Always forward," she echoed.

Carrie smiled as she laid her head on Robert's shoulder. "Always forward," she agreed.

Always forward.

To Be Continued...

*Would you be so kind as to leave a Review on Amazon?
I love hearing from my readers! Just go to
Amazon.com, put Shifted By The Winds into the Search
box, click to read the Reviews, and you'll be able to
leave one of your own!*

Thank you!

The Bregdan Principle

Every life that has been lived until today is a part of the woven braid of life.

It takes every person's story to create history.

Your life will help determine the course of history.

You may think you don't have much of an impact.

You do.

Every action you take will reflect in someone else's life.

Someone else's decisions.

Someone else's future.

Both good and bad.

The Bregdan Chronicles

Storm Clouds Rolling In
1860 – 1861

On To Richmond
1861 – 1862

Spring Will Come
1862 – 1863

Dark Chaos
1863 – 1864

The Long Last Night
1864 – 1865

Carried Forward By Hope
April – December 1865

Glimmers of Change
December – August 1866

Shifted By The Winds
August – December 1866

**Many more coming... Go to
DiscoverTheBregdanChronicles.com to see how
many are available now!**

Other Books by Ginny Dye

<u>Pepper Crest High Series - Teen Fiction</u>

Time For A Second Change
It's Really A Matter of Trust
A Lost & Found Friend
Time For A Change of Heart

<u>Fly To Your Dreams Series</u> – Allegorical Fantasy

Dream Dragon
Born To Fly
Little Heart

101+ Ways to Promote Your Business Opportunity

All titles by Ginny Dye
www.BregdanPublishing.com

Author Biography

Who am I? Just a normal person who happens to love to write. If I could do it all anonymously, I would. In fact, I did the first go round. I wrote under a pen name. On the off chance I would ever become famous - I didn't want to be! I don't like the limelight. I don't like living in a fishbowl. I especially don't like thinking I have to look good everywhere I go, just in case someone recognizes me! I finally decided none of that matters. If you don't like me in overalls and a baseball cap, too bad. If you don't like my haircut or think I should do something different than what I'm doing, too bad. I'll write books that you will hopefully like, and we'll both let that be enough! :) Fair?

But let's see what you might want to know. I spent many years as a Wanderer. My dream when I graduated from college was to experience the United States. I grew up in the South. There are many things I love about it but I wanted to live in other places. So I did. I moved 42 times, traveled extensively in 49 of the 50 states, and had more experiences than I will ever be able to recount. The only state I haven't been in is Alaska, simply because I refuse to visit such a vast, fabulous place until I have at least a month. Along the way I had glorious adventures. I've canoed through the Everglade Swamps, snorkeled in the Florida Keys and windsurfed in the Gulf of Mexico. I've white-water rafted down the New River and Bungee jumped in the Wisconsin Dells. I've visited every National Park (in the off-season when there is more freedom!) and many of the State Parks. I've hiked thousands of miles of mountain trails and biked through Arizona deserts. I've canoed and biked through Upstate New York and Vermont, and polished off as much lobster as possible on the Maine Coast.

I had a glorious time and never thought I would find a place that would hold me until I came to the Pacific Northwest. I'd been here less than 2 weeks, and I knew I would never leave. My heart is so at home here with the towering firs, sparkling waters, soaring mountains and rocky beaches. I love the eagles & whales. In 5 minutes I can be hiking on 150 miles of trails in the mountains around my home, or gliding across the lake in my rowing shell. I love it!

Have you figured out I'm kind of an outdoors gal? If it can be done outdoors, I love it! Hiking, biking, windsurfing, rock-climbing, roller-blading, snow-shoeing, skiing, rowing, canoeing, softball, tennis... the list could go on and on. I love to have fun and I love to stretch my body. This should give you a pretty good idea of what I do in my free time.

When I'm not writing or playing, I'm building I Am A Voice In The World - a fabulous organization I founded in 2001 - along with 60 amazing people who poured their lives into creating resources to empower people to make a difference with their lives.

What else? I love to read, cook, sit for hours in solitude on my mountain, and also hang out with friends. I love barbeques and block parties. Basically - I just love LIFE!

I'm so glad you're part of my world!

Ginny

Join my Email List so you can:

- Receive notice of all new books
- Be a part of my Launch Celebrations. I give away lots of Free gifts!
- Read my weekly BLOG while you're waiting for a new book.
- Be part of The Bregdan Chronicles Family!
- Learn about all the other books I write.

Just go to www.BregdanChronicles.net and fill out the form.